THE FAITHFUL LOVERS

THE FAITHFUL LOVERS

Bridges Over Time
Book IV

Valerie Anand

St. Martin's Press
New York

For my good friends
Pat and Ken Short
and
Kate and Brian Templeman

Library of Congress Cataloging-in-Publication Data

Anand, Valerie.
The faithful lovers / Valerie Anand.
p.   cm. — (Bridges over time ; bk. 4)
ISBN 0-312-10979-2
1. Great Britain—History—Civil War, 1642–1649—
Fiction.   2. Family—England—Fiction.   I. Title.   II. Series:
Anand, Valerie. Bridges over time ; bk. 4.
PR6051.N34F35   1994
823'.914—dc20   94-1243   CIP

First published in Great Britain by HEADLINE BOOK PUBLISHING PLC.

First U.S. Edition: June 1994
10 9 8 7 6 5 4 3 2 1

Sources

A complete list of the books consulted while writing *The Faithful Lovers* would hardly be possible but prominent among them were:

The Roundheads by Jasper Ridley (Constable, 1976)

The Cavaliers by Mark Bence-Jones (Constable, 1976)

The English Civil War by Brigadier Peter Young DSO, MC, MA, FSA and Richard Holmes MA (Eyre Methuen, London, 1974)

The Early Stuarts, 1603–1660 by Godfrey Davies, Hon. FBA (*Oxford History of England*, edited by Sir George Clark, Oxford University Press, 2nd edition, 1988)

The Later Stuarts, 1660–1714 by Sir George Clark (*Oxford History of England*, edited by Sir George Clark, Oxford University Press, 2nd edition, 1988)

The Impact of the English Civil War, edited by John Morrill (Collins & Brown, 1991)

The Century of Revolution 1603–1714, by Christopher Hill (Van Nostrand Reinhold (International) Co. Ltd, 2nd edition, 1991)

King Charles II by Antonia Fraser (Weidenfeld & Nicolson, 1979)

The Diary of Samuel Pepys edited by Robert Latham and William Matthews (Bell & Hyman, 1970–83)

James II by John Miller (Methuen, 1978)

The History of the Town of Penzance by P. A. S. Pool, MA, FSA (Corporation of Penzance, 1974)

Portrait of Cornwall by Claude Berry (Hale, 1963)

The Spirit of Cornwall by Denys Val Baker (paperback division of W. H. Allen & Co. Ltd, 1980)

The Way to Minack, A Cornish Summer, Cottage on a Cliff by Derek Tangye (Michael Joseph, 1968, 1970, 1972)

Old Cornwall, Volume 7, 1969 (Federation of Old Cornwall Societies)

Yesterday's Exmoor by Hazel Eardley-Wilmot (Exmoor Books, 1990)

17th Century English Literature by Bruce King (Macmillan Education, 1982)

The Antique Furniture Trail by V. J. Taylor (David & Charles, 1989)

Seven Hundred Years of English Cooking by Maxime McKendry (edited by Arabella Boxer, Treasure Press, 1985)

Coming of Age in the Milky Way by Timothy Ferris (Bodley Head, 1988)

Acknowledgements

I am indebted to Unwin Hyman (formerly Bell & Hyman) of HarperCollins Publishers Limited for permission to quote from *The Diary of Samuel Pepys*, edited by Robert Latham and William Matthews

and to

Cornwall County Council (Cornish Studies Library) for providing me with a copy of the article on Anthony Gubbes which appeared in Volume 7 of the publication *Old Cornwall*.

In addition, special thanks go to my good friend Shirley Linsell for the gift of *The Diary of Samuel Pepys*, which was not only a goldmine of information but also a delightful read in its own right.

Contents

DESCENDANTS OF RICHARD AND SUSANNAH WHITMEAD

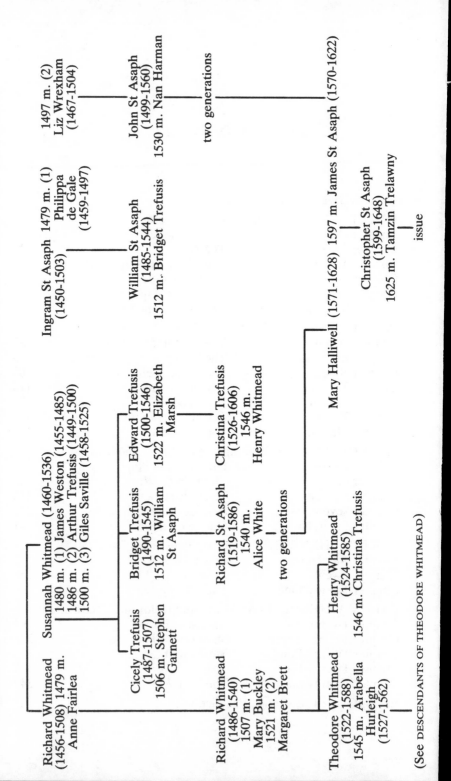

(See DESCENDANTS OF THEODORE WHITMEAD)

DESCENDANTS OF THEODORE WHITMEAD

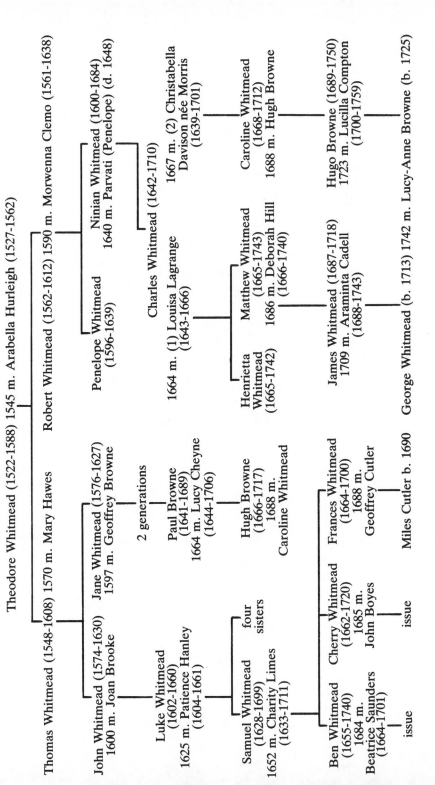

Theodore Whitmead (1522-1588) 1545 m. Arabella Hurleigh (1527-1562)

Thomas Whitmead (1548-1608) 1570 m. Mary Hawes

Robert Whitmead (1562-1612) 1590 m. Morwenna Clemo (1561-1638)

John Whitmead (1574-1630) 1600 m. Joan Brooke

Jane Whitmead (1576-1627) 1597 m. Geoffrey Browne

Ninian Whitmead (1600-1684) 1640 m. Parvati (Penelope) (d. 1648)

Penelope Whitmead (1596-1639)

Charles Whitmead (1642-1710) 1667 m. (2) Christabella Davison née Morris (1639-1701)

Caroline Whitmead (1668-1712) 1688 m. Hugh Browne

Hugo Browne (1689-1750) 1723 m. Lucilla Compton (1700-1759)

Lucy-Anne Browne (b. 1725)

Luke Whitmead (1602-1660) 1625 m. Patience Hanley (1604-1661)

Paul Browne (1641-1689) 1664 m. Lucy Cheyne (1644-1706)

2 generations

Hugh Browne (1666-1717) 1688 m. Caroline Whitmead

Charles Whitmead (1642-1710) 1664 m. (1) Louisa Lagrange (1643-1666)

Henrietta Whitmead (1665-1740)

Matthew Whitmead (1665-1743) 1686 m. Deborah Hill (1666-1740)

James Whitmead (1687-1718) 1709 m. Araminta Cadell (1688-1743)

George Whitmead (b. 1713) 1742 m. Lucy-Anne Browne (b. 1725)

Samuel Whitmead (1628-1699) 1652 m. Charity Limes (1633-1711)

four sisters

Ben Whitmead (1655-1740) 1684 m. Beatrice Saunders (1664-1701)

Cherry Whitmead (1662-1720) 1685 m. John Boyes

Frances Whitmead (1664-1700) 1688 m. Geoffrey Cutler

issue

Miles Cutler b. 1690

issue

PROLOGUE
The Whitmead Legacy

The family which eventually bore the name of Whitmead was founded in England before the Conquest, when there were still slaves in the land. Ivon de Clairpont was a Norman knight who was captured in a political dispute and sold to be a slave on a Northumbrian farmstead. He never saw his home in Normandy again, or the children he had left there. Instead, he formed a new link with another slave, or thrall as they were known, a woman called Gunnor. From that union, the Whitmeads sprang.

Long before the year 1600 when Ninian Whitmead was born, all memory of the family origins had been lost. The Whitmeads had travelled far, in more than one sense. They had journeyed by degrees from Northumbria to Essex and one branch had found its way to Cornwall. They had long since left their peasant status behind. They were people of substance now.

Yet, unknowingly, they carried legacies from both Ivon and Gunnor. The device engraved on the family silver, a pattern of smooth lines arching over wavy lines, like a stylised bridge across a river, had once been the device of the de Clairponts, and the pale red hair so often seen in the Whitmeads had been handed down from Gunnor.

Less physical bequests had descended through the generations, too. From Ivon, an ability to hold on with resolution, even obstinacy, to an unlikely ambition or a difficult marriage; or to the defence of a threatened family or beloved home. And from Gunnor, surfacing only now and then, in a few individuals, a sixth sense, an awareness of impending danger; a gift on occasion of entering and so understanding, another person's mind.

In Ninian Whitmead, all these inheritances came together, and helped to shape his life.

PART I

Ninian:
The Shipwreck
1639–1643

For how do I hold thee but by thy granting?
And for that riches where is my deserving?

William Shakespeare

Chapter One
Ninian Alone

It had not occurred to Ninian Whitmead that a man surrounded by old friends and sincere well-wishers could feel so alone.

But as he stood in the soft March drizzle in Polmawgan churchyard, watching his sister Penelope's coffin descend into the grave, loneliness was as great a part of his distress as grief. Yet he was encircled by people. His Clemo cousins had come in force. The St Asaphs were there and Francis Trevelyan, sympathetic presences gathering round the grave. Thomas Grosse had ridden over from St Buryan; Roger Polkinghorne and the Gubbes family from Penzance were here too, their faces sad. Jane Dewey from Mousehole, who had been one of Penelope's dearest friends, stood staunchly at Ninian's elbow, with Marge Hawkes from Polmawgan at her side. There were tears on Jane's strong face, and Marge, that big, tough fisherwoman, was wiping her eyes with her sleeve.

His bailiff John Treweeke was there and so was Tom Pengelly, who managed the Polmawgan tin mine, and who had turned out in this damp weather even though he had a hacking cough.

Ninian's servants were present too: the Giddys and the Bransons, and Jimmy Tonkin and little Meg Pellowe. It didn't help. None of them seemed to be quite real. When the Reverend Petroc Darracott, in his broad Cornish voice, intoned the ritual words about the sure and certain hope of the Resurrection, Ninian longed to stop his ears. What good was that either to him or Penelope now? She was dead and he must live on in Polmawgan House without her. Even if the doctrine of the Resurrection were true, then it presumably meant that their mother Morwenna, who had occupied the adjacent grave since last August, would rise up too and live again and what a delightful prospect *that* was.

When his mother died, at the age of seventy-seven, Ninian had tried his best to grieve but the fact remained that his sister might have lived longer if Morwenna Whitmead's life had been shorter. He stood now with his back to Morwenna's grave, and it was intentional.

As Darracott picked up the symbolic clod of earth and dropped it on to Penelope's casket, Tamzin St Asaph sobbed. Ninian raised his head and looked across the grave, straight into her eyes. At thirty-five, she was as beautiful as she had been at nineteen, her hair as dark and her brown eyes as steady. She wore a hooded black cloak, holding it closed at the throat to keep out the drifting rain, and the fingers of her right hand were still smooth and slender.

5

Beside her, Christopher St Asaph was bluff and fair. He was putting on weight round the middle and his limp falling-ruff was years out of date, but his mouth and his blue eyes were almost as boyish as when he and Ninian had been lads, swimming and climbing cliffs together with Francis Trevelyan and Anthony Gubbes, and looking for shellfish in the rock pools of Polmawgan Cove.

But so much could and should have been different. Ninian looked down once more at the scattered earth on the coffin and shuddered.

For the first time he squarely faced the fact that he had not only hated his mother but had also to some extent created her, that he had been weak, too intimidated by her to stand up for Penelope as he should have done. Yes, he had been only twelve, and Penelope sixteen, when their father died, and if her husband had lived longer, Morwenna might not have gained so much ascendancy over her children – but that, of course, was no excuse.

Ninian raised his head and gazed about him at familiar scenes: down to Polmawgan village below; up to Polmawgan church, where lanterns hung to guide the fishermen safely in through the rock-strewn sea at night; inland to the vague, rainswept shapes which were the rounded hills of Cornwall and the headland where his own house stood. He realised that these things were so familiar because he had lived here all his life, and that next year he would be forty.

And that in nearly forty years on earth, he had never quite become a man in his own right.

His cook-housekeeper, Hannah Giddy, could always be relied on to do her duty, especially when it came to the repast that by tradition followed a funeral. The inappropriately surnamed Hannah had been a widow when she and her lanky, unsmiling son Uriah who was now Polmawgan's handyman had entered Ninian's service. He had never met Giddy senior but Hannah's husband had surely been of the same ardently Puritan stamp as his wife and son. Ninian suspected that Hannah actually enjoyed funerals, since the requirement to wear mourning black and avoid levity wiped out the distinction, usually so obvious and nowadays increasing, between the Puritan element of society and the rest, and made them *all* look Puritan. She was now carrying in dishes with the help of Eliza Branson and little Meg, and although all of them had been quite fond of Pen and all had obviously shed tears, Hannah could be seen wishing that every social gathering could be as dark-clad and decorous.

However, she had done well today, Ninian thought, as he stood listening with half an ear while the Reverend Darracott made small-talk about the fabric of the church. In the big Polmawgan dining room, the black-draped table held red wine and ale; fresh, warm bread; fish pies; a potage of lamb with cabbages and onions; and a dish of spinach garnished with eggs. There were no sweet dishes; Hannah considered these frivolous. But she had put out the family silver, showing a very proper respect, and certainly no one would go home hungry.

Provided, of course, someone actually called the guests to the table.

6

'. . . Ninian, my dear boy, I christened your sister afore you were born and I know it must seem unconscionable strange now both she and your mother are gone. But if you don't announce the meal, they'll all stand about for ever. They won't sit down afore you tell them and the food's getting cold.'

Ninian looked confusedly round, and found expectant eyes on him. Hitherto, when there were guests in the house, either Morwenna or Penelope had called them to eat. Now he must do it himself. He cleared his throat and Darracott obligingly rapped on the nearby sideboard to command silence for him. 'Please take your seats. The meal is served,' said Ninian, and moved towards his seat at the top of the table. 'Mr Darracott, please sit on my right.'

The chair on his right should have been Penelope's. He preferred not to leave it empty and the vicar was today's chief guest. He let the chair to his left go to whom it would and was glad when his friend Francis Trevelyan took it.

In the past, Trevelyans had coveted Polmawgan property and had bought up some of the land, but if once there had been trouble between them, all that was long ago. Ninian and Francis had been friends since before they could remember.

'You must be feeling very lost,' Francis said kindly now. 'Penelope was a good woman if ever there was one. I always reckoned some man missed a good wife in Penelope.'

'Indeed,' Ninian murmured.

Francis nodded soberly and then a gleam came into his eyes. It was well known to all his associates that Francis Trevelyan was incapable of keeping his face solemn for any length of time and had been heard to refer to tact as mere pussyfooting. His next remark was entirely in character.

'But one could say the same of you, Ninian; the other way round, as it were. And Polmawgan House is lacking a mistress. Why don't you consider getting married?'

There were faintly shocked noises round the table. It was right and proper, once the mourners had walked away from the grave, to begin gently encouraging the bereaved to look to the future. Death came at the will of God and His will must be accepted without undue repining. But the seriousness of the event should not be forgotten either, and consolation must be tempered with propriety. Francis Trevelyan had just breached the conventions.

The scandalised ripple amused him. He grinned, showing strong, white teeth in a healthy mouth. 'Ninian's not offended, he knows me too well. Isn't that true, Ninian?'

'It's perfectly true,' said Ninian gravely and then let himself smile a little because Francis' grin was catching. The Clemos were glowering, but Christopher St Asaph's headshake was indulgent and Tamzin too had allowed her lips to twitch.

'You've no call to be casting the man's single state in his teeth, Trevelyan,' said Darracott, and the laughter lines deepened in his red-veined face, which always looked as though it had been slightly

7

squashed between crown and chin. 'And you a widower yourself these five years. B'ain't it time you were looking round on your own behalf?'

'This is not a proper subject for this occasion,' said one of the Clemo cousins repressively. Clemo had been Morwenna's maiden name and the cousins were the offspring of her brothers. There were five of them, three male, two female, all stocky and dark with watchful, grey eyes and faces which rarely smiled, even at Christmas. Ninian didn't like any of them and was seized with a perverse desire to take Francis' part, just to annoy them.

'Frank means no harm. Penelope was my sister, not my wife,' he said. 'Frank has been trying to marry me off for years. He's for ever suggesting suitable ladies; or in some cases, unsuitable ones. I've grown used to it.'

It was easier to talk in this rallying fashion than to do what most of those present expected, which was to talk about Penelope. He was afraid to do that in case he broke down into grief, or possibly fury. Let Francis burble away about hypothetical marriages, and let Penelope rest in peace.

Francis, head on one side, was quite prepared to cooperate but in spite of the infectious nature of his sense of humour, most of Ninian's guests thought otherwise. Anthony Gubbes and Roger Polkinghorne, both merchants and both aldermen of Penzance, gave Francis reproving glances and began a pointedly serious discussion on whether or not the two shillings all foreign vessels had to pay to tie up in Penzance was too much for the smaller vessels and might drive trade away. Christopher St Asaph in flurried tones said something to Thomas Grosse about the present difficulties of the East India Company. Then Jane Dewey picked up a silver flagon and across all the other conversations, her voice boomed out.

'Mr Whitmead, may I ask what this device is that is chased into your silver? Do you know? Your mother didn't; I asked her once. It's an uncommonly intriguing pattern – looks like a bridge across a river.'

Eating and talking alike were all suspended while everyone attended to Mrs Dewey. Majestically proportioned, she was the wife of a well-to-do fisherman and all her five sons were sailors of one kind or another. All were at sea just now and she had come unescorted except by two meek daughters-in-law. Penelope had loved her because Jane Dewey was everything Penelope wasn't – large and strong and independent of spirit. Today she was wearing a conventional dark dress with collar and cuffs and head-dress of impeccable white, but the face framed by the carefully laundered linen was big-nosed and weatherbeaten. Jane had frequently been seen on the deck of her husband's ship, wearing breeches and smoking a pipe. She knew how to use a handgun and her voice commanded attention like a cannonade. When Jane spoke, people listened.

Ninian found her intervention a relief. 'All the silver with that device on, my parents inherited from my great-aunt Christina Whitmead,' he said. 'She lived at a big house in Surrey, called Ashdon, and my father

8

once told me that the pattern was the badge of that branch of the family. But its significance beyond that, I'm afraid I don't know.'

'Your great-aunt never explained it?'

'Not to my knowledge. My parents had little to do with her until she was dying and the family was summoned. By that time, she was almost too ill to speak. I was only six, then. I can remember going to the house –a huge, decrepit, shadowy barn of a place, it was. And I can remember her lying propped up on her pillows in a great big cavern of a four-poster. It was frightening.'

'And today is the wrong time for such mournful reminiscences,' said Francis. 'Ninian's had enough of deathbeds; recent or ancient.' He picked up a fingerbowl. 'I see that this has the same pattern on it. Amazing. I've been coming here ever since I can remember and never noticed the silver before.'

'We don't use it often,' said Ninian. 'Only on . . . special occasions. And we haven't had that many. No marriages. Only . . . days like this.'

'You should use it much more,' said Jane Dewey dictatorially. 'It's handsome stuff.'

One of the Clemo cousins, a middle-aged man called Ezra, whose religious inclinations were excessively Puritan, remarked that such devices were little but worldly show, and his sister, Mrs Prudence Jenken, nodded, lips severely pursed. Hannah, standing on duty by the sideboard, hands folded at her waist, nodded too. Francis eyed them in annoyance and said wickedly: 'Only noblemen have devices like that. Maybe Ninian is the unacknowledged descendant of some great baron. You must take care to choose a wife in accordance with your station, my friend.'

'No, that's enough, now, Trevelyan.' Roger Polkinghorne was not a handsome man; with his back-sloping forehead and large grey eyes and even larger mouth he had an unfortunate resemblance to a fish. But being an alderman, he had presence. So had Anthony Gubbes, with his long, strong chin and his deep-set blue eyes. Anthony now nodded vigorous agreement that Francis had gone far enough. Ninian gave his friend a small shake of the head.

Christopher St Asaph had been distracted by something outside. He was gazing out of the window and not attending to the conversation. Suddenly he craned his neck to see better, and shouted: 'Damme, if that isn't the *Indian Venus!*'

As a means of creating a diversion, this was even more successful than Jane Dewey's ploy with the family silver. Heads swivelled and chairs grated as the company unanimously turned towards the windows at the end of the dining room, which looked out north-east towards Mount's Bay.

The rain had ceased now but the wind had strengthened, lifting the cloud to form a steely ceiling beneath which the light was clear. The English Channel, grey and streaked with white horses, stretched away to a sharp horizon and St Michael's Mount, crowned with its battlemented castle, jutted miniature but plain in the middle distance. The merchant ship making her way up the Channel from the south was well out, but many details of her were clear. She was a beautiful vessel, sixty feet long, her rigging a mixture of lateen and square, her sails filled by the wind and her figurehead outlined dark against the sea. It was the figurehead which had identified her, for it was highly distinctive, carved in the shape of a woman whose form and head were draped in an un-English fashion, but whose contours were to say the least of it voluptuous.

'Disgraceful heathen thing,' said Ezra angrily.

'Disgraceful *Courteen* thing!' said Christopher, even more angrily, and all of them, with indignant concentration, watched the vessel, sending up white spray as she butted into the cross-seas outside Mount's Bay, slowly pass from view beyond the Mount.

'My eldest is with an East India ship,' said Jane Dewey, 'and they say that William Courteen's vessels are no better than pirate ships. His merchants have been paying the Indian vendors in base coinage. Alan – he's a First Mate now – says that the East India merchants are losing the confidence of their contacts. It's damaging profits.'

'As most of us very well know,' said Christopher with a snort. 'We nearly all have shares in the East India Company. I certainly have! Why did the King ever license Courteen?'

'His Majesty believes that competition is healthy,' said Francis.

'The tale I heard was that Courteen paid handsomely for the concession,' said Ezra Clemo harshly. 'Seems he's a wealthy man. Too wealthy to need to take the bread out of godly men's mouths or even out of heathen mouths. What are the chances of bringing them to the Lord if they think we're all rogues?'

'I'd say less,' grumbled Christopher, 'if the competition were fair. But young Dewey is right. Courteen's ships are privateers and some of his captains aren't even above boarding English ships at sea and stealing their cargoes.'

The conversation settled down on a course which would keep it, for the rest of the meal, far away from either Penelope or Francis Trevelyan's plans for Ninian's future. Ninian, waxing indignant with the rest of them, worrying aloud about the future of his own shares and shaking his head over the state of trade in general, was glad of it.

But when it was time to take leave of them all, he could not avoid speaking of Penelope. He stood at the door, clasping the hands of one guest after another, receiving their final, low-voiced condolences.

'Everyone will miss her. She was so modest and sweet . . .'

'. . . so devoted to her mother. It was the loss of Morwenna that took away her will to live, I feel sure . . .'

'. . . I could never understand why Penelope never married but if she had, there would be a husband and family grieving badly for her now. The Lord knows His own business best . . .'

'. . . a wonderful daughter and a wonderful sister. You should put that on her headstone, Ninian.'

'Indeed, I intend to.'

'. . . Frank's remarks weren't in the best of taste, considering this is poor Penelope's funeral, but I'm damned if he's entirely wrong, y'know, Ninian. Don't take it amiss, but with your mother anu ∠ister both gone . . .'

'I know, Christopher. And I don't take it amiss.'

He was glad when they had gone. But when he went into the parlour he found that after all one guest still remained. 'Can I stay for a while?' Francis asked.

'If you like. Oh yes, please do! The others,' Ninian said, 'were wearing me out. They were saying all the right things and I was saying all the right things and none of it helps. But you're different.' Francis's presence would put off the moment when he was left here, to face the empty place which had been Penelope's. 'Sit down and take a glass with me.'

When they were settled with glasses of Madeira and an engraved silver flagon full of it in front of them, Francis said: 'I wanted to stay, to apologise. I was somewhat crass at the table today. It was the wrong moment to be making jokes about the future and . . . well . . . finding another mistress for Polmawgan House. But I meant well.'

'I know. I minded some of the entirely proper remarks which the others made when they were leaving, much more. They meant well too, but . . .' Ninian shook his head irritably. 'Not Christopher. He understands me, just as you do. But there was Anthony saying that Penelope was a wonderful daughter, and as for Ezra. . . . Well, no doubt he had good intentions.

'Ezra? I thought so. I was watching from the parlour door and I saw your face,' Francis said. 'What did Ezra say that upset you so much? Or shouldn't I ask?'

'Oh, you can ask, and what's more, I'll tell you.' Ninian, glass in hand, crossed his legs and settled back in his chair, catching as he did so a glimpse of his own face in the mirror above the hearth, and noticing how drawn he was. His looks were unremarkable at the best of times; he was well-knit and wiry enough, though not tall, but he had a nondescript face not much improved by nearly white eyelashes, smallish hazel eyes and limp hair of a pale red colour. It could never be coaxed to curl for more than an hour at a time and sooner than have it trailing over his shoulders in rats' tails, he kept it short, which caused many people to assume, inaccurately, that he was of the Puritan persuasion. In truth, he had no strong beliefs of any sort.

'Ezra was saying he couldn't understand why Penelope hadn't married,' he said. 'And I was feeling guilty.'

'Guilty? Why? You can't have . . . damn it, Ninian, you didn't keep your sister from marrying! Surely!'

'No. But I didn't help her as I should, either. There are things I've never talked about much,' said Ninian slowly. 'Things go on inside families that even their closest friends don't hear about. One has one's pride. But I think I'd like to talk to you about it now. If you wouldn't mind.'

'Of course I wouldn't mind. Provided it's something you really want to share.'

11

'It never was before but now, today . . . yes, it is. Pen and I should both have married,' said Ninian. 'Today is a day for looking back into the past and I think I feel like explaining why neither of us did.'

'I must say, I've often wondered. I've tried hard to find you a wife, as you very well know. I've felt that both you and Pen had been somehow star-crossed, as Shakespeare puts it, only I didn't want to probe. But, you say you want to tell me. So – what happened?'

Eliza had lit the parlour fire. Ninian gazed into the flames. 'It was nearly fourteen years ago, back in 1625. Pen and I were both courting at the same time. She was twenty-nine. She should have been wed long before but my mother . . . I suppose you didn't hear what the youngest Mrs Dewey said as she was leaving? She said that it was surely my mother's death which had hastened Penelope's, or words to that effect. Hah! There are times,' said Ninian, with sudden energy, 'when people amaze me. Whether families discuss their private business or not, some things ought to be obvious! But no: it's the convention that all mothers are perfect and all daughters are devoted and people just . . . just *insist* on believing it even when it's patently not true. Frank, my mother *ate* Penelope! Pen was fading to death even before Mother went, because she was sucked dry of hope, of confidence, of vitality.' He paused. 'And now,' said Ninian defensively, 'go on, be shocked and say I shouldn't talk about my mother in such a fashion!'

'I'm not shocked at all. I had a grandmother like that. She used up my Aunt Cathy. Aunt Cathy was her unpaid servant and my grandmother made sure she never had a chance to marry. I take it that's what your mother did to your sister?'

'Yes. She believed that she had the right to be served by Penelope. She could have had all the personal maids she liked but no, it had to be Pen. She . . . she surrounded her,' Ninian said. 'Wouldn't let her go out without permission; kept her from attending parties. I overheard her once telling Penelope what a horrible business it was going to bed with one's husband – I felt very sorry for my father, I must say! – and she used to nag at her, tell her that she was stupid: her sewing was untidy; servants didn't respect her; she didn't know how to choose dishes for a dinner; no man would ever put up with her as a wife.

'Frank, she made Pen afraid to think beyond the walls of this house. And I was too young . . . no,' said Ninian, 'I wasn't that young. The truth is, I was too thoughtless to see how wrong it was, and too damned weak to defend Penelope. I look back now and I castigate myself for that weakness.'

'If I remember aright,' said Francis, 'your mother could be very intimidating.'

'Oh, she was,' said Ninian grimly. 'She'd give you a look out of those cold eyes of hers and it was like having a nail driven through you. I did once or twice say things like: "Oh, but Mother, Pen *can* sew; see how beautifully she has mended my shirt," but she would tell me not to argue, in a tone of voice that shrivelled me – and somehow I couldn't prevent it from shrivelling me. Well, at last, Christopher St Asaph came courting.'

12

'Christopher?'

'The same. Why not? We'd known him all our lives. But he first noticed her properly at the wedding of one of my Clemo cousins. It was a serious affair, as you can imagine. The Clemos don't go in for riotous celebrations. I sometimes suspect,' said Ninian, allowing himself to go off briefly at a tangent, 'that much of what the Puritans call godliness is just parsimony dressed up as virtue.'

'It is with the Clemos,' said Francis with feeling. 'I know! Ezra's a tenant of mine, after all. I've had to speak to him about the way he feeds his plough horses. "How do you expect a horse to do a good day's work on dusty hay and short oat rations?" I said to him. "Do your poor beasts even know what a bran mash *is*?" I haven't seen any improvement, though. I'll have to speak to him again, soon.'

'My mother remarked, more than once, quite candidly, that as long as she had Penelope, she could save the cost of two maids.' Ninian ignored the interruption. 'I didn't hire Meg until Mother was gone. Well, getting back to that Clemo wedding, Pen was allowed to go, for once, and she dressed herself up nicely for it, and there she was, all in pale green, standing out like a beacon among all those Clemo women in dark blue and charcoal. Christopher was there and his eyes were opened. You can imagine what my mother thought about it when he started calling every other day – ostensibly to see me, of course, but always managing to see Pen too – and just happening to cross her path whenever she went to the village or into Mousehole or Penzance. Mother actually forbade him to speak to Pen at one point. She said the St Asaphs used to be Papists and she'd never allow her daughter to marry into such a family. I did object to that. I said that the last Catholic St Asaph had been executed in the days of Queen Elizabeth, and that Christopher was a respectable Anglican. But my mother wouldn't listen. She wanted to hold on to Penelope. She used every weapon she could think of. She swore that she'd never speak to Pen again if Pen married him. She said Pen would find marriage a nightmare; she'd die in childbirth; she was useless as a housewife; how did Pen think her poor mother would manage, left to run this great big place without her . . .'

'A little contradictory, surely?'

'That never worried my mother. You may laugh, Frank. It may sound comical now, but it was deadly serious to Pen and me. Mother wouldn't listen to anything I said and I wasn't determined enough to persist. Or perhaps I didn't have my mind on Pen quite enough. As I said, I was courting too and it wasn't going very smoothly. Her parents didn't think I had enough to offer. Her father was a prosperous lawyer with wide business interests and money salted away, and I had this house which is big, but costly to run, and all I had to run it with was a not-very-productive home farm and the Wheal Susannah tin mine which looked likely to run out of tin at any moment.'

'My family had a share in that mine once,' Francis said. 'My father let yours buy him out and then regretted it when a new seam was found.'

13

'Which wasn't until later and that one's running out now. However. In addition to all my other drawbacks, of course, I had my mother. No one else realised that she was a drawback, naturally, because Pen never complained openly any more than I did, but it made me, well, apologetic.'

Ninian broke off and poked the fire. Francis waited without speaking. 'Eventually,' Ninian said, 'Christopher proposed to Pen. She came to me and cried and said she wanted to marry him but what would our mother say? There'd be scenes, and Mother would never come to the wedding. I said to her: marry him. Elope if you want to. I did offer to help if they needed it. I did do that, Frank! But she'd told Christopher that she must think it over. She was going to give him her answer next time they met. He was growing impatient because she wouldn't make up her mind.'

'And then?' said Francis after a pause. He was watching his friend's face as the firelight played on it. Ninian's brow was wrinkled, not in perplexity, but as though he were in pain.

'In the end,' Ninian said, laying the poker aside, 'she decided to say yes. There was a christening party in Mousehole; we were all to go and so was Christopher. Pen meant to tell him then. Then Mother heard that Christopher was to be one of the guests and she refused to attend and wouldn't let Pen go either. I tried to show solidarity with Pen.' He gave Francis a painful smile. 'I stayed at home, too.'

'And?'

'The girl I was courting was Tamzin Trelawny,' said Ninian simply. 'The baby that was to be christened was her infant cousin. I wasn't there and she was hurt because I'd promised I would see her that day. Pen wasn't there to give Christopher his answer . . .'

'Tamzin? Oh my God!' said Francis.

'Yes. They met, they talked, they commiserated. I don't know the details. I think they were probably angry with us, with Pen and me. I also think that Tamzin's parents encouraged them, as soon as they saw that there was an attraction. Christopher was better off than I was, or am, for that matter. Two months later, they were married.'

'My dear fellow!' said Francis with sincerity.

'I was very bitter, for a long time,' Ninian said. 'But Pen was just horribly hurt. She blamed herself for failing to get to that christening. I blamed myself on behalf of us both. Christopher wrote to Pen to break it off and Tamzin wrote to me when they were about to be betrothed. Well, all right, I hadn't much to offer Tamzin, and I knew it. But Pen was so vulnerable, so put upon, and she loved Christopher so much. He's a good fellow at heart but I think he just didn't notice how much Pen loved him. If someone loves you, you ought at least to notice!'

'I never knew anything of this,' Francis said. 'Perhaps I don't notice enough, either, but I've never been aware of any rift between you and the St Asaphs.'

'I don't think we wanted anyone to know. Pen and I certainly didn't. People do love to whisper. I didn't attend the wedding, of course, but we were all very civil afterwards when we met by chance socially, which

14

was fairly often. We couldn't go to a gathering anywhere in all Penwith without meeting each other. We never went to each other's homes, of course. They've only been in this house twice since their marriage: once for my mother's funeral and then again today.'

'You amaze me. But now I think about it – no, I've never seen them here, except at the funerals, as you say, and I've never seen you at Coombe. I suppose I didn't realise because we were always coming across each other at other places, and I've had you all to Rosnance, all together as often as not.'

'Precisely. And as the years went by, I suppose I've just got used to things. Meeting Christopher and Tamzin, making everyday conversation across other people's dinner tables: all that slowly eroded the bitterness. What had happened, had happened. There was nothing to be done.'

'You have an amiable nature, Ninian. If I were in your place, I doubt if the bitterness would ever have been eroded, as you put it.'

'It's nearly fifteen years. It's a long time. Besides, one's fires die down with age. Wait till you're as old as I am.'

'Oh, Methusaleh! You're only three years older than me.'

'It feels like more, sometimes. Well, that's the story, Frank. I learned to live with it. Eventually, I even admitted to myself that Christopher was still a good fellow and probably hadn't meant to hurt anyone. He didn't understand how Pen felt about him and supposed that I didn't really care for Tamzin. Quite natural! Tamzin had arrived at the same conclusion, as far as I was concerned. But Pen never really got over it. From then on she just . . . faded. Poor Pen.' He smiled wryly. 'Even with me, acceptance went only so far. Every nerve in my body still comes alive when I come into Tamzin's presence and I still find it painful to see her children. Pen suffered over those children, too. I have blamed myself a thousand times over, for her unhappiness and my own.'

'Don't take offence at this,' said Francis. 'But although I was tactless today, my advice was still sound, you know.'

'Find a wife, you mean? Find one yourself, as Darracott said. You've been a widower for years!'

'I'm sorry. You're offended after all. And I stayed on in order to apologise!'

'You didn't offend me earlier and you haven't now. Dine with me on Monday.'

'I'm engaged to have dinner in Penzance on Monday. I could come on Tuesday – or to Sunday dinner tomorrow.'

'Not Sunday dinner. Hannah won't cook on the Sabbath so we just have cold food. Eliza will cook if I ask her,' Ninian said humorously, 'but Hannah resents it. She stands about in the kitchen with her arms folded, staring, and makes Eliza nervous.'

'I keep saying I don't want to offend you but you're incorrigible! If Hannah were my servant, I'd bloody well make her cook the Sunday dinner.'

'You don't know her! Oh, have some more wine and stop trying to change my nature,' said Ninian. 'I want a quiet life from now on. And I don't want to fall in love.'

'It is possible to marry as a practical move, without falling in love. Elizabeth and I got on together very well although we were both sorry not to have children. But I was never in love with her. I married her, because unlike you, I did go to Christopher's wedding, and when I saw his bride, I envied him. I wished I'd found her first. It was after that that I decided I'd better get married myself, as soon as possible. It's odd that we should both have been drawn to Tamzin. She's still a lovely woman and as a bride, well . . .'

'I daresay. I think I shall do better to keep away from affairs of the heart, Frank. One can be so hurt. Pen and I were hurt. I don't want to go through that again, or to give pain to anyone else. I detest doing that.'

'Really? What a kindly soul you are. You mean that if you got the chance to sink a Courteen ship, you wouldn't take it?'

'That would be different!' And for the first time since Penelope had fallen ill with the consumption which killed her, Ninian laughed.

Chapter Two

The Ship

'If someone pays you the compliment of loving you, you ought to notice.'

At the age of six, when that idea first came into Ninian's head, he was too young to frame it in those words; that came later, when he was grown. But it was born in him when his great-aunt Christina Whitmead was dying and with his parents he had travelled from Cornwall to her home in Surrey.

Ashdon House was no longer part of the family. It had been left to his Essex uncle, who had sold it long ago. But he remembered that visit vividly. He recalled his great-aunt, hoarsely whispering from the depths of her shadowy bed, trying to tell his father something about the terms of her will, and how the whisper came out slurred along with a dribble of spit, because her mouth was paralysed on one side.

He could remember too the air of decay in the house and garden. Once, they had been so famous for their magnificence that Queen Elizabeth had stayed there. His mother had said that, as she stared round the great hall, noting its neglected state. He had kept a clear image of Morwenna, wearing a wide ruff and a plate-like farthingale, running a suspicious finger along the top of the sideboard and peering with disapproval at the woodworm in the panelling.

And he remembered too that his great-aunt's servants had apparently loved her and that, according to his elders, Christina had never, all her life, really been aware of it when people cared for her. In Ashdon, listening to the adults, he gathered that she had lavished all her love on the house, not to mention colossal sums of money, and had scarcely noticed her husband until after he was dead. Then she had lived on in the house, apparently communing with it because it held her memories. In the end, she had faded into the dust and the shadows which were more real to her than the servants who cried for her.

At the age of six, too young even to find words for his thoughts, he had nevertheless resolved that when he was grown, he would value those who loved him, and regard his home as merely a place to live.

But it hadn't worked out quite like that. His father's death, when Ninian was still only twelve, had forced him to become the man of the house very early in life. He soon found out that it was his duty to care for the building, and that it was a demanding task, because Polmawgan House, perched on its headland a few miles south of Penzance, was

17

continually exposed to storm winds and driving rain and needed regular repairs. Furthermore, it was big.

It had grown in Ninian's lifetime, for he was ten when his father decided that a separate building behind the house – in the days of armed retainers, Polmawgan's men had slept there – should be demolished. When it was done, there was a sizeable pile of good building stone lying temptingly to hand, and that was how Polmawgan had acquired its new wing, with the big dining room and a second parlour on the ground floor and several new rooms above, mostly used as bedchambers, except for one which Ninian eventually chose as a study. This floor included a remarkable innovation, since the rooms were linked by a passage instead of leading out of each other in the usual way. There were also two extra attic rooms under the roof.

To keep such a house in order meant much expenditure of time and money, whether he liked it or not. In the end, to his own surprise, he found that he did like it, and now that Pen was gone, he would have confessed if asked, that his affections belonged to his home. He was mildly fond of his servants and thought they were mildly fond of him, but that was as far as it went.

No one but Ninian himself thought his feelings for his home were even marginally questionable, for Polmawgan House, as the Cornish folk said, was handsome. Its position might be exposed, but it was also magnificent: three hundred feet above the sea, looking out across the thirty mile-wide expanse of Mount's Bay. To the north, lay Minecombe and the tin mine, Wheal Susannah, and beyond that lay the fishing port of Mousehole and the harbour of Penzance with its little town growing year by year up the steeply sloping hill behind it; both of them places Ninian enjoyed frequenting; both of them part of home.

To the south lay another, deeper combe, running down to Polmawgan Cove and its tiny fishing village with the church just above. The valley's sides were clothed with fields and sheep pastures, some of them Ninian's, the rest Trevelyan land. The village of Polmawgan itself had been owned by the Trevelyans for more than a century.

Jutting between the two combes, the headland fell away in a sheer cliff, with broken rocks in the sea below. At sea-level, there was a cave, running through the headland like a tunnel. When Ninian was a boy, he and Francis and Christopher, and sometimes Anthony Gubbes, whom they had met at school in Penzance, had found that it was possible to explore the cave when the sea was out. Ninian hadn't been down there now for years but the cave reminded him of its existence at every high tide, when the dull boom of the waves crashing into it reverberated up into the house.

The cave too was part of that comprehensive picture which came into his mind whenever he heard the word *home*.

Within the house, he could commune with its memories much as his great-aunt had communed with her own at Ashdon. Polmawgan House held many old memories; not just his own, but older ones still, some of them part of local history.

A woman called Susannah Trefusis had lived there once. Born

Susannah Whitmead, she was of his blood though it was Christopher St Asaph and not Ninian who was descended from her. Legend called her a great lady. The tin miners remembered her for her charity; because of that, Ninian's father had named the mine for her. The records of St Michael's Mount said that her husband had sent her there for a time to attend the wife of Perkin Warbeck, the Pretender who had tried to seize Henry VII's crown.

Susannah had been dragged into great affairs against her will by her husband but when he was arrested, so the story went, she sought audience with the King himself to plead for him. She was still a local example of honourable wifeliness, held up to the maidens of Penwith, as this part of Cornwall was named.

Susannah had left her mark here. She had planted the herb garden, and chosen much of the fine oak furniture which Ninian still used. Above all, she had left her atmosphere. Morwenna had scorned such ideas but Pen had several times said she could feel Susannah in the house. 'She's a gracious presence, Ninian.'

His great-aunt Christina had been her grand-daughter and she too had lived here for a time. She was not well remembered locally but Ninian sometimes sensed her influence too. It was different from Susannah's. Christina's was a hungry, unhappy shade, yearning for something which it could not have, or be. At times, totting up the accounts sent in by builders and carpenters, not all of them for work as essential as repairing storm-damaged chimneys or replacing slates torn off the roof in a gale, he would wonder if he were becoming like his great-aunt. On the whole he thought not but he could see how such things could happen.

The most mysterious thing in Polmawgan was a phenomenon he did not understand at all. He only knew that it was always followed by some alteration in his life. He liked looking at the sea by moonlight and a few nights before the deaths of both his parents and of Pen, he had seen a strange ship, square-rigged and with a forecastle crenellated like the walls of the abbey on St Michael's Mount, glide out of Polmawgan Cove over that moonlit sea. The first time, which was when his father was ill and he himself was only a boy, he had taken her for a real ship and when visiting the village next day had asked after her and been surprised because no one knew what he meant.

He also saw the ship the night before he received Tamzin's farewell letter, although that time, it was in a dream. He had realised then that it was his private ghost, his harbinger of change. He thought that the ship might once have been real, but he did not know its story.

He never spoke of it again, for that could be unwise. It might bring the word *witchcraft* to mind. King James the First, who had been on the throne throughout Ninian's youth, had been rabid, not to say slightly insane, on the matter of witchcraft, encouraging his subjects to believe in it and to hunt down witches with the same virtuous zeal as Mary Tudor had shown in pursuit of heresy. As a boy, he had seen a poor old woman, bent-backed with age, arrested in Polmawgan village and taken away, trembling and protesting, watched by cold-eyed former neighbours, charged with raising a storm and causing a village boy to have fits. She had been heard muttering to herself and she kept a pet raven and that was enough to draw suspicion on her. He had heard afterwards that she had been hanged at Launceston. He knew of another woman, from St Ives, who had been accused of causing her husband's death by witchcraft, and was burned, because her crime was considered a form of treason.

To be old and peculiar and female made one more vulnerable, but they weren't essential qualifications. Young women, even young men, could fall victim to charges of sorcery. Go about saying that you saw ships that weren't there or that you had taken to having prophetic dreams – and the next time a storm blew up from nowhere or someone you knew fell unexpectedly ill, you might well end up on the gallows.

He kept silence, therefore, although he continued to like looking at the sea, both by night and by day. Because he loved books too, he had made himself a study, and the room he picked was immediately above the dining chamber, with a view across the bay. He had had it lined with shelves and provided with a hearth where a fire was always lit in chilly weather. A branched candlestick furnished with candles was always ready, and there was a writing desk at which he could pen business letters or go through his accounts.

When he wished for relaxation, there was a cushioned window-seat, with a folding table beside it, on which books were usually strewn. He would sit by the window for hours, reading, glancing out now and then at the sea, watching its moods alter under the variable Cornish skies.

Ninian sometimes noticed, with mild surprise, that in his nature, alongside his love of books and quietness, ran quite a different strain. As a boy he had been taught swordsmanship and he was actually good at it and often practised with Francis. He was good, too, at sailing his little boat, the *Silver Fish*, which he kept at Polmawgan. He liked the sea best of all when it was either mysterious, as it seemed under the moon, or else stormy. He often chose to walk on the headland in wild weather, preferring it to the days of skylarks and scented thyme and sunlit sea-pinks. He liked to watch the wavecrests roll towards the land, while his leggy, hairy lurcher dogs, Lady and Pol, gambolled excitedly and the wind turned their ears inside out.

In such pastimes, he found his solace after Pen's death. A year later, he said to Francis Trevelyan: 'You know, on the whole I would call myself a happy man.'

'You're incorrigible, as I've told you before,' said Francis. 'Happy, indeed! Detached from reality would be more like it. I'm glad you're overcoming your loss, but when I hear you talk so smugly about being happy while trouble brews all round you, I could shake you.'

'Trouble?'

'Serious trouble. The King and Parliament could end by taking up arms against each other, mark my words.'

'Nonsense.'

'It isn't nonsense. There's no more loyal King's man than I am but he's being very foolish. I went to London last month and I was nearly run down in the street by Archbishop Laud's attendants, clearing the way for him and knocking people aside with staves. Only the King can make Laud mind his manners and he isn't doing so. It's making people angry, especially the Puritans who think bishops are Popish anyway, and Parliament is full of Puritans. They'll call Laud to order themselves soon.'

'I don't go to London often,' said Ninian.

'I know you don't, you stay-at-home,' said Francis mockingly. 'You've hardly ever left Cornwall. You didn't even go away to study! Day school in Penzance and then tutors; that was your education. But even you must have noticed that there's been a certain amount of bad feeling over the Ship Money tax.'

'Oh yes.' Ninian nodded. 'I daresay it's in order to tax people to pay for ships for the realm's defence, but the taxes are too high. I've had to help some of my miners out. One of them had to sell his bedding when the tax collectors came round and I had to buy some more for him. I'm well aware of the strength of feeling about the taxes and everything else, I assure you. But personally, I detest taking sides.'

'You may have to, one day. The trouble's growing. Look at Darracott, changing the form of the morning service in Polmawgan Church last Sunday.'

'Oh, that. He didn't change it very much, and why everyone had to gather in little clusters and whisper about it afterwards, I couldn't imagine. I said as much to you, if I remember aright.'

'And when I said that Darracott was trying to steer a middle course, and simplify his services without exactly abandoning the official Anglican form, to stay on both sides at once, as it were, and please everybody; you just laughed and said that he had merely mystified them. But it's no laughing matter. If a real conflict comes, the people who have tried to please everybody will probably end by pleasing no one, and those who want to stay out will be dragged in regardless. I smell trouble. What does that favourite poet of yours, John Donne, say? *No man is an Island*; isn't that it?'

'I hope he's wrong,' said Ninian. 'Poets don't always actually know things, Frank. They just write down their beliefs in very convincing words, beautiful words – but for beautiful dreams. Or, in this case,' he added thoughtfully, 'alarming ones.'

But, beautiful or alarming, it was true that Donne was a favourite writer of his. A few days after the anniversary of Pen's death, he sat in his study reading Donne's poetry, and thinking both of Pen and of that conversation with Francis.

> Death be not proud, though some have called thee
> Mighty and dreadful, for thou art not so,
> For those whom thou think'st thou dost overthrow,
> Die not, poor Death . . .

He wished he could believe that fourth line, for Pen's sake. But

21

there it was. Part of his dislike of taking sides in the present political squabbles sprang from the simple fact that they were largely a matter of conflicting religions and as the years went on, he believed in religion less and less, although this, like his phantom ship, was not something he mentioned openly.

'I fear,' he said aloud to Pen's memory, 'that the life everlasting comes into the category of beautiful dreams.' The printed page faded in an untimely and livid twilight and the window shook in a gust of wind. He looked up to find that the noonday sky had darkened. Rain was sweeping over the sea, and the boom of the breakers in the cave far below was suddenly so thunderous that the house quivered. He rose to light the candles, and then stopped short, peering out of the window, as the wind tore a gap in the drifting curtain of rain.

For one astonished moment, he thought that he was seeing his phantom ship at noon. Then he realised that the vessel momentarily revealed as though she had square rigging and a crenellated forecastle only because her lateen sails had been torn away and a broken mast was lying in jagged confusion over her bows. She was entirely real and in very serious danger. Abandoning both John Donne and the candles, Ninian rushed out of the room, shouting as he went for Dick Branson, who was Eliza's husband and Ninian's personal man. Dick appeared at the foot of the stairs. 'Sir?'

'There's a ship about to hit the rocks outside Polmawgan Cove!' Ninian leapt down the stairs two at a time. 'She's got a broken mast. Come on, we've got to get down there! *Eliza!* My cloak! Dick, find Jimmy and Uriah and follow me!'

The quick path down to the cove was unsafe in high winds. Uriah Giddy shook a lugubrious head at it, and Dick Branson, square-built and stolid, said: 'No good risking that.' Jimmy Tonkin, who looked like a gnome and rarely spoke at all, was already hurrying off towards the longer track, which led back along the headland and joined the path that ran down from the head of the combe to the cove. The others followed quickly. As they went, they heard the bell of Polmawgan Church clanging out through the noise of wind and sea. Ships ran into danger all too often on this rocky coast; the bell summoned all able-bodied men within hearing to come to the rescue. It also called all poverty-stricken people, women and children as well as men, to hurry to the chance of plunder. When Ninian and his companions at length reached the cove, it was already crowded.

The cove itself was fairly sheltered. A few boats which had been left on the beach had been pulled up to safety, and in the curve of the little quay, the rest of Polmawgan's fishing boats lay in comparative security, lurching and scraping against each other but out of reach of the tide, which was now ebbing, although the wind was slowing it down and the waves were still breaking over the end of the quay.

The Polmawgan villagers had gathered on the crescent of wet sand which the tide had now reluctantly laid bare. Hefty Marge Hawkes stood beside her fisherman husband. The coil of rope round Wally

Hawkes' shoulder might be for hauling shipwrecked sailors ashore, but the immense fishing net in which Marge was draped was probably for the capture of floating boxes. There were many others similarly equipped. At the back of the cove, where a bank of shingle ran up into the shelter of a cliff overhang, someone had managed to kindle a small fire, and some soaking wet children had been gathered round it to keep warm.

Christopher St Asaph was there on the shore, summoned no doubt by the bell. It could be heard from Coombe House, which was a credit to the foundry which made it. The storm was deafening, filling the air, palpable as the rain. Breakers smashed on the headland, throwing up plumes of spray, swirling into the mouth of the tunnel cave, and the wind screeched, buffeting people with invisible fists. Ninian strode out across the sand, and saw Francis emerging from the crowd to meet him, wet strands of hair plastered across his face. 'Ninian!'

'Could you hear the bells all the way to Rosnance?' Ninian shouted.

'No! Someone got on a pony and fetched me!' Francis gestured towards the sea. 'She hasn't a chance! She's going straight for the cliff!' He glanced at Ninian's companions. 'I see you've brought extra help, but she's beyond it.'

Between the rain and the upsurging waves, the ship was only visible in glimpses. She was a mess, wallowing from side to side, all her masts gone now and hanging broken in a tangle of canvas and rigging. She was very close to the headland and the falling tide was no friend to her, for as it sank, the rocks that peppered the sea round Polmawgan Head grew more dangerous with every moment.

Even as they watched, she seemed to check and shudder and then heeled slowly to starboard and did not right herself. A cry went up from the watchers on the shore. 'She's on the rocks!'

They could see, now, the antlike forms of men on her deck and clinging to the rigging on the surviving masts. A huge sea broke over her and there were fewer ants.

The bells had ceased. Petroc Darracott appeared, running towards Ninian through the rain, and Christopher St Asaph came racing to join them.

'There's no reaching her through that sea,' Darracott gasped. 'If only she doesn't break up before the tide drops!'

'She's breaking up now!' Uriah Giddy exclaimed. 'May the Lord have mercy on those souls aboard. They're drowned men, all of them!'

The stricken ship was veiled in white spray. She was at least four hundred yards away, beyond the tip of Polmawgan Head, but Ninian could swear he heard the splintering of timbers above the din of wind and water. A huge breaker rolled in carrying a couple of planks and tossed them like twigs into the mouth of the cave at the headland's foot. Another flung a broken figurehead on the shore, awash with foam but plainly recognisable in the moment before the sea sucked it away again and it vanished.

'She's the *Indian Venus!*' shouted Francis. 'God Almighty, she's the *Venus!*'

'Ah well.' One of the fishermen dropped his coil of rope on the sand. 'Then she idn't much better nor a pirate, is she? Not a lot of point in trying to save the likes of *them*. I had a brother in a ship Courteen's lot sank.'

'They'm sailors in mortal peril and you'll act like a Christian man and save them if you can!' bellowed Darracott. 'Pick up that rope! Give it here!' He had hold of it already and was making it fast round his waist. 'Uriah, take hold, you're strong. Pay it out as I go! If I keep out of the current that sets into the cave . . .'

They rushed to restrain him. 'Don't be a fool, man, you can't get through that!' shouted Christopher.

'If I can get even halfway I might give the hand of life to some poor fellow . . . !'

'There's no poor fellow will live long enough in that to get halfway, in the current or out of it!' Ninian grabbed the vicar's arm.

'She'm coming to pieces now!' Jimmy Tonkin shouted.

She was. Helpless, they stood there, the rain driving through their clothes, and watched her die. Her bows reared upwards as if in some last struggle for breath and then they were gone. The outline of her stern, blurred with rain, showed between the waves, seemingly steady, probably jammed between rocks, but washed again and again by enormous seas. The ants had all vanished. A few black specks appeared in the tossing water for a brief time and then they vanished too. 'God rest their souls,' said Christopher, and crossed himself.

'God'll rest their souls if they're godly men, without that Popish mummery,' said Uriah, and instantly received the flat of Darracott's hand across the back of his head.

'We can do without the cant just now, Uriah! What do you mean by it? Can't you recognise a gesture of respect when you see one? Pity you don't read the New Testament oftener and think more about Christ and less about Jehovah! There'll be bodies rolled to our feet in a moment.'

Uriah scowled and rubbed his head. The fisherman who had not wanted to save the lives of Courteen's men said: 'There'll be barrels rolled to our feet as well. I can see a whole lot out there.'

Others had seen the barrels too. The crowd moved purposefully forward. Darracott shook his head at them but did not protest. Had he seen the slightest chance of saving anyone, he would have kicked and punched his flock to make them help, but there was no such chance and by ancient custom, goods washed ashore belonged to the hands that picked them up. The people of Cornwall knew what it was to be lean with privation. If the sea now brought them a largesse of butter and salt meat which they could eat, or spices they could sell in the markets of Penzance or Marazion on the far side of the bay, he couldn't begrudge it to them.

Automatically, Ninian, Francis and Christopher moved back. The plundered cargo was not for them. It was their part, as it was Darracott's, to stand in the rain and intervene if any squabbling broke out.

It was Ninian, observing in this fashion, who first noticed one particular plank among the objects in the sea. It was being carried along in the current which would sweep towards the cave until the tide had fallen below the entrance. Surely, Ninian thought, peering through the rain, there was something on that plank? The downpour was slackening; he could see better now. Something . . . or someone, who must be either tied on, or else was alive and able to cling. He clutched at Darracott's arm, and pointed.

'The Lord have mercy!' Darracott gasped. 'But . . .' He looked in despair at the rope he was still holding. 'We can't get there!'

'I can!' Ninian had been swiftly estimating the state of the tide. 'I *own* that cave and as a boy I learned a trick or two. Give me that rope!'

He snatched it, flung off cloak and coat, and ran. He heard Francis exclaim in protest, but took no heed. The trick he had mentioned, he had performed only once and in the opposite direction, at that, and he was only fifteen then, but he was spare and active still. Surely, surely, he could do it again.

Because the cave went straight through the headland, the two entrances, both as tall as cathedral doors, were exposed to the waves, which at high tide crashed through to collide in the middle. But the Minecombe entrance on the far side was higher up. It was possible to enter from that end and find the sea already pouring in at the other. It was also possible for a venturesome lad, exploring when the tide was coming up, to get trapped.

At the age of fifteen, one April afternoon, Ninian had gone into the cave from Minecombe, been confronted by swirling water, turned to leave and found that the sea had now risen behind him and blocked his escape.

He could not wade out through either of the rocky entrances, for the sea was already boiling round them with force enough to break him in pieces. He did the only thing he could do. The walls of the cave were rough, with ledges, and he climbed. Perched on the highest ledge he could reach, he watched, awed and panic-stricken as the opposing currents met and the waters shot up in a fountain, booming like thunder and drenching him.

There was a weedy tidemark on the cave walls and he was below it. He could climb no higher. But as he looked about him in desperation, he saw that the ledge on which he stood continued to the Polmawgan cave-mouth and as far as he could tell, round it and out on to the headland.

It meant shuffling along the narrow ledge, digging frightened fingers into whatever crannies they could find. Half a dozen times he nearly slipped. Although he was bitterly cold, the sweat streamed from him.

But he emerged at last round the side of the cave-mouth to find that the ledge continued on, high above the shelving beach. He worked his way steadily onward, skinning palms and knees and elbows until at last he was above boulders which the sea had not yet reached. They were only five feet below. He slithered down, feeling for a gap among them and banging his shins on sharp stone edges. Then he was standing amid the boulders, on a patch of flat sand. A wave swept in as if to pursue

25

him, but it did no more than swirl vainly round his ankles as he scrambled away to safety.

It was a long time before he entered the cave again and when at length he did, he took more care. Never again had he set foot on that ledge. But he still knew how to reach it. Clambering rapidly over the wet rocks which the sea had just relinquished, he found a rock to use as a stepping stone, and was up, slinging the rope round him to leave his hands free. He edged sideways, towards the cave.

The sweat at once broke out on him, just as it had done all those years ago. What the devil was he doing here? But out of the corner of his eye he could see the bobbing shape of the plank and its burden, coming rapidly nearer to the cave-mouth. The ebb would slow it down, but the tide was still high enough to carry it over the rocks into the entrance. Anyone clinging to the plank would certainly drown in the maelstrom where the waves met those coming in from the other side. He must hurry.

Even with the rope, it would be difficult for one man on a narrow, slippery ledge to do anything useful. But he would have to try. Dry-mouthed, he shuffled quickly into the entrance to stand erect inside the cave, breathing hard and pressing his shoulders against the damp rock behind him.

He had thought the world outside was noisy but it was peace and serenity compared to the din inside the cave, where the crash of the colliding seas in the centre and the foaming of the water through the entrances was hurled back and forth from wall and roof in a roar of echo piled on echo.

He remembered vaguely that there was another ledge below him, much lower than the tidemark but probably clear by now. The light was poor but peering down, he saw that he was right and that the other ledge, although awash with spray, was now just above the water and wider than the one he was on. He sat down, slid and perched, dangling his feet just above the sea. With fingers slippery from the wet, he made a loop in the end of the rope.

He was just in time. As he fastened the knot, the plank came in. It was sideways on at first and stuck across the entrance. He could see that it was more than just a plank but a solid piece of timber, with a fragment of railing at one side, and it was to this that its drenched passenger was clinging. Whoever it was, was unquestionably alive. He saw a head lift and fall and glimpsed a face. Then the sea bumped the timber away and it half-spun, so that when it came at the entrance again, it came through.

Ninian, muttering a prayer, knelt up as the impromptu raft came below him and jammed one knee into a crack in the rock wall behind him. It left him in a twisted position but gave him the only purchase he could find. Looking down, he saw hair trailing over timber and floating like weed on the water; saw wide eyes focus on him; saw a hand let go of the rail and reach imploringly up; saw the glint of something bright slipping back down the wrist. He cast the rope. The hand caught the loop and clung on. He hauled with all his strength and then leant

26

forward, grasped a slender forearm encircled by thin gold bangles, threw his weight backwards again, and hauled once more.

His knee ground against the rock and the muscles of arm and shoulder and inner thigh simultaneously twisted and stretched, screaming in unison. Then the light in the cave-mouth darkened and Francis, also coatless, also soaked, opening and shutting his mouth in observations which Ninian couldn't hear but which were probably accusations of insanity, shuffled round the ledge and slid down to lend another pair of hands to the rescue.

The castaway's fingers had lost their weak grip on the rope. But Francis and Ninian, clutching at drenched fabric and a body as icy and limp as a corpse, dragged their prize on to the ledge. It lolled forward and vomited sea water. Ninian, grabbing at it to keep it from slipping back into the sea, inadvertently confirmed what he had suspected as soon as he saw the raft's passenger close to.

'It's a woman!' he shouted into Francis' ear.

'Never mind about that!' Francis shouted back. 'How do we get her out of this cave?' She had sagged into unconsciousness, eyes closed and body continuously shivering. 'We can't carry her back along the ledge!'

But help was coming. The wind had lessened and the tide was going down swiftly. Before long, it was possible to get into the cave by wading, and Dick Branson, followed by Christopher, Darracott, Uriah and Jimmy, came splashing in. The girl was lifted out of Ninian's stiff arms and in a few moments they were all out of the cave and being helped over the rocks towards the smooth sand. Blood ran down Ninian's knee where it had been driven against the rock and it stung in the sea-water. He was glad of Dick's shoulder.

The rain had ceased entirely now. Out among the waves they could see what was left of the *Indian Venus*, a broken-off stern cocked up on the offshore rocks. Most of the villagers were still engrossed with retrieving barrels, but a few ran to meet the rescue party. Marge Hawkes marched up with an armful of coats and cloaks, warmed by the little fire, and handed them out. Somebody else, wrapping a cloak round the rescued girl, exclaimed: 'Why, it do be a female!'

'Aye, it is,' said Uriah. 'And what was she doing aboard the *Venus*? She weren't there for any honest reason, I'll be bound! You should have left her be, sir. Nearly killed yourself, you did.'

'Just now, she's a human creature saved from drowning. Possibly a soul granted another chance, which is more than you'd have given her!' snapped Darracott. 'She's got to be got into shelter. No good taking her to my parsonage, with me being a widower. My housekeeper don't live in. Ninian . . .'

The wind had dropped almost to nothing. Ninian looked up at the headland. 'I think we could use the cliff path now,' he said. 'Bring her to my house.'

27

Chapter Three
Disturbing Influences

Christopher and Darracott chose to stay at the cove. But Uriah and Dick carried the girl up the cliff path, while Ninian followed with Francis. Some of his stiffness eased as he climbed but the air was cold on wet clothing. Jimmy Tonkin, who was quick on his feet, went ahead to warn the women. When amid a duet of noisy barks from the dogs, the damp and shivering party came in through the kitchen door, they found Eliza and Meg, wide-eyed but subdued, busy boiling water and stirring mutton stew, while Hannah stood waiting with mulled wine, warm towels, a pile of clean male garments, and grimly folded arms.

'Who be this, then?' she inquired.

'Through to the parlour,' Ninian commanded. 'Put her on the settle.'

'I said,' repeated Hannah, following them into the parlour, 'who be this you've brought? Jimmy says it's a girl from a Courteen ship. The captain's whore, would she be?'

'We've brought in the only soul to come living from a shipwreck,' said Ninian rebukingly, holding back the inquisitive dogs. 'We'll worry about who she is later. Pol, be quiet! Down, Lady! Did I see mulled wine in the kitchen, Hannah? If so, bring it here.'

'She's coming round,' said Francis.

The girl was stirring. Her eyes opened. Slowly, putting a hand on the back of the settle, she hoisted herself to a sitting position. She was still wrapped in the cloak Marge had provided, but water ran from beneath it, marking the cushions and dripping on to the floor. She glanced in a frightened way at the dogs and said something, timidly and also incomprehensibly. Ninian did not recognise the language.

'Foreign!' said Hannah with disfavour, and then, noticing the ivory tone of the girl's skin, the intense darkness of her eyes, and the bangles which encircled both slender wrists, added: 'Some godless heathen Turk, I daresay. What are we to do with her here?'

Uriah muttered in agreement but Ninian, soaking wet, cold and exhausted, rounded on Hannah. 'Do with her? Get her warm and dry and fed and into bed, of course! Can't you find enough Christian spirit to care for a half-drowned girl just because she's what you call a heathen? Very well. I'll get those wet wrappings off her and bathe her with my own hands if yours are too fastidious.'

It worked. 'For shame!' cried Hannah. 'You'll do no such thing, sir!'

And within a few bustling minutes, a bed had been made in the second bedchamber, and Meg was lighting a fire in its hearth. The girl was carried upstairs and then the door was shut while the women ministered to her. Ninian observed with relief, and Francis with amusement, that Eliza and Meg at least were interested and willing.

The men then withdrew to the kitchen to strip off their own wet clothes, towel themselves warm again, anoint their injuries with goosegrease, don dry clothes and attack the mulled wine and the mutton stew on their own account.

Francis went home in due course and Eliza reported to Ninian that the girl had had some bread and milk and was asleep. 'Hannah and Uriah don't approve of her,' she whispered, glancing over her shoulder to make sure that Hannah hadn't followed her into the kitchen. 'But heathen or not, I feel that sorry for her. I'll see she'm cared for, and I'll patch them torn breeches for 'ee while I'm doing it. You go to bed now, sir, and rest. Drenched and worn out, you be; I can see it.'

Ninian's right knee, which had been badly bruised as well as scraped, was throbbing again. He was glad enough to go to bed. He fell instantly asleep. When he woke up, it was morning.

Stretching within the warmth of his thick bedcoverings and down mattress, he found that after all he was little the worse for his adventure. His knee was less painful and he was hungry.

He was also worried.

Yesterday he had fought the sea to save a life, with no chance to think beyond the moment. But now he saw that he might well have taken on a difficult responsibility. What *was* he to do with a foreign girl whose previous companions had all been drowned? If they'd been saved too, she'd have had people with whom she belonged. As things were, the chances were that the only people or places with which she belonged were on the other side of the world. Too anxious to lie at ease any longer, he got out of bed and was pulling on his dressing robe when Branson came in with his shaving water.

'Ah, Dick. You took no harm yesterday, then? How is she?'

'The wench from the wreck? Poorly, I hear. Running a fever, Eliza says. But she's got some English. Murmured *thank-you* two or three times quite plain, I gather. That'll be a help, if she can talk to us.'

'It certainly will,' said Ninian.

In the second bedchamber he found Eliza tidying the covers as best she could without moving the occupant out of bed while Hannah spooned a herbal febrifuge into the patient's mouth. The girl was swallowing but her eyes were vague and when Hannah laid her back on the pillow, she began to mutter and toss.

'Is she delirious?' Ninian asked anxiously.

'She is. It'll be the will of the Lord, whether she lives or dies, I'd say,' Hannah informed him grimly. 'I'll do what I can, you may rely on that, for all she's maybe one of they murdering Turks. Likely enough there'd be some of them aboard a Courteen ship. Brothers under the skin, Courteen's men and Turkish pirates are.'

Ninian sighed. He could understand Hannah's prejudices. In the previous century, Penzance had been burned virtually to the ground by Moorish pirates. It had been rebuilt, patiently and lovingly, had grown and prospered anew, even outstripping its neighbours Marazion and Mousehole, acquiring shops and warehouses, and fine homes for its merchants.

And then – Ninian had been twenty-five at the time – that prosperous air drew the pirates back again. He had been in the town when the church bells rang out the alarm. He had seen brown-skinned strangers wielding curved scimitars on the quay and two Cornishmen were cut down in front of him. Ninian had rushed into a shop whose owner had a supply of weapons and was handing them out in haste to all comers. He seized a sword, and sprinted out again to wield it as ferociously as he could. He surprised himself by actually causing a pirate to drop his own weapon and run. The enemy had been driven off at last and they hadn't landed again, but they had been a nuisance at sea ever since; Cornish shipping had to be wary. Hannah was not being entirely unreasonable.

'But a young girl like this can hardly be a pirate,' he said gently. 'She's so small; hardly more than a child.'

'Well, I said: I'll do my best for her,' Hannah said and Eliza nodded. 'You can trust us, sir.'

This, he knew, was true. Hannah would never neglect her duty, whatever her private opinions, and Eliza was essentially kind. There was nothing he could do for his guest just now. He looked at her, wrinkling his brow, wondering what it could be like, to find oneself benighted among foreigners so far from home.

'Meg's in the kitchen. She'll make 'ee some breakfast,' Hannah told him.

He was clearly in the way. He removed himself, to exchange his dressing robe for a good blue suit. He was just finishing his breakfast when he heard hoofbeats outside and Dick Branson came to announce that Mr Gubbes and Mr Polkinghorne had called, together with Mr William Norseworthy, the Mayor of Penzance.

'Indeed?' said Ninian. The news of the wreck would have reached the town, of course, and he might have expected Gubbes and Polkinghorne to call. But he scarcely knew Norseworthy. Well, if you were the Mayor, you were licensed to be inquisitive. He went to the parlour to greet them.

All three, like Ninian himself, were in their late thirties. Polkinghorne was in military-style buff and white linen with drawn-thread edgings but Norseworthy wore Puritan clothes, as did Gubbes, although Norseworthy's white cuffs were not so clean. Alice Gubbes, Ninian knew, made a point of supplying Anthony with a fresh set every morning, and laundered them herself, although she had a large and demanding family, and plenty of maidservants. She believed in the virtue of work.

'What a storm yesterday!' Polkinghorne said, advancing straight on their objective almost before the greetings were over. 'Penzance took a battering, I can tell you. My fish-cellar was flooded again and not because it wasn't in a good state of repair this time.' Four years previously, Roger had been fined for allowing his fish cellar, which was used by others as well as himself, to decay. He was still aggrieved about it.

'My younger children were quite frightened by the shrieking of the wind,' Anthony Gubbes took up the conversation. 'And there certainly was a good deal of damage. The sea breached the quay and several ships were torn from their moorings. It may seem strange that we're out of town this morning. But we engaged, some time ago, to dine today with Thomas Grosse and we decided not to put it off, because we could take the opportunity of riding a little out of our way to ask how Polmawgan fared.'

'Ah,' said Ninian.

'Is the *Silver Fish* safe? And you had a Courteen ship piled up on the headland, we hear.'

'Yes. But happily, little harm was done in Polmawgan. All the boats are safe, mine included,' said Ninian gravely.

Anthony suddenly grinned. He and Ninian met quite often socially but in spirit they had drifted apart of late, because Anthony was much taken up with his family and his business, and his increasing interest in religion was not to Ninian's taste. But he was not as rigid a Puritan as some. His shop sold bales of colourful cloth, and he would obtain lace, spices or any other luxury to customers' orders, on the grounds that it was all good business. He still knew Ninian well enough to tell when his old friend was fencing.

'We also hear,' said Mr Norseworthy, deciding to be blunt, 'that there were no survivors of the wreck save for one young woman of foreign origin.'

'That's true,' said Ninian.

'She was brought here, was she not?' said Norseworthy.

'Yes. She's in one of my guest-chambers now, very ill,' said Ninian, and obligingly answered the next question before it was asked. 'She hasn't been able to give an account of herself yet. We fear for her life.'

'I see.' Norseworthy was regretful. 'We wondered if she had given any information about Courteen – future plans, whereabouts of other Courteen vessels, that sort of thing.'

Ninian shook his head. 'She's very young. Somehow I doubt if it's the kind of thing she'd know. We don't even know yet if she speaks English beyond a word or two.'

The main purpose of the visit, as Ninian had guessed at the beginning, was to seek news of the Courteen ships and inquire about the intriguing survivor and since he could tell them little, conversation faltered. Gubbes embarked instead on an account of the latest news from London.

Ninian, who always found political discussion tedious, listened with polite impatience and learned that Parliament had refused to vote King Charles the necessary supplies with which to pursue his war against the Scots, who were resisting his efforts to impose his idea of orthodox worship on them. It seemed that John Pym, the Leader of the House, had made a lengthy speech listing Parliament's grievances against the

King and the upshot, more or less, was that if the Scots wished to abolish bishops, Parliament sympathised.

'As, indeed, do many,' Gubbes said militantly. 'The King should heed Parliament's advice and use less arrogance and so should Archbishop Laud. Laud's outriders have been knocking people down like skittles in the London streets.'

'Yes, so I heard,' said Ninian.

Polkinghorne, who didn't like this kind of talk, said you couldn't believe all the stories. The conversation faltered again, and presently, the visitors left. Ninian saw them off and went thoughtfully to the kitchen where Hannah, Eliza and Meg were already busy about dinner.

'Cook some extra food,' he said. 'I have a feeling we shall have more visitors.'

Eliza looked out of the window. 'Here's Mr Trevelyan now,' she said. 'And the Reverend Darracott.'

Francis and Darracott were not merely inquisitive, however. They rode in with a cloth-wrapped bundle on a packhorse, and fetched the bundle indoors, where Francis, whose knee breeches were stained with sea-water, explained that he had that morning been rowed out to the wreck.

'Her stern jammed on the rocks and stayed put when the rest of the ship broke off. I found the remains of two cabins there, with a few bits and pieces still in them. This was among them. Petroc thought we should bring it to you.'

The vicar removed the wrappings from the mysterious bundle. Inside was a thick pad of damp cotton, and a chest, perhaps three feet long by one and a half feet wide, made of minutely carved, light-coloured wood. It had a flat lid with a broken hasp. Francis unfolded the cotton, which proved to be a long skirt, once blue but now ruined by the sea-water.

'This was in the chest, on top,' Francis said. 'We took it out in case the damp worked through and did more harm. So far, it had protected what was under it, and . . .'

He raised the lid and one by one, lifted folded pieces of fabric and shook them out. Ninian blinked.

There was little bright colour in the parlour. It was furnished and panelled in oak and walnut, with black beams supporting a white ceiling. There were muted blues and rose tints in the carpet and curtaining; that was all. These brilliant silks and cottons in scarlet and peacock, emerald and yellow and azure, burst exotically into the quiet room as though a popinjay had emerged from the egg of a house sparrow. The silk lengths were adorned with embroidery and silver tinsel, and one, a vivid red, had a thick border of woven gold thread.

'Good God!' Ninian took a shining fold between finger and thumb and felt the texture. 'And it was packed in this personal chest? It isn't cargo?'

'No. Nor is this.' From the bottom of the chest, Francis removed a little box in the same light-brown wood. He opened it and tumbled a pile of bright trinkets on to the table, spreading them out with his palm.

'They're not that valuable,' he said. 'Semi-precious stones, most of these necklaces and bracelets. But the bangles are gold and so are these earrings, and that necklace is filigree silver. The chest and the box themselves are probably of some worth. They're sandalwood, I think, and the carving's charming.'

'The thing is,' said Darracott seriously, 'the chest was found in a cabin, not in the hold, and it's very probable that they belong to the girl you saved. How is she, by the way?'

'Very sick,' Ninian said. 'But I will put these things in her chamber. Hannah will mutter about worldly trumpery, no doubt, but if the girl wakes and recognises them, they might comfort her. Thank you for bringing them.'

'You're lucky I'm an honest man,' said Francis, amused. 'I was tempted by some of those silks. I should have liked to present them as a gift to my betrothed.'

'To your . . .? Well, this is news!' said Ninian. 'Since when?'

'Unofficially, for several months. Her father's a Penzance merchant, an old friend of my father's. It would have been announced before, except that her parents thought she was too young. But Miss Mary Nicholls will become Mrs Francis Trevelyan in July.'

'We must drink to your happiness!' said Ninian.

'You'd better get some extra glasses out,' remarked Darracott. 'Because unless I'm mistaken, Christopher St Asaph is just riding up.'

Never since his marriage to Tamzin, had Christopher come uninvited to Polmawgan. 'The stranger in my second bedchamber seems to have much in common with a magnet,' Ninian said.

Over the next ten days, while the nameless girl from the *Indian Venus* lay wavering between life and death, visitors came in what seemed like a constant stream.

All had excuses, mostly flimsy. Meg's sister Polly, who was in service in Mousehole, really had no need to beg an afternoon from her employer and come to Polmawgan the day after the storm 'to see if Meg was all right'. Meg, living in a house high above the sea and sufficiently well fed not to need to snatch floating casks of butter from fortuitous wrecks, was unlikely to have been harmed.

It was of course generous of Ezra Clemo to arrive at Polmawgan the following day offering the gift of a sucking-pig because his sow had farrowed an uncommonly large litter. It was also very uncharacteristic. Ninian accepted the present, listened with amusement to Ezra's probing questions about the girl from the wreck, said sadly that except that she was plainly from some far country, she was as yet a mystery and if she died might well remain so, and then deliberately kept Ezra there for two hours, discussing the weather and farming, while Ezra fidgeted to get away and clearly regretted the sucking pig.

More blatant and more exasperating was the descent of Prudence Jenken (née Clemo), who came openly demanding to know if it were true that Ninian was sheltering a Turkish whore under his roof and expressing fears for the safety of his soul.

'My soul is my own business. I'd be grateful if you'd mind yours,' said Ninian, and sent her away on the plea that he was expecting important company and would have business to discuss. To his amusement, the lie was given substance. Watching from a window as Prudence and her groom rode back along the headland track, he saw them pass a horseman coming towards the house. A few moments later he recognised Mr William Keigwin, a resident of Mousehole. He had met Keigwin only twice, in other people's houses, although he recalled that they had discussed literature, and that Keigwin was apt with quotations.

It hardly amounted to a close acquaintance, however, certainly not enough to justify Keigwin's excuse that he had chanced to be riding this way, had recalled meeting Ninian somewhere or other – Ninian maliciously noted his vagueness about where – and hadn't they talked about books? He had a book of Elizabethan verse which he thought Ninian might like to borrow . . .

Ninian did not care very much what Prudence Jenken thought of him, but if she took Keigwin for his expected visitor: well and good. He was courteous to Keigwin and duly borrowed the book.

He tried to be courteous next day, too, when his mine manager Tom Pengelly, on foot, and Jane Dewey, riding her grey gelding astride in her usual unfeminine fashion, arrived almost together. He liked Jane and was worried about Pengelly, whose cough sounded alarming. But when, the following morning, his tenants Mr and Mrs Treweeke came, along with two sons and three daughters, to make an unnecessary report about a field which they had drained, he was brusque.

The great county families such as the Grenviles and the Rashleighs and the Arundells did not actually put in an appearance – 'But they'd hardly need to. Gubbes and Norseworthy meet the Arundells frequently, and the Arundells know all the others,' he said caustically to Dick Branson. 'The Arundells are related to the Grenviles. I daresay the whole county's talking.'

But gradually, the intrusions ceased. Meanwhile, the girl continued to live, just: tossing feverishly and muttering sometimes in an unknown tongue. Once or twice she roused a little and seemed to notice the silks and trinkets from the chest, which Ninian insisted should be displayed near her bed. Hannah grumbled as he had predicted but she was making an honest attempt to nurse the girl back to health and even Hannah was glad to see her eyes brighten and her hand reach out to touch a necklace.

Hannah and Eliza got nourishment of a sort into her at regular intervals and Meg, young enough to be excited by the break in the routine, ran willingly to and fro with trays. On the twelfth morning after the wreck, Ninian woke at dawn to find Hannah shaking him.

'I'm sorry to wake you like this, sir, but it's her, the girl. You'd best come.'

'What?' He sat up, reaching for slippers and robe. 'What about her? Is she . . . ?'

'Just come,' said Hannah.

In the girl's room, the curtains had been looped back from the bed and the shutters were open. A grey daybreak mingled with the candle-light and showed Eliza sitting beside the bed. 'The fever's down,' she said quietly. 'But she do be too weak to lift her head. It do be touch and go whether she lives or dies.'

Ninian came softly to her side. 'But surely, if the fever's gone . . .'

'Weakness can kill. We've been praying for her,' said Eliza simply, 'through the night. No more we can do but wait.'

'You've done a great deal and much more competently than that doctor we called,' said Ninian. During the girl's first days in his house, he had summoned a physician from Penzance but sent the man away again when he insisted on bleeding the patient and she became visibly more ill before their eyes.

'You're a fool. She needs all her strength,' Ninian had said angrily. 'Don't come again.' Hannah and Eliza, more conventional, were shocked by his rudeness, but Ninian held to his views. 'Give her what will stimulate her,' he had told them. 'Red wine, broth. She's so frail.'

She was still frail, terribly so. Her left hand was outside the covers and it was so thin that it was almost transparent. As the light grew, the sea beyond the window turned to a flat sheet of silver, quiet at the ebb. But Ninian, induced by some instinct to glance at it, saw the smoothness suddenly shiver and break up as though myriad cracks had run across the surface of a mirror.

'The tide's turning,' he said.

'Ah.' Hannah pulled a stool close to the bed and sat down, watching the girl's face intently. 'That's why I called 'ee now, sir. We'll know soon. She'm come through the deep of the night. But it's at the turn of the tide, as often as not, that the spirit decides whether to ebb away or flow back. As if there was some link.'

'You got me out of bed because the tide was about to turn? I'm surprised at you, Hannah. Some of your ideas are almost heathen,' said Ninian, teasing her.

Hannah's face went stiff, but Eliza smiled. Her Puritanism was of a different kind from Hannah's. Hannah was of the extreme and Presbyterian persuasion, and she possessed a marked superstitious streak, but Eliza had a wholesome, moderate faith which Ninian did not share but never disturbed either, for it made her kindly and also appeared to armour her against illogical beliefs rather than encourage them. Eliza did not 'hold with' talk of pixies, ghosts, witches or people whose spirits were linked mysteriously to the ocean.

'You may mock,' said Hannah coldly. 'But look at her. There's a change . . . see it? See it?'

The girl's breathing had deepened. She stirred and drew the thin hand away under the warmth of the covers. Ninian put his palm on her brow and found it cool. Her dark eyes, long doe-eyes in a wasted face which would be exquisite in health but was now only pitiful, opened and focused on his face. They were frightened eyes, full of questions.

36

'She'm given some account of herself, then?'

'Oh yes. She lost her family when she was a child – some sort of pestilence, I think, like one of our outbreaks of plague. She was living in some kind of village near Masulipatnam, I think. She pronounces things oddly, but the East India company has a factory at a place called Masulipatnam, so I've heard the name before. Her parents' house had mud walls and it was thatched, she says. After her parents died, some woman took her in. But a little later – I didn't understand this very well,' said Ninian uncomfortably. 'But she says that the woman took her to Masulipatnam and gave her into the care of a priest of one of their temples. She is sure he was a priest. But . . . he debauched her and then started selling her to men. A lot of them were the sailors who sailed into Masulipatnam.'

'There were some fine scandals about priests in the days of the Papists,' Darracott said from the chair on the other side of the hearth. 'A heathen temple would be worse still, most likely, and sin do be much the same anywhere. Go on.'

Ninian stretched his toes to the fire. 'An East India captain bought her eventually and smuggled her aboard his ship. He kept her in his cabin, in defiance of company regulations. A few days later, his ship was attacked and boarded by a Courteen vessel. I am not offering a reward,' said Ninian, 'for guessing its name.'

'The *Indian Venus?*'

'Yes. Captain Murray appropriated her services. That's one way to put it. But he seems to have been quite kind to her; kinder than the first captain was. He gave her the sandalwood chest and the clothes and trinkets. She grew attached to him.'

'You keep saying *she*,' said Darracott, amused. 'B'ain't she got a name? Even the vessel she voyaged on had that!'

'Yes. But I find it hard to get used to calling someone Parvati,' said Ninian. 'Whoever heard of such a name? Hannah can't get her tongue round it at all. Or won't. Probably it's a case of won't.'

'So,' said Darracott comfortably, 'her name's Parvati. Continue.'

'That's nearly all. She was with Murray for months. She learned to eat meat and drink wine on the *Venus*; apparently she never did before. On board ship there wasn't much choice and luckily most of it was salt pork. If it had been beef, she'd have starved. It's funny. She's so gentle and biddable except in one or two matters. She almost gives off sparks at the idea of eating beef. She thinks cows are sacred. Hannah . . .'

'Never mind Hannah. I can imagine all that. About Parvati. She evidently speaks English quite well.'

'It's broken, but she makes herself understood. She learned from Murray. The *Venus* was making her way to an English port when she was wrecked. I don't know which port. Parvati couldn't tell me. She wasn't interested. All she cared about was Murray. She's wept over his death. More than wept,' said Ninian moodily. 'She made a little doll out of a piece of driftwood from the firewood basket, dressed it in a piece of silk from her chest, put a candle by it and prayed to it to grant Captain Murray wealth and success when he is born again in a new body.'

'She did *what?*' Darracott was horrified. 'I understand that the poor child b'ain't never heard of the gospel. I doubt if any Courteen captain ever did much praying, though I daresay he stammered out a prayer or two when he knew he was going to drown. But – a heathen idol in your very house? Talk of reincarnation? Ninian, we've got to save her soul. That must be what the Lord intended, and we do be His instruments. I will come to your house and instruct her and . . .'

'It's so difficult,' said Ninian awkwardly. 'It's such a disruption to my ordinary life, having her there. I agree that she ought to have the benefit of your instruction. If only you could . . .'

'No, it wouldn't be proper. With me being widowed and . . .'

'. . . your housekeeper doesn't live in, but I am chaperoned by Hannah, who can be trusted to take her duties seriously! I know. Well,' said Ninian with a sigh, 'perhaps we can make her a Christian and then maybe she could go for a maidservant in some respectable house. Hannah, of course, thinks Parvati is going to take my hand in her slender fingers and lead me to damnation.'

'How old would she be?' asked Darracott. 'Parvati, I mean.'

'She doesn't know for sure. But no more than seventeen, I'm certain of that, and maybe less. She became a woman, as she puts it, three years ago.'

'She b'ain't had children? With her history . . .' Darracott paused, delicately.

Ninian threw up his hands. 'One of her belongings that *wasn't* in that chest you and Francis brought me was a packet of something that she used to take each month to . . . er . . . I know,' said Ninian, regarding Darracott's scandalised face, 'but she seems to have no sense of what one can and can't discuss. Darracott, she's so young. I'm so *sorry* for her.'

Darracott narrowed his eyes. He was not much older than Ninian, but in many ways he was much more experienced. He had advised parishioners who sought his help with all manner of temptations; he had at times condemned with wrath those who surrendered to them. He hoped he wouldn't find himself having to imitate Hannah and brandish the risk of damnation at his good friend Ninian Whitmead. Ninian liked this girl very much, perhaps too much. Petroc Darracott could tell.

'When in doubt,' he said, 'seek God's help. Let us pray.'

Chapter Four
Uninvited Guests

During the next few weeks, Ninian scarcely set foot beyond his house and its small terraced garden on the point of the headland. Parvati had taken over his life.

Willy nilly, he had become her guardian. She was so young, so far from home, and so defenceless in the face of his uncomprehending household. His servants had obeyed him, and in any case, Meg was too intrigued by her and the Bransons too goodhearted by nature to be unkind. But they all found her lilting, broken English hard to follow and despite all his strictures, Hannah and Uriah remained disapproving and cold. As a result, Parvati was obviously nervous of being left in the house without Ninian. In sheer pity for her, he had to make her his responsibility.

She was an exhausting one.

She had for a few days wept wildly for Captain Murray, and spent much time staring sadly out to where the remains of the *Venus* were slowly disintegrating into the sea. But then, with a pathetic air of being anxious to please, she dried her eyes and to Ninian's alarm and Hannah's outrage, decked herself in the bright silks and trinkets from her sandalwood chest, and made an evident effort to be attractive to the master of the house.

Fortunately – as Ninian remarked wryly to Petroc Darracott – the Cornish spring that year was wild and wet and it wasn't too hard to convince her that thin silk was ill suited to the climate, and persuade her into some spare gowns of Meg's. They had to be taken in to fit, for if Meg was not large, Parvati was smaller still. But Parvati proved clever with a needle and did the work very neatly.

The gowns made her look more ordinary, but they were all grey or black, the shades which Hannah considered suitable for domestic staff, or indeed, for any respectable woman. Parvati's jewellery looked peculiar with them and she put her trinkets away. The result was depressing. To Ninian it seemed that she drooped, like a plant denied light and water. Even her walk became slower and her smile was dimmed.

Ignoring the predictable Giddy disapproval, he sent Eliza to Penzance to buy something more cheerful at the Gubbes' shop. Eliza returned with a rose-colour, a bluish-green, and some good quality white linen for collars and head-dresses, and helped Parvati make up the materials. Once she was dressed in them she brought her bangles out again and her movements resumed their natural grace. But she remained nervous, mainly because Hannah glowered so much.

She made no difficulty about accepting the Christian religion and Darracott came regularly to instruct her. But Ninian wasn't sure how much she really understood, and was shaken when she told him that she would adopt whatever religion he wished, since she now regarded him as her owner.

'I am not your owner. I am simply looking after you until we can decide what are the best arrangements . . .'

'Arrange . . . ments . . . ?'

'. . . until we can decide what to do next. It may be difficult for you to go back to India . . .'

'I do not want to go back to India.'

'Well, then, you'll have to stay in England and if so, you must certainly become a Christian.'

'But I have said I will. I am learning now, am I not? I have put my Lakshmi away.'

'Your . . . ?'

Parvati took him by the hand and led him up to her room, where she showed him, hidden in a cupboard, the driftwood doll to which she had prayed for Captain Murray. 'That is Lakshmi. But I have put her away in this cupboard.'

'Reverend Darracott told you to *throw* that away, not just to hide it. You call it Lakshmi?'

'Yes, she is goddess of wealth. She gives good fortune.'

'In future, Parvati, you must pray to God and to Jesus His son for good fortune, and for forgiveness of sins, too, which is more important than wealth. You must not keep the image of a heathen goddess in your room, even hidden in a cupboard.'

'Heathen?'

'Not Christian. Heathen means not Christian.'

'And you, my master, you are this Christian? Like my Captain Murray.'

Ninian doubted if he was much like Captain Murray and was coming more and more to the conclusion that he probably wasn't a Christian either. Standing by Pen's grave a year ago, he had been struck by the sheer unlikeliness of the doctrine of resurrection, and since then he had noticed that several more of the required beliefs of his religion were equally unlikely. He found it difficult, for instance, to believe in a virgin having a child. But if you wanted a quiet life, it was best to go along with the conventions. It would be best for Parvati, too.

'Parvati, I want you to be a Christian for your own safety. Many people would be angry if they knew about this image.'

'Others? Like Hannah?'

'There are a great many people like Hannah. You must throw the image away.'

Parvati cried a little but did as he asked and went in docile fashion to

42

her next lesson with Darracott. The lessons did seem to be going well. Ninian was coming to realise that although Parvati was so uneducated that she sometimes appeared simple, this was deceptive. She had learned her Catechism and the Lord's Prayer by heart in a week, revealing that her mind was perfectly sharp, needing only to be stimulated. She agreed without argument to be baptised and to take Penelope as a Christian name. This was Ninian's suggestion, made in a fit of sentimentality. He had missed having a Penelope in the house, he said.

The baptism took place early one morning, in a small private ceremony in Polmawgan Church. But although Parvati entered the church apparently unobserved, half Polmawgan was loitering about outside when she emerged.

When she was first rescued, Parvati had been a subject of curiosity tainted with suspicion because she had been on a decidedly dubious ship for a probably dubious purpose. Later, when word got round about her heathen beliefs and her exotic clothes, the disapproval had deepened. But now she had mended her ways and had been baptised into the Christian community. Polmawgan was still reserving judgement, but the atmosphere was faintly warmer.

As she came out of the church, a diminutive figure in dove-grey, walking beside Ninian, many confined themselves to staring, but one or two, Marge and Walter Hawkes among them, called greetings and one cheeky lad even shouted: 'Looks as if you've married her, master!'

Parvati giggled, but Ninian turned scarlet and hurried her onward, getting her to the headland path and up it to the house as quickly as possible.

Once home, he retreated to his study and sat there with his head in his hands, wondering how long it would be before he could rid himself of this worrying incubus. He had put her into ordinary clothes and made her a Christian, and her English was improving but he couldn't see Parvati becoming ready, in the foreseeable future, for life as a maidservant in anyone else's household.

She was still so timid, which was surprising. It seemed to him extraordinary that a girl who had survived the sexual attentions of numerous sailors and then a shipwreck should be helplessly intimidated by Hannah and petrified by animals. He had coaxed her, with difficulty, not to mind Lady and Pol, even to stroke them sometimes. But she remained afraid of all other dogs, even the hard-working creatures which herded sheep in the combe, and was equally nervous of horses.

Wrapped up in his domestic problems and tied to his house, Ninian did not attend Francis Trevelyan's usual May Day feast, although Francis, calling on him afterwards, told him all about it. There had been some unscheduled excitement.

'A pack of ardent Puritans from Penzance burst out of the crowd and attacked the dancers with sticks and tried to tear the Maypole down. They kept shouting that they were the troops of the Lord, elected to cleanse the world of sin, or some such nonsense. A fight broke out –

well, naturally. The dancers were my tenants' daughters and when their fathers saw them being attacked, they rushed in to defend them. There were any number of bloody noses, believe me. I picked one of the Lord's elect up and ran with him to the stableyard and dumped him in a horse trough. The water was ice-cold well-water; he squealed like a pig. "That'll cool your ardour for you," I told him. But it spoilt the day and that's a fact. My Mary was watching the dancing with me and she was so frightened that she cried. But she cries very sweetly,' Francis said in indulgent tones. 'My Mary's tears are like dew on a rose.'

'Yes, she's very sweet,' said Ninian, who had met Francis's betrothed once, and had not taken to her.

On that occasion, Francis had brought her to Polmawgan on a visit and Ninian, feeling that here was an opportunity for Parvati to learn a little more about English ways, had introduced them. Parvati sat there in her blue-green gown, looking decorative but too shy to do more than whisper a greeting. Mary, equally shy in the presence of this dark-eyed stranger, of whose social standing she wasn't sure, chattered inanely about trivialities, in a childish, high-pitched voice which drove Ninian nearly mad.

She was far more childish than Parvati, for she lacked any experience of the world. If the Indian girl seemed timid, she at least had the excuse that she had encountered danger early in life. Mary gave the impression that she had come out of the egg only yesterday. Fair of hair, with a pretty little snub nose and a pink-and-cream complexion, she was very like the rose to which Francis had likened her, and about as intelligent. The outspoken Francis seemed at the moment to be in a state of soggy besottedness over her but Ninian wondered how the two of them would fare when they were married. They would have children, he supposed, which the first Mrs Trevelyan had not been able to do. Mary would busy herself with her babies and her stillroom while Francis, growing bored, would gradually spend more and more time away from home. It was often the way.

Well, he would go to the wedding, of course. Francis, a generous host, had invited not only Ninian, but Ninian's entire household. Francis was feasting his own servants and those of his guests were welcome to join them. Still doggedly concerned to educate Parvati in English ways, Ninian asked if she could attend. 'She could come with the Bransons. I think she ought to see a little more of our world than Polmawgan House can show her.'

'Of course, of course!' said Francis.

'A marriage party?' said Parvati eagerly when he told her. He had eventually grown accustomed to her name and now used it often in private, somewhat regretting the nostalgic impulse which had made him choose Penelope as her Christian name. It didn't suit her. In public, he called her Penelope or Penny, but never Pen, for that was his sister's name and hers alone. 'Will the bride be in red?' Parvati asked.

'In red? No, of course not . . . oh, is that the custom in India?'

'Yes, oh yes!' Parvati, bright-eyed, began to enlarge but he cut her short.

'You will see what our weddings are like, on the day. We'll ride over; you'll have to manage on Jimmy's pillion. Once you're there, keep close to Eliza and do just what she tells you.'

'Oh yes, I will. I promise.' Parvati was aglow with expectation. 'A wedding! It will be exciting!'

It was.

Francis' house stood in a shallow dip just over the brow of the hill at the end of the headland. It was on what had once been Polmawgan land and from the windows of Ninian's house, one could see the tops of its chimneys. Its carefully cultivated grounds had been created, with imported soil, and much effort, from what had been boggy heath, and Francis' grandfather, its builder, had called it Rosnance, which was Cornish for heathy valley.

Although the Trevelyans had long since abandoned their ancient Celtic tongue, villagers and fishermen and miners spoke it still, among themselves, and it would probably be preserved for ever in the names of people and places. Ninian's name was that of a Celtic saint. Penzance meant a Holy Headland, and Polmawgan itself meant Mawgan's Pool. The cove was roundish and at full tide resembled a pool. Legend claimed that a Cornish saint called Mawgan had once been thrown into it by St Just after a quarrel in which he had accused St Just – known as a notoriously light-fingered holy man – of stealing a jewelled cup from him. 'If I am cynical about religion,' Ninian had once said to Francis, 'can you wonder? Look at the way St Just behaved!'

Rosnance, therefore, was part of a long tradition. Ninian explained it as best he could to Parvati, but she fastened on a different aspect of it.

'It's such a pretty, dancing name,' she said. Parvati loved to dance but the way she did it was highly suggestive and after one demonstration in the parlour, during which all the servants had come to peer round the door with scandalised faces, Ninian told her that she had better not demonstrate again. 'Very well,' she said dejectedly.

'I will teach you our style of dancing,' Ninian said. 'I have a lute.' He kept his word, calling on Meg to help him. By the time the July wedding day came, he thought, Parvati would be able to comport herself fittingly among the Cornish serving people, of whom she would eventually be one, even if the language, history and traditions of Cornwall remained to her a mystery.

The evenings were still long and light and no one intended to waste them. Dusk was falling and still the wedding feast at Rosnance was in progress. They had dined and danced at considerable length and only now was there a move among the women to escort the giggling and more than slightly inebriated Mary to the great fourposter upstairs, hung with new curtains and strewn with rose petals, where Francis would presently join her.

It had been a warm and windless day and it was still sticky. There were sweat-stains under the arms of Francis' elegant wedding suit while Anthony and Alice Gubbes plainly found their decent dark blue clothes over-heavy. They did not dance, but Alice had fanned herself all evening as fervently as though she had been running races. Christopher St Asaph had donned fashionable clothes for a change, but his wide, lace-edged collar was creased and his face was scarlet with heat and wine and, just now, irritation with two of his fellow guests: William Keigwin and Petroc Darracott.

'One can never stop men from talking politics,' Tamzin remarked in mock-despair, as she rose to go with the ladies.

The contentious item was the war which the King had obstinately insisted on pursuing against the Scots.

'. . . well, there it is,' Petroc was saying in his burring voice. 'It do seem to me that this Thomas Wentworth of Strafford has urged the King to go to war against the wishes of Parliament, but that Parliament more nearly speaks the views of people in general.'

'I agree. The war's ill-advised,' Keigwin said.

'Pish!' Christopher huffed with annoyance. 'It's not for the people in general to decide what prayerbook shall be used or when war should or should not be waged. It is the royal prerogative and if that is undermined, all society will fall apart . . .'

'Parliament is very largely Puritan,' Ninian said mildly. 'And you're not that, Petroc. Or you, Mr Keigwin.'

'No, but . . .' They both spoke at once and stopped politely, giving way to each other.

'Mrs St Asaph is perhaps right, that this occasion is unsuited to such a subject.' Anthony Gubbes moved smoothly into the gap in the conversation. 'May I talk of another matter?' He glanced across the table to where Thomas Grosse and Roger Polkinghorne were sitting. 'Parliament's been asked to consider other enemies besides the Scots. We've requested a grant to help Penzance deal with these Moorish pirates. They're growing bold again. Roger, is there any news of it?'

'Not yet,' said Polkinghorne. 'They gave us £600 back in 1625, but now I think they feel that the people of Cornwall should defend their coasts themselves. Personally, I consider that we should have a share of the Ship Money tax.'

There were hearty murmurs of agreement. 'It's only a month since we had nine vessels taken close to our very shores,' grumbled Thomas Grosse and Keigwin nodded vehemently.

All the women had not gone with Mary. The various women servants who had come along in their employers' wake had stayed in the room. Parvati was still there, seated between Hannah and Eliza. To Ninian's annoyance, Grosse suddenly glanced down the room towards her.

'My guest is not a Turk,' he said quietly.

'No, that's very true. Penelope do be a proper Christian now. I can speak to that,' said Darracott with vigour.

'Now, that's odd.' Francis, his head cocked on one side, changed the subject. 'I could have sworn I heard the bell of Polmawgan Church. It can occasionally carry this far when the air is still but why should it be ringing now?'

'It shouldn't. You'm imagining it,' said Darracott.

'Your protégée is very beautiful, old fellow,' said Christopher to Ninian, refusing to be distracted.

He spoke the truth. The hot weather suited Parvati, deepening the ivory of her skin to a warm tawny hue. She had put on her rose-coloured dress and let some of her hair show, and she had added a pair of gold earrings and matching bangles. They were of genuine if very thin gold, and glittered when she moved. Thomas Grosse might regard her only as a foreigner of doubtful origin, but Ninian suspected that Anthony and Roger, now studiously gazing out at the darkening garden and apparently straining their ears for distant bells, were doing so mainly to disguise the fact that they would much rather have gazed at Parvati.

'I can't make it out,' said Francis, puzzled. 'They *can't* be ringing. Well, it must remain a mystery. I think the wine flagons are empty. I must leave you shortly, gentlemen, but first let us have some more wine on the table. Where's my butler? *Marrack!* Where has the rogue got to? My guests are thirsty!'

'I fancy he's answering the front door,' said Anthony. 'Somebody's knocking.'

'Knocking? They're hammering!' said Francis, and started to his feet. 'What in the world . . . ?'

'The Polmawgan bells *are* ringing!' Darracott too rose from the table. 'But . . .'

There was a commotion in the hall. Then Marrack flung open the door and hurried in with half a dozen men, whom Ninian recognised at once as farmhands from the Trevelyan smallholdings, and two fisher-lads from Polmawgan village, crowding after him. Marrack's dignified countenance, which was anything but that of a rogue, was very pale.

'We've run all the way from Polmawgan!' gasped one of the fisher lads. 'Pirates . . . Turks . . . in Polmawgan Cove . . . !'

'It's true! I ran up to the skyline myself to look!' blurted one of the farmhands. 'There's a galley right in the cove! Someone's ringing the church bells to give the alarm!'

Women were pushing into the room now, some of them dragging children by the hand or carrying babies, all of them terrified. 'They Turks are marching up the combe! They'm coming this way!'

'God have mercy!' Darracott looked from one face to another. 'Mr Trevelyan, sir, we've to defend all these good people.'

'How the devil did they get into Polmawgan Cove?' demanded Christopher. 'With all those rocks round it, it's as safe as anywhere could be, I'd have thought.'

'They must have got themselves a pilot,' said Ninian. 'There were two Polmawgan men among those seized last month.'

'Who'd tell the secret of the way in to the likes of them?' demanded Thomas Grosse.

'There are circumstances,' said Anthony Gubbes grimly, 'in which men will tell anything they know to anyone. Gladly.'

Francis, glancing round, picked out a couple of manservants. 'You two: go and fasten all the doors and windows. Quickly! Marrack, I take it your wife's in the kitchen? Send her upstairs to fetch the women down

47

to the cellar.' Marrack hurried out. Francis turned to the men. 'I have an armoury with swords in plenty and muskets too. I can arm us all. We can shoot from upper windows. We may be able to hold them back from actually attacking the house, that is, if they're really coming here. Who knows how to use a musket?'

They were in the midst of laying hasty defence plans when Mary, her cream brocade wedding dress loose at the neck and flapping open at the wrists, as though she had dragged it on again in a hurry after discarding it, burst in on them, with her mother following and protesting that she must come at once to the cellars.

'Francis, what's happening, what's the matter? Why is there such a noise? Why must we hide?'

'Moorish pirates have landed and they're coming this way. They'll be after plunder and slaves. For God's sake, get down into the basement and stay there until I tell you it's safe to come out.'

'Pirates?' said Mary and Mrs Nicholls, once more, tried to pull her away.

'Yes! And they're nearly here!' Tamzin and Jane Dewey came in together, white of face. 'I saw them from the bedroom window,' said Tamzin. 'There's still just enough light. Come with us, quickly.'

'You're the lady of Rosnance now,' said Francis to his bride. 'It's for you to lead the other women to shelter. Mrs Marrack will show you the way. I must organise the defence of the house. Don't just stand there! Hurry!'

Mary's marriage feast had dissolved into a nightmare, and now Mary herself dissolved into panic. With tears streaming down her face, she threw herself into her mother's arms. Tamzin and Jane took charge of the retreat to the cellars. Mary's mother supported her as they went.

Parvati at this point proved herself useful. She might be afraid of dogs and horses and Hannah, but she was calm in the face of pirates and slavery, perhaps because these were to her more familiar perils. She spoke encouragingly to the frightened Eliza, smiled at Meg, and shyly but firmly touched the arm of a paralysed Hannah and coaxed them to follow Tamzin.

'Gentlemen,' said Francis, 'come with me to the armoury.'

The armoury was on the second floor. It contained swords, daggers, pikes, some old-fashioned crossbows and bolts, an array of carbines, muskets and pistols, and boxes of gunpowder and ammunition. 'I hope to God the powder's dry. I don't have to defend my home at such short notice very often,' Francis said plaintively. 'I never expected an attack here. We're out of sight from the sea.'

'Your chimney smoke isn't,' said Anthony, as they helped themselves rapidly to weapons. 'You can see that from well out in the bay.'

Christopher, peering warily from the window, said: 'They're in the garden. Christ, there are hordes of them!'

'We must do our best.' Ninian pushed a pistol into his belt and tested the balance of a rapier.

'*Cry havoc!*' said Keigwin, opening the window. '*And let slip the dogs of war!* Bring those muskets over here.'

'Surely we ought to parley,' said Anthony, persisting with an argument he had been putting forward when Mary interrupted them.

'No,' said Francis shortly, taking aim through the window as dim figures, barely visible in the light of a moon not yet half-full, came slinking across the lawn. 'There are too many of them. We shoot.'

The powder, fortunately, was in good condition. They shot in relays, giving each other time to reload, guests, servants and farmhands together. Their efforts were rewarded with yells of dismay and the collapse of some of the shadowy shapes. Then the garden sprouted flame-coloured blossoms and the window shattered, causing the defenders to throw themselves sideways to safety. At the same moment they heard the crash of breaking glass at ground level and un-English shouts in the house below. Francis, scrambling up from the floor, tossed his musket aside, seized sword and pistol and said grimly: 'Time to sortie.'

'Better lock the armoury behind us,' remarked Anthony. 'No need to present them with your weapons.'

'Do they need them?' inquired Ninian. 'They've enough of their own, it seems to me.'

One of the fisher-lads, gripping a pike, laughed shakily, and Francis grinned. 'Come on!'

He led them out of the armoury, locking it as suggested. Quickly and softly they descended the first flight of stairs, which were lit by candles in wall-sconces, as was the rest of the house on this day of celebration. A bend in the stairs gave them a view into a long first-floor gallery. Cushions lay strewn on the carpet, and a brown hand was rummaging under the lift-up seat of a settle. Then three menacing figures burst up the lower stairs from the ground floor, plainly in search of the defenders who had done so much damage from the upper window. Francis let out a roar of pure rage, and charged to meet them.

It was an extraordinary, confused fight, among the pools of candle-light and the shadows between, in and out of doorways, up and down twisting stairs, round and round the furniture. Two of the farmhands caught a pirate, flung themselves on him and knifed him in an explosion of blood and high-pitched screeches. Ninian had a confused impression of lithe movements and unfamiliar clothes; saw the fisher-lad with the pike knocked down, disarmed, picked up bodily between two intruders and whisked away; and then he was face to face with a hawk-nosed man, wearing a scarlet headband. He saw black eyes in a swarthy face, white teeth grinning a challenge from the midst of a dark beard. His rapier, straight and slender, clashed with a scimitar which was broad and curved, obliging him to invent hasty variations on the classical fencing he had been taught.

He supposed that he was frightened, but there wasn't time to think about it. As in Penzance years ago, he simply fought, doing what was to be done, and it was the rapier, not the scimitar, which went home. The pirate fell, screaming, clutching convulsively at his belly, knees jerking, and there was more blood. Ninian seized the scimitar and straightened up just as another pirate came at him. He fought with the rapier in one hand and the scimitar in the other and the man fled. Ninian tried to give chase but a pistol went off somewhere and acrid yellow smoke blinded him. When it cleared, he found he had blundered into a doorway and there was Francis standing on the petal-strewn coverlet of his marriage bed, slicing with a broadsword at a thickset, half-naked figure. Darting in, Ninian stabbed the pirate from the rear.

'Striking from behind! How unsporting. My grateful thanks,' said Francis, leaping over the body to join him.

'Sporting be damned,' Ninian snorted, and then, from below, they heard women screaming.

There was a further staircase between them and the ground floor. There were three pirates on it. Two had pistols. The pistols spat and Francis and Ninian ducked back. Francis pointed silently. Against the wall at the head of the stairs was an old-fashioned oak chest, hooped with iron. They picked it up between them and threw it. It swept the pirates head over heels to the bottom, bursting open as it went and shedding old candlesticks, disused fire-irons and moth-eaten tapestries over its victims. Ninian and Francis flung themselves after it. They paused long enough to stab the struggling bodies at the foot and then tore on, through the looted dining room, where garlands trailed forlornly and silver plate was conspicuously absent from the confusion on the table. Through the window, they glimpsed laden figures speeding off across the garden. Together, they crashed through the far door, into the kitchen.

The wall sconces were still quietly alight and a pot of something still bubbled on the fire with an absurd air of business-as-usual but the rest of the kitchen was littered with the debris of cookery in collision with war. Drawers had been wrenched bodily from the dresser and emptied and the floor was a welter of cooking utensils; overturned basins; broken glass and crockery; dented pans; the smashed remains of a fruit pie; and a puddle which had once been soup and still gave off an appetising smell.

The cellar door had been broken open and more pirates, shouting and laughing, were dragging the women out. Francis flung himself on a man who had hold of Tamzin and ran him through. Ninian saw Meg Pellowe and two Rosnance maidservants, shrieking wildly, being carried off through the back door. He rushed after them but a huge, bearded enemy rose up from nowhere to bar his way. He was driven back and his foot slipped in the spilt soup. Then in a blur of blue-white steel, a knife hurtled over his shoulder and buried itself in his opponent's chest. He swung round to see Parvati in the basement doorway, a second blade in her hand.

'Good knives in kitchen!' Parvati shouted. 'We took them with us!'

More defenders burst in. The kitchen became the central battlefield. In the mêlée, Ninian glimpsed Keigwin and Gubbes and Darracott; saw Francis and Christopher fighting side by side, backs against the ransacked, lurching dresser. Mary, spreadeagled against the cellar door, her dress filthy with cobwebs and spattered with blood, was screaming Francis' name hysterically. In the cellar, her mother was screaming in reply. Tamzin had been seized by another pirate and was jabbing valiantly at him with a skewer. Another Turk lunged towards Parvati. Ninian attacked with his rapier and Parvati threw her second knife but missed. 'Get back to the cellar!' Ninian shouted.

'Can't! Bodies on steps! Hannah killed one!' Parvati gasped.

Ninian was between Parvati and the pirate. The Turk snatched up the pot that was boiling on the fire. Ninian threw himself backwards and Parvati, with an anguished cry of 'No, not that! I will go! I will go! Do not hurt him!' tried to fling herself past him and into the enemy's arms. Ninian wrenched her back. The pot rose in the air. He was dimly aware of another pistol going off, and that Tamzin's captor had flung her away and was bolting out of the back door, pursued by Keigwin and Gubbes, but it was too late for him. He would be scalded, scarred, maybe blinded . . . Then the pirate reeled and fell and the pot crashed to the floor. Blood and hot meat stock spattered upwards, repellently mingled. Jane Dewey was standing there with a pistol in her hand, which by its unfamiliar design, she must have snatched from a dead enemy. The kitchen was strewn with them; the defenders with superior numbers had prevailed. The surviving pirates had fled. 'Thank you!' Ninian gasped to Jane.

'She shot from behind as well,' Francis panted. 'But one can't always keep the rules.'

There was a shaky, exhausted silence. Gubbes and Keigwin came back from the garden, carrying reddened pikes and empty pistols. 'Have they all gone?' said Anthony.

Tamzin picked herself up and dusted her dress. Christopher peered out of the back door. 'Damme if I can see a sign of them. They've run for it.'

'We've won!' shouted Francis, slapping Christopher on the back. And somehow, because the four of them had been boyhood friends, Ninian and Anthony joined them in a triumphant orgy of shoulder-thumping and loud bellowing, just as they had done in their youth after successfully climbing dangerous cliffs or evading their elders in order to go night fishing.

The rest of the men watched, grinning. Then the moment passed, and not for years did the four of them understand that it was significant, because it was the last time in all their lives that they would all be together even in the same room, let alone bonded like this in comradeship. They broke carelessly apart, still laughing, and Francis went to call the women still in the cellar. They clambered out past the pirate corpses on the steps and as Mary's mother reached the kitchen, her daughter sank sobbing into her arms.

'Well, Frank, you'll hardly forget your wedding day,' said Darracott.

'Now, Mary, m'dear. It's all over. They'm running for their lives, back to their ships.'

'Yes, indeed.' Francis put down his sword and went to his bride, who recoiled with a wail.

51

'You're all over blood!'

'It's all right, my love, my little rose; it isn't mine.'

'And 'ee should give thanks to the Lord for that.' Hannah, who had been terrified when the alarm was first raised, had overcome both fear and foe and marched up the cellar steps grasping a gory kitchen knife. Like Francis, she was copiously smeared with enemy blood. 'Do 'ee show some gratitude, girl. You and your bridegroom could have been slaughtered or taken off to heathen slavery. There do be blood on your dress as well, from the devil's spawn I slew to save 'ee!'

Mary wailed louder, caught sight of Ninian, who was an even more gruesome spectacle than Francis, and buried her face in her mother's shoulder.

'There, there.' The bride's mother was herself white of face and trembling. 'Hush, darling, hush.'

'Pull yourself together, Mary!' said Tamzin, and Parvati, after a rapid and resourceful search of the kitchen, brought some wine in a cup. 'This will help her.'

But Mary, looking at the small, tawny hand offering the wine, and then at Parvati's brown face, shrieked: 'You're just another heathen! Just another Turkish heathen!' and proceeded to have a fit of full-blown hysterics.

There was no wedding bed that night for Francis and Mary. Francis spent it on guard in case the pirates returned, and Mary, after a sedative drink made by Tamzin and Jane, was put to bed in a guest chamber with her mother for company.

But the night was quiet and daylight brought news. Polmawgan House and Coombe were reported to be unharmed, probably because Polmawgan on its headland had been empty and without chimney smoke, while Coombe was less visible from the sea even than Rosnance. The pirates were interested mainly in slaves and the smoke of Rosnance's kitchen, working at full stretch for the wedding feast, had drawn them.

The pirate galleys had gone now, heading south. A whole fleet of them had anchored off the coast; it was a big and well-organised raid. Before Ninian and his people left Rosnance, which was not until past noon, word had come in of valuables snatched and young men and women kidnapped from Penzance and Mousehole and outlying farms. Others had been killed while fighting. Francis' butler Marrack was dead, as were two other Rosnance men, and several were hurt. Jimmy Tonkin had a slash on his forearm and was feverish. Mrs Marrack, despite her tears, was bravely trying to care for the wounded. Mercifully, there had been no children in the house to be frightened or kidnapped. The couples with families, such as the Gubbes and the St Asaphs, had left their young at home, with nurses.

But Meg Pellowe, aged sixteen, Polmawgan's youngest maidservant, was among the missing, along with the two Rosnance girls Ninian had seen being taken away, and the fisher-lad from Polmawgan and two boys who had worked in Francis' stables.

'Poor Meg. Poor child.' Eliza said it over and over again all the way back to Polmawgan. 'Where did she sleep last night? Poor, poor Meg.' That night, Ninian could not sleep. He was thinking of Meg and also of the newly-wed Trevelyans, and wondering what sort of honeymoon they would have when at length they had a chance to begin it. Also, he had been weirdly exalted by the fighting. He had acquitted himself well and he knew it. He never thought of himself as brave but at Rosnance as in the streets of Penzance all those years ago, he had discovered the heartening strength of rage; put to good purpose the fencing skills he had learned in youth and watched himself become formidable. It had made him feel drunk and he wasn't yet sober.

He lay on his back, arms behind his head. He had left the shutters open in the heat and he watched a half moon rising over the sea while he relived the battle. He remembered Francis fighting while standing on his own fourposter bed, and even making a joke when Ninian killed his assailant. Some of the women had been valiant too. Tamzin, jabbing a pirate with a skewer. Hannah – respectable, godly Hannah! – killing one with a kitchen knife. Jane Dewey saving him from hideous injury, standing monolithically in the kitchen with a Turkish pistol in her hand. Parvati . . .

Parvati was worth a thousand Mary Trevelyans. Parvati too had defended him in that kitchen and would have gone back into slavery for him if he'd let her. And with that, overpowering him without warning, came desire. It seized him with such violence that he gasped and sat upright, his body hot and his manhood surging.

He had had, for a few years, a casual, occasional arrangement with a widow in Mousehole, until she remarried. Since then, he hadn't troubled. If he had never called himself brave, he would never have said he was lustful, either. He had never known such an imperative as this. He wanted Parvati, so badly that he could have cried aloud with longing. He was out of bed, already moving across the floor, going irresistibly to her, when his door opened and there she was, a robe thrown loosely round her and the light of the newly risen moon reflected in her long, dark eyes.

She came straight to him without speaking, and put her arms round him. She pressed herself against him and felt his readiness, and sighed. Ninian drew off her robe and dropped it on the floor. He cast off his own. Parvati knelt and with delight and amazement he stood, while she did what the Mousehole widow would never have done, and took him into her warm, moist mouth.

Then she rose fluidly and stood once more in his arms and as their mouths joined, he picked her up and took her to the bed.

The window was unshuttered and the bedcurtains open. In the moonlight, her body was mysterious, made of darkness and silver, a sweet coolness veined with warm crevices; a lithe fierceness tempered with a most tender yielding.

Caressing her, he found a poet's words in his mind. Not John Donne's, but Shakespeare's, and he heard himself whispering them. *'For how do I hold thee but by thy granting? And for that riches where is my deserving?'* But her eyes were full of invitation and he could wait no longer. He drove himself into her as if trying to lose himself there, and she twined her limbs about him and gave to him the grace, the femininity, the wildness that he had missed all his life. He had once hoped for it in Tamzin, but although he had never made love to Tamzin, he knew by instinct that she could never have answered him thus.

But he could not think of Tamzin now. She drifted once into his mind and then was obliterated. The wave broke, beaching him upon Parvati's pale body as though on a shore. He lay spent, his nose nuzzling into her shoulder. Then she laughed and stirred and moved herself astride him, riding him now as though he were the wave and she a vessel borne upon it in the moonlight.

Until, once more, they were swept to their unanimous beach, where, this time, they slept.

Francis had spent the day in getting bodies removed and hurt men cared for, in receiving news, arranging look-outs and comforting tenants bereaved by death or kidnap. Since Mary was still in a state of collapse, he had left her to her mother. But her mother saw her to bed in the restored bridal chamber that evening, and there he came to her at last. He found her watching for him, her eyes large in the light from his candle.

'Well. This isn't quite the wedding night we expected. But I didn't look for such a lot of uninvited guests at the feast,' he said lightly.

'It was h . . . horrible. I wish I could go home.' As he snuffed his candle and came to join her, she shivered.

'This is your home now, sweet, and it isn't usually like this, I promise. Come. Let us put things right. It's giving them the victory, to let them spoil tonight for us. Let us have it in despite of them.'

Mary had been taught her duty. She made no further protest as he moved towards her. But she could not respond to him. She cried throughout and when he had finished what could be called an act of intercourse but could not possibly be described as an act of love, he rolled off and lay staring into the darkness.

'I'm not an enemy,' he said resentfully. 'You may have seen me stained with blood, carrying a sword, but it was in your defence. You could have been sleeping with a Turkish pirate tonight instead of with me. In a stinking hold in a galley, instead of in my down bed.'

'I'm . . . I'm sorry. I'm not brave. Tamzin St Asaph was brave,' Mary whimpered. 'I wish I were like her.'

'So do I,' said Francis coldly.

Ninian sat up and stared in horror at Parvati's tranquilly slumbering face. The house was astir. Branson would appear at any moment with his shaving water. He scrambled out of bed, seized the two discarded robes on the floor and thrust them out of sight in a drawer; then got back under the covers and pulled them up over Parvati's head.

Last night, unbelievably, he had risen to go to her, not to ask her to love him, but to take her, willing or no. That she was willing, was already coming to him, was a miracle which had saved his integrity. The fighting at Rosnance must have driven him temporarily out of his mind. But . . . oh God . . . he loved Parvati now, loved her with the heart and the spirit as well as the body. At the age of forty, he had found out the meaning of love. What was that absurd thing he'd said to Francis, just after Pen's funeral? Something about one's fires dying down with age? What nonsense. Oh, Parvati. How could he now sleep chastely in the master bedchamber while she lay alone elsewhere? His need of her would burn its way through the walls between them.

But still less could he send her from him to servitude in another house.

Branson would be here in a moment. He must compose his face to calm. Calm! What if Parvati were with child?

Meg's body was washed ashore next day in the cove below Coombe. She was pretty and young and the pirates were unlikely to throw such good merchandise overboard. It was far more probable that she had cast herself into the sea.

'And I can't put a suicide in consecrated ground,' said Darracott, distressed.

'But it could have been an accident,' said Ninian. 'How can we know? She could have slipped and fallen overboard.'

'Grant her the benefit of the doubt, you mean?'

'Yes. Lay her near Pen. She was part of our household.'

'Very well. You do be a good advocate, Ninian. Her parents, poor souls, ought to be grateful to you. You've just mentioned your household,' said Darracott. 'It's been on my mind to speak to you on that subject. It b'ain't fitty for this Indian girl, Penelope, to stay in your bachelor home in an undefined manner. What plans do you be making for her?'

'I intend to marry her,' said Ninian.

Chapter Five

The Darkening Sky

Parvati said yes, without hesitation. She wished to stay with Ninian, she said, and to his embarrassment made it clear that in order to do so, she was willing to go through any amount of unfamiliar ceremonies. When informed of the forthcoming wedding, the Bransons looked amazed while both the Giddys gasped in visible outrage.

'I trust you will all wish me happiness, and will help my wife to settle down in her new position,' said Ninian pleasantly, but with underlying steel. He preferred not to know what they said among themselves out of his hearing. In his household, the only congratulations which sounded genuine came from the taciturn Jimmy Tonkin. He had let Parvati tend his slashed arm and it was healing well. He had taken to her.

The wedding in Polmawgan Church was as quiet as the baptism had been. Ninian bought some cream silk from which Parvati made herself a dress and he gave her a string of pearls. The Trevelyans and the St Asaphs attended. Parvati, who was now used to pillion riding, came to church behind Francis, who gave her away at the ceremony.

Jane Dewey was present, as were Jimmy and the Bransons. Uriah Giddy also attended, because Ninian had insisted. But Hannah stayed behind on the excuse that she must watch the dinner and there were other absentees too.

Anthony and Alice Gubbes had sent civil apologies, pleading a previous engagement. Ninian knew that they were shocked. The Clemos had also declined. Well, he could do without *them*, Ninian said. But he was sorry about Anthony.

Once again, a small crowd of Polmawgan villagers gathered outside the church and once again, a few, such as Marge and Walter Hawkes, called congratulations. Most, however, merely stared. Francis helped Parvati up to the pillion of Ninian's chestnut mare Sandy, and they rode back to the house.

A small feast awaited them, which the Bransons served. Hannah, tight-lipped, had prepared it as bidden but now chose to stay pointedly in the kitchen. Francis made smooth conversation about politics and Mary, glancing anxiously at him now and then as if uncertain that she was doing the right thing, attempted to chatter brightly, but the talk was stilted until Jane tackled the situation head-on by calling Hannah into the dining room and stating unequivocally that the wedding heralded a new beginning at Polmawgan, and that young Mrs

Whitmead would need both Hannah and Eliza to help her learn to manage an English house. She gave Hannah a stern glance and added to Parvati: 'My dear, if you should need more experienced advice at any time, please call on me.'

'Thank you, Jane,' said Ninian and tried not to notice Hannah's scowl.

'Well, really, what can he do but marry her? She'll end in the stews of some port or other if he doesn't,' Mrs Dewey had said on hearing of Ninian's plans. 'With lads like my sons spending their money on her and betraying their wives. I call it a soul saved. She's young. She'll adapt. If only some other folk will also do a bit of adapting.'

Unfortunately, in spite of Mrs Dewey's efforts at the wedding feast, this for a long time seemed doubtful.

'Hannah, I know that you've never been willing to cook on Sundays, and you disapprove if Eliza does it, but I have ordered her to cook. The mistress and I want a hot meal today and I insist that you unlock the kitchen door.'

'It says in the Bible that the Sabbath should be a day of rest for thy manservant and thy maidservant and that means Eliza as well as me. There's the food I made ready yesterday, waiting in the dining room, cold. Uriah and me won't be taking dinner at all. In future, we'll fast and pray on the Sabbath. For it do seem to me,' said Hannah stiffly, 'that it's only right to make sure that this house be as godly as may be, seeing that in other ways it's so irregular.'

'*Irregular?* What the devil do you mean, Hannah?'

'You well know what I mean, sir.'

'Very well,' said Ninian sharply, 'today and in future, if the mistress and I want a hot meal on a Sunday, we'll cook it ourselves. If you refuse to share it, that is your business.'

'It's your kitchen, sir, and here's the key, since you want it. But I'd sooner 'ee let things be. It won't be fair on Eliza and me to come down Monday morning and find the kitchen all to be cleaned before we can start on the day's work. It's not fitty for you or the mistress to get down on your knees and scrub the floor. We wouldn't expect for you to do that.'

'I'll clean the bloody kitchen personally, fitty or not! Including scrubbing the floor!' shouted Ninian. 'And if you hold your head up much higher, Hannah, you'll end by getting a very stiff neck!'

'Hannah, the mistress says that she and the master don't want eels on the table again for a bit. It was eel tart yesterday and eels in herb sauce the day before and braised eels two days before that, so can we have something different for a while, please?'

'If the mistress wants to give me orders, Eliza, she'd best come to the kitchen and do it herself.'

'I think she do be frit of 'ee,' said Eliza. 'Last time she come to give orders in kitchen, 'ee made out not to understand her and Uriah's as bad.'

'No more we can make out what she's on about, with her queer way of speaking.'

'Well, I can understand her right enough.'

'Very well, we'll have mussels in broth and stuffed neck of capon for dinner. But I don't like this way of going about things, *that* I don't!' snapped Hannah.

'Hannah infuriates me but she's part of Polmawgan. There's no question of throwing her out,' said Ninian wearily to Jane Dewey, when the latter, having ridden over on a Sunday afternoon, discovered him on hands and knees, washing the kitchen floor, and in her forthright way demanded to know why. 'She hasn't anywhere to go. She comes from Bodmin but she hasn't any family there now. But sometimes I feel like bundling her out of the house at an hour's notice. Eliza's more easy-going but Hannah intimidates her. Neither of the Giddys are more than barely civil to my wife. Par— Penny wants to learn how to do things, but Hannah won't give her a chance. I'm going to have to threaten to give Hannah her notice, I can see that. The trouble is,' said Ninian gloomily, sitting back on his heels, 'I'll have to mean it.'

'You need more help in the house. You've never replaced Meg. Why's that?'

'The mine's running out of tin and owing to the behaviour of the Courteen Association, my East India Company shares aren't producing much income, either.'

'I must think about this,' said Jane thoughtfully.

What made the situation endurable, for Ninian and Parvati alike, was the core of enchantment at night, in Ninian's fourposter. There, shut away from the rest of the house, Parvati was herself, making love in a tradition which had never heard of Puritanism, and Ninian partook joyously of the passion which his life till now had lacked, expanding in it, as if he were a plant hitherto starved of light, and the darkness of the night were a brilliant noonday.

Caught between the splendour of their lovemaking and the continual petty irritations of day-to-day life in the face of household disapproval, he paid little attention to what was happening in the outside world. Now and then, however, Francis would descend on him and bring him up-to-date. 'You need shaking up sometimes, Ninian!'

In fact, the news was disturbing. The Scots had defeated King Charles shortly after Francis' wedding, to the fury of the Earl of Strafford, who had urged the war on the King in the first place. Then in November came horrific revelations.

'It seems,' said Francis, sitting over brandy with Ninian after dinner, 'that at a Privy Council meeting, Strafford suggested bringing an Irish army over to back the King against the Scots.'

'An Irish army? Papists? Here on English soil? I'm not especially interested in politics, Frank, but if that's true, it's scandalous.'

'It's not certain. He could have meant only that the Irish should be brought to Scotland to fight. But he's been arrested for treason all the same. Pym's determined to bring him down. Archbishop Laud's in prison as well.'

'I'm not surprised,' said Ninian. 'Ah well. It's a good thing that Cornwall's a long way from London.'

Francis snorted. 'A long way? The laws they pass in London touch us here as much as they touch the people in Surrey or Essex and if the King and Parliament come to blows, every part of the realm will know it.'

'What a prophet of doom you are, Francis. You sound as though you're hoping for a civil war.'

'No,' said Francis seriously. 'No, I'm not. That would be ugly. Men would be fighting each other who had once been friends and neighbours. The King is trying to save Strafford, of course. I think Strafford was wrong, even if all he did was to suggest pitting the Irish against the Scots, but if he's found guilty and executed, it will be a victory for Parliament over the King and the foundations of the earth will shake.'

'Isn't that a rather melodramatic way of putting it?'

'Not melodramatic,' said Francis. 'Just accurate. Well, we shall see.'

The first thing they saw, however, was Mrs Dewey's solution to Ninian's domestic war. She arrived one December day, riding on a man's saddle, with a dark, plump, merry-eyed girl on her pillion.

'This is Kerenza Penlee. Her people live in Marazion. She's been with me as a maidservant for some months and I think she'd suit as a personal maid for Mrs Whitmead. Kerenza's agreeable to the change.'

'It's very kind of you to take so much thought for us, but we're managing as we are, you know.'

'Maybe, Ninian, but you need someone to take the heat out of the air here and Mrs Whitmead ought to have a personal maid. Kerenza understands all about it. Get down off the pillion, Kerenza, make your curtsy to Mr Whitmead, and speak for yourself.'

Kerenza obeyed, beaming. She had several teeth missing, which spoiled her otherwise pleasant face, but goodwill radiated from her. 'I'd like to be a lady's maid, sir. I can sew and dress hair. And Mrs Dewey do say that Mrs Whitmead be a beauty. I'd like taking care of her.'

'But, Mrs Dewey, when you mentioned this before, I told you how things stood.'

'Nonsense,' said Jane, her stern gaze this time transfixing Ninian, 'the girl will work for little more than her keep. If you like, I'll pay her wages and lend her to you.'

'That won't be necessary!' said Ninian indignantly. 'Very well, Kerenza. If you'll accept modest wages, you shall have a trial.'

In a week, he knew that Kerenza was a saviour. She was bubbly, good-tempered, and adored Parvati on sight, admiring her long black hair, comparing it – without a trace of jealousy – with her own coarse tresses, and she was enchanted by the bright silks which Parvati still wore in private. She also understood stillroom skills and set about showing her mistress how to make cordials from preserved fruit. Unlike Hannah she had no difficulty in understanding Parvati's English.

Best of all, she was a buffer between her mistress and Hannah. She accompanied Parvati to the kitchen to give orders, and translated back and forth, all with a happy giggle in her voice which muffled Hannah's coldness and Parvati's diffidence like a set of fluffy gloves on cold fingers.

At first, Hannah complained to the other servants. 'She fair feeds me up, with the way she gawps at the mistress and hangs on her every word!'

But when Hannah did her complaining in Kerenza's hearing, Kerenza only laughed and said: 'Oh, don't be such an old sobersides, Mrs Giddy!' and when Uriah tried to reinforce his mother's remarks, she gazed at him with sparkling eyes and told him that he talked just like the hellfire minister in Marazion, but the minister was old and wasn't Uriah a bit young to be sounding like him? 'You want to loosen up a bit, Mr Giddy, and enjoy yourself.' Which left Uriah speechless.

Under Kerenza's influence, Hannah and Uriah lost much of their power to make Parvati unhappy. She gained a little confidence and even managed to rebuke Hannah once or twice in person for faults in her cooking.

'I've never seen you flounce before, Hannah,' Ninian said genially, arriving on the scene on one such occasion. 'Take heart. We're all imperfect sometimes. The world hasn't ended. The meat was underdone, it's true, but there was nothing wrong with the pastry. You've still got your light hand there.'

He managed to get a faint smile out of Hannah. But as he smiled back, he suddenly thought of the phrase he had just used concerning the end of the world. According to Francis, it was possible that the world in which they had both grown up might be, if not ending, about to experience drastic change. There was trouble in the air.

On the 12th of May 1641, the controversial Thomas Wentworth, Earl of Strafford, was beheaded on Tower Hill, 'and there were two hundred thousand people there to watch, most of them glad to see him die,' said Francis, with unusual gravity, coming to Polmawgan a week later. He had been visiting London and had been among the crowd.

'And what's going to happen next?' said Ninian.

No one knew the answer to that, but a new atmosphere was developing, all across the land. Whenever a group of people, however small, came together, they invariably talked of politics and religion and disagreements acquired a bitter edge. The infection invaded every town, every village, every congregation. It even split families. Attitudes had polarised. There was gossip of betrothals broken because the families supported different sides, of people withdrawing their custom from tradesmen of the other persuasion, of neighbours no longer speaking.

In Cornwall, it seemed that the general preference was for the King, but if the supporters of Parliament were therefore a minority, they were highly visible. The King had a Catholic wife and himself upheld Anglican ritual, which in Puritan eyes wasn't very different, and there was a strong link between Parliamentarians and Puritans. Puritans dressed distinctively. Those who had once been midway between the two sides, but had decided to back Parliament, now took to wearing Puritan styles.

In the streets of Penzance and Mousehole and Marazion, one could recognise the supporters of Parliament instantly by their tidily cut hair and their dark garments set off only by plain white collars and cuffs. Conversely, those who upheld the King were taking more and more to high fashion. Christopher St Asaph, who had once been content to be an unfashionable country gentleman, now would not appear downstairs without his silk stockings and his ribboned breeches; while Francis burst forth not only into swashbuckling military buff but also into a sash, lace-trimmed boots and a remarkable hat with a long, curled feather, and framed his squarely masculine features in long, curled tresses. He complained that Ninian's short hair created a wrong impression.

'If I grew it, I'd look like a haystack,' retorted Ninian. 'I'm just being myself. Have you bought smart new dresses for Mary, too? I know her mother died at Christmas, but she'll be out of mourning soon, presumably.'

'Yes.' Francis looked tired. 'I've paid for a fashionable dressmaker to renew her wardrobe and I've had some very fine furniture made for her. Anthony Gubbes got a consignment in of a new timber from Brazil – rosewood, it's called. It has a very pleasing deep-red tone. I've had a chest of drawers made for her, with a rosewood veneer over oak. It's beautiful work. Oh, I know what you think. I've seen your face sometimes when I've spoken impatiently to her in your hearing. Believe me, I do try to be kind to her and I know she's been grieving for her mother. But she cries or sulks or becomes frightened over such little things – if a servant answers back or a dress doesn't fit. Then I get irritated.'

'I'm sorry.'

'I thought an older woman's company might help and I asked Jane Dewey to visit us, but she's scared of Jane as well,' said Francis with exasperation. 'Perhaps she'll be better if we have a baby. You . . . er . . . ?'

'Not yet. Penny's very disappointed about that.'

This was an understatement. Parvati, for months now, had been growing more and more distressed by her failure to conceive. 'When it was wrong for me, I would conceive and I would have to dose myself or do things. Now when I want a baby, I cannot,' she sobbed to Ninian. 'I am failing you.'

Ninian suspected that her barrenness now was due to the fact that she had obviously had past abortions, but did not say so because it would have upset her. Instead, he said: 'It is all right. I don't mind.'

'You are kind, but all men want sons. Who will have Polmawgan after you are gone, if you have no son?'

'I've cousins in Essex. In a place actually called Whitmead, as a matter of fact. That branch of the family would inherit, after you. You'd have Polmawgan for your lifetime. I've arranged that.'

'But can a childless wife inherit in that way?'

'Yes, and you would.'

Parvati shook her head in wonderment. 'But you should have a son of your own!' she insisted.

'It might be a daughter.'

'Oh no, it must not be a girl. Girls are worthless.'

'Parvati, you're a girl and you are not worthless. Don't say such things!'

'At least,' said Parvati, 'even if it was only a girl, at least it would prove I can still have babies. I might have a son next. But I cannot even begin. Month after month, I hope in vain.'

'It doesn't matter,' said Ninian.

He was telling the truth. Since his marriage, he had begun to entertain the St Asaphs again and be entertained by them, finding that there was no longer any pain in seeing Christopher and Tamzin together. There was no pain either in encountering their three children. He wanted Parvati's only because she longed for them so badly.

Tamzin and Parvati had even formed a mild friendship, based on an exchange of domestic lore on cookery and the making of ointments for cuts, a subject in which Parvati had some skill. Once, he went so far as to consult Tamzin about Parvati's failure to conceive. But she shook her head.

'Except for prayer, there's nothing one can do. I've helped some of our tenants' wives in childbirth. Jane Dewey is a good friend of mine and she has taught me. She's very skilled in the matter. But conception is in God's hands.'

For just one moment, the past echoed in both their minds. 'Tamzin . . . you are happy? You have no regrets?'

'No, Ninian. None. I think perhaps you and I weren't suited. And I think,' said Tamzin, with the smile which he still thought was entrancing and enigmatic, even though it no longer made his heart turn somersaults, 'that you are very well suited now. Don't worry. The children will come, I feel sure of it.'

But at last, in October, more than a year after their marriage, Parvati began to suffer from nausea and shyly confided that she thought she was with child. It was hard to say who was the most relieved: Parvati or her husband.

Parvati's pains began, a little earlier than expected, in the June of 1642. From the start it was a harsh labour.

'She's very narrow, Mr Whitmead,' said Jane Dewey. 'But she's also young and that's a great advantage.'

'I know you and Tamzin are doing your best.' Ninian's eyes were sunken with tiredness. 'But I've sent to Penzance for the physician. I don't want to give offence but . . .'

'There's no question of offence,' said Jane briskly. 'Where's Hannah with that hot water?'

'Two nights and a day,' said Hannah to the other servants when Jane had seized the basin of hot water and gone. 'And now we're into the second day. It be too long.' She wiped a hand across a sweating forehead. 'She'm a woman like us, I suppose,' she said gruffly.

'I've tried, all these last months, to build her up, get her to eat more,' Kerenza said worriedly. 'But she'm just made small.'

Eliza said: 'It'll break the master's heart if things go wrong.'

The weather, though grey, was muggy. Parvati lay tossing and sweating in a tangle of bed-linen. Tamzin, wiping the small, moist face with a damp napkin, glanced round as Jane came in with the hot water and shook her head. Jane came anxiously to the bedside. Parvati's face was sunken, and her eyes were closed. The mound of her stomach was the only part of her which was filled-out and alive. It was like an excrescence which was sucking the life from the rest of her. As Tamzin wrung out a cloth in the water and laid it on the mound, another contraction seized Parvati. Her eyes opened and widened. She twisted and screamed.

She had been doing this at intervals for a very long time, to no avail. They had tried a whole battery of herbal infusions; they had tried holding pepper under her nose to make her sneeze and they had prayed almost without ceasing. Tamzin had coated her hand in grease and succeeded in establishing that the child was the right way round. But still it could not pass the pelvis.

Parvati heaved and wailed again. As the paroxysm subsided, she gasped: 'My husband. Want . . . husband. Nin . . . Ninian.'

'Now, then, that's not fitting,' Jane said. 'This is women's business, except for the physician. A physician has been sent for.'

'Ninian,' whispered Parvati, and closed her eyes again.

'Rouse up, now!' Jane exhorted her. 'You've a child to bring into the world!'

'Ninian,' insisted the whispering voice.

Tamzin and Jane exchanged glances. 'I've never heard of such a thing before. I can't imagine what Hannah will say,' said Tamzin. 'But I think we should fetch him.'

In the parlour, Francis, who had come to keep his friend company in this dreadful vigil, was hungrily consuming cold meat and wine, but Ninian could touch nothing.

'You ought to. You'll be no help to her if you're ill as well,' Francis said.

'I had some breakfast. But I can't eat now. It's gone on too long!' Ninian cried. 'She's not big and strong enough. Why doesn't Uriah come back with that physician? He only had to go to Penzance. If she loses her life, I'll never forgive myself!'

'Never forgive yourself for what? Getting her with child? Well, neither man nor woman knows what the outcome will be when a child begins,' said Francis. 'But if we all gave up procreation for fear of the consequences, the human race would end.'

'Stop philosophising, Frank. I'm not talking about other people, only me. *I* sired this baby. If only it didn't mean so much suffering. If she's got to die, why can't she die quickly without all this pain?'

Francis was silent.

'Hannah says I should have faith in God,' said Ninian angrily. 'She says I should trust in Him although He slay me. But it's Parvati who may be slain and if God thinks He has the right to kill people at will, I don't see how He can expect to be trusted.'

'Please,' said Francis. 'Please take some food, Ninian. You need it.'

But the door had opened and Ninian had swung round. 'Jane! Is there news? Is the doctor here?'

'Not yet, Mr Whitmead. But your wife is asking for you and we think you should come.'

Francis said nothing, but the pity in his face as he glanced at his friend was enough. Ninian, his stomach cold, followed Jane out of the room.

It was against all custom for husbands to enter the lying-in chamber, and he had to brace himself to cross the threshold into that traditionally female domain. Then he heard Parvati cry out and as he came through the door, he saw her eyes, watching for him. He ran to the bedside and fell on his knees beside it.

'Let her hold your hand,' said Tamzin. 'Put strength into her if you can. This is hardly regular,' she added, 'but she called for you, so . . . Now then, Penny, let us see what you can do now that Ninian has come.'

'Penny?' said Ninian. 'Penny? I'm here.' He took her hand. Her grip tightened and her nails dug into his skin. A fresh convulsion tore through her, and his body shook with hers. She cried out anew.

'Good girl. A strong cry, a strong push. Once more!' Jane encouraged her.

But Parvati had lost strength again. Another convulsion shook her, but this time her cry was one of protest and despair and she seemed to shrink before Ninian's eyes. Her grip slackened. He heard himself crying out in turn, calling her by her true name of Parvati, telling her that he loved her, that she must not leave him alone, that his life would be empty if she were not there to fill it with her brightness, urging her to cling to life as she had clung to the timber that carried her ashore, to fight as she had fought for them both at Rosnance. He shouted and pleaded and knew that his face was streaming, with tears or sweat – he couldn't tell which.

The sound of her real name seemed to rouse Parvati. Her fingers tightened on his once more. He returned the grip. She cried out again. 'I can see its head!' cried Jane. 'We'll do it yet! Tamzin, try the pepper again!'

Tamzin was ahead of her, already offering it. 'Try this, Penny. A good deep sniff, now. And another!'

Parvati sneezed, three times, enormous sneezes. 'And here it comes!' cried Jane.

By the time Uriah, who had had to chase his quarry on his rounds, brought the physician to Polmawgan, Ninian's son had been washed and swaddled and Parvati was in an exhausted sleep.

'Not much for me to do here,' said the physician. 'You don't need my forceps. Give the mother red wine and good meat and mix some gruel for the child. Get a febrifuge ready in case of childbed fever.'

'Gruel?' said Tamzin indignantly, when he had gone. 'Well, perhaps that's what ladies do in London, but half of their babies die. A mother should feed her own baby if she can.'

'I agree with 'ee,' said Hannah, who had come with Kerenza to help wash mother and child. 'Though it do be heathen milk and I hope it carries no distemper of the spirit with it. Kerenza, Mrs *Penelope* needs a clean nightgown.'

Ninian grinned. He had used Parvati's original name several times now in his Puritan housekeeper's hearing, and clearly annoyed her. 'Now then, Hannah,' he said. He felt as if ten years had been wiped off his age. 'This is no time for sharpness. Go down and tell Dick to fetch up my best Madeira from the cellar. We're all going to drink the health of my wife and son.' As Hannah went out, he turned to Tamzin and Jane. 'I can't express my gratitude to you. I owe you both so much.'

'It was you that saved her,' Tamzin said.

He noticed something in her eyes as she spoke, an unexpected wistfulness. It was then that he remembered that although Tamzin had once said that she had no regrets, that she and he were not well suited, she had added only: 'I think that you are very well suited now.' *You*, not *we*. Had bluff, uncomplicated Christopher been a disappointment? Did Tamzin also yearn for some mysterious quality of love which could transcend death? But there were questions one couldn't ask and the fact was that he didn't really care what the answer was. Tamzin had her life and he had his and their paths would not touch closely ever again.

His son was baptised Charles, a considered choice. 'This should make it clear which side I'm on,' he said to Francis during the christening ceremony. The whole of England was in a ferment. The Queen had fled to the Continent, where she was trying to raise money for her husband and, among his subjects, divisions already too deep for comfort were deepening further.

From what seemed like a thousand secret basements and garrets, pamphlets and newsletters were spewing, denouncing the sins of King and Parliament alike, usually in scurrilous terms and accompanied by even more scurrilous cartoons.

Ninian, riding into Penzance to dine with Anthony Gubbes, and enjoying, as he usually did, the look of the steep little streets running down to the harbour, and the sight of the tall-masted merchant ships at the quay, found his pleasure sharply interrupted when a pamphlet was forced into his hand. When he reached the house, he showed it to Anthony, and then wished he had looked at it when alone.

It was by a man called John Lilburne, who had been imprisoned for bringing seditious, anti-bishop literature into England from Holland and whipped for refusing to take the oath in court. It described his treatment in bitter detail. From Anthony, it brought a strong reaction.

'I know something about this,' he said. His long-chinned face, normally pale because of the amount of time he spent in his shop and over his accounts, had reddened. The deep-set eyes flashed. 'He wrote it while he was in the Tower. He smuggled it out, and got his friends to print and distribute it. Oh, these things make me so angry! How can people defend these bishops? Unparalleled act of cruelty and barbarous tyranny is what Lilburne calls it. He is right!'

'I know,' said Ninian. 'I'm glad I didn't witness it. I have never understood why people flock to see these things.'

'And yet,' said Anthony with unusual aggression, 'despite your short hair, you are said to be a Royalist.'

'I am.' Ninian spoke cautiously. 'But I don't bracket the King and the bishops together, as most people seem to do. Attack the bishops and everyone interprets that as attacking the King.' Ninian shook his head as if to clear it. 'Attacking the King . . . I can't accept that. It's like the body turning against the head.'

'When the King and his men behave as they are doing now, one could say the head was turning against the body!'

'Tell me,' said Ninian, 'would you be equally revolted if it were a bishop who had been locked up and beaten instead of this man Lilburne?'

'No,' said Anthony candidly. 'The bishop would be guilty. Lilburne isn't.'

'I see.' Ninian was uncomfortable. As adults, he and Anthony had taken different paths but their shared youth hadn't been forgotten, not even after his marriage to Parvati, much as the Gubbes disapproved of it. Parvati was quite recovered now but she was not on Sandy's pillion today because on the few occasions when she and the Gubbes family had met, the gulf between them was so palpable. The conventional Alice didn't know what to say to the foreigner while Anthony was too painfully courteous. But even so, he and Ninian could still cross the mental ground between them to talk of other things. Until now.

Now, political division seemed to be turning a minor rift into a chasm. 'I can hate Lilburne's treatment,' Ninian said, 'and still remain loyal to the King but . . .'

'So can I. Our quarrel essentially is with the King's advisers and with that Papist queen of his,' said Anthony quickly.

'To the point when you wouldn't pity a bishop who suffered as Lilburne has? I would pity any man who suffered so. I can't pick and choose.'

'There are times,' said Anthony, 'when one must. Who is not on the Lord's side, is against Him. It is weakness to be tender to the Lord's enemies and I call the bishops so. Given time, I believe that they and the Queen would lead us back to Popishness and the days of the Inquisition. Is that what you want, Ninian?'

'Of course not! But nor,' said Ninian sharply, 'do I want to be ruled by impassioned Puritans who won't allow people to enjoy May Day celebrations or hot Sunday dinners. I want a middle road and I find it intolerable that there doesn't appear to be one.'

'May Day celebrations and Sunday dinners are of no importance. One can do without them.'

'I don't agree.'

They were looking at each other with something close to dislike when Alice called them to the table. 'Ah. We are disputing, my dear,' Anthony said. 'But we will not continue over the meal. You will agree with *that*, Ninian, I trust?'

Ninian bowed stiffly. Alice smiled. 'With six children between fourteen and two,' she said, 'I am used to disputes. But they are very bad for the digestion.' She was too modest to add that a seventh child was imminent, but even the very full skirt of her dark gown could not conceal it. Ninian, who had now learned how penetrating the voice of even one baby could be, and had witnessed Parvati's nightmare lying-in, wondered how she could keep so calm, with such a brood. No doubt masculine squabbles seemed very unimportant to Alice.

But this was not unimportant, even though all at table was outwardly smooth, with Anthony becoming a family man, mingling the jovial and the stern, inspecting his offspring's hands and faces to see if they were clean, and saying a lengthy Grace; while Alice, whose social expertise was highly polished when she was not being disconcerted by the presence of exotic foreigners, talked smilingly of everyday matters.

When Ninian mounted his horse to leave, Anthony stood by and Ninian, looking regretfully into his host's face, felt as though he were seeing not a friend, but a stranger: Mr Gubbes, godfearing merchant and paterfamilias, well-meaning and righteous but without the moderating grace either of imagination or self-doubt. He wondered what Anthony saw in his own face. An old associate fallen into error, probably; someone no longer sound. Someone with whom he could no longer pretend to be in accord.

'I rarely see Francis or Christopher nowadays,' Anthony said. 'I last met Francis when I sold him some rosewood – over a year ago. I miss their company, but it is better, I think, to avoid former friends than to quarrel with them. My opinions are very different from theirs – or yours. Forgive me, but . . .'

Ninian searched Anthony's eyes and said it for him. 'You won't ask me to dine again, and if I invite you, you may be engaged elsewhere?'

'It . . . might be best. For the time being.'

'You have my forgiveness,' Ninian said. 'But . . . damned politics. Damned religion. I would rather have friendship than any of them.'

'So would I, but one can't, to please a friend, say *yes, I agree* to things which one's very soul denies.'

'Perhaps not. Well, goodbye,' said Ninian bleakly. As he rode away, he was glad of Sandy's uncritical company. The end of a friendship was like the end of a life.

On his return home, he found that somebody had brought a pamphlet by a lawyer called William Prynne into his house and abandoned it in his parlour. Glancing distastefully through it, he saw that Prynne had lost his ears and been branded for campaigning against the bishops and calling on the King to hang them. Revolted equally by Prynne and what had been done to him, he threw the pamphlet into the kitchen fire.

Since Parvati was in the nursery, feeding Charles, Ninian went down to Polmawgan Cove with the dogs and the three of them went for a sail in the *Silver Fish*. On coming home he took out his sword and put an edge on it before joining his wife, who was now in the parlour, and seeking solace in her presence.

In the worsening atmosphere, Parvati was restful company. Her own land had seen religious conflict, often, and she had understood when he explained about Papists and Puritans. But simply because she was a stranger from far away, she was detached from the conflict. She had no family allegiances to either side, no deep-rooted convictions. She preferred to talk of everyday things, such as the way Charles now quite deliberately bawled at the top of his lungs in order to get himself changed, fed or cuddled, or of the latest plants in the garden and how well or badly they were flourishing.

'You are a centre of peace,' Ninian told her once. 'I wish more people could be like you.'

Very few were. Ministers thundered their opinions from their pulpits; there were cases of people coming to blows in the street; and a band of ardent young Royalists attacked Anthony Gubbes' shop, knocked Anthony unconscious and made off with some of his goods. When the news came at last that the King had raised his standard at Nottingham, it was a relief, as if a hovering storm had at last broken.

Within weeks, Sir Bevil Grenvile of the Cornish Grenviles was sending agents through the county to raise troops and arms and money to hold Cornwall for the King.

Ninian took one last, wistful look round his study, and said 'Goodbye' aloud to his books and his desk and the calm, azure sea beyond the window, where St Michael's Mount swam limpidly in the clear August light. It was hard to believe that he might never see any of them again. Then he went downstairs to bid goodbye to Parvati, knowing that this farewell would be harder still.

But it had to be made. True, many of the Penwith men were staying at home, saying that they would defend their hearths if it came to it but that they were a long way from the Tamar and the county boundary. But Francis and Christopher were going; and simply because they had lost Anthony, the bond between the others had grown stronger. He couldn't stay behind.

'I have to go. Yet I don't want to,' he said to Parvati, as they stood in each other's arms in the hall.

'But it is your duty. I know.' Parvati smiled resolutely.

'I leave our son, and my house, in your care. I have made it clear to all the servants that they must respect you. If they don't, you have leave to dismiss them. Tamzin will advise you if you need it, or Jane Dewey. Remember what Mr Darracott and I have told you about going regularly to church and not giving rise to any kind of talk. I'll write, my love, of course, and you'll write back.'

Parvati had arrived at Polmawgan completely illiterate, but during

69

the past year, he had begun teaching her to read and write. She could manage a simple letter now.

'Yes, I'll write. You will give me your direction,' she said, still smiling valiantly.

Ninian laughed. 'That's my Penny!'

But the tears came at the moment of parting, and Ninian spurred Sandy out of the gate quickly, so as not to prolong either Parvati's distress, or his own.

On the 17th day of August 1642 the Cornish troops mustered at Bodmin race-course. There was a rumour that Parliamentary forces would be invading over the Tamar. 'I told you there would be trouble,' Francis said exultantly to Ninian. 'And here it is.' He laughed. 'Well, Cornishmen thrive on it. Cornwall was a kingdom in its own right once and we're still Celtic by blood, for the most part. We held off the Romans and we held off the Saxons. Now we must hold off Parliament! Have you ever read the tales of King Arthur? Some say Camelot was in Cornwall.'

'I'm only half Cornish and this is real life, not legend.' Oddly, in this time of crisis, it was the vigorous and practical Francis who apparently had his head full of heroic dreams, while Ninian, who, if handy enough with a sword would rather have read a book any day, was the realist. 'You once said,' Ninian observed, 'that this conflict would be ugly. Well, it will.'

70

who spent so much time in his study reading books, would study the writings of Mr Prynne instead of reading all that poetry. His soul would benefit greatly thereby.

And if only, she added herself, her head cocked to the sound of a faint twanging at the other end of the house, Mrs Whitmead would stop making those queer un-English noises on the master's lute. Faint as the sound was, it had begun to eat at Hannah's nerves. She ground her teeth and turned back to her book.

Running Polmawgan House was hard work. Uriah and the Bransons and Jimmy Tonkin all did their bit; Peg Treweeke, the bailiff's eldest daughter, milked the home farm cows and Kerenza had taken over the dairy and the poultry; while Parvati stitched industriously, grew herbs, kept the stillroom in order and looked after her small son.

But nevertheless, between cooking and marketing, washing clothes and endless cleaning, Hannah Giddy hardly had a spare moment, except that at certain times, she insisted on it.

On Sundays after church, and for one hour every weekday afternoon, Hannah withdrew resolutely to the room which, as a housekeeper and a widow of mature years, she had to herself, and there, sometimes with Uriah and sometimes, as now, alone, she read improving books and pamphlets, and prayed.

That weekday hour was for her a tradition. Her father had been literate and on the Bodmin farmstead where she grew up, he had given an hour a day, after supper, to educating his children. No matter how tired they were or how the candles guttered; no matter if linen needed mending or boots needed cleaning, he had kept that hour aside.

Hannah's mother called it a waste of time and Hannah had once thought so herself. Literacy certainly wasn't much use when she went into service, as a kitchen-maid in Redruth. The master and mistress there considered it a drawback in servants, something which made them puffed-up and gave them the dangerous idea that they might be as intelligent as their betters. At the end of her first week, Hannah was caught with a religious pamphlet, whereupon she was walloped with a broomstick, forbidden to read ever again in that house and subjected thenceforth to frequent cutting remarks. 'The meat was overdone today, Hannah. No use in being clever enough to read if you're not clever enough to watch a roast.'

Her second place, in Penzance, was no better. Hannah, bruised in both body and mind, sometimes wished she had never heard of the alphabet.

But when at the age of twenty, she married and left her employment, her husband had encouraged her to read what he called godly books. When he died three years later, leaving her with a small son but no money, she had sought work and come to Polmawgan, although the Penwith servants' grapevine said that the house was lonely and Morwenna Whitmead a demanding mistress. The last cook had walked out in a temper, without giving notice, and Morwenna wanted a replacement urgently enough to take on one with a small child.

Oddly enough, Polmawgan suited her. Morwenna was indeed

demanding and very bad-tempered and Penelope, the daughter of the house, in her late twenties but already visibly turning into an old maid, was too downtrodden to offset it. But demanding or not, as long as the work was done properly, Morwenna didn't mind how her servants used their spare time, and when young Mr Ninian caught sight of Hannah with a book, he didn't chase her with a broom, but told her she might borrow at will from his shelves. From then on the hour of reading which her father had instituted became part of Hannah's adult life.

She read some of Ninian's books of plays and poetry, but her father and her husband had both said that poetry was a waste of time and that plays were immoral, and she felt uncomfortable with them. She began instead to read the Puritan literature which was coming into circulation, the pamphlets and sermons and this book, Prynne's *Players Scourge or Actors Tragedy*, which was so enormous that she and Uriah had bought it between them and had to save up for it for months, at that. But its very massiveness as well as its vitriolic wording seemed to Hannah to be evidence of strong feeling, and she sympathised with it.

If only other people were as clear about the difference between right and wrong. If only the will of God, which seemed so plain to her, were as evident to others. She was not against the King; her employer was fighting on the correct side, in her view. But the King needed to be saved from Papistical and worldly advisers. And Ninian needed to be saved from . . .

It was a grey, sleepy-soft day and warm for March. The sea was slack. Eliza and Kerenza had gone to a fair in Marazion, driven by Jimmy Tonkin in the Polmawgan cart. The house should have been quiet. But the sound of the lute was growing louder.

The mistress was devout in a way, Hannah conceded. She went to church every Sunday and each evening listened respectfully to family prayers in the parlour, conducted by Ninian when he was here, and in his absence – for Ninian had not taken any of his men with him – by Dick Branson. But it was all . . . all . . .

Listening to that faint, infuriating twanging, Hannah groped for words. It was all play-acting, that was it. Mrs Whitmead play-acted the business of being a Christian, just as if she were performing in one of those abominable stage plays. She *still* wore those un-English bangles that jingled when she walked. She wasn't modest, either. She was *proud* of her dewy skin and of the thickness and lustre of her knot of blue-black hair. She gave the master sidelong looks of invitation from those long, dark eyes and didn't care who noticed.

She didn't know that sex was shameful. It was necessary, unfortunately. Without it there'd be no children. But no one ought to enjoy it or if they did they ought to pretend otherwise. Above all no woman ought to walk in that swaying, supple fashion, as though she wanted men to look at her, as though she were rejoicing in her powers.

Hannah, who had once found sex very satisfactory indeed and during her widowhood had spent hours on her knees, praying to be relieved of godless yearnings, wondered what went on between Ninian and Parvati in private and shuddered with anger at her imaginings.

She'd bewitched the master, that's what she'd done. She'd put his soul in peril. Oh, would that lute never stop? Just before Mr Whitmead went away, he'd apparently shown her the fingering. Since then, Parvati had been teaching herself to play. 'And not even English tunes!' Hannah fumed. She was no authority on music, but even Hannah could tell that what Parvati was reproducing on the lute were the chords and rhythms of her own land.

She'd stopped it for a bit after they heard that he was wounded, but then the news came that he was recovering and would soon be returning, and she'd been at it every afternoon this past week.

'But the news is so happy. I must show my gladness,' Parvati had said, when Hannah mentioned that the lute was being heard too much.

'Grateful prayers and a humble mien would be a better way of giving thanks to God,' Hannah had said.

'Oh, but I do pray. I have prayed for my husband since the day he left,' Parvati assured her, and Eliza, who was far too soft in Hannah's opinion, had said: 'Oh well, let her alone. There's no harm in it.'

In revenge for that remark, Hannah had made Eliza empty all the kitchen shelves, clean them and replace their contents, which took an entire morning.

Suddenly, the persistent sound of the lute made Hannah crash her book shut and sit trembling with indignation.

It wasn't right. Such godless noises shouldn't be heard in any Christian household, least of all one where there was a young child. How could the baby – such a fine, strong little boy, too – grow up to be a decent man while his mother set him such an example? Something should be done. A good servant of the Lord would bear witness. She should go straightaway to Mrs Whitmead's room and speak her mind.

But she had promised to be respectful and Parvati had the power to dismiss her, a prospect which frightened her badly. Of course, she had Uriah, who would support her if she couldn't find new employment. But if she left Polmawgan she would have to find a new home among strangers. No matter how often she reminded herself of the horrors that William Prynne and John Lilburne had endured in the name of their faith, she cringed helplessly away even from the minor martyrdom of being cast out of Polmawgan.

The sound of hooves distracted her. Going to the window, she saw Mary Trevelyan riding in, accompanied by her groom. Hannah did not think very highly of Mary, either. Her dappled mare was too elegant, and her moss-green riding dress was of costly velvet, and decorated with too much frippery lace. Her fair hair was in elaborate bunches on either side of her head; her high-crowned hat had a showy green feather in it; and pearls gleamed in her ears. She was worldly.

But she was at least English, and a proper Christian, and since she must have come to see Mrs Whitmead, she would interrupt that music.

Mary dismounted, with some haste, as though her errand were urgent, and Hannah heard Dick Branson let her in. The lute ceased, as though the mistress too had heard Mary arrive, but her door didn't open. She didn't seem to be going down to greet her guest.

75

Instead, feet and voices were coming up. Hannah stepped into the passage just as Mary came hurrying upstairs, holding up her skirts and calling over her shoulder that it was all right, Branson, she knew which was Mrs Whitmead's room. Her voice was bright, but Hannah saw at once that the visitor's face was very strained. Mary made straight for Parvati's door and Hannah clicked her tongue. Guests ought to be properly announced. She stepped into Mary's path. 'Excuse me, Mrs Trevelyan . . .'

'Oh Hannah, there's no need for ceremony.' Mary's hand was on the door-handle. 'Penny, it's me, Mary Trevelyan! I've had such a worrying letter from my husband and I wondered if . . .' Still speaking, and without waiting to be summoned, Mary opened the door. Parvati and the baby Charles were both there. Charles was sleeping placidly in his cradle beside the big bed. The lute had been laid aside but Parvati hadn't stopped playing because of Mary. She had stopped in order to pray.

In a fashion. Hannah and Mary stood transfixed, gaping at the incredible drawing of an eight-armed, dancing figure, which had been propped up on a shelf inside an open wall cupboard and to which Parvati, kneeling with palms pressed together, was evidently addressing her prayers.

She looked round and scrambled to her feet with every sign of guilt and alarm. Mary, distracted from her husband's worrying message, whatever it might be, stared at her and at the drawing and said: '*Oh!*' on a note of horror.

'And what,' demanded Hannah, pointing at the figure, 'what, may I ask, is *that?*'

'I . . . it . . .'

'It's some heathen thing!' Mary's eyes and mouth were wide and round. 'But . . . oooh, I've never seen anything like it before!'

'It's the Lord Shiva,' said Parvati in a defiant voice. 'In my country he is Lord of all. Lord of the Dance, as we say, and . . .'

'A god of dancing!' Hannah screeched, outraged.

'Not dancing.' Parvati tried in a flustered way to explain. 'The dance. The great dance in which all living things take part, as lives cross each other and change each other and fade out of sight and are reborn. Shiva is Lord above all the other gods, and he is both protector and destroyer. I am s . . . sorry.' Their expressions were beginning to frighten her. 'I am not quite used to praying in your fashion, and my husband is not yet home and there is such trouble everywhere. I was praying to Shiva to defend him and destroy any who might do him harm. I . . .'

Hannah stood speechless, opening and shutting her mouth. The sheer unfamiliarity of the figure in the drawing had thrown her into confusion. If it had had the officially recognised horns, hooves and tail, she would have known how to react. But this . . . this multi-armed, dancing thing with . . .

She looked at it again and saw that it was equipped with something else besides dancing legs and eight sinuous arms. Mary saw it at the same time.

'But it's got . . . oh, how terrible . . . Penelope, how could you . . . how could you pray to that?'

Hannah regained her powers of speech. ''Ee've been praying to the devil!' Even Ninian, that bewitched, partisan husband, could not condemn his honest Christian housekeeper for speaking out in these circumstances. Hannah strode across the room, snatched the drawing out of the cupboard, crushed it into a ball and hurled it across the room. 'Wickedness! Profane, filthy, evil thing!' Her whole body shook with fury. 'And you a baptised Christian!'

With an attempt at dignity, Parvati said: 'May I remind you, Hannah, that I am your employer and . . .'

'Employer? Witch, more like! Foreign witch!' Words were no longer enough. Hannah, beside herself, slapped Parvati on the side of the head. Parvati staggered back and with satisfaction, Hannah saw the dark eyes fill with tears.

'I was only praying for my husband!' Parvati pressed a hand to her face.

'Your husband! At least he's supposed to be on his way home!' cried Mary. 'Why should *you* need prayers and spells to bring him? Mine has written to say he is going on to offer his sword to the King himself and he doesn't even tell me where he's going or where I'm to send letters or anything. I came to ask if you knew, if Ninian had sent you any news. But I wouldn't want Francis back if I had to turn to spells and witchcraft to do it!'

Parvati burst into a wild and noisy wailing. Hannah, arms akimbo, stared at her savagely. 'Go on, bawl away! If the Justices get to hear of this, 'ee'll bawl much louder. Thou shalt not suffer a witch to live, that's what the Bible says.' She advanced on Parvati once more, thrusting a suffused face at her victim.

Then the baby woke up and screamed, and on the instant, Parvati's terror turned to rage. 'You're frightening my baby! You wicked woman, you're frightening little Charlie!' She threw herself at Hannah, fingers crooked into claws and raked the housekeeper's face. Hannah shrieked and caught hold of Parvati's knotted-up hair, wrenching the knot apart. Twisting her hand into the long tresses, she dragged Parvati to her knees. Parvati sank her teeth into Hannah's ankle. Mary, watching in horror, set up a cry for help.

Dick Branson was in the room a moment later and hauling the ugly scrimmage apart. Parvati sat gasping on the floor with her hair all awry, while Hannah, scarlet-faced, stood over her. Mary sat down on the bed, aghast.

'Mrs Whitmead! Hannah!' Branson's usually calm, middle-aged countenance was a picture of distaste and his Cornish voice was scandalised. 'Whatever are you about?'

Hannah clapped a palm to her cheekbone and discovered that her scratches were bleeding. 'What have you done to my face, you vicious, evil . . . !'

'*Your* face? You have almost pulled out my hair!' Parvati shouted.

'Oh, my baby, my poor baby!' Charlie's screams had redoubled. Leaping to her feet, she snatched him up and cradled him, glaring at Hannah across him as though daring her to attack *now*.

'Mrs Trevelyan!' Branson said urgently, 'there's remedies downstairs; would 'ee fetch them? There's ointments in the cupboard just inside the kitchen door and water warming in a pot on the fire. No, Hannah, I'd as soon not know what all this is about. For the love of God, tidy your hair, Mrs Whitmead. Why b'ain't Kerenza here just when she's needed? It's as well I came so quickly. As it happens – Hannah, be quiet! – I was already halfway up the stairs. I was coming to tell 'ee,' said Dick Branson, 'that the master is just riding towards the house along the headland path.'

'I have never been so angry,' said Ninian. He could also have said that he had never been so terrified. Even lying wounded on the battlefield, with pike-wielding enemy soldiers at large nearby, he hadn't felt like this. Fear for someone else could be worse than fear for oneself and Parvati was in danger. Witchcraft was a hanging matter and he could not forget the St Ives woman who had been burned. She had been young, like Parvati.

He had come home, lame, tired, riding Francis' spare horse ('I don't want to risk Silver on the battlefield; he's getting on in years. So ride him home and put him out to pasture for me,' Francis had said, making his charity graceful); and what had he found? Polmawgan in an uproar; Hannah trembling with rage, with salves smeared over a scratched face; Parvati wild-haired and in tears; Dick Branson with a set expression, apologising for the disturbance and trying to assure him that it was nothing but 'females having a spat, sir'.

Whereupon, Parvati and Hannah had flung themselves at him to demand protection from each other and Mary Trevelyan who for some reason was also present, decided to feel faint and had to be revived with burnt feathers. 'This is a fine homecoming,' said Ninian accusingly.

He had got them all assembled in the parlour now: Parvati, Hannah, Mary, Dick Branson and Uriah Giddy, who had been working outside, but being Hannah's son had better, Ninian decided grimly, be summoned. Ninian's horse was being rubbed down by Mary's groom, sulkily, since he was aware that he was missing what he called fun. Kerenza, Eliza and Jimmy were apparently out of the house. Just as well, thought Ninian. The fewer people to hear Hannah's accusations, the better.

'I am ashamed of all of you,' he told them. 'Women fighting like fishwives! Branson, how did such a quarrel in the house go so far before you intervened?'

'So!' Hannah's nostrils were actually white with wrath. 'The fighting was wrong and Branson should have been quicker, but what about they symbols of devilry? What about them?'

'There were no symbols of devilry!' snapped Ninian. 'I could forgive your ignorance, Hannah, if you would only realise that you *are* ignorant. You're not fitted . . .'

'My mother b'ain't ignorant!' Uriah broke in. 'She'm a mighty well-read woman and godly too. She knows right from wrong and she knows devilry when she do see it!'

'She does not and neither do you. My wife,' said Ninian coldly, 'was reared in a land where the Christian message has not been heard, where pagan gods are worshipped. But they aren't devils, they're just . . . just . . . ideas that people have invented to fill the place where they know truth ought to be. Can you understand that much, Hannah?'

'Pagan gods and devils; it's all one. Besides, she do be a Christian now. She's heard the Word of the Lord. Yet she still drew this . . . this . . .' Hannah had retrieved the scrunched-up drawing to show him. 'She *prayed* to it, that filthy thing that she'd drawn with her own hands. Worse than worshipping a golden calf, that do be!'

'I was afraid for you. I wanted you to come home so much,' Parvati cried, appealing to Ninian. 'I made that picture to pray to because . . . because . . . I try to be a Christian but Jesus doesn't speak to me. I'm afraid he won't hear me when I pray. Why should he? I'm a stranger from far away. So I spoke to the Lord Shiva because he knows my language and I can talk to him in it and . . .'

Ninian seized the drawing, crunched it anew and flung it into the parlour fire. 'Hannah,' he said, 'if you had been kidnapped by the Turks who seized Meg, you might have been compelled by them to worship as they do. But would you not, in your heart, and when you were alone, have gone on praying as you did at home?'

Hannah threw back her head. 'I'd die before I'd worship like a heathen. I'd jump into the sea first, like poor Meg did.'

'I doubt if Meg jumped overboard for fear of being made a heathen as you call it,' said Parvati furiously. 'You'd have had nothing to dread from the pirates.'

Uriah's face went stiff with outrage. Dick Branson appeared to be holding back laughter. But for Ninian's eyes on her, Hannah would have sprung once more at Parvati. Mary said: 'Oh, please, can't this stop?'

'Yes,' said Ninian. 'It stops now. Penny, come with me. The rest of you go about your work. I will call you together and speak to you later. Mary, please remain until I come back. I shall want to see you too, before you go. Come, Penny.'

He led her upstairs without speaking further. He was slow because his injury made the stairs difficult and she exclaimed over it, but he didn't answer. By the time they were in their room, his silence had begun to terrify her. 'You are angry with me as well as with Hannah?' she ventured.

'Angry! I brought you up here to speak to you in private but I don't know where to begin. I've warned you, Parvati, I've warned you. So has Darracott. He told you never to slip back into your old ways and what people would think if you did. How could you be so stupid?' Ninian smashed a fist into the other palm. 'That drawing . . . it's disgusting, *disgusting*.' The disgust was in his tone and his face as well as in his words. Parvati sank to the floor and began to weep.

Even in this fraught situation, her fluid movements stirred desire in Ninian. He silenced it and turned away from her to gaze about the bedchamber. It was a beautiful room. The windows looked out on the sea and the sky and the wheeling gulls. The fireplace could hold a blaze big enough to keep the winter damp at bay and Ninian's father had had the walls lined with oak panelling. The red velvet hangings of the fourposter bed glowed ruby against it. Here in this room, he and Parvati had known such happiness.

Parvati was crouched, her arms over her head as though she feared a rain of blows. 'I was praying for you, only,' she whispered.

'Then pray to the real God as Darracott has taught you!' His tone now was more weary than angry. I go through the motions of belief as much as Parvati does when she goes to church, he thought.

'But I *can't*,' Parvati said. 'It is as I told you: your god doesn't hear me.'

'He does,' said Ninian, desperately repeating what Darracott would have said. 'God hears everyone who prays to him, no matter where they are or where they come from or what language they speak.'

Parvati leant her head against the bedstead and went on weeping. Ninian sank into a chair. His leg was aching fiercely. Hopelessness overwhelmed him. The future stretched ahead like an avenue to disaster. Parvati would never fit into this world of his. No one in it except Ninian himself would understand her or even try to. Even educated men thought much as Hannah did. There was only one religion: Protestant Christian. Papists were traitors; even ardent Royalists mostly agreed on that, and anyone who wasn't a Christian at all was a devil worshipper needing to be shown the light. While anyone who had been baptised and then turned, or turned back, to a heathen deity, was a witch.

He imagined Parvati being arrested, taken away from him, tried at Launceston Assizes; Parvati bewildered, terrified, tormented, accused of a crime she couldn't understand, executed, perhaps by fire. That was supposed to be only for treason in some form or other, but fear and hatred of the foreigner, allied to superstition, might stretch the law. He had heard of such things. Besides, in these troubled times, the shout of *treason* arose too easily.

'Listen, Penny,' he said urgently, using her European name on purpose. 'Listen. I'm sorry to frighten you but there are things you must try to grasp. I've told you how people here look on heathenism as they call it; I've warned you about the risk of being called a witch, and Darracott has warned you too. But obviously we didn't make ourselves clear enough.'

She listened, still huddled on the floor, while he explained. 'But I am not a witch,' she protested. 'What has this to do with me?'

'Give me patience! If you are known to be worshipping pictures like the one you drew, people will *call* you a witch. They will think you are. Can't you understand that? Dear God, how can I make anything plain either to you or to Hannah?'

Parvati rose and sat on the edge of the bed. Shiny tear-streaks ran down her face. 'I am a nuisance to you, perhaps I am a danger. Perhaps they will say you have done wrong, too, in harbouring me. I will go back to India. Ships go to India from Penzance. I will find a captain who will take me back, the way I came here.'

'What? No, Parvati, no! I only want . . .'

'I think perhaps you wish me to go but you do not want to say so, so I will say it for you.'

'No. *No.*' His anger had all gone now. 'Are you homesick, Parvati? Is that it? Are you longing for your own people, your own gods? You're so far from home. You have to wear strange clothes and speak someone else's tongue, and worship someone else's god. You must feel very lost at times.'

'No. I am not lost. Not when I am with you. What is there for me at home? I was a slave, there. You have made me a wife and . . .'

Her fragile effort at dignity wavered and broke. She rolled sideways and curled up on the bed, her face in her hands. 'I love you so much,' she said through her fingers. 'But I will go away before I bring you to harm.'

Ninian went to sit by her, placing a palm on her shoulder. 'Parvati. I don't want you to go away. I love you. My world was narrow and dark before you came. You pushed open a door and let light and air stream in. God help me, I thought that if ever anyone offered me love, it was my *duty* to pay heed. I never knew what it was like to give love in return. Don't talk of leaving me, my darling. Only don't ever draw that . . . that *thing* again Or speak to anyone of what has happened today. Parvati, sit up, look at me. If you were not here, my life would be like an empty room with nothing in it but dust, and if you came to any harm . . . if anyone hurt you . . .'

His voice faltered. 'If anyone hurt you,' he said at last, 'I would suffer with you. Let me protect you. Listen to my warnings, Penny-Parvati, my only love . . .'

In his arms, cuddled like a child, Parvati said: 'Why did the picture of the Lord Shiva horrify everyone so? It was not just that he is my god instead of the Christian one.'

'No, it certainly wasn't! Is Shiva usually depicted like that? With his maleness so very obvious?'

'I don't know. I have seen only one or two pictures of him and they did not show him thus, no. Shiva is destroyer and creator both, and some of our priests say also that he is female as well as male, and to honour that, they wear their hair as women do, although they marry like other men. But we venerate the lingam and connect it with Shiva. When I was a child, there was a stone lingam, many feet high, in the courtyard of the temple near my home. The women used to wash it.'

'Used to . . . ?' said Ninian faintly.

Parvati nodded. 'Yes. And so I think of Shiva as male, and I made him look male, to make the picture stronger, because I wished my prayers to be answered.'

'A picture can't answer anything. It is just lines on a piece of paper.

But here, it is wrong, improper, to draw the . . . lingam, did you call it?'

'Yes. This,' said Parvati softly, and small, warm fingers found his member and closed on it, while her other arm reached up to encircle his neck.

Perhaps he was indeed bewitched, he thought, as he drew the bedcurtains round them. She transmuted love into a rite. In the holy fire that her soft touch kindled, all anger melted and even the separateness between woman and man was burned away. They were a single flame, enclosed in darkness. Into that darkness, he said: 'I would die for you.'

He had still to deal with the other people in the house and had better do it quickly, before Kerenza, Eliza and Jimmy came back to complicate matters. Presently, leaving Parvati asleep, he limped downstairs and once more gathered the others in the parlour.

Mary Trevelyan and Dick Branson were silent, shaken witnesses, while Hannah twisted her hands and wept and Uriah expostulated. Ninian, reminding them that he had said before he went away that his wife must be treated with respect, proceeded to dismiss Hannah from his service. Uriah must go with her, he said, and he would prefer them to go at least fifty miles away, perhaps back to Bodmin, where Hannah's former home had been.

'All this for speaking out against idolatry and witchery?' demanded Uriah, his face suffused, while Hannah's outcry now threatened to tip over into hysteria. Ninian raised his voice. 'I haven't finished. I intend to give Uriah a good reference. He will be able to find work easily and I am prepared to pay you, Hannah, an excellent pension.'

He had no idea how he was going to afford it. Wheal Susannah was growing steadily less productive and the Courteen Association was still industriously wrecking the dividends from his East India Company shares. But somehow, afford it he must. Hannah and Uriah fell silent, staring at him. 'The pension,' said Ninian, 'will be generous, quite enough to live on. But I will pay it only on condition that neither of you ever speaks of the events of today. If I hear the faintest rumour that you have done so, or slandered my wife in any way, Hannah's pension will cease.'

'Keep your reference! Keep your bloody pension!' shouted Uriah. 'We speak as we find. Didn't 'ee hear my mam say, she'd die for her faith?'

'Oh, do 'ee be quiet, Uriah!' Hannah was wiping her eyes on her apron. 'Die for my faith? Aye, so I would, but to be cast out into the world with nothing; that do be worse than dying. I know about being cold and hungry; we had harvests fail a time or two when I were a child. I'm feared of the cold and walking the roads with no roof and no fireside and not a penny in my hand. It's for me to say yes or no, Uriah; I won't have 'ee speaking for me.' Scowling, Uriah subsided, and his mother looked at Ninian in fear and indecision. 'What am I to say?'

'Take the pension,' said Ninian acidly, 'and Uriah's reference with it, and hold your tongues. I will write the reference now, Uriah. I will state that you are leaving me of your own free will, to accompany your mother, who has a fancy to return to the scenes of her earlier life. You will then, both of you, put your things together and leave my premises. You can put up for the night in Penzance. Your promise of silence begins *now*.'

Uriah tried once more to stand his ground, but Hannah tearfully hushed him. He gave Ninian a glance of sheer hatred, but helped his mother from the room.

'Dick,' said Ninian, 'I hesitate to order you not to talk of the day's events even to your wife, but . . .'

'I'll hold my tongue, don't 'ee fear. Women chatter too much and think too little,' said Branson shortly. 'I don't believe in witchcraft as it happens. I shan't talk to anyone, not Eliza nor Kerenza nor even Jimmy.'

'Thank you, Dick. You will be doing nothing wrong. Once more, I promise you that there was no devil-worship or any nonsense of that kind. My wife is very young, was afraid for me while I was at the war, and foolishly sought to pray for me in the fashion of her ignorant ancestors. It will never happen again. You may tell the others that I gave Hannah and Uriah notice for rudeness. And now, please, I would like something to eat and drink. I've had nothing since I came home.'

He waited for Branson to be out of earshot before he turned to Mary, who was sitting in a chair with her hands clasped, looking nervous. 'I expect you to hold your peace as well, Mrs Trevelyan. If you do not, I think Francis will be displeased to hear of it and I shall make very sure he hears of it.'

His sharp tone annoyed her and she retorted: 'Do you know where he is? If so, it's more than I do.'

'He and Christopher St Asaph have gone on to Devon with the Royalist forces. They have hopes of aid from Prince Rupert, the King's nephew, who came to England last year with a commission from the Queen to act as the King's General of Horse. He won the battle at Edgehill last October. I have a letter for you from Francis, which he tells me will give you his direction. I have a similar letter for Mrs St Asaph.'

'Word from Francis!' Mary was transfigured. She had genuine feeling for her husband, Ninian thought, watching her. Their marriage might prosper yet, as she matured. Perhaps this wartime parting might benefit both of them.

'Yes. I have it here. But Mary, your promise, please. Nothing you have heard or seen here is to be repeated to anyone. Ever.'

'Oh yes,' said Mary with a shudder. 'It was all horrible. I don't want to think about it, let alone talk about it. I promise.'

PART II

Ninian:
The Shadow Ship
1644–1648

No man is an Island, entire of itself; every man is a piece of the Continent, a part of the main.

John Donne

Chapter Seven
Word from the North

The tunnel into the north side of Minecombe was very narrow and grew lower as it went in. Only by bending double and squeezing his shoulders together could Ninian edge up alongside Tom Pengelly and by the light of Pengelly's lantern, examine the newly exposed rockface.

'We were nigh on giving up,' Pengelly said in his chesty voice. 'I was going to tell you that the last of the tin was out and that you were wasting your money on the men's wages. Now I've changed my mind. Just another foot or so, I said to the boys, just to make sure. And then down comes a slither of rock and we find *that*.'

The sentence ended in a burst of coughing, but despite this, he kept the lantern steady, revealing the blue-tinged lines in the newly exposed rock at the end of the tunnel, unmistakable tin-lodes, thickening towards the right-hand corner. 'That's the direction to take,' Ninian said, pointing. 'The tunnel needs to turn.'

'Aye.' Pengelly coughed again, spat, and recovered his voice. 'It'll lead back towards Polmawgan Head. I have it in mind to take a compass bearing and drive a shaft nearer the Head. Likely enough there's plenty of good ore in these hills, if once you know where to dig. The river gravel's run out, all over the county, but most of us reckon there's tin and to spare, and copper too, lying deep.'

'I agree. We'll proceed as you say,' Ninian told him.

They made their way back along the fifty or so yards of tunnel and emerged into the combe, with relief on Ninian's part. The tunnel was damp underfoot, but it was stuffy and smelt of rock grit and his throat felt nearly as scratchy as Pengelly's sounded.

'The open air smells sweet, after the mine,' he said.

Pengelly grunted. 'Maybe. But when you spend most of your life underground, chipping rock, in the end you can't smell anything else. Your nose gets lined with granite dust.' He coughed again. 'So you reckon it's worth trying, sir? The price of tin's not what it was.'

'Nothing's what it was,' said Ninian. 'But even a small profit on the tin would be welcome.'

It would ease the strain of Hannah's pension, for a start. Then perhaps he could get rid of the cheap, ewe-necked and ill-tempered nag which was all he could afford to replace Sandy, and hire more help for the house and stables. It was needed. Despite the lameness which he now knew was permanent, he often lent a hand himself in the stable.

Jimmy Tonkin was getting visibly older and his right arm had been weakened by the pirate's cutlass. He needed assistance.

If a little more money were coming in, Ninian thought, he might even contribute to the royal cause. So far, he had given very little. Tamzin St Asaph and Mary Trevelyan had both sold all their silver plate for the King, but Ninian had held on to his, guiltily but determinedly, feeling that it might in the last resort be an insurance against wagging tongues. He didn't trust either Hannah or Uriah and the silver could buy passages out of the country, if necessary. He did not want to leave his home and he would avoid it if he could, but Parvati must be protected.

He sighed. Above him, the choughs and the seagulls circled in the shining air and preened on the ledges of Polmawgan Head and he envied them their lighthearted freedom. There was little lightness of heart for human beings, these days. His son Charles was two now and was a vigorous, at times even obstreperous, little boy. But into what sort of world had his parents brought him?

There was no sign of an end to the Civil War. Christopher and Francis were still in the field. They were still alive as far as he knew, but they had never yet come home. They had gone on instead with the Cornish Royalist army, following Hopton and Grenvile to claim Devon and Somerset and hold them for the King, and to storm Bristol, which the Parliamentary forces held.

'By God's grace we took the city,' said the letter which Ninian received from Francis shortly after. 'But we have paid a high price, for we have lost so many men that the Cornish army can scarcely be said to exist any longer. I have seen such grievous horrors, I would rather not speak of them. Christopher and I are fortunate in that we remain whole. We are going on to offer our swords to the King's nephew, Prince Rupert, who marched from Oxford to aid in the capture of Bristol. He is said to be a strange man, by turns exultant and melancholic, but he is our hope for the future.'

The letter added, with a glint of Francis' old vitality: 'Though but thirteen years of age, the Prince of Wales supports his father valiantly. We hear that he was with him at Edgehill, where he ran into danger against the will of his mentors. It seems that he provokes his graver governors by laughing at tedious sermons. I can sympathise with him! I believe Christopher has forgotten how to laugh. He was full of fire to begin with but is a simple fellow at heart and the things we have seen have shocked him deeply. But for me, the world still holds absurdity. I derive much amusement from seeing how comical these Parliamentarians look with their hair cropped so ridiculously short. We call them Roundheads. Have you grown your hair yet, my friend?'

Ninian had. 'I'm tired of trying to convince people that I keep it short merely because I like it that way,' he told Parvati. He now cursed it loudly every day, because unless he curled it, it trailed like seaweed. The fashionable alternative of a periwig was not the answer. 'The damned things itch,' he said, after trying one out. 'As well,' he added to a helplessly giggling Parvati, 'as making me look even more foolish than my natural hair does.'

But longer hair was virtually essential in this part of the world, simply for protection. Penwith was staunchly for the King. Anthony Gubbes, who wasn't and would make no pretence about it, had had a hard time and Ninian, remembering their old friendship, was sorry for him. Once, Anthony had been actually arrested for treason, and although he was released, some of his property had been seized.

Names came swirling from the chaos, in a cloud of tales and rumours: sad, funny and hideous. The King's nephew, the moody and darkly handsome Rupert of the Rhine, of whom Francis had such hopes, could lead a cavalry charge with an elan which usually flattened everything in its path, but the sheer speed of it meant that it was slow to respond to any trumpet order to change direction, or retreat. Francis, in a later letter, referred to this dryly as a drawback.

A Royalist colonel called John Hurry had led a charge into a Roundhead camp after dark and overwhelmed the men while they were still scrambling out of their bedrolls. Last Christmas Day, another Royalist leader had put twenty Roundhead prisoners to the sword in cold blood. Ninian wished he hadn't heard that.

And in East Anglia, a new name had emerged. A Roundhead captain called Oliver Cromwell had got into the news-sheets by discovering that the Cambridge colleges were about to sell their plate in order to give the money to the King, and promptly seizing it for Parliament. The same Captain Cromwell had won a number of small engagements in eastern England and then a bigger one at somewhere called Winceby. He was now a Lieutenant-General and among the Royalists, rumour said he was a dangerous man: a frightening mixture of energy, caution and ruthlessness.

Ninian recognised that description. As a boy, learning to fence, he had been told by his instructor that the hardest opponents were those who had learned how to attack fiercely while keeping their own defence unflawed. 'They never give you a chance to get past them but they come at you like tigers.' By the sound of it, this Cromwell was like that.

The latest news spoke of a Parliamentary victory, masterminded by Cromwell, somewhere in northern England, at a place called Marston Moor, although Ninian knew no details. There were conflicts at present in progress in Cornwall, and he was well informed about those, but news from outside the county only reached Penwith in patchy style, mainly from the captains of coastal trading vessels, which still plied, because people were still mining coal in the north and selling it to the south; life had to go on somehow.

Ninian had once had a widely spaced but regular correspondence with his Whitmead cousins in Essex, but the announcement of his marriage had brought solemn warnings from Luke and Patience about the risks of taking a wife tainted by heathendom, and then, at the start of the war, they had written hoping that he would take up arms on behalf of Parliament. He wrote back to say that he was inclined to support the King. Since then, there had been silence.

Parting from Pengelly, he made his way, slowly on account of his limp, back across the stepping stones which crossed the Minecombe stream, and up the steep path to his house. Parvati hurried into the hall to meet him, carrying Charles. She set him down as she greeted her husband, whereupon Charles, who was sturdy and dark, very much on the pattern of the Stuarts for whom he was named, roared with annoyance. Parvati went to pick him up again, but Ninian stopped her.

'No, don't. He's getting too heavy for you and he's more than capable of walking. You indulge him too much.'

'Yes, I know, but how can I help it? He is our only son. I long for another but God is not kind to me.'

Ninian gazed at her with loving regret. She was wearing a blue-grey gown, not Puritan dress, but restrained. He liked bright colours but he had urged Parvati, nevertheless, to 'look as ordinary as you can', and because she had come to understand that vivid clothes made her appear more foreign, she had adopted quiet shades. She had also given up wearing jewellery, even her beloved bangles.

The result was that she had been on the whole accepted locally, though in a slightly guarded fashion, but just as when she first came to Polmawgan, dull clothes extinguished her, turning her skin from tawny to sallow and even, somehow, suppressing the grace of her walk. She came to life again in their private world of the bedchamber, but only there. Ninian grieved to see the colour and joy leached out of her like this, and he knew that because the house was short of servants, she worked too hard.

'God has perhaps been kinder than you know,' he said gently. 'You have enough to do, without the care of another child. What have you been doing this afternoon?'

'I have been sewing in the parlour,' said Parvati. Her English was good now although she still had an accent. 'Eliza and Kerenza are in the dairy. Ninian, I was looking out for you. Tamzin is here and she has bad news.'

'Tamzin? Bad news?' He followed her quickly into the parlour and Tamzin started up from a chair.

'Ninian, oh, Ninian!'

'Is it Christopher? Is he . . . ?'

'Killed? No, no, not that. He's home. But he's lost an arm,' said Tamzin, 'and he's so ill. He wants to see you again, in case . . . well, in case . . . it's infected, you see. It happened in the north, early in July, at Marston Moor . . .'

Ninian nodded. 'Yes, I'd heard there was a battle.'

'Christopher wrote but the letter never reached me. He's brought one for Mary Trevelyan, from Francis. The first she's had for months.'

'What happened at Marston Moor?'

'It was a terrible battle,' Tamzin said. 'Christopher only just escaped. If he'd been caught, he'd have been killed, even though he was wounded. Did you ever think to hear that men would kill wounded fellow-countrymen who couldn't defend themselves? Even in a civil war, can you credit that? And now, to all intents and purposes, Christopher says, Parliament under Cromwell holds the north of England.'

90

★ ★ ★

'It was unspeakable,' said Christopher. He had lost not only his right arm from just above the elbow, but also a great deal of weight. He was sitting up and dressed when Ninian arrived at Coombe, but his coat sleeve had been cut away from the injured arm, which was wrapped in bandages. The rest of the coat hung loose on his wasted frame, and the blue eyes, sunken with pain, held a curious expression of shocked disbelief.

'They cheated,' he said. 'That damned Cromwell cheated. He attacked in the evening – in the *evening*. We'd broken ranks. We were lighting the campfires for supper.' His voice came jerkily. 'Prince Rupert was in his tent already eating his! We didn't know what was happening at first. The Roundheads opened fire but there was a thunderstorm going on. We thought the noise was thunder, not guns, until . . . until . . . suddenly there was smoke and men were falling. A man I was talking to just fell down in mid-sentence with his chest burst open. We scrambled to get into our saddles. Then it started pouring with rain. Cromwell charged us through it. And then . . .' The strained eyes fastened on Ninian's face. 'You remember Braddock Down? All the smoke? The confusion?'

'All too well,' said Ninian.

'This was worse. Prince Rupert rushed out; got us organised somehow. But . . .' He made a gesture like a shrug but stopped it halfway, his face twisting with pain. 'Superb leader. Charged like the wind. Carried you with him. But Cromwell had the advantage. What with the rain and the smoke – couldn't see what we were doing. Rupert tried to get us upwind of the enemy, so as to get away from the gunsmoke. But we couldn't. Smoke everywhere, stinking of sulphur. You could see the flashes of the cannon through it, but damme if you could see much else. And it rained and rained. Bleak sort of terrain at the best of times and in the rain – mud everywhere. Men covered in mud and smoke-stains. Could hardly tell friend from foe. A man would come at you out of the smoke and you wouldn't know . . . whether to kill him or greet him. It was every man for himself. My horse fell and I got mixed up with some musketeers. Ours, I mean. They'd run out of shot and they were laying about them with the musket butts. We crashed into some enemy pikemen. They were wedged together, so tight – there were dead men among them, held upright by the press all round them! I *saw* that. Funny. There was a pike coming at me and everything went slow. I hadn't time to get away but I had time to see that. I remember thinking: we've done the bastards a bit of damage, anyway . . .'

He glanced at his bandaged stump. Tamzin said: 'An army surgeon took the arm off. In a barn! Christopher was hiding in a barn.'

'With the bloody flux on me as well,' Christopher said. 'I got through somehow. My family were always strong. We've lost more men through the flux, and lung fevers after sleeping in the open in the wet, than through the fighting. Lost plenty in the fighting at Marston Moor, though. That pike went through my arm and I fell flat on my face in the

91

mud and it was red mud . . . *red*. Because of the blood in it. I was trodden on; the fight went over me. I crawled away later. There were bodies everywhere, and bits of bodies and some men that weren't dead but couldn't move, crying for help. I couldn't help them,' said Christopher. His voice shook. 'A fellow clutched at me. Wanted me to take a message. To his wife. In York. I asked him for his wife's name but before he could say it . . . he died. Another man wanted water. He was moaning so. Didn't have any water to give him. And there were wounded horses . . .'

'I know. I know.' Ninian remembered Sandy.

'He's no gentleman. That Cromwell. Attacking us in the evening when we weren't expecting him!'

Colonel Hurry, on the side of the King, had attacked a camp of Roundheads when they were already in bed but Ninian did not say so. He only shook his head sadly.

'Never knew . . . there was such misery in the world,' Christopher said painfully. 'I got well enough to ride; arm didn't begin getting enflamed again till I was halfway home. All the way home . . . every farm, every village . . . women . . . begging for news of their men. Slept twice in churches. All spoilt by Cromwell's men. Stained glass windows smashed. Rood-screens ripped out. Saw bits of a lovely rood-screen tossed on top of a fuel stack in a Puritan farmyard. Ugly. Mean-minded . . . I'm sorry. Can't talk any more. I'm so hot.'

Parvati had come with Ninian. 'The wound,' she said. 'Tamzin, what has been done for it?'

'The physician has been,' said Tamzin 'He said my husband had an excess of bile and blood in his system, gave him some medicine which made him sick, bled him and put a concoction on the stump. It hasn't helped. I don't think he knew what to do, any more than I do.'

'The stump was cauterised at the time,' Christopher managed faintly. 'The army surgeon did his best.'

Tamzin shuddered. 'My poor Christopher.'

Parvati said: 'When I was on board ship, a man fell out of the rigging. His arm was smashed and had to be taken off and he was very ill, but he got better. I helped another sailor to let the poison out, and then Captain Murray said the place must be kept very clean, oh, so clean. Tamzin, shall we see what we can do?'

In Rosnance, in a sunny downstairs room, Mary Trevelyan sat at a pretty writing desk of painted and gilded oak. In front of her was the letter from Francis, which Christopher had brought home. Tamzin had dispatched it to Rosnance by the hand of a kitchen boy, together with a note. She was sorry not to bring it herself, the note said, but she was distracted with worry about Christopher. She knew, however, that Mary would want the letter as soon as possible. If Mary was writing back, please would she convey good wishes to Francis from herself and Christopher.

She'd be writing back all right. Mary did not know whether her tears were from sorrow or rage. Hadn't Francis been away at this stupid war for long enough? There was fighting in Cornwall, if fight he must. He hardly ever wrote, and it wasn't just that his letters were going astray. Most of them began with casual apologies for not having written since last winter or last summer or last year, making it perfectly clear that the gap in between was no accident.

According to this letter, he meant to stay with the royal forces until the end, whatever form that might take. If it proved to be his own end, he said, he would be content. He hoped she was well and in good heart and gave her an address through which she might reply. Then came an anxious inquiry about Christopher. 'If this letter reaches you, then I trust it means that Christopher has reached home. I pray you to let me know how he is. Give my greetings to Ninian Whitmead and his wife, and to Tamzin.' Various reminders and instructions about looking after Rosnance followed. There was no word of loving her or missing her.

'I can't bear it,' said Mary. 'I can't bear it.'

She took pen and paper and wrote, not pausing for thought, and certainly not troubling about Christopher – Tamzin could write to Francis about that, if she liked! – but snatching the words straight from her own heart.

'. . . oh, dear God, what I would give to see you. For God's sake write to me soon and come yourself as soon as may be . . .'

But it was a year and a half before Francis came home to Rosnance.

Chapter Eight
The Prince

In such times, to be a timid, comfort-loving woman was a drawback. Mary Trevelyan had damped her pillow over and over, not only with worry over Francis and misery at his indifference, but also with bitter regret that she couldn't be the wife he needed. She'd failed him on their very wedding day and never made up the lost ground since. She didn't know if a child would have helped. There hadn't been one, anyway, and since the war started, there was precious little chance of getting one.

Running Rosnance, even though she had an able bailiff, was a constant worry, too, although the task had helped her not to fret too much over the sporadic outbreaks of trouble in Cornwall itself. The only engagement of any size, near Lostwithiel in north Cornwall, had been won by the King's forces, anyway. But now the main war was edging nearer and the wind which had begun to turn against the King at Marston Moor was continuing to blow.

Since then, that man Cromwell had gathered what he called his New Model Army. One of Francis's infrequent letters described it in horrifying terms. 'The men are hardly human. They are not allowed to swear or get drunk or go with women, although they don't mind killing those they call whores or witches. The New Model soldiers will go into church pulpits on a Sunday and preach and all the ministers can do is listen. They go into battle singing psalms and our spies say their officers fast and pray before an engagement. We would like to think that this will make them weak and feeble in the field, but as yet it does not seem so . . .'

Since then, disaster had followed disaster. The King was somewhere in the north. Some said he had been made prisoner by the Scots; others that he was trying to negotiate a treaty with them. But a Roundhead commander called Fairfax had seized Leicester and Bristol; Sir Ralph Hopton had surrendered and Sir Bevil Grenvile was dead. The Prince of Wales had been trying to hold the south-west, but now he was in retreat, said to be already in Cornwall, with the enemy in pursuit, hard behind.

The nervous gossip of port and market said that Cornwall had no hope. Lostwithiel had been the county's dying spark. The Roundheads were coming.

What would happen, Mary wondered fearfully, if they came to Rosnance? Her husband was with the King's forces. Would they know about that? Would they turn her out? Make her live in the kitchen on bread and cheese? Smash her lovely furnishings?

Rosnance was a fine house and Francis had given her beautiful things to put in it: the painted, gilded writing desk and a chest of drawers veneered in rosewood among them. She valued these, even though the house itself had never felt safe, not since the pirates had invaded it on her wedding day.

It was February and cold, but fear made her so restless that there came an afternoon when she could not bear her embroidery any more. She put on a mantle and went out to pace back and forth in the garden for more than an hour, until the failing light drove her indoors again.

She found a little comfort in the warmth and normality of the house as she stepped inside. She pushed open the parlour door, glad to see the firelight and the candles which had been lit at the first sign of dusk. She would call Kitty, her maid, and they might have a game of cards before supper. Kitty would like that. She was somewhat apt to be lazy but she was always ready to share an amusement. If the Roundheads descended on the house, no doubt card games would be forbidden; Puritans called cards the devil's books.

Better not think about Roundheads. She tossed her mantle across a chair and went to warm her hands at the fire.

'Ah, there you are, my love,' said Francis. 'I was wondering where you had got to.'

Mary screamed, swinging round. Francis was sitting in a chair, close to the fire but drawn into a shadow. He grinned at her. 'That's a fine welcome. Your husband comes home after years away and you shriek at the sight of him.'

'Francis! I thought you were with the King's army!' She went to embrace him, but he disengaged himself after a brief moment and handed her into another chair.

'Sit down, my love. I see I've startled you. I came home very quietly. I came by sea, landed in Minecombe, slipped up here on foot and in by the garden door. I am indeed with the King's army. At least, I'm with the Prince of Wales. He's at Pendennis Castle above Falmouth, just north of the Lizard. The enemy's taken Launceston but the Prince's Council is with him and they hope to fight back and hold Cornwall from Pendennis. Frank Basset who commands St Michael's Mount is loyal to him too. The prince isn't yet sixteen but he's a fine young man; there's a King there in the making. Hair and eyes like coal. He's nearly as dark as Penny Whitmead.'

'But you aren't staying at Pendennis with him?' Mary was half-afraid to ask the question. She sat where he had put her, tense and longing. If only he would say the words she yearned to hear. *I've come home because I want to be with you.* 'You've left the war?' she inquired timidly.

'Oh no.' Francis shook his head. 'I'm here with a commission. The Prince and his Council are always short of money. I'm at large in Cornwall with orders to collect all I can lay hands on. My love, I am sorry to arrive so unexpectedly and only to make disagreeable demands before leaving again, but the fact is . . . I've been to Coombe already and called on the St Asaphs. I was mighty glad to see Christopher again. He was lucky to recover; it was a near thing, Tamzin said. I asked you for news of him, if you recall, but you never gave me any.'

'I thought . . . I thought Tamzin or Ninian Whitmead would send you news,' Mary faltered. 'They knew how he was better than I did. Penny Whitmead helped to look after him.'

'I know. Did you offer to do the same?'

'No, but I have no skill. I thought . . .'

'Or didn't think,' said Francis brusquely. Tears came to her eyes but he took no notice. 'Tamzin and Ninian did write as a matter of fact,' he said. 'Never mind that now. The St Asaphs sold their silver for the cause long ago but Christopher gave me some money, and Tamzin has promised her personal jewels. Can I have yours too?'

'The way to thread a needle,' said Alice Gubbes patiently to six-year-old Tammy (named after Tamzin St Asaph, the wife of Anthony's old friend, in the days before politics had divided them), 'is to hold it up to the light – thus – so that you can see exactly where the eye of it is, and then guide the thread through. Yes, that's right. Good girl. Now show me how well you can sew a button on. You cannot go out this morning in any case. The Parliamentary army is to enter Penzance today, and there may be disturbances.' Alice sighed. 'We have lost many friends in the town over the last few years. But one must be true to one's faith. Always remember that.' She looked at five-year-old Ursula, who was attempting some simple beginner's stitches. 'What is it, Ursula? Why are you fidgeting?'

Ursula looked towards the window. 'Noise,' she said.

'Coming along the street,' said Tammy, large-eyed. 'Mother, what is happening? Is it the soldiers?'

Alice cocked her head. There was indeed a noise, and not the clatter of hooves and the tramp of feet she had been expecting. Instead, there were shouts and – surely – somebody screaming. She went to the window.

The street was full of buff-clad, helmeted soldiers. They were running here and there, in and out of shops and houses, carrying assorted objects. Unusual objects, in the hands of soldiers. Not swords or muskets or pikes, but armfuls of linen, haunches of meat, laden sacks. Mixed up with the soldiers, catching at their arms, shouting at them, being kicked and punched by them, were the townsfolk. She saw two women try to tear a sack away from a soldier and saw him knock them to the ground; and then a man ran out of a house and grappled with another soldier, who was carrying a small coffer. Before her eyes, the soldier, almost casually, stabbed him with a dagger and the man fell down in the middle of the road, blood gushing from his mouth. A woman rushed screaming to his side and sank down, clutching him, shaking him. The soldier walked off as though nothing had happened.

Belatedly, Alice understood. Her husband had been in prison once for supporting the Parliamentary cause, and once, a band of angry

Cornish Royalists – just a mob, including people the Gubbes had once called friends and neighbours – had burst into their shop and stolen some of their goods. Now the Parliamentary army, on entering Penzance, were looting in their turn.

'Mother, what is it?' Tammy was at her side. Alice pushed her back. 'No, Tammy. You are not to look out of the window.'

She made herself speak commandingly, but calmly. One must always be calm. Even when Anthony was arrested, after a pounding on the door in the middle of the night, she had quelled her longing to hurl herself screaming at the constable and his three soldiers, and kept her dignity. She had stood instead with hands linked at her waist while Anthony was manhandled away, and in the morning, had set about raising the money to get him released. When the mob broke in, she had told former acquaintances among them that they should be ashamed of themselves and that God would one day deal with them, but although she had said it forcefully, she had *said* it, not shrieked it.

She must keep her head in the same way now. Surely God would not let them be attacked by the very side they had upheld? Not after all they had suffered already.

But terrifyingly, down below, there was the sound of hammering at their very door. She jerked back from the window just as one of the maidservants rushed into the room.

'Oh, madam, Mrs Gubbes, what's happening? There's someone thundering at the front door and the master's down in the shop all on his own and . . .'

'Mother!' Her eldest daughter Joan ran in, whitefaced. 'Mother, I was reading in my room and I heard a noise. I looked out and there are soldiers everywhere! They were killing someone!' Joan was eighteen and betrothed, but she came to her mother like a child. Alice put an arm round her, wishing she and Anthony had thought ahead more carefully, and gone to their eldest son's house in St Ives for safety.

Anthony Gubbes stepped into the parlour. 'Wife? Don't be alarmed. I'm afraid the Parliamentary army is sacking Penzance but we shall not be touched. Be easy.'

'But they're trying to break in!' cried Joan. 'Listen to them!'

But the pounding had stopped. The uproar in the street continued, but within the Gubbes' house, the only disturbance was that of the latest baby, Frances, crying in another room.

'The soldiers have been let loose in the town,' said Anthony, 'but they had orders beforehand to spare certain households. That hammering was one of their officers putting up a warning sign on our door. I have been speaking with him. Any man who tries to steal from us will hang.'

Alice slid to her knees. 'Praise God who has cast the mantle of His protection over us.'

'Well, in this case,' said Anthony mildly, 'it's more a question of the mantle of Sir Thomas Fairfax. He . . .'

In the street the noise was increasing. Tammy and Ursula began to sob and Alice, still kneeling, drew them to her.

'Some of those who will be robbed and hurt today are still our friends,' Alice said. 'They have not all behaved ill towards us. This is a dreadful day for them.'

There was jeering laughter now under the window, and a babble of desperate protests.

'. . . it's all we've got, you can't take everything . . .'

'. . . how am I to feed the babbies if you make off with every morsel in the house . . . ?'

Then a man's voice, bellowing: 'Put that down, put it down, I say . . . !' The voice broke off with a hoarse shriek and a woman cried: 'Oh God, they've killed him! He only tried to defend what was his . . . !'

'Another!' Alice whispered. Anthony dropped to his knees too, beside her. Joan and the maidservant joined them, huddling close.

'It's horrible!' Alice hid her face against Anthony. 'Horrible. I know those voices; that's Cathy Johnson from next door. The man they've killed must be Jem! He never harmed us or anyone. He's just a decent baker!'

'If the Royalists had won the war, it might have been me,' said Anthony.

'I know. I know. But . . . oh . . . if only there were something we could do!'

'There's one thing,' said Anthony. 'The only thing. They are in God's care, just as we are.' He took her hand and holding it tightly, began in the steadiest voice he could manage, to recite the twenty-third psalm.

'But we cannot just put the silver plate in a sack,' said Parvati. 'The pieces will scratch each other. We must wrap them.'

'Most of it will be melted down, you know,' said Tamzin.

'Yes, and it is such a shame, when so many pieces have the family device on them. I have drawn the device and Kerenza and I have begun to embroider it on the household linen, so that it will not be lost,' said Parvati. 'But what if someone is interested to buy pieces with a family pattern on them? We should keep it in good condition if we can. Kerenza, run and find some old sheets. Quickly. Mr Trevelyan is in a hurry.'

'I certainly am,' said Francis as Kerenza hastened away. 'The Prince is to sail for St Michael's Mount from Land's End tonight. The frigate *Phoenix* is waiting for him and I must go with him, along with all that I've collected.'

'I'm sorry to see our plate go,' Dick Branson said. 'But there, if it's for the Prince, and the ladies are offering their jewellery . . .'

Ruefully, he eyed the precious objects strewn over the table in front of him. They looked out of place in Polmawgan's homely, flagged kitchen, amid the pots and pans and the business-like fire-irons. A shaft of late-afternoon sunlight flashed on Mary Trevelyan's reluctantly yielded necklaces and earrings; and a net of onions hanging from a beam was reflected in one of Ninian's silver bowls. There were several pieces of jewellery which had belonged to Morwenna and Pen, and a few things of Parvati's. Tamzin had brought her promised contribution in person, bravely surrendering ropes of pearls, diamond earrings, and a magnificent set of emeralds.

'These are desperate times,' she said. 'The Prince needs all the loyalty we can give him. There is even treachery inside Pendennis Castle, it seems.'

'A plot to kidnap the Prince in Jack Arundell's very fortress,' Francis said. 'Someone warned the Council just in time. Even so, the names of all the Prince's companions are probably on a Wanted list by now, including mine. But St Michael's is still safe. Frank Basset holds it and he's the most honest Royalist that was ever born.'

'But how long can it withstand siege?' Ninian asked. 'The Roundheads will attack once they know the Prince is there. He ought to go straight on to France or the Scillies.'

'He won't agree to go to France,' Francis said. 'It will link him too closely to his mother and her Papist supporters. The Council want him to keep some sort of credibility in English eyes if he can. So does he.'

'I held on to the plate while the King was winning,' Ninian said. Kerenza ran in with the sheets and they set quickly to work. 'But now, as Tamzin says, the Prince needs all the help we can give. I wish I weren't such a crock.'

Kerenza paused in her task to finger a diamond and ruby necklace on the table. 'Who gave that? I'd have cried, parting with that.'

'It was my wife's,' said Francis shortly and they all knew at once that Mary had indeed cried. All simultaneously imagined Mary's pretty, foolish face blotched with tears over her jewellery.

'Tamzin, you've been more generous than I'd ever have asked you to be,' Francis said. 'I don't believe you've left yourself a single ornament.'

'My wedding ring,' said Tamzin. 'And one strand of seed pearls.'

'If – no, when – the Roundheads come to Coombe,' said Francis, 'what will you and Christopher say, if they ask where your valuables are? I've told Mary to tell them that I took ours away against her will. I'm sure she'll sound convincing! But how will you account for having so little?' Suddenly he raised his head and looked at her directly and anxiously. 'Tamzin, I shouldn't take your jewels. It could be exposing you to trouble.'

'I'll face the trouble,' said Tamzin proudly. 'And so will Christopher. What else can he do for the cause now? Penny's leechcraft saved his life but he'll never be quite himself again. He broods so. He says he'd get satisfaction from looking the Roundheads in the eye and saying that we gave all we had to the King's cause. Let them seize Coombe and cast us out of it! Christopher says he'll never deny his allegiance, and I agree with him.'

'Christopher is fortunate in his wife,' said Francis. 'Ninian, what of you and Mrs Whitmead? What if you are asked why a house of this size hasn't a silver dish to its name?'

'This may be a big house,' said Ninian with some asperity, 'but I'm a poor man. I've a tin mine with a new shaft but the price of tin is so low that all the new workings do is pay for themselves. My shares in the East India Company scarcely pay at all and if I put my money in West Indian trade instead, it wouldn't help because the Dutch are trying to corner the West Indies. The farm just feeds us, I have to pay taxes, and give my old servant Hannah a pension. I sold my plate,' said Ninian in an indignant voice, as though addressing a Roundhead colonel, 'to meet my own commitments!'

'I hope you get away with it!' said Francis. 'But you should be careful. The enemy have been on the rampage in Penzance. We know what to expect from them. Listen, all of you. You could come with us. Tamzin, you could fetch Christopher and meet us at Land's End. Why don't you?'

Kerenza and the Bransons looked alarmed. Tamzin shook her head. 'We can't, Frank. Our servants won't want to be torn from their homes or deserted. Besides' – and once again there was pride in her steady brown eyes – 'you are part of the Prince's entourage and should go with him, but while we can stay without risking our lives, do you think we shall run away from *them*?'

'As I said,' said Francis, 'Christopher is fortunate.' He and Tamzin smiled at each other and Ninian, watching, suddenly sensed that between them flowed something strong and secret, like a subterranean river. Francis had once admitted to being drawn to Tamzin. Was he, perhaps, the man she should have married?

The very air seemed full of that hidden force. To keep it hidden, Ninian broke quickly into speech. 'Tamzin is right. My thanks to you, Frank, but I shall stay and protect my home if I can.'

'You sound as if you've made your plans.' Francis thrust a last piece of wrapped silver into the sack.

Ninian glanced at Parvati. A good wife, she had offered her jewels for the cause that her husband supported, but he hadn't wanted her to lose the last reminders of her homeland, and her silks and her Indian trinkets still lay at the bottom of a chest in their room. But even in her quietest clothes, she still had an air of the exotic. It would make her vulnerable to the hatred of any fanatical Puritan. He might well be very hard put to it one day to keep his home and also protect Parvati.

But he intended to try. He pulled a watch from his pocket. Parvati had given it to him the previous Christmas, having saved up the personal allowance he made her. She rarely went to Penzance because people were so apt to stare at her but Jane Dewey, who like Tamzin had become a friend, had gone to the town and bought it on her behalf. It was a beautiful watch and very reliable, and he had decided that, like Parvati's trinkets, he would withhold it from the Prince.

'We have finished in good time,' he observed, consulting it. 'Oh yes, Frank. I've planned what to do.' Something in his voice made them all look at him in surprise. 'I have decided,' said Ninian, 'to see the light.'

Chapter Nine
The Secret Defiance

'I will repeat my text. The hypocrite's hope shall perish, The Book of Job, Chapter Eight, Verse Thirteen. Make no mistake about it,' thundered Mr Joseph Davies from the pulpit of Polmawgan Church. 'When the Judgement Day comes, every secret little sin will stand revealed. You cannot hide from the eyes of the Lord. Do you, behind closed doors, profane the Sabbath with worldly music and laughter? Or with lust? Even within the bonds of marriage, lust is a sin. The snugglings of the flesh are only to be indulged in for the sake of bringing forth children. But above all, remember that if you pervert the precious hours of the Sabbath in carnality, the sin is compounded tenfold!

'Be very careful.' He raised a finger of solemn warning into the air. 'In the privacy of your mind do you long for sins you do not dare quite to commit? And do you imagine that because you have not committed them but only dreamed of them, that you remain guiltless? There are sins of thought as well as deed.'

He paused, for effect. Joseph Davies was a dark, stocky Welshman with a powerful voice and he was also a natural actor although he would have been outraged if anyone had told him so. Mr Davies believed that all theatres should be closed and all actors imprisoned as vagrants.

His smouldering gaze moved over the faces below, lingering on this person or that. His choice was arbitrary, since he was too new to the parish to know his parishioners as individuals. It didn't matter. In Joseph's experience everybody had something to hide. Select a face at random and stare at it accusingly, and embarrassed guilt would appear. With satisfaction he saw Peg Hawkes, formerly Treweeke, blush and look away and recalled that he did know something about her. The baby she was holding had arrived eight months after her marriage. A couple of fishermen shuffled their feet and a young wife whose husband was away at sea looked ashamed. Lustful dreams, no doubt!

Only four people endured his gaze apparently untroubled. On a bench near the front, Petroc Darracott, whom the new Roundhead administration had dismissed in favour of Joseph, merely scowled at him. Mr Ninian Whitmead and his swarthy foreign wife also kept their countenance. The wife perhaps did not fully understand the sermon, but Ninian's limpid eyes annoyed him. The fourth unmoved member of the congregation was Ninian's small son, who was under six, but was looking at Davies as though the parson were some kind of strange animal, such as a giraffe.

He returned to his sermon, dropping his voice to an ominous note of warning.

'Be it known to all of you that of all sins, that of hypocrisy is among the gravest. The sinner who deceives, who lives a life outwardly godly, but cultivates wickedness in secret, shall on Judgement Day be more blackly condemned than those who indulge openly in wrongdoing. He will see the men of righteousness, yea, his own brothers, turn from him before he is led away to his doom. And what a doom it shall be! For him,' thundered Mr Davies, 'the fires of hell shall be especially stoked! *Such are the paths of all that forget God, and the hypocrite's hope shall perish!*'

He crashed a fist on to the edge of the pulpit. His congregation flinched. He leaned towards them again and once more his eyes travelled, lingered, travelled on. 'Are *you* so sure that you have no hidden sins?' His voice was now ominously soft. 'What will happen to *you* on Judgement Day? Will *your* hope perish?'

'A magnificent sermon,' said Ninian, shaking Davies' hand as they filed out of the church. 'I feel sure that we shall be searching our consciences and cleaning our souls out like kitchen cupboards.'

'If my poor words have moved any hearts towards God, I shall not have wasted my breath, or my hours of prayer,' said Davies, eyeing him thoughtfully. Ninian's manner was solemn, and all the Whitmeads were dressed most decently in black with clean white collars and cuffs, and so were the servants who accompanied them. *But . . .*

Mr Whitmead claimed to be a most ardent Puritan. Yet his son was named Charles and his wife had apparently come to Cornwall as an unbaptised heathen, after being washed ashore from a ship – having, very probably, been on the ship in the first place for some dubious reason. He had already gathered that although Ninian was popular, some of the Polmawgan people weren't at ease with Mrs Whitmead. There was a story that she had used foreign arts to heal Christopher St Asaph, who had been wounded fighting not for Parliament, but for the King. As far as he knew, the St Asaphs and the Whitmeads did not now meet, but the Whitmeads lived retired lives up there at Polmawgan and there was something about Mr Whitmead which hinted at a secret levity. Levity was irreverent. In Mr Davies' eyes, the Whitmead household was suspect.

Peg Hawkes came out of the church with her fisherman husband, Marge Hawkes' son John. The baby in her arms crowed with pleasure at being carried out into the July sunshine. Mrs Whitmead turned at the sound, halting her family and letting other worshippers stream past them. Her face broke into a smile. 'How is he, Peg? Is he better after his teething?'

'Aye, he's better. We'll see 'ee tomorrow as usual, then?' Peg said. Her tone was a nice balance of the villager addressing a lady, and one woman speaking to another. Davies' thick eyebrows rose and Peg explained. 'Mrs Whitmead do so enjoy being with children. She comes to see us Mondays, me and my two sisters-in-law, Polly and Betsy, what's married to my husband's brothers . . .'

'Peg, you're a chatterbox.' Hawkes had joined his wife. 'Give over ploughing the sands with your tongue. The reverend gentleman won't want to hear all this.'

'Not at all. I'm most interested,' said Davies. 'I wish to get to know my flock. How is it that Mrs Whitmead visits you each Monday, Peg?'

'Well, Polly's sister Meg that's dead now, she used to work at Polmawgan, and my family work on the farm, so there's a link with Polmawgan, like,' said Peg. 'Anyway, me and Polly and Betsy, we've all got babbies. Mrs Whitmead comes with Kerenza – that's her maid – on Mondays and they keep an eye on them while we get on with the wash.'

Polly and Betsy, with their infants, in turn emerged from the church. They greeted Mrs Whitmead politely but with reserve. Betsy, who was stout, drew an incipient double chin back into her neck while saying good-day, a sign which did not escape the minister. No, the Polmawgan villagers were not comfortable with Mrs Whitmead. Interesting.

Because of his lameness, Ninian rode home from church, taking the longer track and carrying his wife on his pillion. The rest of the household walked sedately home by the cliff path. A cold meal awaited them, and in the stableyard, Jimmy Tonkin had all the horses' feeds measured out so that they had only to be put in the stalls, with the minimum of work. After dinner, there would be two hours of prayer and Bible readings in the dining room, which was cold and dusty because it had been used very little since that day in March 1646, nearly a year and a half ago now, when Ninian had called the household into it and announced, with absolute seriousness, that he was turning Puritan. Henceforth, Polmawgan was to be a godly household where the Sabbath would be kept as the Lord intended, where food and clothes would be plain and fripperies such as damask table linen would henceforth be outlawed. Master and mistress would eat in the kitchen with the servants, off a scrubbed wooden table. The dining room would be used only for prayers. Polmawgan would be a house where Oliver Cromwell himself would feel at home.

This announcement had at first produced a shattered silence, until Eliza Branson blurted out: 'Do this be because them Roundheads are a'coming?'

'Aye. I reckon,' Dick said, and chuckled softly.

'No,' said Ninian clearly. 'It is not. I have for a long time been troubled by the Papistical leanings of King Charles and by the behaviour of some of his supporters in this county. My good friend Anthony Gubbes has suffered cruelly at their hands, and only for standing by his principles. I will respect a king who proves himself to be respect-worthy, but I fear that our present sovereign has not done so. However, these matters are for greater men than myself to decide. I will put my trust in God, and henceforth, I will run my house accordingly. My wife agrees.'

He took Parvati's hand, and in her pretty, lilting voice, she said: 'I agree with my husband. Please, in future, all of you, act as he wishes.'

From the point of view of his servants, Ninian had undergone a complete change of character. Out of his hearing, they puzzled over it, but at first could find no chinks; the alteration was like a solid wall. Ninian behaved as though he meant it.

Kerenza was severely upbraided and her wages reduced for a month because one morning she put a red ribbon in her hair. The St Asaphs and Mary Trevelyan were quietly dropped and if Mrs Whitmead missed Tamzin, she didn't say so. Guests were few altogether. Jane Dewey came now and then to see Parvati, but her calls were informal. She usually wore respectfully quiet clothes but avoided all mention of either politics or religion, and conveyed, with a subtlety remarkable in the outspoken Jane, that she didn't believe in Ninian's conversion but wasn't going to argue about it.

Ninian also made an abortive attempt to renew social contact with his Clemo cousins. But after his marriage, they had virtually ignored him beyond the occasional chilly nod in the streets of Penzance, and since the outbreak of war, had ceased to acknowledge him even by that much. Now, they continued to keep their distance, and would not come to his house or ask him to theirs.

'Ah, well. They're terrible bores,' Ninian said, and that was the first time his mask slipped, for he was careless enough to let the Bransons overhear him, which caused them to exchange thoughtful glances.

Where Anthony Gubbes was concerned, Ninian himself preferred to keep aloof. Anthony, hearing of events at Polmawgan, offered his friendship again but Ninian, though cordial when they chanced to meet in Penzance, politely refused Anthony's invitations to dine, and offered none. 'You must excuse me. My wife much prefers to live quietly and I was always something of a recluse.'

The only time Polmawgan entertained on any scale was the day a Roundhead captain called William Beresford-Higham arrived with ten troopers at his heels. Ninian greeted them as brothers and offered them the best the household could provide. Captain Beresford-Higham raised sarcastic eyebrows and regarded Ninian, of whom he had apparently heard, with evident suspicion but could find nothing to substantiate it.

Eventually, he and his men left. Since then, he had requisitioned Coombe as a soldiers' billet, and had himself taken over Rosnance. The St Asaphs had taken the proud line that Tamzin promised and been ejected from their home for it. They were at Rosnance now with Mary Trevelyan, who had been more conciliatory and so had been allowed to stay at Rosnance and even to offer shelter to her neighbours, albeit in uncomfortable conditions.

Neither Mary nor the St Asaphs, Ninian knew, could afford to buy their way out of trouble. Thomas Grosse had apparently paid to make terms with the new Parliamentarian authorities and so had William Keigwin of Mousehole but they were said to have paid high. The Roundheads were in a position to dictate what terms they liked. St Michael's Mount had yielded after multiple desertions from a despairing garrison and Pendennis Castle likewise after a five-month siege throughout which the crash of the Parliamentary artillery had been heard for miles, week in and week out. At night, when the clouds were low, the reflected flash of the cannon had been visible in Penzance, and even at Polmawgan – where Ninian remained in undisturbed possession, at no charge.

'I reckon he's putting it on. The master, I mean,' Dick Branson said to his wife in the privacy of their bed. 'He timed it just right. But he let out what he really thinks of them Clemos. That were an accident, if you ask me! He can't keep it up quite all the time. I reckon he keeps clear of Gubbes because Gubbes knows him too well and might see through him. But I doubt even Gubbes could fault him that easily.'

'I hate Sunday afternoons now,' said Eliza. 'Religion's all very well but this 'ud be too much even for Hannah!'

On this particular Sunday, however, it seemed that the routine was going to be interrupted for once. They were hardly indoors before the dogs began to bark, announcing a caller. Kerenza answered the door and brought him in.

It was Uriah Giddy.

'What brings you here, Uriah?' Ninian ushered his visitor into the study and closed the door after them. 'And do I understand that you have been travelling on a Sunday?'

'Don't 'ee give me that,' said Uriah. Now in his early thirties, he was as lanky and unsmiling as he had always been, and his grey eyes were chilly. They were also defiant. He was no longer Mr Whitmead's employee, but old habits were persistent. Uriah was nervous. 'I take leave to say, Mr Whitmead, that I could have danced all the way from Bodmin, leave alone walked a few miles of the way on the Lord's Day, and it 'ud be nothing to you.'

'You do me an injustice,' said Ninian gravely. 'But you came with a purpose, I take it. Tell me what it is.'

'My mother's pension, that's what,' said Uriah aggressively. 'It's due for the quarter, ain't it? I was in Penzance on an errand, so I come up here to get it.'

'It isn't ready. I'll be sending it as usual at the end of the month.'

'My mother wants it now. She's short. Prices go up all the time but not her pension. It's scarcely worth half what it was. She'd like an increase, too.'

Inwardly, Ninian groaned. Poor as tin prices were just now, he had been relying on the latest sale to make just enough profit to cover Hannah's pension. But the money wasn't back from Bodmin yet. He probably had sufficient sovereigns in his personal chest under his bed, but . . .

'I will let you have this quarter's pension, yes, Uriah. But an increase is another matter. I doubt if I can.'

They stared inimically at each other. In his forties, Ninian had acquired more presence than he knew. His facial bones had grown heavier and his sandy hair had begun to retreat in front, leaving him

107

with a high, gleaming forehead. It made him seem taller and put Uriah at a disadvantage. He loathed Ninian for it and this gave him, paradoxically, the courage to persist.

'If the pension ain't worth what it was, Mr Whitmead, that means it buys less. For us and for you too. You know as well as me what you're buying with it.'

'I also know, Uriah, that if you carry out the threat I think you're making, the pension would cease altogether.'

Uriah was gaining confidence. 'That might be small comfort to you and Mrs Whitmead, sir.'

'It might be even less comfort to your mother.' Ninian, however, judged it wise to give in a little. 'I'll see what I can do. How much extra does she need each quarter?'

'Ten shillings, Mr Whitmead.'

'I'll give her eight,' said Ninian, wondering how.

'You're not in a position to chaffer, Mr Whitmead.'

'You're wrong. Your mother wants to keep that pension. Be careful, Uriah. Don't demand too much. Think twice before taking any unwise action. There is such a thing as overplaying your hand.'

'That's a card-players' phrase, ain't it? I wouldn't know the meaning of it,' said Uriah woodenly. 'Since I reckon card-playing is ungodly.'

'Quite,' said Ninian and added silkily: 'We are about to dine. You had better join us. And do, please, stay for prayers this afternoon.'

To the infinite regret of the Whitmead household, the arrival of the visitor didn't shorten the afternoon prayer meeting in the least. On the contrary, it went on for a punitive three hours instead of two. Even Uriah showed visible relief when it was over, and left the house to start his journey home without delay.

The interminable prayers, the silent evenings of private Bible reading and serious conversation, the supper of bread and cheese and ale, were all over. Charles – the only one spared the tedium of the prayer meeting because nothing would have made him sit through it quietly – had been put to bed.

Now, darkness had fallen. Ninian and Parvati, the last to retire, went quietly upstairs and bolted the door of their room behind them. No one else slept close nowadays, not even Kerenza. They were private, as they only were at night.

Ninian drew curtains over the door and window and made sure that the window too was fast. Parvati went to a chest. It was not the Indian sandalwood chest from the wreck, which had been damaged by the sea and had long since fallen to pieces. But from under layers of dark garments, she removed a sari of gold-bordered red silk, and the sandalwood trinket box, from which she chose a set of bangles. She also lifted out Ninian's lute, which he took from her.

'Poor Uriah. Did you see him, Parvati? I kept them all kneeling so long that I think he got pins and needles. He was in an agony, trying not to fidget.'

'I nearly giggled. Ninian, you are so naughty!'

108

'Shall we profane the Sabbath, with worldly music and laughter, then? Shall we practise the sin of lust? Take off that white head-dress, Parvati. Shake down your hair. Shed that dark gown and put on your sari and your bangles and dance while I play for you the music of your land.'

'Is it safe? It is such a still night. There is hardly any wind. Will the sound carry?'

'I think not, but what use is there in worrying? I can't keep my godly pretence up if there isn't this. I nearly slipped, talking to Davies at the church door today. I made some sarcastic remark about kitchen cupboards. Never mind. Forget it. We've shut out Cornwall with her misty Celtic past and her righteous Puritan present. Dance for me, Parvati. Make India for me.'

She raised her hands to her head and took the head-dress off. 'What would Davies say if he could see us now?'

'He'd have an apoplexy. Probably two.'

'Oh, Ninian. I wish I could see him having two apoplexies!'

'So do I!' said Ninian. 'Come!'

Laughing, she changed into the glistening red silk sari and the tinkling bangles. Ninian sat down cross-legged on the bed and softly fingered the lute. On small, bare feet, Parvati began to dance, one hand on her hip, one arm and hand undulating in gestures of invitation, of coquettish denial, of imperious summons. The bangles glittered. The rhythm of the music quickened. The little feet stamped, whirling her near to him and then away. Her body rippled as though she were boneless. Save for a few silvery marks on her taut abdomen, there was no sign that she had ever borne a child. As she finished the dance, she sank effortlessly to the floor, head bent, hair swirling. He laid the lute aside and drew her up.

'*To our bodies turn we then, that so, Weak men on love revealed may look; Love's mysteries in souls do grow, But yet the body is his book.*'

'That is your John Donne?'

'It is.'

'They are lovely words. They have a strong sound, like the sea. But I like Shakespeare best; those words you said to me our first time. That was the first time,' said Parvati, 'that I ever gave, instead of being simply taken.'

'*Was* it?' Shaken, he recited: '*For how do I hold thee but by thy granting? And for that riches where is my deserving?* Were those the words? Here are some more. *Being your slave, what should I do but tend upon the hours and times of your desire?* You have always given yourself to me, my heart. I would never . . . just take.'

'Take,' said Parvati softly as he lifted her on to the bed. 'And be welcome!'

Ninian deliberately left the bedcurtains open and the candles lit. 'I expect Davies thinks that even on a weekday, a couple should lie together in the dark,' he whispered. 'If they saw each other, the sight might give them pleasure. How dreadful! Parvati, you are so beautiful. You gleam like amber. You are so taut and yet so soft. I adore you.'

'Mr Davies would not think you should say that.'

'You sound so prim,' said Ninian, chuckling, 'but how your eyes shine.'

'I wish we could have another child.'

'One day we will. Come, my darling. Let us profane the Sabbath once again!'

Some days later, Kerenza developed a rash on her forehead, and then fell ill with a fever. The day after that, Peg Hawkes sickened, and her small son, and Betsy her sister-in-law.

Within a week, it became plain that the plague had come to Cornwall.

It had most probably arrived by sea. Vessels came into Penzance from everywhere. Timber, iron and salt; sometimes more exotic goods such as wine and raisins, were unloaded on its quay, alongside the mackerel and pilchards brought in by the fishermen. Much of the salt went to preserve the pilchards and much of the timber to make hogsheads to put them in, and ships set sail on every tide, bound for the Mediterranean countries with holds full of pilchard casks. They would come back with more iron, more salt, more raisins, beginning the cycle again. From those warmer climates, they might also bring back an invisible and unauthorised cargo, and often did.

The plague concentrated most of its vicious energies in Penzance, where thirty-four coffins were laid to rest in a single month, borne to their graves by frightened bearers. Nervous mourners followed, armed with clove-stuck oranges, and the committal was read by ministers who stood well back from the grave. But the pestilence migrated too, across the peninsula to St Ives, down to Land's End, northwards through Cornwall all the way to Bodmin.

In their rented cottage at Bodmin, shortly after Uriah came back with her pension, Hannah got up one morning, said she felt ill, returned to her bed, and was dead by nightfall, with dark marks like bruises all over her body, and buboes like huge, throbbing fruits in her armpits.

Uriah did not run away. 'You're a good son. Some would have left me to die,' Hannah whispered once.

'Whether I live or die is in the Lord's hands. It must be a terrible thing,' Uriah said, 'to have no faith.'

'I've brought you up right. Wish your father could see you,' whispered Hannah. 'I'm mortal afeared of dying, son.'

In a gentle fashion which would have astonished Ninian, Uriah brought her a cup of water. 'You'll mend. But if you don't: you're a good woman, and there's nothing to fear.'

Hannah tried to smile and drink the water, but swallowing was very painful. In the end, the pain was so bad that the darkness of death was welcome.

Uriah saw her decently buried, bullying the minister in order to make sure that all was carried out in good order. He did not feel well at the funeral but thought it was grief. By the next morning, he knew it was the plague. It took him two days to die, and before the end, anguish and fear had destroyed all the faith that Hannah had taught him.

His landlord, when at length he faced the task of clearing up the cottage, did not know if there was anyone who should be told. But he found a reference which a Mr Ninian Whitmead of Polmawgan in Penwith had written for Uriah, and for lack of any other contact, he wrote to Ninian.

On learning that the Giddys were dead, Ninian's chief feeling was relief. They knew too much that was dangerous to Parvati. Mary Trevelyan could be intimidated and the down-to-earth Branson was loyal, but he had never trusted the Giddys. Parvati was that much safer, now.

Thirty-four coffins that July in Penzance; three more in Polmawgan. Healthy people did sometimes recover from the plague and Peg Hawkes' sister-in-law Betsy was one of them. But Peg and her little son were unlucky and so was Kerenza. No one else in either the village or Polmawgan House sickened, but Kerenza's family feared the infection too much even to attend her funeral, let alone take charge of her body, and left the arrangements to her employers. Parvati and Ninian saw Kerenza to her burial in Polmawgan churchyard.

Four hired men from Penzance carried the coffin to the grave and Joseph Davies conducted the service. He did so with dignity, not standing back. When it was over, Ninian thanked him and the bearers and paid them and then he and Parvati lingered for a while in the churchyard, looking at the recently heaped mound which hid Peg and her baby, and at Pen's grave nearby.

'We should let Kerenza's parents know how we have put her beside your sister Pen,' Parvati said. 'They will like that; it was respectful. How strange your customs are. We burn our dead in fires and cast their ashes into a river. Widows often burn themselves on their husband's pyre, or are put there by his family. You have no such custom here?'

Ninian stared at her. This happened every now and then. Parvati would make a casual remark and suddenly he would glimpse the alien hinterland behind her eyes. 'You mean . . . women who have done nothing wrong are thrown on to bonfires because they are widowed?'

'Yes. Women do not marry again as they do here; they are part of their husbands and die with them.'

'But don't the women resist?'

'Sometimes, but they have no choice.'

'They are just thrown on the fire, then, like used rubbish?' said Ninian, outraged. 'And what of the men? How can a man who loves his wife bear to think of such a thing being done to her? Don't the men themselves rise up against such a horror and put a stop to it?'

'No. It is a matter of family honour. Often the women go willingly.'

'Willingly to *that*?' Ninian felt ill. The familiar Cornish landscape swayed. He had never seen a burning. But more than once, people who had, had told him more than he wished to hear before he could stop them. 'Honour?' he said. 'The murder of the innocent – and by such a means – a matter of *honour*? Oh, Parvati, thank God you are here with me. For our son's sake, too! A nice thing for the children, I must say, to murder the mother if the father dies! Why, here, if I die, you can marry again.'

But what other man would understand her as he did? For there were fleeting moments when her past did not seem so alien to him, when he saw in his head small, bright pictures which could only be of India, and when he shared what he had learned was her sense of life as a helpless drifting on tides of fate. These experiences were rare and puzzling and he had no idea that the power was inherited and had been passed down to him through centuries.

But from this deep knowledge of Parvati's mind came a grim certainty that she would surely come to grief, alone in England without his protection. Tenderness for her filled him. 'Don't be afraid,' he said. 'We shall both be here to see our son become a man.'

'If only he wasn't our only child. If we lost him, what would we do? Oh, Ninian, if *only* . . .'

'Don't think about it.' Ninian glanced inland, to where cloud from the west was veiling the hills and threatening rain. 'At the moment,' he said, as he led her out of the churchyard, 'Charles is healthy enough and driving us all to a frenzy with his roars and his demands. He's spoiled, I'm afraid. He needs a firmer hand.'

They were hurrying now, as quickly as Ninian could manage, past the slate-roofed stone cottages of Polmawgan. 'There's Polly Hawkes,' Parvati said. 'Just coming out of their cottage. Poor John Hawkes, to lose both Peg *and* his son. Polly! How are you? How is Betsy now?'

Polly came towards them with obvious reluctance, pausing several paces off. There was no smile on her small, neat-featured face. 'Good day, Mr Whitmead, Mrs Whitmead. Betsy is up again, thank you kindly, and by God's grace, the rest of us are still well. That's how it be, sometimes. But it do be very strange.'

'Before long, I'll be coming to help you with the children on Mondays as I used to do,' Parvati said. 'I'll bring my new maid with me, when I find one. We can—'

'There's no need for 'ee to trouble. We can manage.'

'But it is no trouble. I like to play with the children so much.'

'That's as may be. Begging your pardon, Mr Whitmead, but there's times it's best to be frank. Mrs Whitmead, you may like to play with our children, but we're not so keen on it ourselves, not now. The plague started after you'd been to see them, and then Kerenza got it, up there at your house. Who's to know how a plague begins? Some say it comes off the ships and some say it's the will of God, but maybe it comes from something that's neither of those.'

'Polly,' said Ninian quietly, 'just what are you saying?'

Embarrassingly, one or two other people had drifted up to stand in apparently casual neighbourly conversation, just within earshot. There were a couple of fishermen; three older women with very clean linen head-dresses and wind-reddened faces which should have been rosily benign but were oddly stern instead; and two young wives whose air of assured respectability was so noticeable that it had to be deliberate. A frisson ran down Ninian's spine.

'I'll say no more, sir. But with respect, Betsy and me'd sooner see to our own babbies and our own washing days in future. Good day to you, Mr Whitmead, Mrs Whitmead.'

'Polly!' Ninian stopped her as she was about to walk away. 'One moment.' Unwillingly, Polly waited.

Ninian disliked almost everything he had heard about Oliver Cromwell and did not approve of Colonel John Hurry either, but he had more in common with them than he knew. He too believed in carrying a war into the enemy camp.

'Tell me,' he said, 'would you happen to know of a girl who might be interested in Kerenza's place?'

It was no use. 'No, sir,' said Polly. 'Sorry, sir, but I wouldn't. And now, if you'll excuse me, I've things to do. My mother-in-law's not so well. Oh, not the plague. But the joint-evil keeps her from getting about as she used.'

She went on her way. Ninian, acutely aware of the watching bystanders, said to the stricken Parvati: 'I think it's going to rain. We should make haste,' and urged her onwards, hobbling rapidly beside her, aware of the eyes on their retreating backs.

'What did she mean?' Parvati burst out. 'Why am I not welcome to play with the Hawkes children? I loved them. I did not give them the plague! Perhaps Kerenza did but I did not. And why does no one want Kerenza's place? It is well paid, comfortable; we do not mistreat our servants!'

'I don't quite know what she meant,' said Ninian grimly. 'But, Parvati, my dear love, whatever is behind this, I think that from now on, you shouldn't go to Polmawgan village very often, and never go alone.'

Chapter Ten
Distant Thunder

The big first-floor parlour at Rosnance had pleasing furniture, an Oriental carpet in cool blues and greys, and a westward view of smooth-crested green hills. It smelt of beeswax-and-resin polish and at the moment, it had a deceptive air of ladylike peace. Garments and linen in need of repair were piled in a basket on Mary's pretty writing desk and three feminine heads, every hair neatly concealed beneath white linen head-dresses, were bent to the task of mending. It was very quiet. The September day was cool and drizzly enough for candles and a small fire, but even the driftwood only ventured an occasional splutter. When the ladies spoke, their voices too were soft. Herein lay the deception. The thoughts inside the heads of Mary Trevelyan, Tamzin St Asaph and Prudence Jenken bore no relation whatsoever to their words.

'May I have the white thread, Mrs Jenken, please? Thank you,' said Mary Trevelyan sweetly.

And if I have to spend many more days like this, she added silently, putting together a torn seam in a shirt belonging to Captain William Beresford-Higham, I shall forget myself and scream out loud and bang my head on the panelling. Those Roundhead beasts have been living in my home for over a year now and if I'm not sewing for them, I'm rolling pastry or sweeping floors. Having to make do with nearly all the servants sent away, and no maid to help me. Poor Kitty, just turned off for no reason. It's Prudence's fault, telling the Captain I didn't need a maid. She looks like a horse and behaves as if she were our governess. Who does she think she is? She's only the wife of the man who sells horse-fodder to the Captain. She may have come here to escape the plague in Penzance, but I wish she'd stayed there and died of it!

Tears filled her eyes and she ran the needle into her forefinger. She gripped the place hard to keep the blood off the Captain's pristine shirt. Oh, Francis, where are you? Why don't you come home and save me? But Francis doesn't care about me any longer.

Tamzin, stooping to take another piece of driftwood from the wood-basket, remarked: 'We need more wood. Whoever goes downstairs next should fetch some.'

In Mary, bitterness suddenly surfaced. 'Fortunately, we can get driftwood. Otherwise, we should have to ask the Captain for permission to buy coal. Very likely he'd make us chop up the furniture first. He's hinted as much.'

Mary worries me, Tamzin thought. She burns inside. I've done my best, telling Captain Beresford-Higham that we couldn't work if we didn't have enough to eat. I managed to be firm and calm. But Mary is the kind to seethe inside and then lose control. One of these days, she *will* lose her temper and that will be dangerous. I wish Jane Dewey could come and see us but as long as the plague is in Mousehole, the Captain won't allow visitors except for men like Anthony Gubbes. I suppose he has to keep in touch with local supporters. But Jane might put some heart into Mary. She could certainly put Prudence in her place. I'm going to have a try, one of these days, but Jane would do it better.

Oh, how I hate this life. Losing Coombe, and then there's Christopher . . . He's lost heart, lost hope. I'm glad we sent the children to his cousin in France but how I miss them. There'll be no more children now, with Christopher like this, staring out of the window all day, brooding. The only time he stirs himself is to go to the shore for driftwood. I wonder where Francis is? Will he ever be able to come home again? How long must we go on just existing, while Beresford-Higham and his psalm-singing crew look at us as though we were blackbeetles and expect us to mend and patch for them?

Without raising her eyes from her work, Prudence Jenken said: 'It is as well for Mr St Asaph that he can help by gathering driftwood, even though he has only one arm. He must be glad to know that he can still contribute. You mustn't think I don't realise how difficult life is for you now, Mrs Trevelyan. No doubt Captain Beresford-Higham seems severe. But he only wants to help you pay off the new taxes. You will lose Rosnance altogether if you can't pay. You are fortunate. Now, your husband could have paid, could he not, Mrs St Asaph? But it was not permitted. That was very sad.'

'Yes, that's true,' said Tamzin, carefully toneless.

'The Captain is only acting under the orders of General Fairfax, of course,' Prudence said dulcetly. 'The General has at least shown consideration for Mrs Trevelyan's deserted state, since Mr Trevelyan has apparently vanished.'

You St Asaphs always were lazy and stuck-up. And Mary is a fool. Prudence stitched briskly at an elbow patch, rather enjoying the contrast between her controlled movements and the raging hatred in her mind. I'm as good as you are. I was born a Clemo and the Clemos have come up in the world since the days when my Aunt Morwenna was Robert Whitmead's housekeeper before he married her. My husband is one of the most prosperous feed merchants in Penzance; we've got a fine house right at the top of the town and three barns full of fodder. We can pay our taxes and I could wear all the silk and lace I wanted if I didn't know it was vain show. But you still think of me as someone not quite good enough to mix with you.

Well, provoke me, my dear ladies, and I'm in a position to see that you regret it. How I wish I could catch Mary out in treasonable correspondence with Francis. I don't think she is, which is a pity. But meanwhile, spying on her most certainly has its compensations. She's so frightened of me. Look at her now. She doesn't answer. She daren't.

'I fear, Mrs Trevelyan,' said Prudence aloud, in reproving tones, 'that you still somewhat resent the presence of the Captain and his men in your house.'

'That censorious note is hardly fair, Mrs Jenken,' said Tamzin coldly. 'No one likes it when strangers come into their home without a by-your-leave.'

'Oh, come. Mrs Trevelyan has only been asked to accommodate a few men and to accept some guidance from Captain Beresford-Higham in the management of her estate. You are *very* fortunate, Mrs Trevelyan.'

'No, I'm not!' Mary's face suffused. She jumped up, dropping her work on the floor. 'I'm not fortunate! I have to put up with *you* in my house, moralising and preaching. I wonder if you'd be so complacent about having soldiers billeted in *your* house?'

'Mary!' said Tamzin warningly.

Mary paid no heed. The breaking point had come. 'Guidance, you call it! The bailiff has to report to Captain Beresford-Higham instead of to me; the Captain controls all the money and just doles out to us what food he thinks fit; I and my guests have to live in one wing while the Captain and his men make free with the rest and they're *ruining* it!'

She broke off with a sob. She had never much liked Rosnance, or thought she hadn't. But to see it misused by the soldiers, the dining table unpolished, the candlesticks left dull, the carpets trampled; this had hurt more than she had dreamed possible. She had saved her writing table and her rosewood-veneered chest of drawers, but they were hostages for her good behaviour, as Kitty had been. If she displeased the Captain again, he would find an excuse to destroy them.

'Come, now,' said Prudence. 'The Captain wouldn't like to see his shirt flung on to the floor like that. You must not give way to passion.'

'Why not? I've every reason!' Mary snatched up the shirt and jumped to her feet. She threw the garment at Prudence. 'Here! *You* mend it!' she shouted, and fled from the room.

Prudence removed the shirt, which had fallen over her face. She had gone rather red. Tamzin said quietly: 'You did provoke her, you know. She is indeed living like a poor relation in her own home. You have never actually said that if she complains, you will use your influence with the Captain to make life harder for her, but you have hinted it, have you not? That was wrong, and it's time someone told you so.'

'I don't need you to instruct me on good and bad behaviour, Mrs St Asaph! I'm ten years your senior and I have the right to insist on respect.'

Tamzin, refusing to be outfaced, kept her brown gaze on Prudence, and Prudence fell silent. 'Shall we continue with our work?' said Tamzin evenly. 'Since Mary has presumably gone downstairs, I hope she thinks to fetch some wood.'

Mary, biting her lips to keep from bursting into tears, ran down the stairs, and came face to face in the hallway with Captain Beresford-Higham.

'You seem to be in a hurry, Mrs Trevelyan. Is anything wrong?'

His eyebrows were rounded like Norman arches, giving his face a constant expression of disbelieving inquiry and his fastidiously curved nostrils implied that the whole world smelt unpleasant. She not only disliked and feared him, but was piqued by him. She had been pretty Mary Nicholls, whose parents had called her their angel and whose merchant father had given her dresses made of the costliest blue cloth in his warehouse, because it matched her eyes. Both her parents were dead now. What would they have said if they knew this man was looking at her like this?

His disdain, coming on top of the quarrel with Prudence, now annoyed her so much that her tears dried. She bobbed a curtsy which was nearly an impertinence. 'I'm going to fetch some firewood, Captain.'

'In such haste? You came down the stairs as though you were a deer fleeing the hounds. And you've forgotten the wood-basket.'

His tone was not exactly unfriendly. His expression did not change but his voice was mildly teasing. Through her distraction, Mary noticed and took advantage of it.

'I intend to bring another basket. Please excuse me. I said I would be quick,' she said in her sweetest voice, and tried the effect on the Captain of the first smile she had ever given him. Francis had once said that when she smiled, it wrinkled her snub nose and made him want to kiss it. She was gratified to see a flicker of response in the Captain's chilly eyes as with a small bow, he stepped aside for her.

She escaped into the garden and then found that the drizzle had now become heavy. She couldn't just stay out in the rain. Presently, she'd have to go back to that parlour, even if it did have Prudence in it. Well, she was supposed to be going to the woodshed and it would at least be dry. Hurrying across a once-lovely rose garden, now as neglected as everything else at Rosnance, she went through the gate to the yard. Christopher was just entering it from the opposite gate, which opened on a lane leading down to Minecombe. He was leading a pony laden with panniers which he had industriously filled with driftwood. He must have been on the beach for hours, to find so much. Mary stopped short.

She longed to pour out to someone an account of her quarrel with Prudence and her fears for the outcome, but Christopher wasn't the right person. Since he had been here, she had scarcely had anything she could call a conversation with him. He was locked into a private world of resentment over his disability and the loss of his home and it was no use trying to talk to him about anything else. Remark to him that it was raining, and he'd reply: 'It was raining when we had to move out of Coombe. And we had to walk, with what we could carry. They kept our horses.'

But as she hesitated, Christopher caught sight of her and beckoned. She went slowly to meet him.

'Come along,' he said impatiently, heaving a pannier off the pony. 'Help me get these into the shed. They've got to be emptied and the wood spread to dry. While you're doing that, I'll see to the pony.'

Something was different about him. He had never of course stopped being outwardly a bluff, red-faced country gentleman, but at Rosnance, he had appeared smaller, shrunken. Now, mysteriously, he seemed to have filled out again. He looked . . . *excited*, that was the word. How strange. 'Has something happened?' she ventured as she lifted the pannier.

'Happened? Of course not. What are you talking about? Let's get these baskets inside.'

From the shed door, she watched him lead the pony away. He was even walking differently. Something *had* happened; he was lying to her. She was shut out of most of her house, out of her husband's love, and now out of the confidence of her friends. She sat down on the floor and cried, until Tamzin appeared, twenty minutes later, in search both of Mary and firewood. 'I've had a few words with Prudence,' said Tamzin, more brusque than sympathetic. 'She won't say anything more. Really, Mary. Fancy weeping in an outhouse!'

Ninian lowered the sail on the *Silver Fish*, ordered the dogs, who were used to the routine, to lie down, took out the oars and manoeuvred the boat deftly towards the deep green water which wound like a curving lane amid the submerged rocks, into the mouth of Minecombe.

No fishing village had ever grown up beside Minecombe's river. Its V-shaped outlet ran into a cove which was peppered with rocks, as was the shingly little beach to the north of the river. For boats, Minecombe was far more dangerous than Polmawgan and for the most part, the little cove was the province of the seals which lazed and sang on the rocks and the cormorants which perched there to dry their wings.

Small, shallow draught craft could find a way in, however, if their skippers knew the cove well. Francis knew it, and had used Minecombe in order to slip to his home and demand Mary's jewellery. And Ninian knew it, and was able to use it because the *Silver Fish* was only sixteen feet long.

But even for Ninian, negotiating the cove required concentration. The *Fish* was in the mouth of the stream and Pol had got up and put his paws on the gunwale, preparatory to scrambling out, before his master even saw the man who was standing on the bank.

'*Francis!*'

The dogs leapt out to jump up at Francis with licks and joyful barks. Ninian followed, more awkwardly.

'I recognised the *Fish* a mile away. I've been waiting for you,' said Francis, as Ninian moored the boat where a jutting outcrop provided a natural harbour out of the current, above the reach of the tide. 'Pengelly told me you'd moved her from Polmawgan. Yes, Pol, you've washed my face quite enough. Down, Lady! How old are they now? About twelve?'

'Yes.' Ninian heaved a basket of eels out of the boat. 'This will make

119

today's dinner. What the devil are you doing in Cornwall, Francis? You're a traitor in the eyes of the Roundheads. Suppose they caught you?'

'They'd take me in for questioning,' said Francis. The wind snatched at his broad-brimmed hat and he slammed it haphazardly back on to his head. He was as dishevelled as a tinker, even though the clothes beneath his stout cloak were costly. A generously cut linen shirt bulged through the slashed sleeves of a dashing blue doublet, and his velvet trunks were tied below the knee with enormous satin bows, while his wide collar and turned-back cuffs were edged with lace. But everything was creased and grimy; only his insouciant grin was unchanged.

'I expect they would,' Ninian agreed. 'You've been associating with the Prince of Wales.'

'And no doubt they'd like to know what plans the lad is making to come to his father's aid. The King is still more or less a prisoner on the Isle of Wight, is he not?'

'He is. But I daresay you know more than I do. I've been keeping out of it and avoiding trouble. How long have you been here? Where are you staying? It can't be Rosnance.'

'No.' Francis nodded towards the narrow path which led up the combe to Wheal Susannah's original entrance and the miners' cottages higher up. 'I'm staying with Pengelly. That poor devil's slowly wheezing to death. He's not afraid of the Roundheads. He told me that anyone who killed him would be doing him a favour.'

'I know. He hasn't left his bed now for months,' said Ninian. 'But I ask you again: why are you here?'

Francis did not answer at once. He sat down on a rock and studied Ninian thoughtfully. 'I've seen Christopher,' he said. 'Pengelly told me that he'd taken to gathering driftwood here – not what he's used to, poor fellow – and I waited for him. He was overjoyed when he came across me. But he tells me you've turned Puritan, and that you're avoiding him for that reason. Judging by the clothes you're wearing, he's right. Or is it just a protective disguise?'

'I fancy you assume the latter. At least, you seem quite sure I won't inform the militia that you're here.'

'I am. This abominable war has divided friend from friend and even split up families, but I don't see you knocking me on the head and handing my unconscious body to General Fairfax. But what's the truth of the matter, Ninian? Are you genuinely Puritan? Or not?'

He couldn't pretend with Francis. They'd known each other too long. 'I'm wearing a disguise, because it's safest for my wife. These Puritans pick on anyone who's in the least different from themselves. If you want to know,' said Ninian bitterly, 'I wish the Parliamentarians would all go walking in a mist and step off the edge of a cliff. No fairs, no Maypoles; they're trying to shut down the taverns and people scowl at you in the street if you put a feather in your hat. The latest is that they want to bring in the death penalty for adultery. As for the sermons Joseph Davies preaches . . .'

'Pengelly has a young nephew with him. According to the nephew

Davies preached a sermon last week on the text *Thou shalt not suffer a witch to live.*'

'Yes, he did,' said Ninian belligerently. 'What makes you mention that, particularly?'

'I heard why you moved the *Fish*. The Polmawgan people were hinting things about Penny, weren't they?'

'Yes, they were, the fools. They've always been suspicious of Penny and now they're under Davies' influence. He encourages superstition. I thought of taking Penny away but we have nowhere to go and she herself wishes our son to be brought up in the home he will inherit.' Ninian shook an exasperated head. 'As for me, I love Polmawgan and I don't want to leave. We live a godly life and avoid the village except for going to church, and hope the talk will die away. And now you've come back to Cornwall to stir up trouble. Because that's it, isn't it? You're here to launch a new campaign for the King.'

'If the King is to be restored to his proper place and his family enabled to rejoin him, it can't be done without a campaign and without stirring up a great deal of trouble.'

'I daresay not. But if you have sought me out to ask me to enmesh myself in it, the answer's no. I'm prepared to wish you well and forget I've seen you, but that's all.'

'Indeed?' With misgiving, Ninian saw the familiar, mischievous sparkle in his friend's eyes. 'Tell me, Ninian,' said Francis persuasively, 'what if there were a real chance of turning the tide?'

'I said, I'd wish you well.'

'You don't like the Roundheads but you wouldn't be prepared to lift a finger to help?'

'I would prefer not to, Frank. It would endanger my wife, for one thing.'

'Good God, man, she'd be safer under the King's rule than under these Puritans!'

Away at the mouth of the stream, a wave broke in spume. The dogs rubbed their heads against him and Ninian fondled them absently. 'I know,' he said. 'And Cornwall is the logical place to start. Sea on three sides and the River Tamar on the fourth. A defensible land, if only we have the defenders. I know all the arguments. But the enemy is in control on the wrong side of the Tamar and you have no organised resistance.'

'We're unlikely ever to acquire it if all the able-bodied men devote themselves to protecting their own safety. Or even that of their wives.'

'I don't mean to offend you, Frank, but what's between me and Penny – well, between you and Mary, it isn't the same.'

'I know, but I can still understand what you mean. Only,' said Francis strongly, 'it shouldn't make a difference. Our cause matters too much. I'm not a fanatic, as these Puritans are. But for that very reason, breaking their hold is too important for any personal consideration.'

'It's more than a personal consideration.' Ninian regarded his friend with exasperation. 'I am tired to death of the Puritans, yes, but can't you understand that I feel just as sick and weary inside when I think about the King? He demands the loyalty of his subjects just because he is King, but what has he ever done for us? Among other things, he once entertained the idea of letting an army of Papists step on to our soil . . .'

'That was to fight the Scots.'

'But would it have ended there? This king, who demands our unquestioning loyalty, and says he rules by the will of God, has a Catholic queen. Suppose we found ourselves under an Inquisition! Dear God, Frank, can't you see? I came to Braddock Down because you and Christopher were there and because I was younger then. I've had time to think, since. I know now that I want neither Catholic rule nor Puritan. I don't want a king who thinks he's substitute for God, any more than I want Joseph Davies and his sanctimonious maunderings. I want to live a peaceful life under sensible, moderate rulers. Failing the sensible, moderate rulers, I've taken cover behind a suit of black clothes and a suitably long face, and got on with my own life in private. I support neither side now. Can't you grasp that?'

'I think,' said Francis, 'that you are forgetting one vital thing. That the King of whom you disapprove so much has an heir who is virtually a grown man. I have met Prince Charles, and I can tell you that he is not like his father. He could well be the reasonable and moderate ruler you so much desire. Provided,' said Francis, in his dryest voice, 'he is allowed to inherit. Provided he lives long enough.'

There was a pause. Then Francis said, seriously, with all the dryness and the mockery gone: 'You want to withdraw, to stand alone. But you can't. You used to like the writings of John Donne. Do you still?'

'Yes. Why?'

'Do you remember I once reminded you of something he wrote? *No man is an Island, entire of itself; every man is a piece of the Continent.* You said he was only putting beliefs into convincing words; that he didn't *know.* But I think he was right. The rest of us make up the continent and you're part of us. Are you sure that to deny that is truly the best way to protect yourself, or your wife?'

'How can I know? I can't foretell the future; I can't know which side would win, if there were a rising!' There was another pause. 'I might join a rising if it had a real chance of success,' Ninian said at last. 'But not otherwise.'

'But only loyal support will give it that chance.' Francis got to his feet. 'I must go. I have others to contact. Think about it, Ninian. If you want to hear more . . . go and see Pengelly.'

'Pengelly?'

'Yes.' Francis offered his hand. 'Meanwhile, let us part as old friends should. But I hope to see you again soon, Ninian. I do indeed.'

'Wait!'

Francis paused in the midst of swinging his cloak jauntily round him. 'What is it?'

'Your wife, Mary. I haven't seen her for a long time but news filters. Penny's maid Kitty used to work for Mary and she has told my wife that Mary misses you. You say you've seen Christopher. Have you been in touch with Mary?'

'No,' said Francis, 'and I think it better not to. Mary is easily frightened. It wouldn't be safe.'

The new workings in Wheal Susannah had two entrances, one through the old diggings in the valley and one driven into the side of Polmawgan Head itself. There were several levels by now, and places where the miners must descend vertical shafts by ladder. But for the purpose of a secret meeting, it was only necessary to be out of sight of anyone above-ground. The hurriedly convened and unofficial council for the recapture of Penzance for the King met in a candlelit rock chamber reached merely by creeping fifty yards along a sloping, low-roofed tunnel.

Even so, there was an uncomfortable awareness of the mass of Polmawgan Head above them. The little room, shored up with stout timber supports, had been hacked out to accommodate a rope and winch by which buckets of ore could be drawn up from a deeper level. The wheeled winch took up a good deal of space and so did the shaft into which its rope vanished. Somewhere down there, water dripped slowly with an intermittent *plink-plink*. Beyond the shaft was the dark mouth of a further tunnel, from which a cold draught came. The air smelt of dust and damp combined. Christopher St Asaph and William Keigwin, who had never been into a mine before, kept glancing uneasily upwards. Thomas Grosse, who was currently the Mayor of Penzance, looked as if the place offended him.

'Are we all here?' Francis, sitting cross-legged on the floor, raised his lantern and scanned the tightly packed group round him. 'Christopher, Ninian, Will Keigwin, Mayor Grosse, the Reverend Darracott. Good.' In the golden light, his eyes danced wickedly. 'I told Prince Charles that Penwith was still Royalist at heart. I am sorry about this peculiar venue, but I am known to have been with the Prince. I prefer not to risk being seen anywhere, and above all not to be observed entering any of your houses.'

A pickaxe rang in the distance. 'Pengelly says we cannot rely on all the miners,' Ninian said. 'They have been given orders to work elsewhere in the mine today. They don't know the reason. But I believe that many would join us if once we mastered Penzance.' He glanced sidelong at Christopher. It was the first time they had met for well over a year. 'I do mean *we*. Whatever you may have heard, and in spite of the depressing way I'm dressed, I am with you.'

'Damme if I ever really doubted it,' said Christopher. 'We were boys together and I know you.'

'I must apologise to you, Ninian.' Darracott's hair was now entirely white but his red-veined face was pugnacious. 'I feared you'd gone and turned Puritan properly. I should have trusted you. God knows, my former flock have given you cause for this masquerade. That man Davies has done them no good, with his sermonising.'

'Oh, let's get to business,' said Grosse irritably. He did not match his name, being a small man, though tough, his sleeves and stockings bulging out with muscle. He was wearing his chain of office, which

123

looked absurd, and this had probably exacerbated his evident ill-temper. 'A fine thing, the Mayor of Penzance conspiring down a tin mine! We must take Pendennis Castle and the Mount and hold them, which is more than Arthur Basset did when he had the Mount. It was a bad day when Frank Basset died, and left his brother to defend it.'

'Arthur Basset withstood siege as long as he could,' said Keigwin. 'What did you expect him to do – hold out until he was in the Mount all alone? He was running out of food and the garrison were deserting in droves, sneaking off over the causeway every time the tide ebbed after dark.'

'He lost over a hundred men that way,' Francis agreed. 'Maybe he held out too long rather than not long enough. But he's in the Scillies now with his officers, and they'll come back if they see there's a cause worth joining. What we have to do, is to create one.'

'Can it be done?' Keigwin had a fastidious, scholarly face, with thin furrows deepened by worry on either side of his mouth. 'We could be killed trying,' he said, 'and leave nothing for our children but a tighter regime than ever, and fewer goods to inherit because the Roundheads will have seized our substance.'

They stared at him in disapproving silence.

'We must be sure of what we're doing,' Keigwin told them. 'Otherwise, we may as well keep out of trouble. Eat, drink and be merry and try to avoid dying tomorrow.'

'It's to give people the right to be merry that we don't want to keep out of trouble!' snapped Francis, and Christopher was so incensed that he tried to scramble to his feet in order to shout at Keigwin. There wasn't room in the chamber to stand upright, and he knocked his hat off and lurched into one of the timber supports. It creaked ominously and grit showered round them. Grosse exclaimed in alarm and Ninian pulled Christopher away.

'Stop that! Don't knock those supports about!'

Christopher sat down again but spoke his mind just the same. 'I never heard such traitorous talk! What are you doing here, Keigwin, if that's what you think? Let them get away with it: the men that lost me my arm and took my home away from me? Damme if I wouldn't have called you out for that when I was whole!' He had gone scarlet.

It was the grumpy Grosse, who said: 'Leave it. He's only playing devil's advocate. He won't let us down.'

'He'd better not,' fumed Christopher.

'You misunderstand,' said Keigwin. 'This is not traitorous talk, but the opposite. I'm merely trying to impress on you that if we lay a plot, it must be sound. I'm saying that if we act, we must not fail. This is not a game. I repeat: *We must not fail.*'

'I'm with you there,' said Ninian. 'Wholeheartedly.'

'Well, we knew all that before,' snorted Christopher.

'Did we?' said Keigwin. 'We'd better be sure of it. We must not risk making mistakes.'

'We are not going to make mistakes. I think,' said Francis briskly, 'that we should list the points we must cover. We have to arrange supplies of arms, safe hideaways for men as they move into the district, a date for the rising and a rendezvous. But first and foremost, there's the business of assembling supporters. I have collected some names. To start with, there are two men Sir John Arundell knows well – Captain Maddern of Penzance and Captain Tresilian of St Levan near Land's End. I've seen Arundell and he says he'll contact them. We might also approach . . .'

'What's that?' said Christopher sharply.

They sat still, listening. Someone was coming towards them from the direction of the entrance. They exchanged sharp glances. No miners should be coming this way today and besides, this didn't sound like a miner. They were used to underground travel, like moles. They didn't huff and puff and bump like this. There was another rattle of falling gravel, which made them all stiffen anxiously, and someone exclaimed: 'Damned low roof! That was my head! How much bloody further?' It was a woman's voice. Then a boy's voice said deferentially: 'The tunnel do be narrow, but if ee'd just crouch down a bit more, it do be only a yard or two further,' and there was some more puffing but, mercifully, no more rattling, and Jane Dewey, head-dress filthy and twisted over one eye, emerged into the chamber on hands and knees.

'There you be, then,' said Tom Pengelly's nephew, following her, lantern in hand. 'Here's everyone.'

The new arrival sat down on the floor and breath was thankfully released from six ribcages. The young Pengelly, who was aged about thirteen, said he'd better get home, then, and vanished, eel-like, into the tunnel.

'Mrs Dewey,' said Francis in astonishment. 'What in the world brings you down here? It's no journey for a lady.'

'Now don't you give me that.' Jane Dewey rearranged her head-dress and her thick brown skirts, and propped her back against the rock. 'There was no one else could come. My eldest boy's halfway to India and all the rest of my menfolk are out after mackerel. There's a shoal been sighted off the Lizard and nothing gets in between my men and a catch that good, not even the King's business. But they had a message for you and they said to bring it to Pengelly and *he* sent me down here. Pengelly doesn't talk nonsense about no journey for a lady, not when the lady's me. I've been out in gales, hauling nets full of mullet and mackerel on to the deck myself in my time and he knows it.'

'And the message?' said Francis.

'From Sir John Arundell. We took dinner with him not two days ago and after we'd all tiptoed round in circles for a while, it became clear that we'd all heard from you, Francis. Arundell wants to let you know that he has seen both Maddern and Tresilian and they've agreed to join us, and bring more men. Also, my husband is willing to use his ship to transport arms. They'll be coming from France, I take it?'

'Some will,' said Francis. 'We'll have to buy gunpowder from abroad. But we're short of money. Most men will have to arm themselves. With Ninian's permission, we can hide the armaments here in the mine.'

'A very good idea.' Jane Dewey chuckled. 'No one's likely to trip over them when out for a morning stroll down here. What a horrible place this is. Is that roof safe?'

'Good enough, as long as no one knocks the supports about,' said Ninian.

'It isn't fitting for you to be down here,' Christopher said. 'My wife is privy to our plans but I wouldn't bring her to our councils, dammit. You should have sent word by someone else.'

'Why? Got to be careful about trusting people,' said Jane. 'Young Pengelly couldn't have remembered it all and I'm not stupid enough to write it down. You take it in person, Jane, I said to myself, and then you'll know it's got there. Talking of who's trustworthy: I don't want to annoy you, Francis, but does *your* wife know about this?'

'Mary doesn't even know I'm in Cornwall,' said Francis.

Christopher said gruffly: 'Tamzin's promised not to tell her. Sounds odd, I know. But . . .'

'It's best,' Francis assured them.

'Quite right.' With an air of relief, Jane fished in her skirts, found a pocket and pulled out a pipe and tobacco. She lit up, enjoying their expressions. 'Mary might panic,' she said. 'You've done right. Now then, gentlemen. How can I help? Women can go about, visiting other women all they like even in times of plague, within Penzance, at least. I'm at your service.'

Ninian said, slowly: 'We must plan for the worst as well as the best. What if we have to hide in this mine as well as store arms in it? I can stop the men from working here. Jane, can you arrange some supplies of food – stuff that will keep – and lanterns and tinderboxes and blankets and the like?'

'Leave it to me,' said Jane.

'Something's going on,' said Anthony Gubbes to his wife, as they stood at the parlour window. 'I can feel it. With the plague on the rampage, people have been staying at home and avoiding each other. But now there are knots of them talking on every corner. Today, there was a little group of six who fell quiet as I went by, and then stared after me. I don't like it.'

Alice nodded. 'I took the children to the harbour this morning, because they must have air, and some women talking in a doorway gave me such a strange look. It was – triumphant. But about what? And Sampson and Thomas have both had other boys catcalling after them, jeering at them for being Puritans. In public!'

'Mr Gubbes!'

'Yes, Parrish?' Anthony, standing on a ladder to stock-take the contents of the upper shelves in his warehouse, peered down at his clerk with slight irritation. Trade was poor in these days of high taxes and plague but if God spared him and his, the disease would abate in the winter and then the customers would reappear. Slack times were when one saw to the tasks which were so often put off when trade was good, and he was busy.

Then, seeing the worry on Parrish's face, he scribbled '3 rolls unbleached wool cloth; 2 rolls Watchet blue' on a slate, and backed rapidly down the ladder. 'What's the matter?'

'I've just been down to the harbour, sir, to pay the port dues for your cloth consignment, like you told me, sir. The Dewey fishing vessel, the *Foweymoor*, was just in and being unloaded. Sir, it was carrying small cannon.'

'Cannon!'

'Yes, sir. I asked a bystander what they were for and he said they were for extra defence against pirates. But we've had no attacks recently. It seemed odd.'

'Indeed it does,' said Anthony grimly. 'We already have cannon positioned to defend us against attack from the sea and if Penzance had asked Parliament for more ordnance or the money to buy any, I would know. There has been no such request. Odd?' said Anthony. 'It's suspicious.'

'Cannon, Alice! And I'll tell you something else. Yesterday, when I was exercising my horse, I saw the cart that takes the tin ore from Polmawgan to the smelting works outside Penzance, on its way back to the mine. It should have been empty but it was loaded with something, covered up. I pray that whatever is afoot, my old friend Ninian isn't in it. He seems to have become a Puritan, but he has held aloof from all my olive branches.'

'Should you do anything about all this, Anthony? Report it to someone?'

'Not until the plague abates. Travellers from Penwith aren't welcome outside it.' He sighed. 'I have lost too many friends lately, Alice. Norseworthy's dead of the plague – how I wish I could discuss this with him! – and others I've lost through my beliefs, though I still think of them kindly. I've found new friends, such as Captain Beresford-Higham at Rosnance, yet it remains strange to me to visit Rosnance and not see Francis. But there it is. Parliament is our only bulwark against the Papists. When travelling is feasible, I'll go to Bodmin and report what I've seen and heard to the Justices. I think I must, though I shan't enjoy it. Sometimes the Lord is a hard taskmaster.'

'The fools! The fools!'

Anthony strode about in his wife's parlour, and banged a clenched fist on the table. Alice quietly drew her needlework out of harm's way and with a movement of her head, sent her young daughters out of the room. 'Would the Justices not listen, Anthony?'

'Oh yes, most politely! They assure me that a few people gossiping, an unexpectedly laden cart and the arrival of some extra cannon in a port prone to attack from pirates, have no significance. But they have! I called at Rosnance before I came home, and Beresford-Higham agrees with me.'

'So do I,' said Alice. 'I am sure I saw powder kegs on Penzance quay yesterday. And there are strangers in the town, carrying arms and dressed in Royalist fashion.'

Anthony threw himself into a chair and put his head in his hands. 'I'm exhausted, Alice. It's hard riding through this winter weather. But there's a Grand Parliamentary Committee soon in Launceston, so Beresford-Higham says. He recommends me to get there if I can. He can't leave his post. If only they'll pay me just a little attention!'

'You should have told me!' Mary screamed at Tamzin. Prudence Jenken, fortunately, was not there to hear her, having at last returned to her home. 'You should have told me before! I had the right to know! Oh my God, Francis has been here, living in Minecombe with Pengelly, since last year and I never knew? He's my husband! He's *my husband!* Why didn't you tell me?'

'Because he forbade it. He knew that you would be worried, frightened, if you knew what was afoot. I have broken his instructions now because, frankly,' said Tamzin with annoyance, 'it seems safer than having you continually harping – and in Captain Beresford-Higham's hearing at that – on how odd it is that Christopher should choose to go off to visit relatives and not ask his wife to go with him, and how much you'd have liked to go too, as my companion, and how thoughtless it was of him to leave his womenfolk behind, and after all, we're not actually prisoners and it would be quite easy, Captain, to engage some temporary help while we're away. You would *not* be quiet, would you? I kept on making faces at you, but you can be amazingly stupid sometimes, Mary.'

'I'm not stupid. How dare you call me stupid? If I'd known Christopher had gone to join the rebels, of course I wouldn't have said anything. I *should have been told.*'

'Well, you've been told now. If all goes well, we'll have Penzance soon, and then, God willing, we'll seize Pendennis and the Mount as well. This could be the turning point.'

'But Francis should have let me know he was here. You knew and I didn't!' The hurt wouldn't subside. Tamzin was regarding her with a mixture of sympathy and disapproval. She was seventeen years older than Mary and to both of them, the gap sometimes felt more like a century. 'I'm frightened,' said Mary, trembling. 'What if the rebellion fails? What will happen to us then?'

'Mary, don't.' Suddenly, Tamzin too was trembling. 'I wish I could see the future,' she whispered. 'If only this war would end. If only Christopher could be himself again. Oh God, this war will be the ruin of us all!'

'But Ninian, you said you would not go to war again, because you cannot ride or march far, or fight well. Why you must go?'

'It should be why must I go, not why I must go. You still put words in the wrong order sometimes.'

Ninian said it lightly but there was no lightness in their hearts, though on this last night they were trying to keep up a pretence. Ninian had brought a flask of wine and two glasses to bed, and they caressed as they drank, trying to lead each other towards the act of love. But Parvati's smooth, naked skin tormented his stroking palm, because he could not get rid of the worm of fear in his stomach: fear that he would never caress her thus again, that he would die in the conflict ahead, and that she would be left alone here to face the world without him.

She had not loosed her hair. It hung over one shoulder in a long, thick braid. She took his wrist and wrapped the braid about it. 'See, I am putting chains on you. I will not let you go to war.'

'It isn't going to war, precisely. This is a matter of simply taking control of Penzance and holding it, and drawing others to join us. Christopher has joined in, despite his one arm. I have lent my mine tunnels for meetings and to store weapons. I'm part of it already, in the background. But – it isn't always enough to stay in the background.'

With a sigh, Parvati released his wrist. 'Come home safe. That's all I ask. Come home safe.'

Ninian set his wine-glass aside and took her narrow shoulders between his hands, turning her towards him. Her dark eyes searched his face. They held an expression which he did not understand.

'You are full of mystery, Parvati. There are memories lodged in your mind which I can't even imagine. What are you thinking at this moment? Is there something you want to ask me? Or tell me? There is something! Parvati, what is it?'

Parvati shook her head. 'It is only my worry for you that you see in my face. Take Penzance and hold it, you say – but until when?'

'I don't know. But Penzance isn't far. Take heart from that. I shall find moments in which to come home.'

'I will pray for you. I will think of you every moment until I see you again.' She drew herself away and tried to appear practical. 'Have you weapons and men enough?'

'We have a good cache of arms in the mine, and cannon already in Penzance. It was no use putting those down the mine; they have to be where they're wanted on the day we strike. I wasn't happy about that,' Ninian admitted. 'The damned things had to be brought into the town much too openly. But opinion there is fairly solid against Parliament. Even some of the Puritan families are tired of the taxes.'

'I shall miss you every day that you are gone.'

'Take care of yourself. Eat well, take the air.'

'Yes, I will. I still cannot eat beef,' said Parvati, 'but I will eat mutton and bacon. And I will walk.'

'Take the dogs out on the headland. You're fond of them now.'

'Yes, although they don't mind me as they do you.'

'They'll come to no harm and they'll guard you. Go to Polmawgan only to church, with the rest of the household, and even on the headland, always have Kitty with you.'

'Kitty will not like that,' said Parvati, trying to laugh. 'She is lazy; she dislikes walking.'

'She'll be company, nevertheless. She seems good-natured. I don't want you to be lonely and I do want you to be safe.'

'You are the one who is going into danger. God be with you,' said Parvati.

'Dry your eyes, Mary, quickly!' said Tamzin, fiercely scrubbing at her own with a handkerchief. 'Never mind what I should or shouldn't have told you. Listen! That's Prudence downstairs!'

'Oh no, not Prudence now!'

'Sit down and do some mending,' said Tamzin, setting the example. 'Look ordinary!'

Their everlasting mending was to hand, as usual. Mary did as she was bid. Her hands shook. The door was flung open and Prudence Jenken, stately in her black stuff dress and her head-dress and collar of virtuously sparkling white, stood on the threshold. Tamzin rose with words of polite welcome, but was cut short.

'I have come to bring you tidings,' said Prudence. 'The evil plot laid by the Royalists and Papists to overthrow the godly rule of Parliament in Penwith has been foiled!' She threw back her head, enjoying the drama of the moment. 'Your husbands were in it: oh yes, all is known!'

Mary opened her mouth and then, wisely, shut it again. Tamzin said coldly: 'My dear Prudence, you're posturing like a play-actor. What on earth are you talking about?'

'I'm no play-actor. You don't know what I'm talking about? Really? There was a Royalist riot in Helston last night,' said Prudence. 'That's news to you, is it? And you had no idea that your husbands are with a party of insurgents? Christopher has been seen with Francis Trevelyan, who is a wanted man, and Mayor Grosse, a known Royalist, outside Penzance with a gang of armed men. But it has been known for weeks that the plot existed. Reinforcements for Parliament are on their way from Devonshire. Get to your knees and ask for the mercy of God for yourselves and your men, for there will be little enough mercy from us!'

Black skirts swirled and she was gone. Mary's face was ashen. 'They know! They know all about it! Oh, Tamzin, what are we to do? And why did Prudence come here like that?'

Tamzin's hands were clenching and unclenching on the napkin she had been darning. 'Why did she come? To crow, of course. She is full of smug malice. As for what we are to do . . . I suggest,' said Tamzin, 'that we set about looking as stupid, terrified and innocent as we can. That way we may ward off retribution and retain some freedom of action. We must make Beresford-Higham despise us as negligible. Then if our husbands contact us for help, we shall have a better chance of giving it.'

'Give them *help*?' Mary cried. 'My husband neglects me and neglects me, year after year, takes my jewels to pay for his plots and gives me nothing in return, and you think I would risk my life to help him? Or . . . do you mean we might have to flee into exile with them? Oh, *no*! I couldn't!'

'I could,' said Tamzin.

Chapter Eleven

Penzance

'Betrayed.' Francis's voice was bitter. 'That presumably, is why our supporters in Helston went on the rampage too soon. They'd heard something. We've lost good men through that. Not that it'll make much difference in the end. There's an army on the way from Devon and we've no *time*.'

'I intend trying to seek a parley,' Grosse said. 'If it's fixed for a few days ahead, it'll give us a breathing space. Meanwhile, we can still make a bid to take Penzance. Do that, and we'll have a chance still. Otherwise,' said Grosse in a growl, 'we can kiss goodbye to Pendennis Castle and the Mount. If I knew who betrayed us . . .'

'The cannon are there. They need only to be positioned,' said Keigwin.

'Aye. Turn back now and we do be done for,' Darracott agreed. 'Press on and we've a chance yet.'

Ninian shifted uneasily, his leg aching because his foot had been too long in the stirrup. He had just arrived, and hadn't dismounted since he left Polmawgan. Relieved of the burden of Hannah's pension, he had been able to buy a good horse; his new blue-roan mare Venus was easy of pace and sweet of temper. But nothing, now, made riding pleasant.

Least of all when he was riding off to an enterprise which endangered both his wife and his home. Only now was he fully aware of how badly he wanted to go on living in peace, not only with Parvati, but at Polmawgan.

He ran an eye over the men who had collected on the road leading towards Penzance. They included tenants from Polmawgan and Rosnance and Coombe; others attached to Keigwin and Grosse and Tresilian, the broad-spoken and weatherbeaten captain from Land's End; and a dozen men from the household of Captain Martin Maddern, who came from Penzance itself. Jane Dewey's husband Peter was here with two of his sons, and there were a number of other fishermen, farmers and miners. Most were on foot although all were now well armed with the pikes and muskets and ammunition which had been fetched from the mine the night before. But a whole cartload still remained undistributed. This otherwise promising array had one serious drawback.

'There are only two hundred of us,' said Ninian grimly. 'I've been doing a head count. What good are all those weapons if we haven't got the men to use them?'

It was the 17th of May, fresh spring weather. There was a thin haze over the hills inland but otherwise the visibility was good and they could keep watch on their surroundings. The road stretched away north and south and but for themselves, appeared empty. Below them was the town and beyond it the flat, sparkling expanse of Mount's Bay, also empty. St Michael's Mount, conical and lonely, crowned with battlements, looked as always slightly unreal, as if it ought to house a bewitched princess or a treasure-hoarding ogre. It was actually in Parliamentary hands and contained a highly dangerous garrison.

Well to the north was Helston, where somebody, last night, had got excited and started the insurrection too soon and beyond Helston, lost now behind that drifting haze, were the cliffs of the Lizard, and beyond that was Pendennis Castle, also in enemy hands. Sir John Arundell, who had once held Pendennis and in this rising had claimed the responsibility of seizing it back, had not come.

'We will still enter Penzance,' said Grosse. 'I trust to find more supporters there.'

'You will,' affirmed Maddern.

'I hope so, because we've precious little option. What else can we do? Tell these good fellows here that it was all a mistake; some other time, maybe; for now, kindly pack up and go apologetically home? You said something, Keigwin?'

'My library of plays and verse,' said Keigwin, 'is already packed and stowed in a boat at Mousehole. I can always unpack it if we win, of course.' He touched spurs to his horse. 'Forward to Penzance!'

Ninian already knew, they all knew, that the enterprise was doomed. He rode, in his painful fashion, into Penzance and along its upper street, high above the shoreline, looking at the familiar houses, at the shops and booths and the gleam of the sea visible every now and then between the buildings, with affection and regret and no hope at all.

But the inhabitants of Penzance were more sanguine. Maddern was right. People came to their doors and leaned from their windows to shout encouragement and men can running out to join them. More awaited them in the little market square. They drew rein and Grosse ran a dourly efficient eye over the assembly.

'About three hundred, at a rough estimate,' he commented. 'Some armed, some not. Keigwin, bring up that cart. Now then!' He rose in his stirrups. 'Welcome, good men of Penzance! This day with God's help, we shall prevail and turn back the tide of the Roundheads.' Someone in the crowd inquired: 'Like bloody Canute?' but was peremptorily shushed by his neighbours. 'Those who have weapons, to my right, over there! Those without, to the left. Form a line. Those who can handle a musket, take one pace forward. Weapons will be issued. Whitmead! St Asaph!' Ninian and Christopher rode forward. 'You can see to the cannon emplacements. Take what men you want.' Grosse gestured to the recruits who had marched in with them. 'St Asaph, attend to the overland approaches: Whitmead, take charge of the shoreline from Marazion and join St Asaph when it's done.'

Ninian found himself dismounting, beckoning a boy to take Venus and find her a stable, gathering some helpers and making for the harbour.

An attack on Penzance could come from any of five directions, the most probable being along the main road which led to Devon. But a crafty commander might also lead his men across country from the other side of the peninsula, and into Penzance through the tracks and lanes over the hills; or bypass his objective, double back and arrive from the direction of Land's End. Or the enemy could approach by sea, or round Mount's Bay on the lower coastal land from Helston, via Marazion.

The cannon already set up to guard against pirates pointed out into the bay. Clearly they could also be used to defend the shoreline but the town's prospective defenders had quickly seen that if an assault came from both the sea and the shore at once, they would need extra artillery. It had been provided, but the extra guns had been hidden for the time being, albeit close by, in one of the fish cellars belonging to Ninian's old friend Alderman Roger Polkinghorne.

Ninian now discovered that close by did not necessarily mean convenient. Because of the steep rise of the land round the harbour, the guns had had to be hauled to their hiding place on carts; now they must be manhandled out and then rolled downhill again, carefully, using chocks and ropes to keep them from running away. Also, all the local men hadn't gathered in the market square. Some of them were down at the harbour, raising objections.

'I'm not against getting rid of they damned Roundheads but I don't want cannonballs scuttling my ship just the same,' said one indignant fisherman. 'Nor do any of us. Look where we'm anchored! Sink us two at a time, you could, if you don't turn them cannon mouths away a bit.'

'The cannon have to face that way and the shot will go far over the top of your boats,' snapped Ninian. 'Shift the boats if you're still worried!'

'I'm glad to see the back of those,' said Polkinghorne later, as he and Ninian stood in the fish cellar to watch the last two guns being dragged from behind a row of pilchard barrels and hauled up the ramp down which fish carts usually rumbled for unloading in situ. 'They're taking up good barrel space. It's bad enough being nearly taxed out of business, without half my premises being requisitioned for guns.'

'You'll be grateful once the Roundheads are out of power. We'll get rid of the taxes,' said Ninian.

Polkinghorne's codfish mouth opened in a sudden grin. 'That'll be a happy day.' The grin disappeared. 'But we've yet to win it.'

Ninian, moving to give orders as a rope slipped and a gun carriage swung sideways to jam against the edge of the cellar door, pretended not to hear.

He saw the last cannon but one brought into the street and watched as it was taken tenderly down the hill and placed at the edge of the harbour. These guns would ensure that they had enough artillery on the coastal side of the town, but was there enough to guard the landward approaches against a determined assault? That too could come from several directions. Would there be time to shift the harbour cannon? Would it help to keep the last gun up here as a reserve, to be taken wherever it was required? But he had had no orders to that effect.

'All right,' he said as his men came back up the hill. 'Take the last one down.'

He wished he knew more of military matters. He had, quite simply, never been interested in them. Swordplay he liked because he had once been good at it, but his knowledge of guns was sketchy. He knew how to use a musket but would rather not, and would all his life recall with loathing, that monstrous moment at Braddock Down, when he had seen foot-soldiers hit by cannon fire and been showered by dismembered limbs and a spray of blood.

At which moment, another rope slipped and the gun, veering, pulled its other cable free of the hands trying to hold it, and trundled off downhill by itself. Ninian shouted and the men who had been steering it gave chase. He watched them nearly catch up, saw the gun, as if coy or else possessed of a diabolical sense of humour, gather speed just as they were grabbing for the rope which still trailed behind. Once more, it escaped them. It hurtled down on its brother cannon at the harbour's edge. Some of his men were there, along with some onlookers. He saw them scatter in fright. The runaway gun collided with the standing cannon with a crash of iron on iron which sent sparks into the air. A cannon muzzle reared up, outlined against the bright sea, and then both the guns on their wheeled carriages toppled over the edge with a noisy splash and a burst of white spray.

Later in the morning, with a heavy heart, he made his way back towards the market square to make his report to Thomas Grosse. The cannon had been hauled out of the water, but they were not only saturated, they had landed on rocks and been damaged. Unwillingly, he must go in person to report the catastrophe and see if at least one more gun could be found from somewhere. He hadn't, Ninian thought dismally, precisely covered himself in glory today.

Although he would feel worse about it if he thought it mattered. It didn't, not really. It would make no difference if they had cannon enough to make a continuous wall all round Penzance. It was men they needed, support from outside as well as in, a movement in the spirit of the whole county of Cornwall or better still in the whole land of England, and more than that: training, a fighting force which in the hands of experienced leaders could be wielded like a weapon.

They had neither. There was no general mood towards a rising and the enemy now advancing on them from Devon was professional and highly trained while they themselves were only amateurs. A couple of cannon in the harbour were neither here nor there. Ninian trudged the last few yards to the market square. Ahead of him he could hear a good deal of noise and vaguely, he wondered why.

Then he rounded the last corner, and saw.

In Polmawgan, Polly Hawkes and her sister-in-law Betsy technically lived in adjacent cottages but neither they nor their menfolk thought of it that way. They washed clothes together, sat together to do their mending, cooked together as often as not. Most often, they did these things in Betsy's cottage, because it pleased Marge Hawkes, who had lived there now for over a year, ever since Wally and his boat were lost in a storm.

Rheumatism and stoutness had crippled Marge of late years, so that she could go out very little and had to sleep downstairs because she couldn't climb the staircase. But she had kept her essential tough-mindedness and when the plague struck it was Marge who looked after Betsy and hobbled painfully across the street to nurse Peg and her baby. 'It don't matter if it takes me; I'm a right useless hulk.' It hadn't taken her, but it took Peg and the baby, and this, coming so soon after her husband's death at sea, had done her harm. She had pulled Betsy through, but it wasn't enough.

During the long hours of watching by the bedsides, she had occupied herself in her usual way with knitting, going slowly because of her swollen finger-joints, but managing. But after the crisis, her fingers suddenly seized up altogether and nowadays, although she still insisted on being helped out of bed every morning, she did little but sit by the hearth. She grumbled a good deal and so did Betsy and Polly, for the business of feeding her and helping her from chair to bed to privy meant such a burden of extra work.

But it still came as a shock when, after going out to the well for water and a nice gossip with the other women, they came back full of the exciting news that there was a rising on the brew, and found no one to tell. Marge was still sitting where they had left her, propped among her cushions, but she had lurched sideways, her head flopping over at a horrible, coy angle. Her eyes seemed to be staring at them, but their gaze was blank.

'She'm dead,' Betsy whispered.

'Where are the children? Playing at the back, with their friends, b'ain't they? Best make sure they don't come in till we've got her tidy,' Polly said. 'She'm not a fitty sight for little ones. Lord save us.' Her voice was awed. 'She do scare me, staring like that. Like as if she saw the angel of death coming for her.'

'I feel that shaken.' Betsy, whose own tendency to stoutness sometimes made her short of breath, sat down suddenly on a stool. Her face had gone very white. 'She looks that awful. I feel faint.'

Polly went hurriedly to the ale cask in the corner and drew a mug for each of them. 'This'll put heart into us. We've got to get her laid out decent, and quickly. You know, it's maybe not that surprising. She went downhill after we lost Peg, there's no doubt about it.'

Betsy gulped the ale, regaining a little colour. 'There's been no luck hereabouts since that foreigner come to Polmawgan,' she said angrily. Her lips folded into a grim knowingness and her eyes bulged at Polly, who had drained her mug and was pulling the patchwork quilt off Marge's bed. 'Just nothing but trouble. Father-in-law dying, and Peg and her boy and now Marge.'

'You might be right,' Polly said. 'But meanwhile, we've to see to this. We can put this quilt over her. You feeling better yet?'

'Yes. No good giving way, I suppose.' Betsy put her mug on the floor and came to Polly's aid. Marge continued to be an unpleasant sight, but blaming it on somebody else made one feel better. 'How're we to do it? If you can take her feet . . .'

They lifted Marge's sagging weight between them and staggered to the bed with her. Polly, trying not to shudder, closed the staring eyes and put the coverlet over the body, hiding the face.

'We'd better take the children along to Mrs Veale or Mrs Goble for a while,' she said. 'Until we're finished.'

They went out through the back door. It gave on to the grassy bank at the foot of the hill, where the village children customarily played. Their three were there, along with several others. They were sitting in a semi-circle in the sunshine and listening to a story.

'Ooh!' said Polly in outraged tones.

The story-teller, squatting among them with a grey-muzzled dog on either side, was that Mrs Whitmead, the foreigner from the big house. Her maid Kitty, who was sitting on the grass beside her, was the first to see the approaching women, and interrupted her mistress, pointing. Parvati broke off and stood up, looking nervous.

'What's all this?' demanded Betsy, marching forward.

The dogs were on their feet too, and one of them was growling. Parvati gentled them both. 'Betsy . . . Polly . . .'

'I thought we made it clear,' said Polly, 'that we'd as soon you left our babbies alone.'

'I'm . . . I'm sorry.' The lilting foreign intonation was always more noticeable when Parvati was flurried. 'I took the dogs walking. My husband asked me to. But they wouldn't come back when I called and I came after them. They led me down here. And I saw the children and . . . I meant no harm. I was only telling them a story.'

'She was telling we as how she come to Cornwall on a big ship and it sank and she come ashore on a bit of wood,' said one of the older children. There was eager assent from the others. Boats and the sea were part of their world and all the Polmawgan children were enthralled by tales about them.

'Came to Cornwall on a broomstick, more like!' snapped Betsy and then, her eyes popping with a new idea: 'Did you look into our house, Mrs Whitmead? Did you?'

'What? Why, no, I . . . no, I wouldn't do that. You would not wish it and so . . .'

She was telling the truth and did not understand the note of accusation in Betsy's voice, but it frightened her. She stammered and to Betsy and Polly it sounded like guilt.

'Yes, you did!' shouted Betsy. 'You must've. You looked in our cottage and saw my mam sitting there and you put your evil eye on her. She's dead! We've just found her dead! Found her set in her chair and her head all sideways and her eyes all staring, we did. God, oh God, I won't never forget it, I won't never sleep again, I'll see her eyes in my dreams, I will! She comes down here and people die, that's what it is! Witch! Witch! Get away from us!' She raised her right hand with little finger and forefinger extended and pointed it at Parvati. 'Get away!'

'But she was tellin' us a story!' protested the small boy who had spoken up the first time. Betsy rounded on him.

'You don't want no tales from the likes of her. She'm a witch, she is. She'll make you look at her and look at her and she'll look back at you and then you'll die.'

'They won't die! I'd never harm anyone. I made Mr St Asaph better when he lost his arm!' Parvati cried. 'I saved him when the physician could not!'

Other women had come up, drawn by the sound of raised voices. They were catching their children to them. 'And how'd you do that, except by the black arts?' one of them shouted. 'How'd you know better than a doctor?'

'That be how witches work,' said another, knowingly. 'They do heal when they want to, to get people into their power and on their side.'

'That's right, Mrs Veale, that's right. Witch! Get away from here! Go!' shrieked Betsy. She snatched up a big stone and hurled it at Parvati. It struck her in the stomach and she doubled up with a cry. Some of the children, forgetting the interrupted story and excited by the shouting, joined in with more stones. So did several of the women, including Polly. The dogs, although not attached to Parvati as they were to Ninian, nevertheless recognised that one of their own human beings was under attack and ran at the women, barking and baring their teeth. But they met a hail of stones and fled yelping back to Parvati's side. Parvati herself reeled back, one arm over her head and the other across her stomach.

Kitty, who had been standing open-mouthed, as if paralysed, caught at Parvati's arm and they both ran, Parvati half-doubled over and Kitty hurrying her on, steadying her when she stumbled. The dogs had already fled ahead of them. The women chased them for a little way, still hurling stones and clods. A lump of earth, fortunately not solid, struck the back of Kitty's head and she sobbed and rushed them on faster. Their pursuers, satisfied with their departure, fell back, jeering triumphantly.

'Oh, madam, Mrs Whitmead, we shouldn't have come. Oh, do hurry!' Kitty gasped.

'I can't . . . go any faster.' They reached the cliff path and began to climb, but Parvati, her forearm still across her abdomen, stumbled again and again. A few yards short of the top she stopped, and collapsed against a granite outcrop. 'I feel so queer. Kitty! What are you staring at?'

Kitty's face was aghast. She was pointing. Parvati looked down. The grass at her feet and the base of the granite outcrop were crimson. She was standing in a pool of blood.

Eliza did not think very much of Kitty, whose big brown eyes were too bovine for her liking, and who didn't, in Eliza's opinion, work nearly hard enough. Nevertheless, Kitty supported her mistress bravely over the last short distance into the house, and her shouts for help at least had the effect of bringing Eliza at a run. Eliza took one look at the state Parvati was in, swept them all into the parlour, threw a cloth over the sofa, and snapped: 'Quick, get her lying down here. She's never just come on. Not like that! What's happened?'

'The women in the village stoned her! They *stoned* her!'

'Stoned her? And injured her? Mrs Whitmead, where are you hurt?'

'A stone hit me in the stomach. I'm three months gone,' said Parvati faintly. 'I didn't want to say till I was sure and then by the time I was, my husband was planning to go to war. I didn't want to tell him in case it pulled at him, took his mind off fighting. But now . . . what's happening to me? Am I losing it?'

'Looks like it,' said Eliza grimly.

She and Kitty did their best, but Kitty was young and Eliza childless and they had not had enough experience.

'We need help,' Eliza said urgently to Dick. 'I can't take the responsibility. You'd best ride to Rosnance. Mrs Tamzin St Asaph do be there and she knows about these things. Tell her Mrs Whitmead's miscarried and she's bleeding too much. Tell her to hurry.'

A trial was in progress in the market square of Penzance and the defendant, who stood with his accusers on a cart, in lieu of a platform, was Anthony Gubbes.

Friendships might fade and friends be torn apart by differing allegiances, but Ninian had no sooner understood who the prisoner was, than he was thrusting his way purposefully and instinctively to Anthony's aid.

Alice Gubbes came struggling through the crowd to meet him, her children following her. She was obliged to struggle because few would move aside for her and some of them even jostled the children. The two eldest, boys of fifteen and thirteen, jostled angrily back and exchanged insults. Alice's carefully maintained composure had gone. She caught at Ninian's arm. 'They're going to hang Anthony! They say he brought the enemy down on us. But he's honest and decent, you know he is; he did what he thought was right . . . Can't you do anything? Please!'

'All right. All right.' Ninian thrust at backs and shoulders, forcing a way through. Alice and her family turned round and came with him. Someone had climbed on to the cart with a coil of rope and an argument had apparently broken out about what, if they were going to hang Anthony Gubbes, they proposed to hang him from. Grosse and Maddern and Tresilian were there, grim-faced, and Darracott, with a forefinger keeping a place in what looked like a prayerbook. Francis was beside him. When Ninian reached the cart, Francis was essaying a protest.

'. . . this is not a properly constituted court. We should be sitting in a courtroom, with a jury, and if the jury decides it's a hanging matter, it should go to Launceston Assizes . . .'

'What good's the Assizes?' demanded Grosse. 'The law's in the Roundheads' pockets! As for courtrooms, we're holding the trial out here so that all passers-by can hear the charge and know it's just! Can't be more correct than that!'

'I second that,' said Maddern. He had hard features at the best of times. Now they were implacable.

The foot of the cart was guarded by a row of pikemen. 'Let me through!' said Ninian urgently to the man who was presenting a pikehead to his chest. 'Damn you, I've got to get up there!' The pike didn't waver and its owner didn't reply. On the cart, Francis was appealing to the minister.

'Darracott! You're a man of God. Say something, can't you?'

'I'm a man of God, Francis, but what this here man's done 'ud condemn him in the eyes of most honest men. I've been asked to give him counsel on the eve of eternity . . .'

'I don't want your counsel,' said Anthony loudly.

'. . . but I b'ain't got any quarrel with the judgement,' finished Darracott.

'Right! Let's go through it again!' Grosse shouted. 'Let's ask the good people of Penzance to judge. Hear me, fellow-townsmen! This man stands accused of sending warning of our plans to the enemy. His eldest son is with them now! We say that his goods and his life are forfeit! What say you?'

There was a chorus of agreement. Anthony stood still, his face paler than usual, but held his head up. He made no further attempt at speech. Ninian said: 'In God's name, *let me through*!' and was once more ignored.

'Tie a noose in that rope!' shouted Grosse. 'Any tree will do.' He caught sight of Alice and the children. 'And someone get that woman and the young ones away from here.'

Given warning to the enemy. Oh no, Ninian thought. Typical Anthony: solid, law-abiding, following his Puritan conscience, putting God first. If all his friends had been dragged away to traitors' deaths, he'd have grieved for them sincerely and no doubt prayed for them. He deserved to hang!

But it was *Anthony*. It was his own boyhood, being threatened with oblivion on the end of a rope. And what *about* Alice and her family? One of the children, held in the arms of an older sister, was scarcely two.

Judging by the way Francis was glancing from Anthony to the Gubbes family below, his mind was working along similar lines. Suddenly he raised his voice. 'Mayor Grosse!'

Grosse turned to him. 'What is it, Trevelyan?'

'I wish to make a suggestion. You say we're going to seize Gubbes' goods, but if the Roundheads win Penzance, they won't be much use to us. We haven't time to turn them into cash. But some cash in the hand could be very useful; something to take with us to the Prince if we have to run for it. I daresay the Gubbes' gold and silver are well hidden but why not offer him his life in exchange for three hundred pounds in coins?'

141

Anthony was once more roused to speech. 'Not one penny will I give to a Papist cause! Not even to save my life!'

'Oh, be quiet, you fool! We're not all prepared to throw our old friends to the enemy like bones to hungry mastiffs. Try profiting from my example!' Francis growled it in an undertone, but Ninian, who had now stopped trying to climb on to the cart, because he couldn't in any case think what he would do if he got there, was near enough to hear.

Anthony stiffened and raised his chin and Ninian saw with despair that the mantle of martyrdom had fallen on his old friend. Alice cried Anthony's name and he looked towards her. 'Wife! Worse things have happened to others in the past who would not give up their Protestant faith or betray their principles. Where they led we must be prepared to follow. If I die, go to our son Joseph. He is already sheltering our Joan. He will take you in. If necessary, apply to Cromwell in person for relief.'

Francis raised his eyes heavenwards and with shoulders and hands made an I-give-up gesture. Darracott, his mouth tightening, raised the prayerbook and seemed about to begin reading from it. And Ninian, inspired at last with a practical idea, raised his voice and shouted, as Francis had done, to Mayor Grosse.

'What is it?' Grosse peered down testily. 'Ninian Whitmead? Weren't you placing cannon?'

'Never mind the cannon! There is something I must say to you concerning Gubbes. Will you come down for a moment?'

Grosse complied, if in an irritable fashion. Ninian caught his arm. From the corner of his eye, he could see Alice, her eyes full of a hope which frightened him because he feared to disappoint her.

'Well?' demanded Grosse. 'What have you to say?'

'I have an offer to make,' said Ninian.

He made it in a low voice, not wanting Anthony to hear and intrude with obstinate protests. Grosse's grumpy face lightened with surprise.

'Can you put your hand on three hundred pounds, just like that?'

'Not quite like that. But I own a tin mine worth £70 a year, approximately. I will give the mine to the Royalist cause. The cause can have the income, or else sell the mine outright. Not quite cash in the hand, no, but a healthy addition to Gubbes' goods.'

'Wait there.'

'And don't shout it out to everyone, please.'

'Why not? It might induce Gubbes to pay up after all.'

'I don't particularly want some of our more hotheaded supporters to know that I'm buying a traitor's life. You can tell Gubbes quietly, afterwards,' said Ninian. 'I've known him for a long time, as you're no doubt aware. As Francis says, we don't all desert our old friends. You can rub that into Anthony, with my good will.'

'All right.' Grosse climbed back on to the cart and began a quiet consultation with the others. To Ninian's relief, their faces changed. Tresilian was thoughtful; Maddern appeared to be doing arithmetic on his fingers and arriving at tempting answers. Darracott closed his prayerbook. Francis gave Ninian a questioning look but Ninian nodded vigorously and Francis, turning back to his companions, could be seen urging agreement.

Around Ninian, an argument had broken out, involving both the crowd and Anthony's boys.

'Hang Gubbes and let's be done with it!'

'I don't like this much. He's been a good enough neighbour to me.'

'Bloody good neighbour, I must say! Barefaced treachery, and you call 'un a good neighbour!'

'Look here, we've ourselves to think of. Kill 'un and if so be the Roundheads get into Penzance, someone'll be accused of murder.'

'T'ain't murder; it's an execution. Oh, hush your snivelling, woman!'

'Let my mother alone!'

'Leave her be; she b'ain't accused of nothing. Reckon my own wife'd cry if that were me up there.'

'Bah! Her man's a traitor and these are traitor's spawn and . . . ow, ow! Did 'ee see that? Young limmer kicked me in the shins!'

'I'll kick you somewhere else if you call me traitor's spawn again!'

'Don't, Sampson, don't antagonise them!'

'Here, give the baby a sweetmeat. It be a bit fluffy from my pocket but it do be fresh otherwise . . .'

'Hang Gubbes!'

'Oh, leave off. We go hanging someone outside the law and they Roundheads'll be stringing up a few of us; mark my words.'

The group conferring on the cart were speaking in low voices, but the crowd was not and the last telling point was heard. Ninian, watching, saw the balance tilt. The conference reached a rapid conclusion.

'So be it,' Grosse said. Anthony started, running his tongue round his lips, clearly wondering if this meant life or death. 'Have Gubbes and his family escorted to their home.' He surveyed the crowd while behind him, Anthony closed his eyes and his lips moved, as if in a prayer of gratitude. Then his eyes opened again in surprise, as Grosse announced: 'We need a conveyancing lawyer. Can I have a volunteer?'

The bewildered Anthony was escorted away, with Alice and the younger children clinging to him as though afraid he would suddenly vanish, and the two older boys following, still exchanging insults with the crowd. When they had gone, Grosse came down to talk to Ninian.

'You're a sentimental fool and I'd suspect you of being a Parliament man if I didn't know that boyhood friendship was at the bottom of this.'

'Quite,' said Ninian. And set gloomily about explaining that two of the Royalist cannon had just been raised, much the worse for wear, from the bottom of Penzance harbour.

143

Chapter Twelve

The Homecoming

Parliament was once more in control in Penzance. Grosse and his men had long since been driven back from their cannon emplacements. The cannon themselves were in enemy hands and now as the defeated Royalists fled through the town, there was nothing left to do but hope to get out of Penzance alive.

Dodging as fast as Ninian's limp would let them, through streets hazy and pungent with gunsmoke, Ninian and Francis once again took cover behind a tree from a burst of enemy musket fire. 'Up that lane,' muttered Francis. 'When we can.'

They waited their moment and made another dash. The lane led to a row of shops. They barged through a pie-shop where the owner and a frightened assistant were crouching under the counter; tumbled out of the rear window into a kitchen garden and trampled the cabbages before swarming over a fence into a hideous street, where bodies lay like bundles of bloodstained clothes and reddened puddles were slowly drying to rust-colour. As they slipped through an alley to plunge under a tangle of bushes in somebody's garden, Ninian noticed cynically that the topography of Penzance had undergone a remarkable change.

When he rode into Penzance to go to the market or dine with friends, the things he noticed were the ships in the harbour; the houses whose owners he knew; the shops he patronised; a garden he particularly liked because it was so well kept; trees which gave shade or were especially shapely.

Penzance as a battlefield was a completely different place. A hunted man needed to remember now not only who lived or traded in such and such a street, but also whether it was a trap without side turnings, or offered an escape route. No tree was more beautiful than one which had a big enough trunk to shelter a man's body from musket fire. The garden in which Ninian and Francis were now crouching was not at all well kept but just because of this, its overgrown bushes provided a hiding place. It met a new ideal of loveliness.

They glanced towards the house to which the garden was attached. It was shuttered and silent. The owners might well be shivering inside as the conflict swept to and fro in the town and cannon smoke filtered under their doors. 'I think we've shaken the hunt for the moment,' Ninian whispered.

'Have we? Listen.'

Their dash through the alley had brought them into a street on the south-eastern side of Penzance. The garden opened on to the street which, to the right, led to the open country towards Polmawgan and Land's End. But on their left, it led back into the heart of the town. Somewhere in that direction, was a confused uproar. It was coming nearer.

They edged back, glad of the foliage and the low wall which screened them from the road. The vague racket crystallised into booted feet, running, and shouts from further off. Somebody snapped: 'Over here, quick!' and peering through the leaves, they glimpsed several men vaulting the wall. They glanced at each other and pulled out their daggers. Then Thomas Grosse, his clothes torn and his face smeared with smoke, crashed in on them, and threw himself down beside Francis. 'Oh, put that ironmongery away, you fools. It's us.'

'Us' meant William Keigwin and Christopher St Asaph, who now plunged into the shelter on Grosse's heels. They too sank down, hauling long breaths into their lungs. Christopher's face was scarlet with exertion.

But above them, the branches were quivering, and more booted feet were pounding up the road. 'Can't stop here!' growled Grosse. 'Bloody bushes . . . shaking . . . they'll give us away. There's a way round the side of that house. Come *on!*'

The overgrown bushes had almost choked the way into the narrow gap between this house and its neighbour. They made a dash for it, and fought their way through, to find themselves suddenly out of the undergrowth, and close to a side door into the house. Ninian seized the knob but the door was locked. Behind them, the pursuit had indeed seen the disturbed branches and cries of triumph broke out. Then a voice shouted: 'Thomas Grosse! Can you hear me?'

Ninian raised his head sharply at the sound of the voice but otherwise remained motionless. 'You should have listened to me that day in the mine,' Keigwin remarked. 'We could all have been at home, eating, drinking and making merry.'

'Hold your noise, Keigwin. Swords out!' hissed Grosse. 'Christ, we need guns. I gave you a musket, Ninian. And you, Frank. What the hell have you done with them?'

'I ran out of shot and dropped mine down a well,' said Ninian briefly. 'It was heavy and I find running hard enough, as it is. I'd sooner use a sword, anyhow.'

'I used the butt-end of mine on somebody's helmet and broke it,' whispered Francis. Christopher muttered that he had killed four men already, with the sword in the only hand he'd got.

'Grosse! Keigwin! St Asaph! You may as well come out and surrender!'

They waited, hands clenched hard on swordhilts. Then Christopher, nudging his companions with his one arm, used his chin to indicate the side door. It was opening.

It opened no more than a crack. A clawlike hand emerged, beckoning. One by one, as silently as possible, they crept through and into a dim kitchen. The fire was lit and the room was warm, but the tiny, aged woman who had let them in was huddled in shawls as though this were the depths of January.

'Thank you!' said Francis in a low voice. 'We are grateful. But you are putting yourself at risk for us.'

'My two grandsons died for the King at Bristol. All the family I'd got left, they were. I'll do anything to put they Parliament noses out of joint.' She spluttered when she spoke, because her discoloured teeth were few and widely spaced. She had a nutcracker profile and hairs on her upper lip and a watering eye. But the other was sharp and bright and expressed the utmost contempt for Parliament and all its works. 'I b'ain't 'feared of they. What can they do to me? Over eighty, I am. Bit of rough handling and I'll just die on them. No good standing here chattin'. This way, now.'

Scuttling rapidly ahead of them, she led them through to the back of the house and pointed to some more overgrown garden. 'Through that, quick. There's open hillside going up beyond but where the garden ends, there do be a ditch. You can't hardly see it unless you know it's there. Looks like just a slit. But a man can get into it and you can follow it right out of Penzance. Might be wet, but it's deep; it'll hide you.'

Keigwin seized her mottled hand and kissed it. '*She is kind as she is fair, for beauty lives with kindness.*'

'Get on with it, Keigwin,' said Grosse impatiently, but he too paused to grasp her hand before hastening out of the back door, and so did all the others.

They were only just in time. Musket fire broke out in the front garden and as they fled they heard men thrusting through the bushes at the side, and, right through the depth of the house, a furious hammering on the front door and the sound of breaking glass.

The ditch was certainly hard to see. They found it only because they were looking for it. They slithered down, Christopher coming last. There was water at the bottom but it was only ankle-deep and the grass at the verge was long and met across the channel. If they dropped to all fours, it would close over their heads.

They were barely under cover when they heard their aged rescuer scream. They raised wary heads to peer through the grass stems. Two soldiers were dragging her into the garden, shouting at her and shaking her. Between them, she was like a little, shawl-wrapped doll.

'. . . they were in your house . . . damp footmarks and leaves in your kitchen . . .'

'. . . are you hiding them, you treacherous old witch?'

'No, I b'ain't! Let me go!'

'. . . did they run out this way? Show us where they've gone! Speak up! Do you want to find yourself at the Assizes?'

'. . . you'll burn for treachery and witchcraft, you disgusting old hag.'

'Think I'd live long enough, you sons of whores? Frail as a twig, I be!'

'And you'd burn like a twig, you wicked old besom. You'll last long enough to repent, I'll warrant!'

A fist swung, and there was another scream and another: dreadful

147

proof that death could be too tardy even for the old and fragile. 'Oh, God!' said Grosse, his fingers gripping the edge of the ditch.

'We've got to. We can't leave her to them.' Keigwin was already heaving himself up in order to race, however suicidally, to their benefactress's aid. Francis and Ninian, glancing at each other in despair, were doing the same.

But Christopher, who had been last into the ditch, was the first out of it, bursting back across the garden with his sword raised before the others were out of concealment.

His suddenness took both his friends and the soldiers by surprise, and his attack was over almost as soon as it began. Steel clashed and sparked and more men came racing from the house. One of the soldiers still had hold of the old woman and was fighting with one hand while holding her in front of him as a shield.

It could have been an accident, or perhaps it was not quite an accident but only a swift death given on impulse by Christopher as being better than the Assizes and a witch's end. But a swordstroke took her in the neck and she collapsed in a fountain of blood. An instant later, Christopher too went down.

'God have mercy on him,' Francis whispered. Ninian had closed his eyes and leaned his forehead against the muddy side of the ditch.

'Come,' said Grosse. 'We can do no good here. Quickly.'

It was against all nature just to creep away but they would not bring Christopher or the woman back to life by dying too. They went, crouching and crawling, along the ditch, under the curving grasses. They heard shouts behind them and the sound of musket fire and more bushes being broken down, but the enemy evidently did not realise where Christopher had come from, and did not explore far enough to find the ditch, no doubt dissuaded from it because all they could see beyond the garden was a completely empty grass-grown hillside. As night fell, the fugitives, well clear of the town, crept out of their muddy shelter.

'I'm making for Mousehole,' said Grosse. 'I might steal or borrow a boat there.'

'The enemy may be waiting for you,' said Ninian. Earlier in the day, he had seen Darracott with a crowd of other Royalists ambushed at the harbour and hunted along the quay. From a perilous vantage point crouched in a warehouse doorway, he had seen them driven at swordpoint into the sea. Darracott was gone, drowned with the rest.

'The darkness will help,' said Grosse. 'I'm local. I know the place well. Who's with me?'

'I'll come with you,' said Keigwin.

Ninian said: 'I'm going home if I can. I'll go to Pengelly first and find out if the enemy's been to my house. I fancy he'll know. If they haven't, I'll return and try to look as if I've never left. You've all been identified, but as far as I know, I haven't, except by Anthony and I fancy he won't betray me. Rather ungrateful of him if he does! I want to see my wife and I don't want to end my days in exile if I can help it. Francis?'

'I'm going to the Scillies,' said Francis, 'but not instantly.

Christopher is dead and there's something I have to do about that before I leave. I can't explain now.'

'You'd do better to come with us now, both of you,' Grosse said. 'God knows when we'll all meet again, or where or if. But there's no time to argue. We must go our ways.'

It was also against all nature for those who had been bound together in such warfare, to part without ceremony, but there was no time for ceremony. They embraced and were not ashamed of their wet eyes, and then separated into pairs without further delay, Grosse and Keigwin moving off across the darkening heath towards Mousehole while Ninian and Francis, with great caution, keeping away from the lanes, set out towards Minecombe, slipping along in the shadow of bank and outcrop and gorse clump, while the moon swam up over Mount's Bay and cast a long, silver path on the sea.

They were not only tired but also lightheaded with hunger and they spoke very little, except that once, Ninian said: 'The officer back there, the one who shouted to Grosse and the others to surrender: I recognised his voice.'

'Who was it?' Francis asked.

'My cousin, Ezra Clemo. We never liked each other very much,' said Ninian bitterly. 'But he was at Pen's funeral if you recall; we still thought of each other as members of one family, then.'

They plodded on. Ninian, exhausted, began to feel as if he were walking in a dream. He wondered what had happened to his mare Venus and wished he were riding her now. His bad leg ached and even the stirrup would be more restful than this endless trudging.

Once, looking towards the sea, he thought he saw a ship in the moon-path: a square-rigged vessel, with a crenellated forecastle. Then Francis caught his arm and he realised that he had nearly fallen asleep even while he limped painfully over the tussocky ground.

'There's a light ahead,' said Francis. 'I think it's Pengelly's cottage. Wake up, Ninian! Am I right?'

'Good,' said Tamzin. 'You've finished it all: hot soup to put heart into you and red wine to put the blood back into you. Not that you're losing much now. It's stopping.'

'If only I had not gone to Polmawgan,' Parvati mourned. 'If only Eliza had not told you about those women, and the stoning. I did not want Mrs Trevelyan to know.'

'You keep saying that, Penny. But Mary won't gossip, I promise. I have told her that she must not. I said it would give the Roundheads a weapon against your husband, and would do harm to our cause,' said Tamzin.

'That was clever,' said Parvati weakly. 'But Mrs Trevelyan doesn't approve of me.' Mary had seen the picture of Shiva which had shocked everyone so much and made Ninian so angry. But she mustn't speak of that. She closed her eyes.

'Now, you're not to fret,' said Tamzin. 'Are you comfortable? I'll send up some more linen cloths presently.'

'I can change them myself, now,' said Parvati. 'I have been out of bed. I went to the window.'

'Penny! I told you to stay put, with your feet up.'

'I am none the worse. I heard gunfire. I wanted to know where it came from. But I couldn't tell.'

'We've been hearing those guns all day. I think they're in Penzance; there's a smoke haze over the town. But that's all one can see.'

'There were some boats putting out. I saw those,' said Parvati. 'But there's no news, no word of Ninian. Oh, how I wish he'd come back.'

'He will,' said Tamzin, hoping it was true. 'Penny, you mustn't upset yourself. It's bad for you.'

'But I've lost his baby. What will he say?'

'Oh, *Penny*, you sound as if you put it down somewhere and forgot it! It wasn't your fault and there'll be another time.'

If Ninian came back. If the hatred of the Polmawgan villagers didn't grow into a deadlier threat than a handful of stones. And why did Penny seem so afraid of Mary?

Tamzin knew no answers. She took the dishes away to the kitchen, where Eliza was washing up after breakfast. In the parlour, Mary could be heard trying to teach Charles his alphabet. Tamzin hadn't particularly wanted her to come to Polmawgan too but Mary, who did not like Tamzin much but also clung to her because she was the stronger character, had refused to stay behind. 'I'll be so alone. Captain Beresford-Higham and his men have gone to Helston and I'd feel safer if they were still here. Anything could happen. There could be fugitives breaking in and I'll be so frightened.'

'Well, you'd better make yourself useful, then,' said Tamzin.

Mary's attempts at usefulness were being less than successful by the sound of it, although it might not be all Mary's fault. Charles was approaching his sixth birthday and had discovered that he possessed a forceful personality. Parvati, when well, petted him atrociously and in his hearing referred to 'my son' in tones which would have made it plain to a much more stupid child than Charles that she thought him something very, very special.

The results were now becoming all too plain. Tamzin flinched as Ninian's son and heir let out a loud screech and demanded to go outside and play.

'It's time Ninian got a tutor for that boy,' she said.

'I'd agree with 'ee there. A man's hand, that's what he needs, and a firm one,' said Eliza. 'His father's too mild and Dick and Jimmy Tonkin b'ain't tutors, for all they've done what they can. How is the mistress today?'

'Much better. You didn't need me, you know. Nature has done most of it.'

'Maybe, but I said at the time, I felt that responsible. I was right glad to see 'ee and Mrs Trevelyan the other day. Can 'ee stay on a bit? She'll start fretting herself again soon if there's no word from the master.'

'She's fretting now.' Tamzin decided not to comment on the fact that however glad Eliza might be to see Mrs Trevelyan, Parvati didn't share these feelings. 'Let me wipe those dishes. Kitty ought to sit with her this morning. She could take up some fresh linen. Where *is* Kitty?'

Eliza let out a snort. 'In the parlour along of Mrs Trevelyan and the boy. She'm mending a hem for Mrs Trevelyan.'

'Oh, is she, indeed? She's Mrs Whitmead's maid now, not Mrs Trevelyan's. I'll have a word with her about that,' said Tamzin. She paused, listening. 'There's no gunfire this morning. Oh, if only we knew what was happening!'

The tapping on the kitchen door a few moments later made them both jump. Opening it, Tamzin found a skinny boy of about thirteen outside. 'Hullo. Who are you?'

'I'm Dan Pengelly but everyone calls me Tom Pengelly's nephew, 'cause everyone knows who Tom Pengelly is.'

'Pengelly!' Tamzin was alert. 'Have you a message from . . . your uncle?'

The boy edged into the kitchen, peering suspiciously round it. 'You b'ain't Mrs Whitmead. I've seen her.'

'I'm Tamzin St Asaph. I'm looking after Mrs Whitmead. She's ill and can't leave her bed.'

'She'm all right, Dan,' said Eliza. 'You can trust Mrs St Asaph.'

Dan nodded. 'Any of they Roundheads here yet?'

'No, Dan,' Tamzin said. 'No one's been here.'

'Because Mr Whitmead, he wants to know if it's safe to come back to the house. They Roundheads have got Penzance but Mr Whitmead's all right. He'm in the mine,' said Dan.

'In Wheal Susannah? And safe?' cried Eliza.

'Yes 'm.'

'Oh, run, Dan!' Tamzin cried. 'Bring him, *quickly*! Mrs Whitmead will be so glad to see him!'

'There's one thing more,' said Dan. 'Mr Francis Trevelyan, he'm in the mine too.' From the depths of his dirty jacket, he produced a folded sheet of paper. 'They thought to put writing things in the mine as well as food,' he said in an awed voice. 'If you'm Mrs St Asaph, this is for you. He said to give it to you only and not in Mrs Trevelyan's hearing. Thought I'd have to go to Rosnance with it, I did. Well, you're here and I see Mrs Trevelyan ain't, so . . .'

'She's in this house,' said Tamzin, taking the letter from him. 'She has a nervous nature. I daresay, Eliza, that it contains a message for her, which I am to deliver soothingly.'

'Then you'd better have a calming posset first,' said Eliza shrewdly. 'Your hands are shaking.'

'I lost the baby. It was three months, and I lost it.' Parvati clung to Ninian's hand as though afraid that he would vanish again if she let go, but her head was turned away from him. 'I went to Polmawgan and they stoned me. I didn't mean to go, but the dogs ran away and I had to follow them and then I saw the children and stopped to talk to them . . .'

'Hush, hush. Tamzin has explained it all to me.'

151

'Tamzin has cared for me so well,' said Parvati. 'But I have failed you. No baby, and now we have Mrs Trevelyan in the house and you can't want that. You must be so angry.'

Ninian took hold of her chin and turned her face towards him. 'Mary Trevelyan will soon go home. I'm not angry, except with those silly women. Too foolish to know they're foolish, that's their trouble. They are responsible for this, not you. I shall have words with Joseph Davies over this. He has encouraged their nonsense.'

Parvati, it was clear, hardly dared to believe in his forgiveness but she let herself be comforted against his shoulder. 'I am glad to see you home. I have been so frightened for you. We could hear the guns but we did not know what was happening. I do not care that Penzance is lost, if you are safe.'

'Well, I hope I'm safe. I think I can get away with pretending I haven't left home. The only alternative would be for us to flee abroad and we couldn't do that until you've recovered, anyway. I'm gambling on being able to stay. When Dan Pengelly said that no Roundheads had been here yet, I told Francis he could take the *Silver Fish*. He's got to get away, although why he's waiting until tomorrow, I can't think. He's still hiding in the mine, with some mysterious errand to perform before he goes. Listen, Parvati. I must speak to Tamzin again. I will get Kitty to sit here until I come back but I must go to Tamzin because I have some dreadful news to break to her.'

Parvati's dark eyes widened. 'Her husband?'

'I'm afraid so.'

'Oh, poor Tamzin. Poor Tamzin. Let me get up and come with you. She helped me; I will help her now if I can.'

'No, stay there and rest.' Ninian pushed her gently back. 'I saw him die. I will attend to it.'

'I should have told you at once,' said Ninian. 'But . . .'

'You had very little chance.' Tamzin brushed the tears from her eyes. 'There was all the confusion about Penny. And besides: I already knew.'

'You knew? But how?'

'Dan brought me a note from Francis.'

'Good God. So that's what he was scribbling by candle-light last night in the mine. I thought it was a letter for Mary. Tamzin, I'm so very sorry. Your husband: my friend. I can't think of anything comforting to say except that he died very bravely, and it was quick. I am not lying about that, I promise.'

'I am thankful that it was quick. He had suffered so much. If I seem too calm, Ninian, shedding only these few tears, well, Christopher has been far away from me in spirit for years, ever since he lost his arm. He doesn't seem so very much further, even now. He said to me, more than once, that he was tired of living. I lost him long before this.'

'I am more sorry than ever,' said Ninian. 'I wish with all my heart that he and Francis could be escaping together tomorrow. I've told Francis to take the *Fish*. He'll set off at dawn tomorrow, as soon as it's

152

light enough to see the rocks. For some reason he wouldn't leave today. I hope to God he doesn't run into any more danger.'

'It was rash of you to give him your boat. What if you need it?' said Tamzin. She added: 'His note says he's going to the Scillies.'

'Yes,' said Ninian. He was puzzled. Something was obscurely wrong with this conversation. Tamzin should be talking about Christopher, not Francis. 'I hope he has fair weather,' he said. 'The *Fish* isn't very big. That's really why I'm letting Francis take her. If Penny and I do have to get away, I'd sooner we did it on a bigger vessel. I daresay I could always steal one from Polmawgan. Penny doesn't like the sea anyway, and I married her to protect her, not to put her at risk. Tamzin, why did Frank write to you, and not to Mary?'

Tamzin sat in the window-seat of the parlour, hands now quietly folded. 'Francis has his reasons for everything he does, Ninian. In fact, there was a message for Mary in his note. He instructed me to tell her that he had sailed already. He thought we were both at Rosnance, of course. It's lucky that you haven't let out to her that Francis is still in Cornwall. I think, in fact, that you should give her his message. It would come more naturally from you, since she's here in your house and you have just left him.'

'He wants us to lie to Mary? But why?'

'I think we should just do as he asks.'

Ninian studied her, more puzzled than ever. Her tears had vanished; she was quite serene; indeed, her face was almost happy. There she was: Tamzin, the girl he had once longed to marry. She was still beautiful, with that entrancing smile and those steady eyes, but although her face was familiar, the Tamzin behind it had become a stranger. What had her life with Christopher been like? And what was she thinking now?

'Tamzin,' he said, 'what is going on? I don't wish to pry but . . .'

She shook her head. 'Leave it, Ninian. You will understand soon. Listen to me instead. In my opinion, even though the *Fish* is so small, I think you would be wise to take your wife away now. She is fit to travel in an emergency. You should accompany Francis. Because of the stoning if not because of the Roundheads. I would do whatever was necessary to help you. I mean . . . even if . . .' She broke off short.

'Those fools of women!' said Ninian.

'Fools can be dangerous. By the bye, Mary knows about the stoning and for some reason Penny is very worried about that. Do you know why?'

Ninian hesitated. 'There was an occasion when Mary showed that she didn't understand that to be brought up in a heathen land is one thing and being a witch is another. That's all.'

'Mary is a fool too at times,' said Tamzin briskly. 'I should know – I've been living at Rosnance with her! Ninian, whether or not you manage to convince the Roundheads that you've never left Polmawgan, I think you and Penny should go to the Scillies, if not with Francis, then soon.'

'Stop trying to slide out of that door, Kitty my girl, and put Mrs

Whitmead's napkins to boil, will 'ee? And there's no need to look as sour as a wig over it, neither. I need a bit of help and I won't get it from the ladies, that's plain, what with Mrs St Asaph shutting herself in her room and Mrs Trevelyan pining in the parlour. All right, so her husband's gone out of the country and not written a line to her, but I'm still run off my feet. It's a good thing I'm still spry. I'd like a hand with the pastry as well, *if* you can find the time, my girl.'

'I'm doing my best, Mrs Branson. But Mrs Trevelyan keeps wanting me to stitch this and patch that for her and . . .'

'You'm Mrs Whitmead's maid, not Mrs Trevelyan's. You just tell her no and get on with your proper work.'

'All right,' said Kitty, brightening somewhat.

It was in fact the first time anyone had ever recommended her to say no to a job of work. Even when she got the place with Mrs Trevelyan, who had told her that all her tasks would be light, they had nevertheless come in a ceaseless procession like the drips from a leaky barrel. 'Oh, my cloak needs brushing, Kitty. Will you see to it?' 'Kitty, can you stitch up the seam in my cream dress?' 'Kitty, would you fetch my workbox . . . my fan . . . a posset . . .' It was what she was paid for, but it was still maddening.

She'd been both angry and distressed when Captain Beresford-Higham sent her away from Rosnance, but it was true, what the Captain said. Mary could easily have done all Kitty's jobs herself. In fact, for Kitty, it had worked out well in the end. Tamzin St Asaph had given her a note to bring to Polmawgan, and Mrs Whitmead took her on. Mrs Whitmead was a bit odd, being a foreigner, but she was kind enough and it had been an easy place until the trouble with those bitches down in the village and the arrival of Mrs Trevelyan along with Mrs St Asaph.

She'd been glad to see Tamzin, but why had Mrs Trevelyan had to come too? It was awful now, what with the work she had to do for her sick mistress and Mary Trevelyan behaving as if Kitty were still working for her, and driving her mad with her non-stop stream of odd jobs . . .

Mary was now waiting for her to come and repair a chemise. Emboldened by Eliza's orders, Kitty took her time over taking Parvati's stained cloths out of their cold salt-water soak and putting them to boil clean, before going to the parlour to say that she couldn't do the chemise just now and enjoying Mary's affronted expression. She was crossing the hall on the way back when there came a commanding knock at the front door. Being handy, she opened it, to find the Polmawgan minister, Joseph Davies, on the doorstep.

'Are Mr and Mrs Whitmead at home?'

'Yes, sir. Please come in.'

'Who is it, Kitty?' Mary came out of the parlour to see who the new arrival was. Mr Davies swept off his hat.

'Ah. Mrs Trevelyan. I thought you were at Rosnance.'

'No. We came over, Mrs St Asaph and myself, to look after Mrs Whitmead. She's been ill.'

'Indeed? She and her husband were not in church yesterday. I wondered why. So that is the explanation. Her husband would not wish to leave her, of course.'

'Quite,' said Mary warily, aware, like Kitty, that he was snooping. He had probably hoped to find Ninian mysteriously absent. He would be disappointed.

'What is the nature of Mrs Whitmead's illness?' Davies inquired. 'Is she making a good recovery? I believe there was some . . . trouble in the village recently. Some of the women have mentioned it to me.'

'Them! The silly fools,' said Kitty contemptuously. 'They don't know their heads from their hindquarters. Mrs Whitmead's had a miscarriage, that's what. And it was their fault!'

'Kitty, be quiet,' said Mary sharply. 'Mrs Whitmead is still in bed, Mr Davies. But if you'll wait in the parlour, we'll call Mr Whitmead. He's sitting with her now. Kitty, go and fetch him. Oh, and when you come down, bring me my blue slippers from the cupboard in the room Mrs St Asaph and I are sharing. It's too warm for the ones I'm wearing. Luckily, I put both pairs into my bundle when I came here. I missed you, I must say. I had to do all my own packing.'

Kitty duly fetched Ninian, but decided to forget about the slippers. Instead, she followed Ninian quickly downstairs. Through the open parlour door she glimpsed the chagrin on Mr Davies' face as Mr Whitmead, neatly dressed and shaved, and looking as if he'd never heard either of guns or tin mines limped briskly in and went straight into the attack with: 'Ah, Davies! I'm glad to see you. I have a complaint about the behaviour of your flock!' Disappointingly, she heard no more because he then shut the door, excluding her from the exciting conversation on the other side of it, and she saw that steam was drifting from the kitchen into the hall. The cloths she had put on to boil clearly needed attention. She went regretfully back to them.

She was still stirring them with a long wooden spoon, when hooves clattered outside, and there was another commanding knock at the door.

'Dick's seeing to the master's muddy things. Just answer that, will 'ee, Kitty,' said Eliza. 'And please God it b'ain't any of they Roundheads, come prowling, not that they'll find anything out of order in this house.'

It wasn't the Roundheads. It was Jane Dewey. She stepped quickly inside, inquiring: 'Is Mr Whitmead here?'

'Yes, 'm. He's in the parlour with Mr Davies from Polmawgan church.'

'Oh, damn,' said Jane Dewey, causing Kitty to giggle. '*Damn.*' She frowned. 'I hear that Mrs Whitmead's ill. Is that right?'

'Ill? Why, yes, she's had a miscarriage, but . . .'

'Well, I've come to ask how she is. Go and tell Mr Whitmead I'm here.'

But in the parlour, Ninian had heard and recognised Jane's voice. He came quietly out, once again closing the door after him. 'Jane?'

Rapidly, in lowered tones, Jane said: 'Grosse and Keigwin are safe

155

away, on the *Foweymoor*. Roger Polkinghorne's said to have got away too.' More loudly, and as though continuing a sentence already begun, she added: '. . . should have sent for me at once when your wife was taken ill. How is she now?'

'Tamzin was nearer,' said Ninian. 'The worst is over but Tamzin is still here, and Mary Trevelyan. The cause of the trouble was a disgraceful episode in the village. The minister's here now and I've been having a few words with him about it. Come in and join us. Mary's there.'

They went back to the parlour. Once more, the door closed between Kitty and the enthralling conversation on the other side of it, and once more, she trailed back to the kitchen.

'Was that Mrs Dewey?' Eliza inquired. 'And is she staying to dine as well? What a day. We won't get dinner till four of the clock at this rate of going. The master'll be shouting for something for his guests to eat and drink in a minute, too. I b'ain't never been so distracted. Now, get them cloths in to rinse and clear my range. Then maybe you'll get round to helping me line these pastry dishes . . .'

Mary was not at ease with Mr. Davies, although to begin with, it was highly entertaining to sit in the parlour, nibbling almond cakes and listening while Ninian put the minister down and Mr. Davies bridled.

'. . . really, Mr Whitmead. I can't be held responsible for something that happened when I wasn't even there. Oh, yes, Betsy Hawkes told me all about it when she came to me to arrange Marge Hawkes' funeral . . . I would have come before to ask after your wife, but I have been helping to arrange food supplies for the Parliamentary relief force . . . The women may have been in error but old Mrs Hawkes had just been found dead and there are all too many cases of witches causing harm. They are usually female. The weaker sex are vulnerable to the devil's persuasions.'

'Or to absurd accusations. Years ago, a poor old woman in Polmawgan was supposed to have bewitched a boy who'd irritated her. He had fits and she was accused of causing them. And last year in Redruth, two old ladies with hardly a penny between them were accused of giving a youth they scarcely even knew pins and needles and bad dreams. I wondered why they should bother,' said Ninian.

'Any wretchedness caused to the godly is a pleasure to a witch, Mr Whitmead. The power to cause it is the price they receive for their souls.'

'Don't you ever ask yourself why they don't stand out for a better price? Nearly all these so-called witches are poor and old. In their place, I'd want youth and wealth. And perhaps,' said Ninian thoughtfully, 'some armed retainers to protect me from witch-hunters, too!'

'All witches are not poor – or old,' said Davies significantly. Ninian regarded him coldly, leaning back on a settle and crossing an ankle over a knee. 'You are pleased to be cynical, Mr Whitmead. But the existence of witches, and their malign influence, has long been proven. In the Bible, it says—'

'Nothing to encourage the persecution of the innocent. My wife has been made seriously ill, and my unborn child destroyed, by your silly parishioners. And while we are on the subject, this is a godfearing household. My wife was born a foreigner but she is now a thoroughgoing Christian. She is not a witch. Is that clear?'

'Quite clear, Mr Whitmead. I assure you that your wife has my good wishes and I trust we shall soon see both of you in church again.'

It was all so amusing that Mary forgot her own disapproval of Parvati and sat nodding in agreement with Ninian. But just after that, Jane arrived, another person with whom she was not at ease, and the conversation ceased to be interesting. Mr Davies aired his opinion of the rising in Penzance and said that no Royalist was any better than a Papist and they were all damned for ever in the eyes of God.

'You must greatly regret, Mr Whitmead, that you are not fit enough to join the Parliamentary forces. How you must long to lend your good right arm to bring Penzance back to the rule of Parliament and godliness.'

'Ah, well. Did you know I hurt my leg at Braddock Down, fighting for the King? Lying on my bed of pain,' said Ninian solemnly, 'I came to my senses. But for this injury, all those years ago, I might have been in Penzance on the wrong side. God sometimes moves in a strange fashion.'

Jane nodded in sober agreement and Mary wondered how they could do it. Mr Davies glanced at her.

'I daresay we are offending Mrs Trevelyan. Her husband, of course, is a Royalist.'

'But it was most kind of her to come to help my wife,' said Ninian. 'I appreciate it.'

'Oh, quite, certainly. You have had no word from your husband, Mrs Trevelyan?'

'No,' said Mary, and succeeded, barely, in not bursting into tears. According to Ninian, Francis had gone away to the Scillies. He had neither sent her a letter nor found a moment to visit her, and Ninian, looking apologetic, said he hadn't mentioned sending for her to join him. She didn't know if she would ever see him again and it was so humiliating, to be ignored like this. It would hurt less to cry for a dead husband than it did to weep over a neglectful one.

To add to her discomfort, the day was growing steadily warmer, and her feet in their thick slippers were now disagreeably hot. 'Excuse me,' she said abruptly. 'I asked Kitty to bring my lighter slippers but she has forgotten. I think I must fetch them myself.'

She almost fled from the parlour. She wanted privacy in which to shed her tears unseen. She was exasperated to find that after all, her bedchamber offered no solitude. Tamzin, who shared it with her, was there. She was piling her gowns and linen on the bed as though she were packing.

'Tamzin! What on earth are you doing?'

Tamzin swung round. 'Mary! You made me jump. Must you creep about like that?' For some reason, her face had flushed red. 'I'm just making a few preparations in advance. We'll probably go back to Rosnance tomorrow. Penny doesn't need us now.'

'You must be eager to go back!' said Mary. 'I can't say I am. We don't have to help scrub the floors here. I came up for some slippers. Did you know Mr Davies was downstairs? I think he's prying.'

'Oh, is he, indeed?' said Tamzin militantly. She rolled up her belongings, fastened a strap round them and tossed the bundle into the chest under the window-seat. 'I had better go downstairs and give my support.'

She went without waiting for Mary, who found her slippers but didn't put them on. She dropped them beside the bed and sat down on the edge of it. It was always the same. Always, she was shut out of things, but worst of all was being shut out of Francis' heart. She lay down on the bed, buried her face in her arms, and, alone at last, surrendered to her tears.

The dinner gong called her downstairs again. She wiped her face and went down but had little appetite and was embarrassed by her reddened eyes, although she soon realised that no one could see them, for just as dinner was served, the wind rose, and the warm spring day was suddenly swallowed by dark clouds. A violent rainstorm began, and it was necessary to light the candles.

Over dinner, the weather was the main topic of conversation. Davies had not stayed to dine and Ninian said that he hoped the minister had reached Polmawgan before the storm began. Tamzin hoped the storm would clear up before the morning. Jane Dewey agreed with her and Ninian inquired if Jane would like to stop the night. 'It'll be a wet ride home for you.'

'I'd be grateful,' Jane said. 'All my men are at sea and I'd be glad of company. Not that I fear for them on account of the storm. They've sailed in worse than this many a time and the *Foweymoor*'s the best ship on this coast. But seeing who they've got on board – well, I hope they're not pursued, that's all.'

Mary took little part in the conversation. Francis' rejection seemed to be sinking more and more deeply into her, hurting more with every moment. She did not care whether it rained or not, whether Mr Davies got wet or not; the *Foweymoor* could sink with all hands as far as she was concerned. Tamzin was oddly fidgety, continually turning to look out of the window, and her restlessness made Mary want to scream. When the wind suddenly dropped and the rain eased, Tamzin settled down but by then Mary was exhausted by the effort of restraining her irritation. She went to bed early.

She found it hard to sleep, however, and when she did finally doze off, it was a light slumber, from which she woke, suddenly, at dawn. She sat up, wondering what had roused her. Then she saw that Tamzin's bed was empty.

Somewhere in the house, on the ground floor, a door was closing.

On impulse, she slipped out of bed and lifted the lid of the window-seat. Tamzin's bundle of clothes was gone.

Lowering the chest-lid, Mary stared out of the window. The world outside was barely visible, the dark masses of hillside and outcrop emerging faintly as sky and sea turned from black to grey. But she could make out the path down into Minecombe, and the figure hurrying down it. The figure was not yet far away; it was possible to tell that it wore long skirts, and carried a bundle.

Surely, surely, it was Tamzin.

Chapter Thirteen
The Ship Sails

Once again, something was going on and once again she hadn't been told. Well, this time she wouldn't sit meekly by while they all ignored her. Mary dressed, more rapidly and haphazardly than ever before in her life, leaving her hair uncombed, ignoring stays and stockings and head-dress because they took too long to fasten, stamping her feet into their shoes, wrapping a shawl round her for warmth, and tossing a hooded cloak on top.

She went downstairs, quickly and quietly. The two dogs, Pol and Lady, appeared from somewhere and Pol barked once, but she gentled them both and since they knew her, they became quiet. She found the side door unbolted; Tamzin no doubt had gone out that way. The dogs, hopeful of an early walk, tried to push through it with her, but she thrust them back and shut them inside.

Out in the wet, grey garden, she made for the grassy bank which bounded it on the Minecombe side. There was a gap where the track down to Minecombe began. The light was good now, colour coming back into the world – a pearly sky changing to blue in the east; gorse flowers showing gold in the furze; dew flashing on the grass and the sea-pinks; the sea turning turquoise and beginning to sparkle. The first larks were singing invisibly, high above. She saw Tamzin as soon as she reached the track, a small, hurrying figure already at the foot of the hill. Slipping and scrambling, her leather shoes rubbing painfully on heels which had never before been exposed to them without an intervening stocking, and a fresh breeze blowing her hood back, she hurried in pursuit.

She lost sight of Tamzin on the way down but not before she had seen her cross the Minecombe stream on what looked like stepping stones, and then turn along the bank towards the shore. She herself did not know Minecombe; she had often seen it from above but could not recall ever having been down it before. She went astray once, where the path forked, and found herself, as she rounded a granite outcrop, confronting a tunnel mouth in the side of Polmawgan Head. An entrance to Ninian's mine, she supposed, as she backed hurriedly away from its threatening gape.

Retracing her steps, she tried the other fork. The side of the combe grew steeper and the path zig-zagged, but it was taking her steadily downwards. Presently, dishevelled and breathless, she arrived at the bottom. The flanks of the combe, clothed with grass and granite and scattered gorse bushes, soared on either side and the stream flowed swiftly through with a trodden path along each bank. As she had thought, there were stepping stones. She crossed, wobbling somewhat, and turned downstream. A moment later, rounding a spur from the side of the combe, she caught up with her quarry. A boat was moored in the stream, in a natural harbour behind an outcrop, and in the boat, engaged in hoisting a sail, was Tamzin.

But she was not alone. Another pair of hands was beside hers on the halyard. 'Francis! Francis!' shrieked Mary, running forward. The boat was still moored but she tore her palms, clutching at the painter as though to hold the boat back. 'What are you doing?'

They stared at her, two aghast faces, two open mouths. Mary stared back, equally aghast, for she already knew the answer to her own question.

She was seeing a man and a woman who belonged together, who stood side by side, cooperating on the halyard with the complete assurance of a mated pair. The very way they stood, each with the same tilt of the head, made them look as though their bodies were ruled by a single mind.

'What are you doing here, Mary?' Tamzin asked sharply. 'Did you follow me?'

'I woke up and you were gone. I looked out of the window and saw you . . . why shouldn't I follow you?' cried Mary. 'And what are *you* doing here, with Francis?' She might know the answer, but she wasn't going to give in to this awful revelation without a struggle. 'Ninian said he'd gone to the Scillies! Why do people lie to me? Francis, what are you *doing*?'

'Tell her,' said Tamzin tersely.

'Mary, it would have been better if you'd stayed in bed,' Francis said. 'The rising has failed and yes, I am bound for the Scillies. Christopher St Asaph is dead. And Tamzin is coming with me.'

'What do you mean? I am your wife. I am the one who should come with you!'

Francis shook his head. 'It would mean a life in exile, with no settled home, and perhaps no future – beginning with a voyage in a very small boat in dangerous seas. Can you face all that, Mary? You know you can't, and I would be wrong to ask it of you.'

'But I'm your *wife*!'

'Mary,' said Tamzin. 'Go back to Polmawgan. I'm sorry you followed me, sorry you saw us here together, but you must go back.'

'If Kitty hadn't forgotten my slippers,' said Mary in a high-pitched, near-hysterical voice, 'I wouldn't have come upstairs when I did, yesterday, and I wouldn't have seen you packing. If Kitty weren't lazy, I'd never have known where you'd gone. It's quite funny, isn't it? Such a little thing, to break my heart.'

'We didn't want to break your heart,' Tamzin said. 'But I am going away with Francis, and there's nothing to be done about it. I would never have left Christopher while he was alive but now he's gone and . . .' She made a gesture which said: *I can't explain any further.*

'We should never have married, Mary,' said Francis. 'You were never happy with me; I always asked too much of you. Let me go now.'

'But . . .' Mary looked from one unyielding face to the other. 'How can you prefer her to me? She's *old*!'

'I'm forty-two,' said Tamzin 'Not too old to begin again. I've spent four years in the wilderness, ever since Christopher came back from Marston Moor. I'll stay in the wilderness no longer.'

'But I can be left in it! Is that when this started? When Christopher came back? Has this been going on for four years? Another thing that I didn't know, another thing that was kept a secret from me?'

'Would you have had us tell you this?' Tamzin asked. 'You ask how long? Two years, not four. When Francis came back in secret to gather funds for the Prince of Wales; that's when it began. He came to Coombe and I was in distress because Christopher was drifting further and further away from me and I couldn't get him back. I opened my heart to Francis . . . sometimes, Mary, there are no words for these things. I am sorry.'

'Listen, Mary,' Francis said. 'After a while, you will find that you're happier with me gone. You have eaten your heart out for me, all these years; I know that. You can have peace, now.'

'*Peace!*' Mary felt her eyes going hard and her mouth contorted with rage and misery. 'How dare you? You're adulterers! Do you know what the Puritans are going to do if they get enough power? They'll make it a hanging offence! For once, I think they're right. I'd like to see you both hang. Especially you, Tamzin. You've stolen my husband, you . . .'

She tried to climb into the boat to attack Tamzin but Francis was out of it instantly, blocking her way, catching at her wrists. 'Stop that! Mary, stop it, stop it!'

'Let me go!' Mary kicked out, struggling to be free. 'She's not going with you, she's not. *You* go back to Polmawgan, Tamzin. I'm going with Francis, not you; I'm his wife, how dare you steal him?'

'I'm not an object to be stolen, Mary. I am not your property, nor am I Tamzin's.' Francis' grip was savage. 'Believe me,' he said, 'if Tamzin were wiped from the face of the earth, I would never come back to you. When was ours ever a marriage?'

'You wouldn't let it be! You went away and never sent me word. I wanted you to love me, to be kind to me, and you wouldn't, you wouldn't!'

'Go home, Mary.' Francis released her but stood between her and the boat. Mary stood there, crying desperately and rubbing her wrists. The worst of it was that he was right. The thought of being out on the sea in this small boat, with no idea what kind of roof or food or bed awaited her at the end of the voyage made her feel even more sick than the prospect of being abandoned by Francis. She hated him and Tamzin, and hated herself even more.

As he turned to get back into the boat, she made one last bid for him, trying to put her arms round him and hold him, but he slid his hands down to her elbows and pushed them away from him, stepping backwards, out of her embrace. 'Go!' he said.

163

She could make no impression on either of them. They were utterly sure of themselves, invulnerable as the cliffs. Weeping in defeat, Mary fled.

Normally, Kitty slept in a small room with Charles but while Parvati was ill, they were sharing a truckle bed in Parvati's room, so that Kitty could look after both her mistress and the child. Ninian, sleeping next door, woke in the night when Charles called out for a drink of water, and after that failed to fall asleep again. His bed seemed narrow and lonely and he longed for Parvati. He rose and went to his wife's chamber. Kitty, attending to the little boy, politely ignored him and he slipped quietly through the bedcurtains to join Parvati. She was asleep but as he edged himself under the covers, she stirred.

'Parvati? It's Ninian. Is it all right? Not to do anything, but just to be here.'

Parvati turned over and her arms slid round him. 'Yes, of course. It is no more now than it is each month. I have missed you.'

He pulled her more firmly against him. 'And I you. Let us go to sleep like this.'

When he woke for the second time, he was still wrapped in Parvati's arms, but the daylight was full. Somewhere downstairs, the dogs were barking. Kitty and Charles were evidently up, because Charles too could be heard downstairs. And Dick Branson was shaking his shoulder.

'Wake up, sir. Please wake up!'

'Thanks be to the Lord that you'm here!' Eliza was also in the room. 'When we found you gone from your bed, we thought, he'm vanished too!'

'Vanished too? Who else has vanished? What's all this?' Ninian struggled out of the depths of slumber and sat up.

'Mrs Trevelyan and Mrs St Asaph, they'm both disappeared,' said Eliza distractedly. 'We come up to call all of you because that Captain Beresford-Higham's here, with a whole lot of men, saying everyone's to gather downstairs. But the two ladies, they'm *gone*. There's the beds been slept in but the ladies, they'm just spirited away and when Dick see your bed empty too . . . ! If Kitty hadn't said we'd find 'ee here . . .'

'Beresford-Higham is downstairs?'

'Yes, Mr Whitmead.' Eliza's voice dropped. 'He'm looking for men running away after Penzance.'

Ninian pushed back the covers. 'I'll come down at once. Did you tell them that my wife was ill and confined to bed?'

'I am better now.' Parvati was sitting up too, pushing her long hair back and fastening it into a knot. 'I have walked about in this room; I can dress and come down with you, Ninian.'

'Are you sure? You must be careful.'

'I am quite sure. I will tell them how you have scarcely left my side, all this last week.'

'Very well, but you must come back to bed if you feel too weak. Eliza, I don't understand all this about Mrs St Asaph and Mrs Trevelyan. They slept in their beds but aren't in the house now? My watch is in the other room but I think it must be quite late. Perhaps they're in the garden, or walking on the headland.'

'They'm not in the garden, Mr Whitmead, I've looked, and if they'd gone out for a proper walk, Mrs St Asaph would have thought to take the dogs. She'm that kind of lady. Besides, Mrs Trevelyan's left half her things behind . . . I mean things no lady is dressed without.'

'Does the Captain know the ladies were here? I understand he had left Rosnance before Mrs St Asaph was sent for.'

'He asked who was in the house,' said Eliza miserably. 'So I told 'un. How were I to know half the souls under this roof would vanish in the night?'

'You weren't.' Somewhere, Jane Dewey's voice could be heard, joined with Kitty's in quelling Charles' uproar, but the dogs were still barking. 'Go down and offer the Captain some breakfast. And Dick, try to quieten those dogs.'

'I can assure you, Captain,' said Ninian coolly, 'that I am not hiding any fugitive Royalists in this house.' He needed a shave but getting downstairs and taking charge of this new situation had been more important. He had contented himself with donning his most sombre black suit, with fresh white linen, and in order to appear more militantly Puritan, he had added a sword. Parvati was in dove-grey, her hair packed away in a clean head-dress and her face shiny with washing, the epitome of a good Puritan wife, were it not for the grace of her walk, and her dark almond eyes, and the amber of her skin.

The parlour was full. Jane Dewey and Kitty, also in grey and looking as near to demure as either of them could manage, were sharing a settle, with Charles on Jane's knee. Jimmy Tonkin and the Bransons, all visibly ill at ease, stood in a cluster. There were also six Roundhead troopers with helmets and pikes, and Captain Beresford-Higham. Ninian felt as though he could hardly breathe.

'Your household doesn't seem to be quite in order, however,' said Beresford-Higham. His face and his voice and his cold grey eyes as usual expressed sardonic enquiry. 'You appear to have mislaid two of your guests.'

'That puzzles me as much as it does you,' said Ninian. 'It seems they rose early and went out together. But I'm sure they'll soon come back.' He hoped it was true. He had looked into their room and been considerably taken aback by the sight of Mary's stays, head-dress and stockings thrown across the foot of her bed.

'You'll have no objection, Mr Whitmead,' said Beresford-Higham, 'if my men search the house for fugitives?'

'Not the least in the world,' Ninian assured him cordially. 'Every room is open to you. There are no secret passages here but some of the rooms are panelled. Don't omit to tap all the panels to make sure none of them sound hollow. Look under all the beds. Oh, and there are tall cupboards in some of the bedchambers, big enough to hold a man. Make sure you examine them all carefully.'

Beresford-Higham's arched eyebrows rose even further than usual. 'Your tone isn't all it should be, Mr Whitmead, any more than your house.'

'I'm offended, Captain. I'm a good Puritan and an ardent supporter of Parliament. You should know that this is the last place to look for Royalist fugitives. If I sound caustic, it's because I feel caustic.'

Beresford-Higham stared at Ninian long and hard and Ninian stared back. Finally, the Captain turned to his men. 'Search the house and the outbuildings. But with care. You are seeking men; there is no need to pry impertinently into chests of drawers and small cupboards, and no need to damage anything. The attics and the stable loft are more likely hiding places than the bedchambers.'

The troopers went out. Beresford-Higham turned to Jane Dewey. 'Mrs Dewey, isn't it? What brings you here?'

'Mrs Whitmead has been ill and I came to ask after her. Penny, sit down. It'll do you no good to stand about like that.'

'Your husband is at sea at present?' inquired the Captain.

'Fishing,' said Jane. Her tone carried a faint tincture of 'Try and prove otherwise' but her face was amiable. Charles exhibited restlessness and she jigged him up and down. 'I'm on my way home this morning, Captain.'

Upstairs, the heavy tread of the troopers moved to and fro. Doors opened and closed. Lady and Pol, who had been shut into the kitchen, still barked intermittently and somewhere outside, poultry cackled as more soldiers searched the yard.

'Are your men harassing my hens?' asked Ninian acidly. He moved to look out of the window and then stopped short at the sight of Mary, who with tangled hair flying and cloak clutched round her all anyhow and her shoes in her hands, was half-running and half-limping across the garden to the house.

Beresford-Higham had seen her too. He was out of the room at once, making for the side door, and a moment later steered a distraught Mary into the parlour. 'Calm yourself, Mrs Trevelyan! Tell me what has happened. Has there been an accident? Where is Mrs St Asaph?'

'Accident!' If Mary had looked a mess from a distance, she was at close quarters even worse. Her face was blubbered and dirty, and raw, bleeding patches on her heels showed why she had taken off her shoes. The soles of her feet and the palms of her hands were grazed and her dress was stained with blood from them. She looked as if she had run a long way and fallen down many times in the process. 'Accident? No, there hasn't been an accident!'

'But you have hurt yourself.' Beresford-Higham pushed her, not unkindly, on to the settle next to Jane, who moved quickly up to make room for her. 'Where have you been? Tell us what's the matter.'

'I've been down in Minecombe! Tamzin's run away with my husband, that's what's the matter!'

166

'What are you talking about, Mrs Trevelyan? Your husband? Francis Trevelyan? Has he been here?'

'No. He hasn't been here. But Mrs St Asaph's run off with him just the same,' Mary informed him.

Jane Dewey, as if to free her hands for some difficult task, handed Charles over to Kitty. 'Explain yourself, Mary. You sound hysterical to me. Tell us plainly what you've been doing. Look at the state you're in.'

'I'm telling you that Tamzin St Asaph and my husband have been lovers for God knows how long and now they've run away. How many more times?'

'Did you know Francis Trevelyan was in Cornwall?' said the Captain to Ninian. 'Did he contact you?'

'He knew better than to do such a thing,' said Ninian virtuously. A picture was shaping itself in his mind; a memory of a day when he and Tamzin and Francis were all together in the kitchen of this very house, wrapping silver to be given to the Prince of Wales; when Tamzin and Francis had exchanged smiles and he had sensed, almost heard, the secret current that rushed between them. He had thought of it then as a might-have-been.

Mary was staring at Ninian. He stared back at her, willing her not to speak of what she knew, such as his own part in the rising and the message from Francis. She was quivering with her rage and the burden of her knowledge but mercifully, she only said: 'He got word to Tamzin all right.' And then out tumbled the story of how she had seen Tamzin bundling her clothes, how she had woken to find Tamzin and the bundle gone; how she had seen her going down to Minecombe; how she had followed and found Tamzin with Francis and a boat. And how they had told her bluntly that they were going away together. 'I couldn't bear it! I ran away. I wish I was dead. How could they? I was always faithful to Francis; why couldn't he be faithful to me? Oh, Francis!'

'You,' said Beresford-Higham to Kitty. 'Fetch Mrs Trevelyan some wine. Mrs Trevelyan, please accept my sympathy, but try to answer some questions. Have you any idea how Mrs St Asaph and your husband arranged their assignation?'

'None of us have any idea,' said Ninian. 'But if they were lovers, no doubt they had their own ways of communication.' He glanced anxiously at Parvati. 'I hope this isn't too much for you, Penny.'

'I am all right,' said Parvati quietly, and Ninian went to her side and rested his hand lightly on her shoulder.

Mary regarded them with hatred, possessed once more by the feeling that other people were a solid wall of indifference on which she could make no impression, concealing secrets from which she was excluded and love from which she was shut out. Ninian and his wife were like Tamzin and Francis in their solidity and tenderness for each other. She could scarcely endure the sight of them.

'I think,' said Jane, 'that you should lie down, Mary. Here's Kitty with the wine; take some. We'll dress those cuts for you and then you can go upstairs and . . .'

'I don't want the wine!' Mary turned her head away from the glass Kitty was offering her. 'I want Francis and he's gone away for ever with that whore, that . . .'

Kitty looked helplessly at the wine-glass and Parvati, rising softly, took it from her. 'Oh, Mary, we all feel for you. You mustn't think we don't. This is a terrible thing that has been done to you. We would not have helped Tamzin to run off with Francis, you know. I am truly sad for you. Please take your wine. You will feel better.'

She held the glass out persuasively. It was the same gesture exactly as the one she had made long ago in the kitchen of Rosnance, and on that occasion Mary, wild with terror of the pirates, had looked at the brown hand so close to her and gone into a frenzy.

Now, equally wild with grief and jealousy, she looked once more at Parvati's hand, offering her something to drink, and history repeated itself.

'Don't touch me! I don't want your sympathy. Leave me alone, you foreign witch!' shrieked Mary.

The quality of the silence that followed, and the sudden fear in Parvati's face, told Beresford-Higham more than Ninian would have wanted him to know.

'Witch?' he inquired. His eyes scanned Parvati, visibly taking in the un-English face, the sinuous body. 'Are you merely hurling abuse, Mrs Trevelyan? Or do you mean what you say?'

'I . . . I . . .'

'Well, Mary?' said the Captain, using her given name, as if speaking to a servant or a child. 'Come, answer.'

'Stop talking to me as if I were a little girl!' Mary flung at him. 'Stop pitying me because I'm hysterical! Why shouldn't I be hysterical? But no, I'm not just hurling abuse.' She stared furiously at the trembling Parvati. Ninian put his arm round his wife. 'Why should you have a faithful husband when I haven't?' Mary shouted. 'Did you give him a love philtre? A love philtre!' The idea, having sprung into her head, entranced her, uplifting her on the instant from failure to victim, offering her, at last, a way to undermine these smug human cliffs. She got up and pushed her face at Parvati. 'Did you give a magic potion to Mr St Asaph to heal his wound? And did you sell a philtre to Tamzin so that she could steal Francis away?'

Horrified exclamations burst out. Ninian shouted at Mary to stop talking nonsense. Charles added his voice to the confusion, demanding loudly to be put down. When a measure of quiet had been restored, Beresford-Higham said sternly: 'That is a very serious accusation, Mrs Trevelyan.'

Mary turned to him. 'Do you know why she's been ill?' She pointed at Parvati. 'She had a miscarriage after the women of Polmawgan village stoned her for being a witch. She put the evil eye on Marge Hawkes and killed her, that's what they said. I'll tell you something.' Mary's eyes were bright with malice. 'Years ago, I came on her when she wasn't expecting me and I saw her worshipping a picture of the devil. What about that!'

'I've never worshipped the devil. It isn't *true!*'

'Of course it isn't true!' blazed Ninian. 'Mary, how dare you invent such lies?'

'*He* told me I wasn't to tell anyone.' Mary's pointing finger veered towards Ninian. '*He* said that Francis would be angry if I did. But Francis has gone away now so it doesn't matter any more. You made a big mistake when you sold a love potion to Tamzin, didn't you, Penny Whitmead?'

'But I never . . .!'

'I think you helped Francis to leave me. You could, because you worship the devil. *I saw you with my own eyes!*'

'One moment. Am I to understand, Mrs Trevelyan, that you saw the devil being worshipped and you said nothing?' Beresford-Higham had the air of one who wishes to get a complicated situation clearly explained.

'Mr Whitmead said it wasn't the devil. I didn't know what to think, *then*. And I told you: he said Francis would be angry if I ever talked about it. But now I think it *was* the devil, and Dick Branson there, he saw it too. Ask him!'

Beresford-Higham turned to Branson, who regarded him stolidly. 'I never saw any such thing,' Dick said. 'This is all moonshine, Captain. The poor lady's off her head, and no wonder, with her husband running off like that. But this that she's saying: it's not the truth.'

'It is, it is! I won't be branded a liar when I'm not, I won't!' Mary stamped her foot. 'What about the women in Polmawgan? They *did* stone her! Kitty was there, ask her.' Kitty's mouth dropped open. Her grip on Charles slackened and Charles, who had identified Mary as some kind of enemy, yelled: 'Stop shouting at my mother!' and rushing up to Mary, began to pummel her. She thrust him off. 'The minister knows about the stoning!' Determined to justify herself, she forgot her dislike of Davies. 'Ask *him*. He'll tell you!'

'Davies?' said the Captain. 'Of Polmawgan Church? A good, reliable man. He's organising a system of look-outs for us, to catch any fugitives who try to steal boats from Polmawgan. Mr Trevelyan was fortunate in being able to obtain a boat from Minecombe, Mr Whitmead. Did you really have no idea he was there? Certainly I shall speak to Davies. Mrs Trevelyan, where did you see this drawing of the devil?'

'In her room,' said Mary fiercely. 'She had it in her room.'

Kitty got hold of Charles once more and sat down, holding him firmly. Beresford-Higham went to the door and shouted for a trooper. They heard him say: 'My orders are changed. Search all rooms thoroughly. Look for the emblems of witchcraft.'

'You will find nothing in my wife's room, or anywhere else in this house, that shouldn't be there,' said Ninian as the Captain came back into the parlour. 'I am surprised at you, wasting your time over this nonsense.'

'I've never seen anything in Mrs Whitmead's room that shouldn't be there. She's a good Christian,' Kitty agreed, entering the fray on the side of her mistress.

'One may hope so,' said the Captain. 'But witchcraft is not nonsense. We are warned against it in the Bible.'

Mary sat down on a chair. She held up her head and her face wore a righteous expression but she avoided the eyes of the others. Jane and Eliza in particular glared at her in vain. Ninian led Parvati to a seat and stood beside her, grasping her hand tightly. Both of them stared at the floor. There was a prolonged and frightful wait.

Presently, a trooper came back, carrying a lute, a carved sandalwood trinket box and an armful of glistening silks. 'We've found these, sir.'

'The lute is mine,' said Ninian. 'I gave up playing it some years ago and put it away. The silks, the box and the little things inside, my wife brought from her homeland. Is there anything remarkable about that?'

'We also,' said the trooper, pulling a piece of paper from his coat, 'found this. They were all in a chest, sir. And this paper was under them.'

Beresford-Higham took the paper and spread it out on the table and Shiva, multi-armed and dancing and equipped with the mighty lingam which was Parvati's personal way of visualising him, lay shockingly exposed to the eyes of Puritan law and order.

'Whatever's that?' gasped Kitty.

'Why?' said Ninian despairingly to Parvati. '*Why?*'

'I was afraid. All these disturbed times. I was afraid. I needed Shiva. I asked him to protect you. But I hid him, oh, so carefully. I hid him,' Parvati said faintly.

'Oh, *God*,' said Ninian in a desperate voice.

'Don't be angry,' whispered Parvati. 'Please don't!'

'How can I help it?' said Ninian. But he did not let go of her hand and when he moved it was only to put himself protectively between Parvati and the Captain.

Of all the people in the room, the least shocked appeared to be Jane Dewey, who looked at Shiva and merely snorted. 'My eldest son's with the East India Company. He's told me about the people there. *That*,' said Jane with contempt, 'is merely one of the gods they worship. It's got nothing to do with witchcraft.'

'Of course it hasn't!' said Ninian angrily.

'But it must have! Look at it!' Mary shrilled.

'Mary, you're making a fool of yourself!'

'Asked it to protect her husband, did she?' The trooper stared in fascination at Shiva's remarkable appendages. 'And what was her husband doing that put him into danger? Not upholding Parliament, not with a wife who prays to that, sir. Maybe he *was* mixed up with the Royalists, sir.'

'If so, this could be witchcraft for the purposes of treason,' said Beresford-Higham.

'And that,' said the trooper, 'might be a burning matter.' He looked at Parvati and suddenly, nastily, licked his lips.

'All this is completely ridiculous!' Ninian shouted.

'That will be for a court to settle,' said Beresford-Higham grimly. 'I am placing both you and Mrs Whitmead under arrest, on charges of being concerned in witchcraft and also on suspicion of aiding and abetting the escape of Francis Trevelyan. Go and call the men back here, Mileham. The servants will be kept in this house, and will hold themselves ready for questioning . . .'

Eliza and Kitty cried out and in Kitty's arms, Charles struggled, calling for his mother. 'I tell you that drawing means nothing.' Jane was exasperated. 'Why can't you listen to me, Captain? I know what I'm talking about.'

'I fear you're biased, Mrs Dewey. Mary, I thank you. You have acted rightly, although you would have done better to speak sooner. However, your feminine frailty and ignorance may perhaps excuse you.'

'At least,' said Jane roundly, 'let me take that child to my own home. You presumably don't want to question *him?* Or me, I trust.'

Beresford-Higham considered her thoughtfully. 'I'm not holding you at the moment, Mrs Dewey. Yes, take the boy if you want. But don't leave Penzance.'

Without answering, Jane lifted Charles bodily out of Kitty's grasp and carried him over to his parents. 'Kiss your mother and father. You're coming to stay with me for a while,' she said to him. 'Not for long!' She spoke some low words of reassurance to Ninian and Parvati as they said goodbye to their son. Then she carried Charles out and they heard the dogs bark as she passed through the kitchen.

Mileham was coming back with the other troopers. Ninian, his face very drawn, urged his wife gently to her feet. Then, as the soldiers came back into the room, he put two fingers in his mouth, and whistled.

The dogs arrived like hairy thunderbolts, hurtling out of the kitchen and into the parlour, through the doors which Jane had whispered that she would leave ajar. The taciturn Jimmy burst into unexpected whoops of encouragement to them to attack the troopers and suddenly the room was a chaos of snarls and yells and curses. Ninian gripped Parvati's arm and hustled her out of the door.

Lurching on his damaged leg, he got them both to the side door into the garden, and through it. Behind them, there was a gurgling yelp as one of the dogs was speared. It must have been Pol, for suddenly Lady was bounding alongside as they stumbled across the garden. Heavy feet were close behind them when they reached the gap in the bank. 'Get them, Lady!' Ninian shouted, and the dog whirled, growling, to guard their retreat. Without looking back, Ninian dragged Parvati on down the path towards Minecombe and round the first bend of the zig-zag track.

Behind them, a pistol spat and Lady's snarls ended in a pitiful howl. 'Oh, the poor dogs!' Parvati moaned.

'It'll be poor us in a minute.' Ninian threw a quick glance at the hillside below. 'Neither of us can run fast. Quick. Short cut. Straight down. Fall and roll!'

They slithered and rolled across grass and heather and a few stray sea-pinks, landed on a lower stretch of the path, heard another pistol shot and slithered again as earth flew up from the track. Above them, three of the troopers tried to follow in the same fashion but, lacking Ninian's minute local knowledge, picked too steep a place and fell heavily, tumbling downwards in a heap.

'Where . . . are . . . we going?' Parvati panted.

'I've a plan. Nearly there.' They reached another stretch of path, beside a granite buttress. Ninian hurried them round it. In front of them was a hacked-out wound in the side of the hill, a dark entrance the size of a small door. Beside it was a mound of excavated rock and earth, covered thinly with grass.

'It's the Wheal Susannah,' Ninian said.

Parvati had seen the mine entrance from a distance, but had never been close to it before. She looked at it in alarm. 'But they can follow us in there!'

'Leave that to me. Come on!' said Ninian.

A few yards inside, the rocky roof sank, forcing them into a half-crouch. Ninian's stiff leg dragged awkwardly, but he led them through the dusty darkness as quickly as he could, until a space once more opened out round them and, pulling them both upright, he felt for what he knew was there; a rocky shelf where candles and tinderbox were stored. A moment later he had lit a candle and the little chamber where he and Francis had hidden, where once a party of conspirators had met, wavered out of the darkness.

Parvati looked fearfully about her, at the timber supports, the winch and the shaft and the winch-rope which stretched over the edge of it to disappear into the depths. In a corner of the room lay some water flasks and some leather bags, a pile of rugs and a couple of buckets. The smell of ordure mingled with the throat-drying tang of rock dust.

'Is the roof safe?' Parvati whispered, pointing. 'That slab is only being held up by one timber! And what is in those bags?'

'Food. Never mind the roof.' Hurriedly, Ninian lit a second candle from the first. He thrust it at Parvati, grabbed half a dozen candles more, and pushed them in one of the bags, then rammed a couple of flasks in on top. 'Take these and go on through that other tunnel. Careful of the shaft.'

'But what are you . . . ?'

Ninian was already beside the shaft and hauling on the rope. Something clattered in the depths and a bucket came up. 'Go on, quickly! I'm coming in a moment. Go *on*!' Ninian snapped.

She entered the tunnel, stooping. Glancing back, she saw Ninian unfasten the bucket and begin winding the rope round the timber support. Then he was coming after her, urging her on, dragging the winch with him on squeaking wheels and paying out the rope as he went. 'Go on, go on, further. We've no time. They'll probably fetch lights before they follow us in but they won't take long over it. Quickly, quickly!'

A few yards further on, he said: 'Far enough. Stop. Now help me wind. Hurry!'

Parvati put down the bag and joined him at the handle of the winch.

172

It spun easily as it took up the slack of the rope but when the rope tautened, it jammed.

'*Wind. Make* it move . . . *make* it . . . !'

'What are we . . . doing?' panted Parvati. 'That piece of timber . . .'

'They won't . . . follow . . . if they think . . . we're dead under a . . . rockfall . . . *Wind* . . . There's another way . . . out. We'll . . . escape . . . that way . . . It's coming . . .'

They heard the groan of timber under stress. Then came a menacing crack, which made Ninian hesitate, wiping sweat from his forehead with the back of his hand and looking upwards, as if suddenly unsure how far the collapse would extend. But it was already too late. A new noise, more threatening still, had begun; a low rumble which grew into a roar. A dust-laden blast of air came down the tunnel. They coughed and choked, turning their heads away and shutting their eyes against the flying grit. Ninian instinctively shielded his candle, but Parvati's went out.

Quiet fell. Ninian relit Parvati's candle. 'It's all right. Let's get to where we can see daylight. We drove a link tunnel to the old workings last year and we can walk straight through. It's fairly smooth going though we'll have to stoop a little. We shan't meet any miners. Pengelly had the work stopped so that we could use the mine to store arms and as a hideaway.'

The link tunnel ran almost straight, leading downhill. It became uncomfortably warm and also damp. Their feet squelched in puddles and the candle-light showed moisture sweating from the walls. Ninian pointed out the tin lodes, running in horizontal lines like streaks of bluish ink but Parvati, glancing uneasily from side to side, did not reply. Then they were going uphill again. The floor became dry once more and at last, ahead of them, there appeared a slit of brilliant light.

'The entrance on the other side of Minecombe,' Ninian said. 'This is far enough.' He stopped, blew out his candle and sat down on the floor. 'The whole combe will still be seething with the Captain's men, I don't doubt. We must wait. Come, sit down. How are you feeling, Parvati? This can't have been good for you.'

Parvati slid down beside him, trembling. 'It is no use to worry. I don't think I am harmed. I am only weak. Oh, Ninian. What have I done? Your poor dogs. You loved your dogs. And now . . . where will we go? It was because I was so afraid for you, when you went to fight in Penzance. I made the drawing that same night and I asked the Lord Shiva to protect you and scatter your enemies. I knew I should not but I was terrified for you and I never meant anyone to find it. I am sorry. I am sorry.'

'I know that.' Ninian sighed. 'Listen, my Parvati, you haven't done as much harm as you think. The dogs were growing old. In quite a short time now, they would have died, or I might have had to end their lives myself.' He blinked, but did not give way. There would be time later to mourn because he would never again hear them bark, or be greeted by their waving tails and eager leaps. 'I might have had to leave them behind, anyway. Our life in Polmawgan was probably already over. I put it in jeopardy myself when I joined the rebellion and again when I let Francis take the *Fish*. Don't blame yourself. Do you think I don't understand how isolated you are, cut off from your beginnings? You still can't eat beef; I know by that the past hasn't just vanished for you.'

'I am only lost when you are not with me, Ninian. When you are there, I am at home,' Parvati said. 'But when you go away – then it is true, yes, I thirst for my own gods.'

'I know. Well, I have been more careless with our safety than you have. I am in no position to be angry.'

'What . . . what will we do now?'

'We'll try to reach the Scillies.' Suddenly, Ninian pummelled his temples. 'I wanted us to keep our home. I thought I could keep up the pretence of being a good Parliamentarian but . . . How can I be sure that no one saw me in Penzance, who would betray me? And there was your trouble in Polmawgan. Tamzin tried to warn me. If we'd stayed, anything could have happened. And I've let the *Fish* go. I've been such a fool!'

He checked himself, then continued more calmly. 'Now, listen. We have to reach Polmawgan Cove and steal a boat from there. Davies is organising a watch for fugitives so we'd better avoid going over the headland and use the cave that goes through it instead. We can only go through at low tide, so we'll have to time it carefully. The evening will be light until late but the tide will be dropping just before dawn tomorrow. There are usually a few boats pulled up on the beach, so we needn't go to the harbour.'

He felt in his jacket for his watch. 'Do you remember giving me this, Parvati? It's very reliable. We can tell the time at least. Look, undo that bag and we'll have something to eat. There's dried fruit in there, and smoked meat and hard-tack cheese. I've only got a sword-edge to cut it with, I'm afraid. We shall have a long wait here but I think it would be the safest thing to do.'

'Ninian, if we're caught . . . I'll be taken up for witchcraft, won't I? And if they say I used it for some treasonable purpose, they could . . . I could be . . .'

'No,' said Ninian, and closed his eyes as if to shut out some intolerable image. 'I won't let it happen.'

'I knew Mary was dangerous,' Parvati said. 'I was frightened as soon as I knew that Eliza had told her about the stoning. Oh, Ninian, she has parted us from our son!'

'He'll be safe with Jane. When we've reached safety ourselves, we'll find a way to send for him.'

'I've told you, haven't I, about what happens to widows sometimes in India? I . . . I saw it once.'

'What? You . . . ? Oh, my dear. Parvati, don't be afraid. I will never let that happen to you. *We are going to escape.*'

'Promise. Promise that you will never let me burn.'

A genuine Puritan would turn faint at the thought of swearing on such a Popish symbol as the cross. Ninian, without hesitation, laid his hand on the crosspiece of his sword and said: 'I swear.'

And then he set about giving them both some food, in the process discovering that it was easier to tear meat and cheese apart than to cut it with even a well-sharpened swordblade.

Dawn was barely glimmering when they crept out of their hiding place and stole down through Minecombe. Parvati had borne up well, sleeping a little in the mine with her head on Ninian's shoulder, but Ninian, as he guided her down to the shore and across the wet shingle towards the cave entrance, cursed himself again and again for his stupidity in not taking her away before. They should have gone with Francis. He had tried to cling to Polmawgan for too long – and see what had come of it! 'Careful,' he said, as Parvati tripped on the loose stones.

The tide was ebbing but the waves were still powerful, thundering round the headland's foot and flinging up clouds of spume which gleamed in the daybreak. Water swirled round their feet as they clambered over the wet rocks at the cave entrance. Gulls called their disapproval of the intruders and Parvati caught at Ninian's arm. 'Was that a shout? It's getting lighter. Someone may have seen us!'

'It's only the gulls. Look out for these rocks. They're slippery with seaweed.'

They entered the cave. The sea was still rolling in at the other end. Parvati looked round her, awed.

'This is the place where you saved me? I have never been here since. It is so high.' Craning her neck, she peered upwards, to where the cave roof vanished, narrowing, into the shadows fifty feet above. 'How the sea echoes here!'

'You were pulled up on to that ledge there. There's the tidemark, can you see? You were swept in through the other entrance.'

'This is where it began, then. Where we began, I mean. I can hardly remember it. I remember the wreck and being swept off the boat and clinging to something. Then it is all blurred. I can remember being pulled out of the water, I think. Not much else. What do we do now?'

'We wait until the further entrance is clear, and then,' said Ninian, 'we peer out. Cautiously.'

'If only,' breathed Parvati, like a prayer, 'there is a boat within reach.'

The sea was receding. Presently they were able to walk over the wet sand of the cave floor and peer out of the far entrance at the cove, where the light was steadily broadening. 'There are three boats,' said Ninian. 'There, look, dragged up on the shore. If only they have oars and tackle in them.'

'There is no one about.' Parvati's eyes roamed, taking in the cove, the cottages clustered below the church, and the mass of boats bobbing in the harbour beyond the quay on the other side. 'If these boats will not do, surely we can reach the harbour.'

'Getting out of the harbour would take time and the village isn't as quiet as you think. Those masts belong to fishing vessels and they probably haven't been in long. There will be men still aboard some of them, sorting out the catch and stowing their sails. We must pray we can take one of these.'

He led the way out. The nearest boat was empty of oars, sails or mast. But the second had them all. It was small, smaller than the *Fish*, but it would have to do. They began moving it towards the water, slowly, because Ninian could never put his full weight on his damaged leg, and Parvati was breathless and to his alarm kept dropping a hand to her side as though she had a stitch. They were at the very water's edge when they heard the shouts from the direction of the quay.

'It's Davies!' Parvati's eyes were wide with fear. 'And there are men with him!'

'So I see,' said Ninian, in despair.

There were six of them, with Joseph Davies in the lead, running across the beach towards them.

'Get it into the water!' said Ninian, hauling at the boat. 'Launch it – quickly! Heave at your end!'

But it was too late. They were still struggling, knee-deep in the chilly water, when their pursuers pounded up and caught hold of the gunwale.

'I knew you were a tricky bastard, Whitmead!' Davies called. 'I told the Captain so. Mark my words, I said, Ninian Whitmead is not buried under any rockfall in his mine, not he, nor that sorceress who has bewitched him! We have been on the lookout, for fugitives and for you.'

He made a *take them* gesture to the fishermen with him and in a flurry of splashes, Parvati fled round the boat to Ninian's side. She put her arms round his neck and kissed his mouth, fiercely and briefly. 'Remember what you swore,' she whispered. And then, turning away from him, she ran headlong into the sea.

'Parvati!' Ninian swung round to go after her. But a fisherman was reaching to lay hands on him and the others were already thrusting the boat off in order to give chase. He wrenched out his sword, scrambled aboard and proceeded to defend himself.

He had always been good with a sword. Tired and despairing and lame though he was, his arms retained their skill, and the hilt of the sword, which carried his promise to Parvati, seemed to burn strength into him.

It was recorded afterwards in the annals of Polmawgan church, by the hand of a disgruntled but truthful Joseph Davies, that Ninian Whitmead, whose wife had been accused of witchcraft, stood alone in the boat with a sword and held it against six men for long enough to let the sorceress escape from justice by drowning herself.

Neither I nor any of my honest companions were killed, for which mercy God be praised, but three were injured, and one will never use his left hand well again. Mr Whitmead had till then had the reputation of a godly man; a sorry thing it is to see how a witch's wiles can corrupt and ensnare even a baptised soul, wrote Davies.

Ninian himself never afterwards remembered the episode with any

176

clarity at all. He fought by instinct, balancing himself somehow despite his faulty leg and the awkwardly shaped interior of the boat, his body faithfully performing the task he had set it while his mind tore apart between his longing to throw the sword away and fling himself after Parvati to rescue her; and the oath he had sworn her, which he could not now redeem unless he let her die.

When they overpowered him at last, it was because he knew that Parvati was no longer in the world. Her spirit brushed his in passing and with that, his strength failed. They hauled him from the boat, wrenched his sword away and attacked him with their fists. A powerful set of knuckles, hardened by years of exposure to sea-water, struck his jaw and he blacked out.

When he came to himself again, he was sprawling face down on damp sand, throbbing throughout his whole body and filled with an enormous sense of grief and loss over something which he couldn't at first remember. Rolling painfully over, he opened his eyes and vaguely observed a sunlit beach on which most of Polmawgan seemed to have congregated. Captain Beresford-Higham, hands on hips, was standing over him. Beside the Captain was Joseph Davies and half a dozen troopers were gathered round. Dazedly raising his head, he saw two horsemen also making their way down through the combe.

'He's come round,' said Davies in tones of satisfaction. 'Watch him, Captain. A slippery one, he is. How did he organise that rockfall, I wonder? More sorcery, perhaps.'

'Don't be a bloody fool,' said Ninian weakly. 'I pulled a roof support down with a rope.'

'On your feet,' said Beresford-Higham. 'You're under arrest. Come on. Up!'

Ninian tried to obey but turned dizzy and sank back. Beresford-Higham dropped to his knees and pushed his arm roughly under Ninian's shoulders. 'Up!'

'Give me a moment. Where did you spring from, anyway?'

'You were seen creeping into the cave through the headland this morning. We were on the watch for escaped Royalists. When we got down here, we found that Davies had caught our quarry for us, and that it was you.'

'So the cry my wife heard wasn't a gull after all. But you haven't caught *her*,' said Ninian. 'I promised her she wouldn't be taken.' Memory had returned. Parvati was gone, drowned. He hadn't been able to save her. He had had, virtually, to help her perish. 'Are you proud of what you've done? And you, Davies?' He looked up at the minister. 'My wife was a stranger from a far country, where customs are different. But you think anyone who is different from you is in league with the devil, don't you? She was quite innocent and still very young but you'd have killed her, maybe even burned her. Well the sea was kinder. Oh God, she's *dead*.'

He still couldn't quite believe it. His arms remembered her still; he could feel her against his body, hear her voice; when he closed his eyes again, her dark gaze looked at him within his eyelids.

No one deigned to argue with him. Rough hands dragged him to his feet and he stood swaying. Opening his eyes again, he found that he was being gripped by Beresford-Higham on one side and Joseph Davies on the other, while Trooper Mileham was standing in front of him with a pike. Somewhere behind him hoofbeats were approaching over the sand; the two riders he had seen coming down the combe, presumably.

'How many men do you need to arrest one middle-aged fugitive who's lost his sword?' he said. 'The whole damned Parliamentary army?'

'That's enough,' said Beresford-Higham. 'March!'

'On the contrary,' said the familiar voice of Anthony Gubbes, in tones of authority. 'Let Mr Whitmead go at once.'

For a moment, Ninian thought he was hearing things. But his captors had evidently heard it too, for although they didn't precisely obey the order, the fingers grasping his arms eased enough to let him turn his head and discover the source of this timely interruption. Jane Dewey was just dismounting from her grey gelding, which she had been riding astride in her usual swashbuckling fashion, and beside her was Anthony, on a blue roan which Ninian dimly recognised as his own mare Venus. Jane, thrusting her reins into the hands of a staring trooper, strode up and snapped: 'Didn't you hear Mr Gubbes? Let him go!' and actually slapped Davies' hand away from Ninian's elbow.

The Captain maintained his hold. 'This man is under arrest, on suspicion of aiding Royalists and being involved with sorcery.'

'Mr Whitmead,' Anthony barked, 'has been aiding *me*! Mrs Dewey fetched me, Ninian. She knows what you did for me in Penzance. Her husband was there and heard it all. She reminded me of the debt I owe Ninian here. It was late last night when she found me; I was from home, helping to scour the town for Royalists. But we came to Polmawgan House early this morning in search of you and the Captain. What has happened and where is Mrs Whitmead? Is she safe?'

'No,' said Ninian savagely. 'She's dead. She drowned herself for fear of being taken up for witchcraft.'

'Drowned? Oh, dear Lord.' Anthony pulled off his tall black hat. 'If only we had reached you sooner.' His deep-set blue eyes were full of distress. 'Ninian, my poor friend! Mrs Dewey has told me all about this silly witchcraft charge. I'm surprised at you, Beresford-Higham. Why did you listen to Mary Trevelyan? She is a foolish, credulous woman. Mrs Whitmead was a foreigner with foreign ways, but to call her a witch because of that is rubbish.'

'Did I understand you to say,' inquired Beresford-Higham, still holding Ninian's arm, 'that Mr Whitmead's been in Penzance?'

'Certainly. He came into the town at the height of the rising, to save my life by buying it from the insurgents who wanted to hang me. They might well have hanged him too!' Anthony declared. 'I don't know who informed you, Ninian. But I do know that you came to my aid at once and took a terrible risk for me. I'll be grateful all my life. Captain, are you going to let go of him, or do I have to draw my sword and make you? Ninian is the best of Puritan gentlemen. Under arrest, indeed!'

Davies began to protest, but Jane rounded on him, ordering him fiercely to hold his tongue. Beresford-Higham slowly relinquished his hold. Ninian was not sure that he could stand unsupported, but Jane came to his side and he leant on her. Anthony dismounted as well. 'Here. Help him on to his horse. It actually does belong to him; he left it behind in the town.'

Venus looked to Ninian as tall as a house, but Anthony was lengthening the stirrup, to make mounting easier, and Jane was encouraging him kindly. 'We must get you home. Oh, Ninian, I am sorrier than I can say about . . .'

'What's that in the sea?' said Ninian.

Something had caught the corner of his eye. He broke away from Jane and stumbled to the water's edge. In the slopping waves, a bundle swayed and rolled. But it was not just a bundle. Long hair trailed like seaweed; a hand, palm upwards, showed momentarily upon the surface.

He stooped, with difficulty, and in his weary arms, he lifted Parvati from the sea which once had brought her to him living, and now had given him back her body for burial.

The night before Parvati was buried in Polmawgan churchyard, close to Ninian's sister Pen and close also to Kerenza and Meg, Ninian kept vigil beside her body and Anthony came to Polmawgan House to share it with him.

Sometime in the small hours, Ninian broke a long silence. 'But for you . . .'

'I owe you my life,' Anthony said simply. 'And as it happens, I don't believe in witchcraft. I will get that man Davies removed from office. I have influence enough, I think. I'm glad he isn't conducting the service tomorrow.'

The candles flickered, troubled by a breeze, and the shadows danced in the room where once Parvati had danced for Ninian.

'He refused. But I wouldn't have let him, anyway. The minister from Marazion seems kindly, and he's a stranger. That's best, I think.'

They fell silent again. There were too many things which must not be spoken. In death, Parvati had become acceptable to Anthony and Alice Gubbes as she never was in life. It was Anthony's insistence that she was not a suicide, but had drowned while fleeing in panic from arrest on a false charge of witchcraft, which had won her a place in consecrated ground; and it was Anthony's insistence that Ninian was a good Parliamentarian who had foiled a Royalist attempt at murder which had kept Ninian free.

Very probably, Anthony didn't believe either of these things, but he would never say so, and Ninian would never ask.

'Who will come, tomorrow?' Anthony asked at length.

'Jane Dewey. Not many others. Most of my friends are dead or fled,' Ninian said. 'Mary won't be there, of course. I hear she's ill in bed at Rosnance. Tom Pengelly would have liked to come but he can't leave his bed, either. He's coughing his lungs out, I'm afraid. Dan will represent him.' The candles flickered again, playing across Parvati's quiet face. 'Anthony, will you leave me alone with her, just for five minutes?' Ninian asked.

'Of course.'

Anthony took a candle and left the room. Quietly, Ninian went to the chest that stood by the wall, just as it always had. Opening it, he took out Parvati's carved sandalwood casket and her gold-bordered red sari. Beresford-Higham had returned her belongings, if disapprovingly. He took a few trinkets out of the casket and returned them to the chest, where Parvati's other silks still lay. He looked for a moment at the pieces of jewellery which remained in the casket and touched them gently. Then he closed the lid, wrapped the casket in the red sari, and slid the gleaming packet into the coffin under Parvati's body.

She was so far from home, and she would be laid in foreign soil, by the rites of an adopted religion. She should have something of home to go with her. The things still in the chest should be his keepsakes. When Anthony came back into the room, Ninian was sitting quietly beside his wife, as though he had not moved.

'Your mine revenues will be legally restored to you, of course,' Anthony said. 'I shall see to it personally. Once Parliamentary rule is secure, many things will be set to rights. We intend to deal with the Courteen abuses too. We have all lost money through them.'

'Forgive me, Anthony. But I don't feel as if anything will ever be set to rights. I can't think of mines and shipping now. I wish I'd drowned with her, Anthony, and that's the truth.'

'What? Ninian, you can't say that!'

'Why not?'

'Have you forgotten?' said Anthony. 'You have a son.'

PART III

Louisa:
Waiting on the Quay
1664–1666

When we could endure no more upon the water, we to a little alehouse on the Bankside . . . and there stayed till it was dark almost and saw the fire grow; and as it grow darker, appeared more and more, and in Corners and upon steeples and between churches and houses, as far as we could see up the hill of the City, in a most horrid malicious bloody flame, not like the fine flame of an ordinary fire . . . We stayed till, it being darkish, we saw the fire as only one entire arch of fire from this to the other side of the bridge . . . It made me weep to see it. The churches, houses, and all on fire and flaming at once, and a horrid noise the flames made, and the cracking of houses at their ruine.

Samuel Pepys, 2nd September 1666

Chapter Fourteen

Drama at the Play

'. . . *and Crispin Crispian shall ne'er go by, from this day to the ending of the world . . .*' said Louisa Lagrange, and then stopped, because her gentle, feminine voice had been drowned out entirely by the raucous din two rooms away. She looked at her mother apologetically.

'The trouble with the gentlemen,' said Clemency Lagrange, 'is that when they get together over their card-playing, they insist on getting together over the brandy at the same time. At least, when your father is the host.'

Louisa laid Shakespeare's *Henry the Fifth* shakily down on her lap. It was so difficult to appear serene, to make conversation. Reading aloud was easier; the words were set down for you. 'I never remember them being so noisy when I was a child,' she said.

'They weren't. We had Puritan rule, then. I wouldn't wish it back,' said Clemency frankly. 'It was a joyless time. One Christmas, we actually had our kitchen invaded by soldiers who took our roast beef out of the oven and threw it out of the window, because they said it was against the law to celebrate Christmas like a pagan festival. So absurd! When your father and his friends played cards then, they did it very quietly, behind locked doors and curtained windows. But now, things have gone to the other extreme and I can't say I like that, either. No one nowadays seems to behave with any restraint whatsoever.'

Louisa nodded. Her tightly laced pearl-grey satin bodice made it difficult to breathe and the nearby masculine racket made it difficult to think. 'Mother . . .'

'I quite like a hand of cards myself,' said Clemency, continuing her own train of thought and not even hearing her daughter's timid interruption. 'But only when other ladies are present. Talking of amusements, I really must arrange some musical evenings this winter. You are twenty-one and your elder sisters are married and your future ought to be settled soon. It is a pity nothing came of the introductions we arranged this year, although I have to admit that neither of those young men were quite right. Young Mr Dixon may be the son of a Master Woodworker like your father but I used to watch him and wonder if he were actually trying to swallow his adam's apple. As for Mr Brent . . .'

She paused, expecting Louisa to say something. 'I couldn't,' said Louisa, doing her best. 'I really couldn't. He talked about varnishing and japanning all the time, as if I were an apprentice he were instructing.'

'Not *all* the time,' said Clemency. 'I'm sure I heard him mention the weather at least twice.'

Louisa forced herself to laugh. Clemency laughed too. 'We will do better than that for you, my dear,' she said.

I wish I could die, thought Louisa. Here and now. Anything, so that I don't have to tell her. Anything, so that I don't have to open my mouth and say those terrible words which will destroy the kindness in her face for ever.

'There should be no difficulty,' said Clemency amiably. 'You are very pretty, my dear, probably the best-looking of all my daughters. Our swarthy King Charles has made dark hair fashionable and you have an excellent complexion. Never a single spot, even when you were in your teens. When I think of how your sister Catherine cried over her spots! I scarcely knew what to do with her. And you have fine, slender bones and a nice shape, fortunate child!' Clemency's own waist had long since vanished and her sensible face was comfortably padded out with flesh. 'I must take you shopping for some new gowns.'

I've *got* to speak. Oh, why can't one turn time back and undo the past? But if people could do that, I expect King Charles would turn time back and do something differently so that his father wouldn't be beheaded after all and then everything in the world would be different and perhaps I wouldn't be sitting here like this now, trapped and petrified . . .

'I think,' said Clemency, 'that we could have the musical evenings after Christmas. Your Aunt Faith will have come and gone by then. She'll be here next week but she'll go home before Christmas if the roads aren't too mired. She still holds by Puritan ways and wouldn't approve of frivolous music. Ah, well. She disapproves of noisy card-parties, and your father has a healthy respect for her, so I daresay that while she's here, we won't have to put up with them.' Clemency chuckled. 'It's strange that your father should have such a stiff elder sister. But, of course, he left home early to do his apprenticeship; I expect that's why he's so different.'

'I . . . I didn't know that Aunt Faith was coming to stay.'

'Oh, did I not tell you? We had a letter from her last week. She wishes to hear some of the famous ministers who preach in London. You remember her, I daresay? You must have been about sixteen, the last time she visited us.'

'Yes. Yes, I remember.'

I remember very well. What will Aunt Faith say to this? Oh, God help me!

'We shall all have to be careful what we say while Aunt Faith is here,' said Clemency, rearranging her face in lugubrious lines. 'She doesn't approve of King Charles and his lax ways either. Oh dear. On balance, I think I'd rather have these rackety card-parties – listen to that! Someone's broken a decanter, by the sound of it. But when your aunt is with us, we shall all have to nod gravely when she says what a loss Oliver Cromwell was, and how much better it was when there were laws against loose morals, and the playhouses were closed . . . Louisa? What's the matter, my love? *Louisa!*'

The Shakespeare had slipped from Louisa's satin lap. She was trembling all over. She looked into her mother's face, into the kindness and concern she must soon forfeit for ever, and threw herself into Clemency's arms, sobbing with grief and fear, and babbling incoherently.

Two words emerged recognisably from the babble.

'Charles Whitmead?' said Clemency. 'I might have known!'

The crisis had had to come, but it was the prospect of a visitation from Aunt Faith, combined with the one word *playhouse* which brought it on at that precise moment. The playhouse, the King's Theatre in Drury Lane to be exact, was where the disaster began.

Yet they had set out, that day last February, in such excitement. *The Indian Queen*, the new play from the pen of John Dryden (though some said Sir Robert Howard had written part of it) was London's talking point. Everyone was going. The King had attended it, and his mistress Lady Castlemaine; if you hadn't seen *The Indian Queen*, if you hadn't an opinion on whether the rhymed dialogue were an enhancement or a drawback to the drama, and if you couldn't comment on the spectacular and barbaric scenery and costumes, you were out of fashion, the equivalent of a mere rustic.

And besides, Barnabas Lagrange, Master Woodworker, whose fine oak and walnut furniture had been bought by the aristocracy, and who could afford a comfortable house with stabling at the back, just off the fashionable Strand, had lately acquired a private coach with a pair of matched bay geldings to draw it. He wished to show it off, and driving to the King's Theatre to see *The Indian Queen* was a splendid way of doing so. Half of fashionable London would be crowding into Drury Lane at the same time.

Louisa was familiar with playhouses, of course. Her father loved the theatre and even at the height – Barnabas called it the depths – of the Puritan rule, all the playhouses hadn't closed. In defiance of edict and fine and onslaughts by wrecking squads, one theatre, the Red Bull, kept in business throughout. Louisa could dimly remember being taken to a performance there when she was about ten, and since the Restoration four years ago, her father had taken his family to the theatre often.

Although she was only seventeen when Charles the Second came home to claim his crown, she was sharply conscious of the new freedom to enjoy oneself. The narrow London streets, darkened by overhanging upper storeys, the muck underfoot and the continual risk of getting one's purse snatched in a crowd hadn't altered, but the people had. Overnight, it seemed, a population which had been quietly dressed and muted in speech, became colourful and rumbustious. Beggars who had once stood raggedly on street corners asking alms for the love of God and moving off in a hurry if they saw officialdom approaching, now played fiddles and bagpipes for pennies; and if the costermongers had always bawled their wares with a fair amount of noise, they hadn't hitherto declared that their apples were ripe and sweet as young maidens, or drawn bawdy comparisons between firm, fat cabbages and a wet-nurse's breasts.

It made life exhilarating. But from the start of that outing to the King's, Louisa was exhilarated beyond the usual, aglow, as though sensing that the day would be momentous and the whole world were about to change.

Unfortunately, she took it for granted that if so, the change would be for the better.

If she had foreseen its true nature, she would have shammed a blinding headache and taken to her bed, with the curtains drawn round it, until the danger had gone by.

Barnabas had obtained a box at the King's, in which he was lucky, for the theatre was crowded. The much-vaunted play proved, as far as Louisa was concerned, to be all that was claimed for it. It was a drama of a contested throne, conflicting loves and noble self-sacrifice, with a heroine whose plight and bravery moved Louisa to tears. The rhyme and metre she thought only made the feeling more piercing and the costumes she was sure had been borrowed from the royal palace.

By the time Act IV had ended, with the Inca's gallant daughter Orazia apparently doomed without hope, she could hardly sit still for wanting to know the outcome.

'Well, you must be patient,' said Clemency, amused, when Louisa said so. 'Try looking at the audience to pass the time. I always find that entertaining. Now, why are those two elderly ladies down there sitting in such cheap seats? Those purple gowns must have been costly; they can't be poor.'

'They look like sisters,' said Barnabas. 'Perhaps they were well-off once but are fallen on hard times and they're using up their good clothes. The Restoration has meant serious reverses for some people. Some of the Puritan leaders who were granted property seized from exiled Royalists have been dispossessed again. It's hard on their families.'

Louisa wasn't listening. Her eye had now been caught by a handsome, dark young man who seemed, in the midst of this periwigged crowd, to be wearing his own hair, and who was bowing to a young woman with butter-coloured ringlets, sitting in the box opposite that of the Lagranges. She was bowing back and smiling, but the young man's companion – an older man, perhaps his father – appeared to be taking him to task about it.

People were getting up, to use the interval in order to parade in the aisles and galleries. Barnabas, leaning over the edge of the box, cut off Louisa's view of the two men. Someone below had caught his attention.

'I do believe that's William Beresford-Higham. There, just passing below us with a lady in blue on his arm. He ordered a matching set of oak furniture from me last year. But how he's changed!'

'Changed, dear?' Clemency also leant inquiringly forward. 'He looks just the same as everyone else to me.'

'Exactly. Wig down to his knees,' exaggerated Barnabas, whose own wig was both luxurious and glossy. 'And coat-skirts full enough for a ball-gown, and a very pretty way of strutting, and a wife in the top of fashion. Last year he was still wearing a black suit and a Roundhead crop and the one time I caught sight of his wife, she was all slate-grey and white linen. Well, well.' His normally beaming features expressed pure astonishment. 'He used to be the most passionate of Puritans. He was a captain in Fairfax's army. What a transformation! He doesn't seem to have lost by the Restoration, anyway.'

The Beresford-Highams passed from view and Barnabas sat back. Down in the audience, the dark young man and his older companion were still in their seats, but the woman with the butter-coloured hair had left her box and the young man was looking elsewhere for amusement. He saw Louisa and his olive face was lit by a flashing smile. He blew her a kiss.

'Oh,' said Louisa, confused.

Clemency had seen. 'Better pull your chair back a little,' she advised.

'Oh, who would be a mother?' Louisa turned to her inquiringly, and Clemency patted her daughter's shoulder. 'You'll find out one day. I've been through it all before, twice, with Catherine and with Jemima, but it's still a worry. One wants one's daughters to marry well, and that means ensuring that they are seen and admired. But not too much. And oh dear, what a fine line there is between too much and not enough.'

Barnabas's mind was still on the Beresford-Highams. 'When I had dealings with the Captain over that order for furniture, I gathered that he is quite a friend of the Duke of Monmouth. That would be because Monmouth is very decidedly a Protestant. It is to be hoped that the Queen has a healthy son soon, or there will be trouble over the succession. The King's brother is Catholic, they say, and Monmouth is only the King's son out of wedlock.'

'The King,' said Clemency, 'has made love affairs fashionable. Hence the need for caution, Louisa, my dear. Be not over-retiring, but careful.'

'Yes, Mother, of course,' said Louisa, and wondered, privately, who the darkly handsome young man might be.

Then she set him aside because people had returned to their seats and Act V was about to begin and the scene was opening, amid gasps from the audience, on the Mayan Temple of the Sun, covered in what looked like authentic gold leaf. Four horrible, barbarous priests in cloaks of scarlet and white feathers, stood ominously beside an altar which had been artistically stained reddish-brown as if with old blood; waiting to sacrifice the Inca and his general Montezuma and his noble daughter Orazia. 'Ooh!' whispered Louisa in appalled delight.

'I'm so glad Orazia wasn't sacrificed after all,' Louisa said as they made their way out of the theatre. 'It wasn't really a tragedy, was it?'

'No, indeed. But the changes of fortune were too sudden for my taste,' said Barnabas. 'I thought that was too contrived. But it was a spectacle; no doubt about that. Lord, what a crush.'

Outside, the daylight was fading and the wind struck raw. It had been raining and Louisa lifted her skirts fastidiously clear of the muddy road as they made their way towards their waiting coach, through a throng of people on foot, grooms bringing saddle horses and vehicles manoeuvring. Imperious voices demanded right of way or loudly discussed the performance. Barnabas' bays were tossing their heads nervously, upset by the noise. Trying to hurry, the Lagranges were delayed by two men walking just ahead of them and going slowly because one was lame and leaning on a stick. He too was talking about the play, which he had apparently hoped would be about India. 'I might have known that the Indians would be American. The Americas are all the rage.'

'They certainly are,' said his companion. 'So many disgruntled Puritans have sailed off to start new lives there. I wonder what they'll make of the American Indians – or the Indians of them?'

He turned his head as he spoke and Louisa, close behind, recognised him as the dark young man. She wondered again whether the older man with him was his father. Except that they had similar black velvet cloaks and that neither wore wigs, they were not much alike. The younger man was taller, and his companion's thinning grey hair, which was shorter than fashion decreed, had originally been not black but sandy. A trace of ginger still showed in it.

'Come along, where are you wandering to?' Her father pushed her towards their coach. 'Ah, there are the Beresford-Highams again; that must be their coach in front of mine. I'll just have a word with them. They're good customers. Clemency, you and Louisa get in. I won't be long.'

To Louisa's surprise, the sound of her father saying 'The Beresford-Highams' had a galvanic effect on the man with the walking stick. He stopped short, apparently searching the crowds, saw Barnabas' acquaintances, then seized his companion's elbow and began to march them away as fast as his lameness would allow, almost bumping into the Lagranges as he did so. The young man, expostulating, jerked his arm free and his cloak swept in an arc across the muzzle of Barnabas' nearside horse, which promptly squealed and reared. The coach rocked and Louisa, in the act of setting foot on the step, lost her balance and fell. For a terrifying moment, she was face down in the mud, with her outflung hand only inches from a wheel.

She heard her mother shriek from inside the coach and her father shouting her name as he ran back to her, but the dark young man got there first. Strong brown hands, scattered with blue-black hairs, caught her up to safety and set her on her feet.

'Are you all right? I beg your pardon; it was entirely my fault. I frightened the horse. Are you hurt at all?'

'I . . . no, I don't think so.' Confused by the brilliant dark eyes now fixed so penetratingly on her face, Louisa could only stammer. 'I must be very muddy.'

'You've grazed yourself.' He took her wrist and turned her hand palm-upward. 'Allow me.' He produced a fine white handkerchief and carefully cleaned away the dirt and blood from what, after all, was a very small scrape. 'That's better.'

The coachman, shooting unfriendly glances at the cause of the trouble, was at the horses' heads, soothing them. Clemency was climbing out hurriedly and the older man was anxiously telling Barnabas that he was exceedingly sorry; he and his son – yes, they were father and son – had turned back suddenly on catching sight of someone they didn't wish to greet; they could only hope no harm had been done . . . He spoke with a trace of some regional accent which she couldn't identify, and had a high, polished forehead running up into a receding hairline. He had considerable presence, but between his pleasant hazel eyes was a deep vertical furrow, as though he were no stranger to anxiety or grief.

'Yes, well,' said Barnabas brusquely, and pushed past him, to join Clemency who was now kneeling at Louisa's side, thanking God that she was not harmed, and bewailing the state of her dress.

'I'm quite all right,' said Louisa, speaking to her parents but still unable to drag her eyes away from the young man, who had now released her hand and was putting the handkerchief away. He had turned to his father. 'I'm afraid we've caused an upset to these good people. Should we not introduce ourselves?'

'*We* caused an upset?' said the lame man dryly, but then his face lit up with a smile. 'But I am indeed forgetting my manners. Ninian Whitmead, at your service, and this is my son Charles. May I know . . . ?'

While Barnabas introduced the Lagrange family, Charles Whitmead turned to Louisa once more and smiled at her. She smiled back. It was extraordinary. She knew nothing of this young man beyond his name, yet when, presently, her mother nodded farewell to the Whitmeads and drew her away to the coach, the effort of detaching her gaze was so great that it almost hurt, and where his fingers had held her wrist, she thought that they had burned her skin.

'Just what was all that about? *Why* did you veer round at the sight of that harmless middle-aged couple as though they were covered in plague buboes?' said Charles, as he and Ninian resumed their slow walk homeward.

'Harmless? Those, my boy, were the *Beresford-Highams*. Mr Lagrange knew them; he shouted out their names.'

Charles stopped dead. 'I didn't hear him. You mean that woman was Mary Trevelyan? The one who . . . ?'

'Yes. Because of that woman, I was placed in such a position that the kindest thing I could do for your mother, whom I loved, was to let her die. I knew that Mary and her new husband lived in London now but to come face to face with them in the street like that was a shock. I never want to set eyes on Mary Beresford-Higham again, let alone speak to her.'

* * *

A Master Woodworker like Barnabas Lagrange did not spend all day in his workshop. It was Barnabas' habit to work in the morning, make sure that his foreman, his two journeymen and his current apprentice understood precisely what they were supposed to do in the afternoon, and then to go home for dinner. After dinner, he would take his family out or take himself by river into the City of London to meet acquaintances in one or other of the coffee-houses which had sprung up in the last ten years to sell the fashionable new beverage.

He had moved to the Strand when he could afford it because it was smart but the Guilds, including his own, were based in the City. Although his old friends were willing enough to come to his card-parties and invite him to theirs, he sometimes missed the vigorous pulse of the City, the close daily proximity of others like himself, craftsmen who worked with their hands, with skill so hard-won that it gave them an exceptional dignity. He rejoined them when he could.

Barnabas considered himself the equal of any man in the land except possibly the King, and he resented the sometimes patronising attitude of his wealthy customers at the western end of London. He'd like to see some of those elegant swaggerers, with their ruffled shirt-cuffs drooping over their wrists, dovetail the corners of a drawer so smoothly that a fingertip couldn't detect it or lay two pieces of veneer so that together they made a seamless grain.

As a lover of music, conversation, good food, cards and dancing, Barnabas had not enjoyed the Puritan regime but at least, he had once said crossly to Clemency, they valued people who worked. Some of his customers seemed to think they were superior merely because they didn't. On the Day of Judgement, said Barnabas, though cheerfully rather than sanctimoniously, they'd be in for a shock.

The City and the company of his own kind, therefore, drew him irresistibly. On each of the three days following the theatre visit, he spent the afternoon in the same City coffee-house with the same cronies. They discussed the latest Woodworkers' Guild politics; the likelihood of a war with the Dutch who were still doing their best to steal England's foreign trade; and the desperate need for King Charles to have a legitimate heir, because a choice between James, Duke of York (legitimate but Catholic) and James, Duke of Monmouth (illegitimate but Protestant) was too appalling to contemplate.

On the third day, however, the conference over the coffee tables was interrupted. Barnabas came home with news.

'Guess who walked into the coffee-house this afternoon and sat down at our table?'

His wife and daughter, exchanging amused glances across the hearth, played the game as he expected.

'Now let me see. Your sister Faith, up in town unexpectedly? One can never keep her out of coffee-houses and taverns,' said Clemency solemnly. 'So shocking.'

'I should love to see Faith in a coffee-house,' said Barnabas. 'I really would! No.'

'The King?' offered Louisa.

'The ghost of Oliver Cromwell?' said Clemency.

'No, you're all wrong.' Barnabas beamed. 'It was the Whitmeads. What do you think of that?'

'The Whitmeads?' said Clemency, puzzled.

Louisa, on whose memory every detail of that encounter outside the King's Theatre had been printed in jet-black embossed lettering, said: 'You mean the father and son we met when I nearly fell under our coach in Drury Lane?'

'The same,' said Barnabas. 'They were with a Mr Edward Davison, a very well-spoken man; he holds quite a position on the Navy Board. The Whitmeads' business is concerned with the sea; that's how they know him. Like attracts like. Ninian Whitmead owns shares in merchant vessels and his son is on his way to becoming a ship's captain. They didn't stay in the coffee-house for long, but Mr Davison did. I gather that he and his wife are fond of entertaining, and I have an invitation for us all to join them next Saturday evening for a supper party, with cards and dancing. I have accepted, of course. They live quite near Drury Lane.'

Louisa's eyes lit with pleasure but her mother frowned. 'Louisa,' said Clemency, 'I think we would like a little music before supper. Will you fetch your lute?'

Louisa, aware that she was being got rid of, looked momentarily mutinous, but went. Barnabas raised inquiring eyebrows at his wife, who said bluntly: 'Did the Whitmeads put this Mr Davison up to issuing this invitation? Are they going to be there?'

'They didn't say.' Barnabas was surprised. 'Possibly. The Whitmeads entertain very little themselves – Ninian is a widower – but they seem to be popular. They live in Wych Street, quite near the Davisons. Does it matter?'

'It might. There was something about that young man, Charles Whitmead, that I didn't take to. And I had a feeling that he was attracted by Louisa. Well, it's time to find her a husband, but I assume that we want her to marry someone in your own trade or an allied one, as Jemima and Catherine did. Charles Whitmead doesn't strike me as being what we had in mind.'

'Young Whitmead? I fancy he isn't all English,' said Barnabas easily. 'I daresay that's what you noticed. But he's due to go to sea in March; sailing to the West Indies as First Mate on a ship called the *Salisbury*. He won't be back for months. If he attends the party, it's neither here nor there. Not that I feel there's anything against him. Any well-off young man with good prospects is worth considering.'

'Hm,' said Clemency.

The Davisons' party at first showed every sign of being a disappointment. The Lagranges considered themselves to be comfortably off, but Louisa was completely overset by the smartness of the Davison house, the elegance of the other ladies, the astonishing number of bowing servants and the extravagant brilliance of so many candles.

She was then overset anew when her father presented her to their host and hostess, because the latter, Mrs Christabella Davison, turned out to be the young woman with the butter-coloured hair, who had been in the opposite box at the theatre – being bowed to by Charles Whitmead.

At close quarters, Louisa saw that Christabella Davison had a strong, experienced face, with a short upper lip and eyes of a surprising, deep pansy-brown. She wore tawny satin with huge skirts and quantities of lace and ribbon. Louisa was in white silk with silver trimmings, in which she looked virginal and naive and knew it. Christabella's knowledgeable eyes took her in and visibly dismissed her as negligible. Louisa blushed helplessly.

Edward Davison was a portly man, much older than his wife. He took Barnabas off to join a group of gentlemen at one end of the room while Clemency, unsure where she and Louisa should go, stood hesitating. Christabella visibly took that in, too and let the hiatus become awkward before remarking coolly that the evening was quite informal, and perhaps they would care to join the other ladies in the drawing room while she finished receiving.

'Really,' said Clemency in an undertone as she led Louisa towards the door Christabella had indicated, 'what is the matter with the woman? We were invited here! She's positively hostile. What a pity we can't just go home.'

Christabella came into the drawing room ten minutes later and proceeded to hold a kind of court among her female guests, drawing them round her in a semicircle. Matters for Louisa and Clemency at once became worse. Somehow, and there seemed no doubt that it was intentional, Christabella manoeuvred them to one end of the semicircle where they had to stand, smiling and silent, while their hostess talked of places and people they did not know; made jokes they didn't understand; was elegantly applauded for them; and never once let her gaze travel round as far as the Lagrange ladies. Clemency's expression became furious.

It was a relief when the musicians appeared and began to tune their instruments. The gentlemen came in and the door to a card-room was thrown open. Barnabas instantly made for it along with Edward Davison and several others, but the younger men came to join the ladies. A strong brown hand closed on Louisa's elbow.

'So you came,' said Charles Whitmead softly. 'I hoped you would. I told Davison that he must invite you. He found out through the Woodworkers' Guild where your father lived, and then someone there told him to try the coffee-houses near the Royal Exchange. We found him at the third try.'

'You mean you *arranged* for us to be asked here?'

'Of course. I wanted to see you again. Ah, Mrs Lagrange!' Charles bowed to Clemency. 'May I have the pleasure of treading a measure with your daughter? Don't refuse me, I implore you. I'm about to go to sea and the only thing I shall dance between now and next autumn will probably be a sailors' hornpipe.'

Clemency looked as if she would love to refuse. But she had no excuse. She consented.

'Tell me about yourself,' said Charles, as they emerged laughing from the set. 'I know your father is a Master Woodworker, and your name is Louisa Lagrange, but who is Louisa Lagrange? What is she like?'

'My father's well-known in his trade,' said Louisa. Charles was an excellent dancer and easily the best-looking man in the room, with that brown face and flashing smile, and that romantic sailor's queue of hair. She pretended not to see her mother beckoning, and let him lead her to the supper room and help her to cheese tart and olives of veal. 'I'm the youngest of his three daughters; I practise music and study geography on my globe, and read Shakespeare and do my embroidery. And you? I know your name is Charles Whitmead and that you are a seaman, one day to be a captain, but . . .'

'But who is Charles Whitmead? I am the son of Ninian, whom you would like if you knew him better because he too is very fond of Shakespeare, and also of John Donne. I was born in Cornwall though I don't remember it well because we left when I was about six, under dramatic circumstances.'

He paused, as he always did at this point, when telling anyone of his childhood.

'I am telling *you* the truth,' his father had said when Charles was sixteen and Ninian judged him old enough to withstand the facts of his mother's death. 'You have the right to know it and I think it best that you should. But I would advise you not to go about saying that your mother was accused of witchcraft. She was innocent, anyway. Tell other people the story I've let you believe up to now.'

Charles had recognised it as sound advice and although he always stopped to consider before reciting the edited version of his early years, he had never yet found a reason to abandon it in favour of the real story. He now had a fleeting impulse to see what effect it would have on this girl with the admiring, innocent eyes, but quickly suppressed it. He didn't want to shock her. 'There was a Royalist rising in Penzance during the Civil War . . .'

'Penzance?'

'Your geography lessons clearly leave something to be desired,' said Charles indulgently. 'Have some syllabub.' As he handed her the syllabub glass, she looked again at those brown, beautifully shaped hands with their scattering of strong, blue-black hairs, and felt as though something were melting inside her. She did not understand herself.

Charles was still telling her about himself. 'Penzance is a Cornish port and our old home was near it. My father was in the rising and when it was put down by the Roundheads, my parents tried to flee abroad in a small boat. They were pursued and attacked. Father was brought back, but my mother was drowned. Father couldn't bear to stay in Cornwall after that. We came to London that same year.'

'But if he was brought back . . . wasn't he arrested? Wasn't he imprisoned?' Louisa asked.

'No. It seems that there was no proof against him and many people were sorry for him, losing his wife. Even some of the enemy knew him well. During the war, friends and neighbours were often on opposing sides.'

'Oh yes, I know. When I was small, my parents lost some friends because one evening when they were with us, my father suggested a card game and they told him he should give up cards as the devil's works. There was such shouting. I got out of bed and peered through the banisters and heard it all. I was scared! But Father never asked them back.'

'Chatterbox,' said Charles, and smiled down at her as he escorted her towards a couple of chairs. 'We can sit here. Let me finish. A Roundhead friend of my father's, called Mr Gubbes, spoke up for him. So we were free to come to London.'

Later, while they were dancing again, she learned that in London, whatever his opinion of Cromwell's rule, Ninian had done well in business. 'My father never remarried and always says that it helped him to save. Will I see you again, Louisa? Bachelor households like ours don't often entertain ladies, but perhaps we may meet again through the Davisons. I hope so.' He glanced down at her, sidelong, as he paraded beside her, one hand on his hip, the other holding hers high. 'I hope we meet many, many times,' he said.

Louisa looked straight ahead, confused. The set ended and he released her hand, but the feel of his fingers still lingered glowingly.

He returned her to her mother but stayed to talk about his prospective voyage to the West Indies. Other guests gathered round, interested. Clemency began to signal with her eyebrows that she wished to take Louisa elsewhere but again Louisa pretended not to notice. Charles was now telling everyone about navigation: the difficulties of estimating a ship's longitude position, and what it was like, sailing at night by compass. If a compass could feel, she thought, then when the north pulled at it, it would feel as she did in Charles's presence.

Her mother's irritation was becoming noticeable, when Christabella interrupted them. 'So here you are, Charles! I do believe you have forgotten you promised to dance with me tonight. How could you?'

She gave Clemency a cursory nod and ignored Louisa altogether. Louisa gazed at her in surprise, thinking how odd it was that eyes as softly brown as pansies in colour could be as hard as agate in their expression, even when their owner was being arch.

'My dear,' said Charles. 'Do forgive me. Excuse me, everyone, but I have been caught out in lack of gallantry.' He gave Christabella his arm, smiled at them all, and went.

As though released from a spell, the little group broke up. Clemency and Louisa were left alone. Clemency drew an exasperated breath. 'Really, Louisa. You have been in that young man's company for half the evening. I've always told you never to grant your company too easily or for too long.'

'I'm sorry, Mother. But I was fascinated when he began to talk about his voyages and . . .'

'I'm not referring to his conversation just now but to your constantly dancing with him, and going in to supper with him. From now on, Louisa, stay close to me.'

Clemency, however, was as liable as anyone else to the calls of nature and half an hour later withdrew, leaving Louisa in the company of an elderly lady who was a mere acquaintance of the evening. Charles, his duty to Christabella presumably performed, immediately pounced. 'I have her mother's permission,' he said blandly to the elderly lady. 'Come and dance, Louisa.'

'I shouldn't do this. And we *haven't* got my mother's permission,' protested Louisa as he led her to the floor.

'But you are doing it and you're glad I lied.'

She couldn't deny it and preferred not to answer him. She changed the subject. 'I don't think Mrs Davison likes me very much. Why is that?'

'Our Christabella? She has paid you a compliment, if you did but know it. Christabella Davison likes to be the queen bee. She disapproves, on principle, of any woman who is young, lovely and unattached. Ignore her.'

Clemency was tight-lipped and disapproving when Louisa returned to her for the second time, and her displeasure deepened when Barnabas emerged from the card room on the best of terms with Edward Davison and Ninian Whitmead and announced that he had asked them both, along with Christabella and Charles, to a return supper party in three days' time. The invitation had been accepted, however, and she could not express her outrage. She could only simmer in silent fury.

Louisa, on the other hand, was thrilled.

At the return supper party, Christabella was sweetly civil to her host and hostess and their daughter; flirted in a discreet manner with Charles while showing her husband every wifely deference; and found an opportunity to murmur to Clemency that Charles was a dear boy, but somewhat given to trifling. 'I should keep a benign eye on your daughter if I were you, Mrs Lagrange. She is so charming, but a little young for her age, and Charles is, shall we say, experienced?'

She made sure that Charles did not overhear these barbed observations, but took no care to prevent Louisa from hearing them. Louisa, speechless with annoyance, was then even more annoyed by her mother's response.

'We have made a point of keeping our daughters young in a sense, Mrs Davison. We are no Puritans. No one enjoys everyday pleasures, such as good food, or a little dancing or theatre-going, more than we do. But we still value modesty and a touch of unworldliness in our girls, and we think the two attitudes not incompatible. Louisa is indeed somewhat innocent. She is meant to be. We shall take care of her.'

And thereafter, the secretly enraged Louisa found her mother keeping a close watch on her, not by excluding her from the party in any way, but by keeping her both occupied and in full view, singing to the lute and helping the maidservant Katie bring in the refreshments. As a means of keeping her from any delicious tête-à-têtes with Charles, it was most effective.

She sent him several despairing glances, and once or twice was rewarded by a smile deep in his dark eyes but to her disappointment, he presently turned away and said that he would play a hand or two of cards with Barnabas and Ninian. A moment later, he had left the room with them, remarking as he went that since he was the youngest gentleman, he would take it on himself to put his head into the kitchen to bespeak fresh supplies of hot chocolate for the ladies, and some wine and wafer biscuits for the card-room. Louisa was left sitting dejectedly amid all-female company, while her mother remarked triumphantly that a ladies' party was always such a pleasure.

But a few minutes later, as the ladies were sipping their chocolate, they were startled by the sound of breaking glass and cries of distress from Katie. On hastening to the scene, they found that while carrying a laden tray through a door which Charles was chivalrously holding open, the maidservant had somehow managed to trip over his feet and send the tray and its contents hurtling to the floor.

While Clemency scolded and Katie in floods of tears protested that it hadn't been her fault, and the Davisons surveyed the disaster with an air of tolerant amusement ('Such a thing would never happen in *our* house,' said their expressions), Charles came quietly up to Louisa, cupped his palm under her elbow and guided her back to the room where the ladies had been sitting and into a curtained window-bay. He jerked one of the curtains across, screening them from the rest of the room.

'At last. I've been wanting to get you to myself all the evening!'

'Charles, whatever happened?' It felt as though they had been in some kind of wordless conspiracy and Louisa, bright-eyed, forgot to be shy with him. 'Did you trip Katie up on purpose? *Did* you?'

'What a thing to suggest. As if I'd dream of it! There was Spanish sack and good Bordeaux claret and broken wafers all over your father's carpet. That's not the way for a guest to behave.'

'But did you, all the same? Oh, do tell me!'

'You really are a chatterbox, aren't you, darling? Well, I know now that you sing as sweetly as you talk, but did no one ever tell you, my love, that when a young man and a young woman are alone together, both singing and talking are a waste of time? There's another thing for lips to do.'

She had seen men and women kiss before, but she had never imagined how warm a man's lips would feel on hers, or how exciting the trace of roughness where his shaven bristles were beginning to grow. He lifted his head away once, in order to murmur: 'Open your mouth,' and when she did so, presented her, to her amazement, with a tongue which curled itself round hers and coaxed her into reciprocating.

She freed herself with a sudden jerk, eyes wide, and involuntarily glanced down. Charles laughed.

196

'Have I shocked you, darling? Has no one told you about men and women?'

'Yes, of course! My mother told me about . . . about marriage, long ago. But . . .'

'There's no magic in a few words spoken by a parson, or a magistrate. The magic is in us, my sweet. That was my magic you felt, pressing against you just now. Come here, sweeting. Don't be afraid of it. It's the source of the greatest happiness in the world. Give me your hand.'

Katie was still making a frightful noise. Louisa, behind the curtain in the window-bay, engrossed in Charles's crash course in masculine mechanics, suddenly wondered if he had bribed the girl as well as tripping her up, for she was certainly providing them with time.

When calm was restored and Clemency returned, she was relieved to find Charles and Louisa in decorous conversation in front of the hearth. 'The card game is about to begin now,' she said to Charles, who gracefully excused himself and withdrew.

Louisa sat for the rest of the evening with her mother and Christabella, sipping chocolate, discussing fashions and servants' wages and feeling in her palm the hot, pulsing member Charles had made her hold, and the stickiness of his seed; and deep within herself, a huge, unsatisfied ache of sheer desire. And remembering the final words that he had said to her as he drew her to the hearth, just before Clemency came back.

'I'm going to the West Indies soon but I'll be home in a few months. Wait for me, darling, and when I come back, I'll take you all the way to heaven.'

She did not see Charles again before he sailed, and that summer, they exchanged no further visits with the Davisons. Life settled almost into its old pattern, except for a new purposefulness in the social occasions which they shared with Barnabas' various friends in his own and related trades. They saw two families in particular on frequent occasions: the Dixons and the Brents. Philip Dixon had been an apprentice alongside Barnabas and was now a Master Woodworker holding office in the Woodworkers' Guild, and Isaac Brent was a craftsman in lacquering and japanning. Both were men of substance, growing a little pompous and inclined, like Barnabas himself, to embonpoint.

Each had an unmarried son, already qualified in his father's trade, and in a position to wed.

'If only,' Clemency repined bitterly later on, 'either the Dixon boy or the Brent boy had been tolerably attractive!'

Louisa made no comment, but she knew that it would have made no difference. If Oliver Dixon and Mark Brent had been respectively King Charles the Second and the sun-god Apollo, instead of a callow youth with a bulging adam's apple and a habit of convulsive swallowing, and a seamless bore whose speaking voice was pure monotone, Louisa would still have rejected them. That they were so very unappetising merely saved her from having to resist her parents' urging.

For whenever she looked at them, or at any other young men, Charles' brown face, with its flashing smile and deep, dark eyes; Charles' strong and flawlessly shaped hands, came between.

She belonged to Charles now, and when he came back from the West Indies, they would be betrothed. She had no doubt of it. She had only to wait, and hold off other offers until then.

In September, her patient vigil was rewarded.

Louisa didn't know it at the time, but at the last moment, the reward was almost snatched away.

Clemency had few opportunities for privacy with Barnabas. On weekdays, he rose early, put on the working shirt and breeches to which the aromatic sweetness of woodshavings always clung, and set straight out on foot for his workshop. If he came home to dine, Louisa was usually there, and perhaps guests, and Katie would be coming in and out. He was out on most afternoons, and if he were home for supper, it was as communal a business as dinner. On Sundays, they all went to church in the morning and nine times out of ten, the rest of the Lord's day for Barnabas, whether he went out with his friends or stayed at home, would be sociable, surrounded by others.

But there was one place where Clemency could be sure of being alone with him and that was behind the closed curtains of the marital bed. The best time to talk was on a Sunday morning, for then they rose later. On the second Sunday in September, she seized her chance. 'Barnabas, I am concerned about this invitation for Saturday next. I don't know this Alexander Morris.'

'Morris? I know you haven't met him but he's a thoroughly well-bred man. In fact, he's at court. He's a gentleman usher to His Majesty and a member of the Royal Society too. You should hear him discourse on the mountains of the moon. Astronomy and mathematics are all the rage nowadays, my dear. King Charles is fascinated by them. If a man wants the King to take an interest in furthering his career, I gather he can't do better than be gifted in such ways. There's a man at Oxford, called Christopher Wren, whom the King regards as exceptionally talented and would like to employ as an architect, except that Wren prefers astronomy—'

'Barnabas, I don't want to talk just now about either the King or Christopher Wren, whoever he may be. I don't understand figures or science and I really don't feel that being able to talk about the mountains of the moon is necessarily a character recommendation either. This Alexander Morris—'

'It's astonishing,' said Barnabas, unabashed, 'how this interest in science has burst forth, so suddenly. I was talking to Morris about it in the coffee-house. He said that it isn't really so sudden, that it must have been growing, quietly, underground, all through those long years of solemn religion and witch-hunting and so forth. We're moving into a new world, he says, led by the King's cousin Prince Rupert, who is something of a scientist, and the King himself, who would like to be. Morris actually has a telescope in his own house near Whitehall Palace.

His wife is in poor health and stays in the country but his sister acts as his hostess and they entertain a great deal. The party next Saturday should be a delightful occasion.'

'But the sister,' said Clemency, raising her voice and making her point with determination, 'is Christabella Davison. I had hoped we had seen the last of the Davisons.'

'Now what is the matter with you?' Barnabas sat up, his face pinkly indignant under his nightcap. 'They have brought me some good business by recommending me, and Alexander Morris commissioned a very fine tallboy cabinet last summer. He's a good fellow and we've had many an interesting talk over our coffee and Madeira. What are you objecting to?'

'I keep myself informed of more than you perhaps realise,' said Clemency. 'That young man Charles Whitmead sailed to the West Indies in the spring on a ship called the *Salisbury*. I happen to know that she docked in London last week. The invitation specifically includes Louisa. What will you wager, Barnabas, that the Whitmeads will be at this supper?'

'Well, why shouldn't they be?'

'If they are,' said Clemency resolutely, 'it's a reason for us to stay away. That young man was undoubtedly sniffing after Louisa and he's *not* what we want for her, and well you know it.'

'Why are you in such a fuss? He can't marry her without our consent. Anyway, what's wrong with him?'

'There is just something about him that I don't like. I'm sure you're right about the foreign blood, for one thing . . .'

'Well, really; does it matter?'

'If he were different, perhaps it wouldn't. But he's . . . I don't like it, Barnabas. I wish you would make an excuse for us not to go, or at least to leave Louisa behind.'

'Now look, Clemency.' Barnabas pulled off his cap and scratched his balding head crossly. 'Just see here. I've told you: Alexander Morris is in the King's suite. He has influence. He is already a customer of mine through the Davisons and I look to all of them to bring me more custom still in the future. I don't want to offend them.'

'Before this, you have always avoided meeting customers socially. You once refused an invitation because the Beresford-Highams were going to be there.'

'I had lower standing then. As time goes on, one's attitudes have to change. We're coming up in the world, Clemency.'

Clemency, albeit annoyed, gave up.

Whether Clemency approved of the invitation or not, Louisa could not be the guest of a gentleman usher to His Majesty looking anything but her best. Her dress for the occasion was a new turquoise silk and Clemency paid careful attention, with a pair of tweezers, to her daughter's eyebrows. 'You have lovely eyes, my dear. Grey eyes are so often just pale, but yours have that rare, deep tone. I will lend you my pearl eardrops and necklace and you must have shoes to match your dress. A hooded cloak for the journey, of course. We're going by water and it's always so cold on the river. But, Louisa . . .'

'Yes, Mother?'

'Our hostess is Christabella Davison. Frankly, neither of us like her. But the host will be her brother who is apparently quite a personage. Of course, King Charles is accustomed to mingle freely with all kinds of people, or so we hear, and society takes its tone from the King. But it is quite surprising that we should be invited. So be careful how you behave.'

'Yes, Mother.'

Louisa's eyes were downcast. But her pulses were thudding. She knew already who the hostess was to be; Barnabas had told her. She also knew that the *Salisbury* was anchored in the Thames. She had seen it, while taking a hired boat down the river. She could guess who had arranged their invitation. Surely, surely, Charles would be there!

They often travelled by water, in one of the boats which plied for hire on the Thames. It was frequently the most direct route from one place to another but it tended to be chilly. The night of Mr Morris' gathering was clear, but a sharp breeze was whisking the river into choppy wavelets and Louisa was glad when they drew in towards a private landing stage, attached to a big house which had an unusual tower at one end, with a multi-sided top which seemed to be all windows, even its roof.

'That will be Mr Morris' observatory,' Barnabas said, pointing and then clutching at the gunwale as the wind gusted, blowing Louisa's hood off, and making the boat bounce. Their boatman edged his craft in just behind another which was delivering two passengers to the same place. One of them turned on the landing stage, saw the Lagranges, and waited for them. Calling to the boatman to throw him the painter, he looped it round a bollard and reached out a hand to help the ladies.

'I recognised you as soon as your hood blew off,' said Charles to Louisa as his fingers closed about hers. 'So did my father.' In a whisper, he added: 'Hello, my love.'

Alexander Morris had his sister's brown eyes but whether or not he had her butter-coloured hair it was impossible to say, because his fashionable wig concealed it. He was taller and thinner in build than Christabella, and gracious in manner. He was dressed with formal elegance, complete with sword, and was inclined to double-edged remarks.

'So this is Louisa. I have heard about you, my dear. Edward says you have put my sister in the shade. Poor Christabella!'

Louisa, not knowing what to do with a compliment which sounded like an accusation, turned pink and said nothing. Clemency, at once awed by her surroundings and annoyed with Mr Morris, said in a voice which was just a fraction too regal: 'I believe you are a member of the Royal Society, Mr Morris? You are something of an astronomer, are you not?'

'He tours the lunar mountains on every moonlit night,' said Charles.

'An exaggeration. But certainly I have a telescope,' said Mr Morris.
'Ah, Christabella. You know Ninian and Charles Whitmead, I think, and the Lagrange family . . .'

'Yes, indeed. How delightful to see you all,' said Christabella, her eyes on Charles.

The house was extensive, its rooms large and with higher ceilings than Louisa had ever seen before, even at the Davisons'. The rooms led in and out of one another and the party, which was crowded, circulated through them as people sought out acquaintances, paused to admire paintings and fine furniture, and gathered up refreshments from the trays offered by an army of liveried servants.

Barnabas and Edward Davison quickly vanished in the direction of a card-room and Ninian Whitmead, whose stiff leg seemed to be paining him, sat down on a couch. Charles too disappeared, melting into the throng with Christabella on his arm. But when music struck up for dancing, he came back, alone, to seek Louisa as a partner. Clemency refused before her daughter could speak.

'Please excuse my daughter. She has been unwell.'

'But, Mother!' Louisa whispered fiercely as Charles withdrew. 'I'm perfectly well!'

'Yes, dear. I know.'

In anguish, Louisa stared after Charles, who had turned his back and moved away to talk to Alexander Morris.

'It's unfortunate that we know so few people here,' Clemency said. 'You and I must talk to each other, my dear. In a moment, perhaps we will go and find some supper. I saw some tables being set out in the next room.'

Louisa was beyond answering. Charles was here but she wasn't to be allowed to dance with him and he hadn't stayed to talk to her. She wanted to cry, or stamp her foot, or just leap up and run away from her mother. She dared do none of these things but to speak normally was out of the question. Then Alexander Morris, accompanied by a footman with a branched candlestick, made his way towards them. 'Mrs Lagrange! You showed some interest earlier in my telescope. I am taking a few of my guests up to see it now. Would you and your daughter care to come? There's something to see, I promise you. The moon is almost full and the night is clear.'

'Certainly, Mr Morris. We should be most interested,' said Clemency and added to Louisa: 'This will be far more instructive than merely dancing.'

'Of course, Mother.' Across the room, positioned so that Clemency couldn't see him, Charles had turned round and was winking at her. She didn't quite see how a visit to the observatory tower was going to help them get together but she was willing to trust him. She rose with alacrity.

Morris and his footman led the way, collecting more people as they went. Louisa, her senses attuned to Charles to a degree which verged on the psychic, was aware of him falling in behind. Presently she heard him breathe the words: 'Just hang back a little,' into her ear. She lagged accordingly, and the two of them were among the last to enter the small, round room where Morris halted his party. A spiral staircase, lit at intervals by candles in sconces, led upwards into what Louisa realised must be the tower they had seen from the boat. Clemency, turning to see where her daughter was, caught sight of Charles and frowned, but had no chance to comment, for Mr Morris had taken the candlestick from the footman, and was holding it up, counting heads.

'How many would-be astronomers have I got? Ah . . . ten of us altogether. Well, we can't all squeeze into my little observatory, I'm afraid. I'll take you up in two groups.' And smoothly, as if by accident – except that Louisa, giggling secretly, guessed that it was no accident but had been arranged between Mr Morris and Charles – he picked out five guests, including Clemency but not Louisa, and invited them to follow him up the stairs.

Her mother could hardly refuse to leave Louisa behind in a room full of people merely because one of them was Charles. It would sound absurd. Louisa, gleefully, knew it. Clemency knew it, too. She gave Louisa a stern glance, but followed her host obediently. Charles instantly pulled Louisa through a door into a tiny room, little more than a store cupboard. He shut the door. 'They'll be half an hour up there and none of the others will care a farthing about us.' And then they were in each other's arms.

Half an hour. But it wasn't enough; not nearly enough. Caressing feverishly, they exchanged eager questions and answers, but the time was gone before they had said a quarter of the things they wanted to say, or Charles had coaxed Louisa into anything like the intimacy he wanted.

'What were the West Indies like?'

'Hot. Oh, how I've missed you. No, darling, let me put my hand there; don't hold yourself away . . . You haven't promised yourself to anyone else while I was gone, have you . . . ?'

'No, of course I haven't: I wouldn't. Was the voyage stormy? I was afraid for you. Oh no, Charles, you mustn't . . .'

'I must. Why not? There's no harm in it. Let me hold your breasts. They're like melons. Have you ever seen a melon? The voyage was ghastly. There's hardly any room to move aboard ship and the food's horrible. Hammocks all squashed together, rats getting at the stores and yes, there were plenty of storms. I was nearly washed overboard three times. Oh, my darling, my love, I've starved for you!'

It would not be proper to say that she had starved too, but she did not have to say it. Despite her shyness, she was responding to him and he knew it and so did she. But already the time was gone and they could hear people coming down the spiral stairs.

'We must go. Let me go, Charles!'

'I don't want to. Damn them!'

'Charles, you must! Oh, quickly!'

Louisa pulled herself free and they slipped from their haven and into the outer room, to stand there, well apart, as the first party of visitors came down from the observatory, with Clemency in their midst. Louisa was glad that in the candle-light, her untidy hair and reddened lips would not be easily noticed. Mr Morris was already ushering his second party towards the staircase. She climbed with the others, conscious of Charles just behind her, wondering if they would succeed in being alone again; or if those few urgent fumblings, which had left her so excited and so unsatisfied, were all they were to have.

The observatory was octagonal, cramped inside because the long telescope on its wheeled stand took up so much space, but commanding magnificent vistas from its windows and skylights. The telescope could be swivelled and wheeled to poke out of any window its owner chose. Morris opened some of them, letting in cold blasts of wind, and his shivering guests peered out, to admire the moon-blanched Thames and the roofs of London stretching away to the east.

Apart from the telescope, the only other object in the room was a table with a star-chart pinned on it. Morris showed it to them, explaining that it showed the night sky in winter, pointing out the Pole Star and the Plough and the constellation of Orion. Then he explained the workings of the telescope, and invited each of them to peer in turn through the eyepiece and look at the moon.

Afterwards, Louisa thought that it was a pity that this rare opportunity to gaze at the moon through a telescope should be so confused by strange physical sensations. Charles stood beside her and put his hand over hers as she held the stem of the eyepiece, and she could feel the heat of his body close to hers. She was surprised to find that one did not look straight up the tube of the telescope but down into it through a smaller tube which joined it at right angles, but into her surprise and then her wonder when she saw the strange, pitted face of the moon brought so near, the nearness of Charles continually and disturbingly intruded.

And then the demonstration was over. People were going one by one down the staircase. Louisa was not surprised to find Charles' hand on her arm, holding her back, until they were alone together in a room lit only by the moon. 'Wait a moment. We can go down last. Oh, Louisa, come here.'

It wasn't quite rape. Charles knew his business too well for that. He had made her ready for him; he had made her want him. When he pushed her backwards across the table and the star-chart and his face in the moonlight turned suddenly narrow-eyed and hard, as though he were not seeing her any more, she could have tried to thrust him off, could have screamed or kicked, and she did none of these things.

She struggled once, more in protest against a stab of pain than against Charles, and then was swept exultantly up into delight. Engrossed only in her hammering pulses and in the marvel burgeoning within her, Louisa surrendered herself and her virginity and came, in time with him, with a surge which left her gasping.

Charles lifted her off the table, stroking her hair. 'As if you'd been at it all your life, my love,' he said. 'And now we must catch up with the others.'

Dazed, acutely conscious that despite her bodily ecstasy, something was missing, some dimension of depth and tenderness, loving words that hadn't been spoken and promises of commitment that hadn't been made, Louisa smoothed her clothes. She peered once at the table and saw a single dark blot on the constellation of Orion. She touched it with her finger and when Charles guided her down the stairs and back into the realm of candle-light, she saw that her fingertip was red.

That was the middle of September and now it was nearly halfway through November. In almost two months she had not heard from Charles or seen him. He had never sought her out again, let alone come to see her father or asked for her in marriage.

And though she had waited and worried, had looked at the calendar, and tried to believe her calculations were wrong, and prayed for divine aid when she could pretend no longer, she had lost not one single drop of blood since the one she had left on the constellation of Orion.

Chapter Fifteen

The Shining World

'You are bigger than I am, and I'm lame,' said Ninian to his son. 'Or I'd thrash you half to death.' His lameness had increased in the last year and he spent more time now just sitting in his chair, but his stick was always to hand and his arms and shoulders were strong. He kept a small boat on the river at Temple Stairs, coped with the stairs themselves by willpower and taking them slowly, and was quite capable of hoisting the *Penelope*'s sail, or rowing her for miles. He was seated now but he shook his stick at his son with genuine menace. 'What the *devil* did you think you were about? Your continual affairs with women of experience are bad enough. But to seduce an unmarried girl from a respectable family and not even trouble to inquire if there have been results or not . . . words fail me. I did my best to rear you properly; where did I go wrong?'

'Nowhere, Father,' said Charles blithely. 'I was born selfish, as a succession of tutors, schoolmasters and tearful ex-mistresses have told me. I was also spoiled as a child, I believe. I know my mother thought I was the most marvellous being ever to enter the world. I can remember her,' he added thoughtfully, 'saying that.'

'And I can remember telling her that she said it too much,' said Ninian grimly. 'However, I suppose wondering how you achieved such heights, or depths of irresponsibility isn't the point. What is the point is that Barnabas Lagrange wishes to know what you propose to do about his daughter. I told him I would speak to you as soon as you came home from wherever you had roamed off to – I won't ask where you were all last night – and wait upon him and his wife as soon as possible afterwards. You know what I shall have to say, don't you?'

Charles sighed. 'Yes, Father. How ill-arranged these things are. Fancy having to pay for a lifetime for a few minutes' hurried amusement in Alexander Morris's observatory.'

'Louisa is no doubt of the same opinion. Why the observatory, by the way? An odd place to choose for a seduction, I would have thought.'

'I didn't choose it. It was so difficult to shake off Clemency Lagrange. I had to get Alexander to connive with me. "Very well," he said to me. "I'll separate mother and daughter and the rest is up to you." And a tiresome, rushed business it was too.'

'I have never liked Alexander Morris. The man is a mischief-maker. He seems to have no loyalty even to his sister.'

'He believes, and so do I, that when women obviously long for a man's caresses, it is ungallant to refuse them.'

'I strongly suspect that you know very well how to lead an inexperienced girl on until she hardly knows what she's doing and that that is what you did to Louisa.'

'All right, don't go on. I admit the child is mine, if only because getting past Louisa's mother is so hard that I doubt if anyone else has managed it. I'll marry Louisa if that's what you want.'

'It is most certainly what I want. You'll marry her, or leave my house without a copper farthing to your name. Do you understand?'

'Really? Would you do that to me? To Parvati's son?'

Ninian levered himself to his feet, stepped across the floor with the aid of his stick, and boxed Charles' ears.

'Never abuse your mother's memory in that way again.' Charles blinked, startled by the assault and unexpectedly shaken by the undisguised pain in his father's hazel eyes. 'She is dead,' said Ninian, 'and not to be used as a lever against me. But I will say this. Your mother was once a helpless castaway, dependent for her very life on my care, my goodwill. Now, it seems to me that Louisa Lagrange is also in a sense a castaway, and dependent for her future on *your* care and goodwill. They had better be forthcoming.'

Charles recovered himself. 'Well, I've said I'll marry her. As a matter of fact, I don't really mind. It's time I married and she's a charming girl. Shall I come with you to see Barnabas?'

'No,' said Ninian.

'My son is willing to do his duty and will call on you and Louisa whenever you wish,' Ninian said to Barnabas. Both men had dressed carefully for this difficult meeting. They sat in the Lagrange parlour, warily studying each other. 'But I decided,' Ninian said, 'to come by myself first so that we two fathers could settle things in a business-like fashion. I would like to repeat what I said this morning: that I apologise for my son's disgraceful behaviour. I have no doubt that this calamity is more his fault than hers. Now, we have to think about Louisa.'

Barnabas's round grey eyes met Ninian's steadily. 'If you're agreeable and so is your boy, then maybe we can settle things without quarrelling any further, which we'd best not do if we're to be related henceforth. I recognise I can't hold you responsible for what your son has done. I'd like to get one or two things clear. I'm a tradesman, Mr Whitmead. But I'm a master in that trade and well-to-do. I keep a coach of my own and it isn't everyone who can say that. I can settle a respectable dowry on Louisa, as I did for her sisters, which is fitting, since I believe you're gentlefolk, though Louisa tells me that you sold your land in Cornwall. I can assure you that Louisa's well-educated and can take her place in any society. Having said that . . .'

'Please, Mr Lagrange! I've no doubt that Louisa is all you say. I have met her only once or twice, but she seems very sweet-natured and I will gladly receive her as a daughter. I only wish the circumstances were happier.'

'So do I, and I wasn't afraid you'd think Louisa not good enough,' said Barnabas frankly. 'Far from it, Mr Whitmead. I was going to say that although I reckon I've no choice but to promote this marriage, I'd still like to know precisely who she's marrying. What family does Charles come from on his mother's side?'

There was a pause, while Ninian chose his words. Barnabas watched him. 'I can tell you little about my wife's forebears,' Ninian said. 'My Penny arrived in Cornwall by way of a shipwreck. She was born in India, of Indian stock. But she was a good Christian and the best wife a man ever had.'

'Charles is half-Indian?'

'Charles,' said Ninian, 'is the son of my beloved wife Penelope.'

Barnabas took the hint. 'What happened to her?' he asked.

'She was killed after I was involved in a Royalist rising. She was a casualty in a most thoroughly English civil war. I prefer not to discuss the details. But her death was why I sold my Cornish lands. Some memories are intolerable to live with. I took a small house in London, in Salisbury Court, just off Fleet Street, and put the rest of the money into shipping. I have to admit that Cromwell's regime did a great deal for trade. The Dutch are still a menace but he put an end to the Courteen nuisance. I did astonishingly well. We were able in a few years to move into our present house, which is quite large. There is plenty of room for Louisa and Charles to live there.'

'Ah. I was going to ask about that. Yes, it would be best for Louisa to have company since her husband will be at sea a good deal, presumably. She'll need a respectable personal maid.'

'I'll see to that,' Ninian said. 'I am quite able to provide your daughter with the comforts she has been used to. I've never bought a coach, as it happens. Charles and I live simply on the whole and I put my profits back into the business. I keep a small boat – I can still limp to Temple Stairs and even up and down them if I take my time and I'm at home on the water. But I will get a coach if you wish, for Louisa.'

'No, there's no need. It takes two to get a child. I reckon your son led the way, and that maybe he's had practice, but Louisa should have known better than to let him go so far. He didn't force her; she admits it. If she has to miss a few luxuries, it won't hurt her. A respectable maid she must have, but a private coach she can well do without. There are a couple of things more that I'll ask of you, but a coach isn't one of them.'

'Yes, Mr Lagrange?'

Barnabas sighed. 'Let's be clear. I want this marriage to save my daughter's good name. But . . . left to myself, I would have chosen a husband for her from a trade family like my own, with a solid London background. But it's not to be and there's one thing:

207

I've taken to *you*, Mr Whitmead. I'm happy to know she'll have you as her father-in-law.'

'Thank you,' said Ninian and waited for Barnabas to get to the point.

'But since her good name is what's in danger, I'd like the wedding held as soon as possible,' said Barnabas. 'And will you arrange, if you please, for Louisa to be out of town when the baby's born, so as no one here quite knows when that is? Then there won't be any scandal.'

'Agreed,' said Ninian.

'It's all decided,' Ninian told Charles. 'A quiet Anglican ceremony at the end of the week. The excuse to the vicar for all the haste is that you are insanely in love, and expecting to be summoned to sea at any moment.'

'But I'm not.'

'Oh, don't be provoking, Charles. The Duke of York is proposing to sail against the Dutch in the English Channel at any moment and we shall probably have a full-scale war against the Dutch starting after Christmas. You're a seaman. As far as the vicar or anyone else knows, you could have volunteered for the war. As far as your new in-laws are concerned, that is just what you have done. Everything has to look thoroughly proper. Barnabas Lagrange has a sister coming to stay within the next two or three days. She'll be at the wedding and she is apparently still an old-fashioned Puritan. Barnabas is very anxious that she shouldn't sense that anything's amiss.'

'Oh, God.'

'Just behave yourself, that's all. And Charles . . .'

'Yes, Father?'

'Try to make Louisa happy. Make an effort to be a good husband. And try to give the poor girl a little real romance on her wedding night. Alexander Morris' observatory must have given her a strange idea of what lovemaking is all about.'

'She has a natural talent for it. I don't expect to be greeted with distaste.'

'And don't discuss her with me in that manner, please, Charles. Dear Lord,' said Ninian wearily, 'sometimes I feel old. When I was born, Queen Bess was still on the throne. I can remember my mother in a ruff and a farthingale. There were Puritans then but they weren't in the ascendant; people wore fine clothes and went to theatres and feasted at Christmas just as they do now. But the way your generation talks and behaves would have been unthinkable, just the same. I admire King Charles – what he is doing for science and in tackling the Dutch at sea is admirable – but in other ways he's setting a poor example.'

'Well, there it is, Father. Times change.'

'And yet,' said Ninian slowly, 'it's strange, but some things linger on, too. You would never have met Louisa Lagrange if we hadn't come face to face with the Beresford-Highams outside the King's

Theatre that day and I hadn't turned us round to avoid speaking to them.'

It was ten years now since Anthony Gubbes had written to Ninian, telling him that Francis had died in Cologne, of a lung inflammation after a bitter winter. Tamzin had remained abroad, apparently finding shelter with the cousins who were caring for her children. And Mary, who had gone on living at Rosnance while William Beresford-Higham had gone on being billeted there, had married him.

Something had been quivering in the air between them, Ninian remembered, even when he last saw them, although the laws against adultery brought in by the Puritans had probably held them apart until Mary was widowed. Even so, when she married Beresford-Higham, she would only have been in her thirties and she had kept her looks, for she still had them in her forties, when he saw her in Drury Lane. She had kept them too well for Ninian's taste, appearing in front of him like a spectre from the past; instantly recognisable, still fair of hair and elegant; still with her air of expecting to be indulged. By the look of her, Beresford-Higham the former Puritan had decided to do precisely that.

Mary had lost Ninian his wife and now she had, more or less, presented him with a daughter-in-law. It was as though he could not free his life from her persistent influence. He could only hope that the result this time would be happier than before.

When Charles came to see her, Louisa scarcely knew what she would say to him. Part of her longed to see him. But he had paid no heed to her after his conquest; he had left her alone to face the consequences which were now pushing impatiently at her waistline. She was expanding early and the pregnancy would soon be visible.

She watched his arrival from the window, and waited in the parlour for her parents to send him in to her. When he came, she met him with her head up and when he offered his hand, did not take it. She took care not to look at it, either. Charles's hands were so beautiful; so very beautiful.

'I have come,' said Charles, 'to ask you to marry me.'

'I know,' said Louisa. 'And of course, my answer must be yes. I hope to be a good wife to you. I will certainly try my best. But Charles . . .'

'Yes, my love?'

'I want to ask you something. After we . . . I mean, after the evening we visited the observatory, why did you never arrange to see me again? Or ask after me?'

Charles had expected that one.

'I wanted to, my heart. I tried to. But plans kept on falling through for one reason or another, and I was much caught up in business, too. I was helping my father and also trying to arrange the provisioning of the *Salisbury* for next season's voyage. I should have managed to meet you before very long. But your mother doesn't like me. I could hardly come

to the door and ask for you, and still less inquire after your health in any
. . . er . . . particular way.'

'Oh. I see.' Louisa felt foolish. Charles, who had intended precisely
that, watched her with amusement.

'My sweet,' he said, 'let us not begin our betrothal with a
disagreement. We will be married within a week! Come and kiss me and
tell me what your wedding dress will be like.'

'It is being made,' said Louisa, allowing him to embrace her. 'But the
groom must never know any details of it beforehand.'

The hurt at his neglect was still there but he was right; they mustn't
squabble when marriage was so inevitable and so close, and his
explanation was reasonable. He was very resourceful but he wasn't a
magician and their meetings always had been difficult.

'That girl!' said Christabella, her nostrils pinched white with rage, a
phenomenon visible even in the shadowy surroundings of a curtained
bed. 'How could you, Charles? Not that I'm surprised! From the
moment Edward told me that you wanted him to help you meet this
Louisa Lagrange, I *knew*. I wouldn't mind so much if she wasn't such a
stupid little innocent, but to be set aside for such a baby . . . !'

'No claws, now! I can't go to my wedding with a scratched face! Stop
it, Christabella . . . damn you, you bitch, stop it . . . oh, all right, if you
want to play rough games . . . !'

Some time later, he said: 'I've warned you, Christabella. I won't be
tied. You don't own me. No one owns me. I give my services freely . . .
or not.'

A little later still, Christabella said drowsily: 'When you say that no
one owns you, does that include Louisa?'

'Of course,' said Charles.

Despite the inauspicious events which had led up to it, Louisa's
wedding day went well. Aunt Faith was there, even wearing lavender
for the occasion instead of the gloomy black which was Louisa's only
memory of her. She was a large woman with a deep voice in which she
lectured them both about the seriousness of matrimony, the likelihood
that all would turn to dust and ashes in this vale of tears and the
unwisdom of marrying in the kind of haste they were displaying.
However, she clearly did not suspect the reason for the haste, and even
unbent enough after the ceremony to wish them happiness.

The whole party presently repaired to Ninian's house and there,
amid noisy well-wishing and ribald jests, Louisa and Charles were
shown to their room and their fourposter bed and left in it together.

Ninian had told Charles to make the occasion romantic and Charles
had no objection. Once again, but this time on the comfort of a down
mattress, Louisa experienced the burgeoning delight and the surging
climax which she had first known on top of Alexander Morris' star-
chart.

She woke in the morning to find herself snuggled tight against
Charles, and filled with a happiness which she hardly knew how to

contain. All the longing and secrecy, the guilt and fear were over and out of them had come this. She was safely married to Charles, and she loved him. She would never look at anyone else as long as her life lasted. Her world was shining.

Chapter Sixteen

The Olive Branch

'Your hot chocolate, Mrs Whitmead,' said Molly Meade, whose name suggested a milkmaid but who was actually a dignified widow approaching her fifties. She was Louisa's personal woman and it was Molly who, during the hard frost of January, had decreed that her mistress should start each morning with a cup of hot chocolate in bed and was still bringing it to her each day, now that it was March.

Louisa sat up. Outside, London was waking up. Wheels rumbled and hooves clattered, and an approaching milk vendor shouted his wares. Wych Street was nearer the heart of things than the Strand and therefore noisier. An out-of-tune skirling came from a few yards away: Piper MacPherson, who played the bagpipes – not very well – for coins. Charles said it was a horrible noise and that most of the coins were attempts at paying the drunken old devil to shut up.

But Charles wasn't here now. Louisa closed her hands round the cup as though to find comfort from its warmth. In the comfortable crimson-hung fourposter, she was alone. Yesterday, she had stood by the Thames and seen the *Salisbury* sail away. She wasn't bound for the war against the Dutch, but Louisa knew that her West Indies destination was as perilous as any war, and that even if Charles avoided pirates and fevers and hurricanes, he would be months away. The child kicked and the chocolate jolted, spilling a little on the bedcover. Louisa, absurdly, sobbed.

'Now, now.' Molly came briskly to her side. 'I once saw my husband off to war, and I know how you feel. But it's no use giving way to it. Now, what dress will you wear today?'

'I feel as though I'd rather stay in bed,' said Louisa sorrowfully. 'Or wear mourning.'

'You'll get up and you'll wear your tawny grosgrain and your mood will change to match your gown,' said Molly, quite as firmly as Clemency would have done. 'Pining isn't good for the baby. Come along, now. Mr Whitmead will think you're ill if you don't come to breakfast.'

In the Lagrange household, breakfast had been of no importance. People there rose early and went about their day's business, swallowing a buttered bread roll and a beaker of ale or cup of chocolate in passing, as likely as not without even sitting down.

The Whitmeads, however, consumed their rolls and chocolate at leisure from a table adorned with a cloth. Ninian liked tablecloths at all

213

mealtimes and Louisa knew now that this was bound up with the fact that his dead wife, Charles' mother, had embroidered the motif at the corners of all the table linen. The motif consisted of wavy lines like rippling water, and curved lines arching over them like a bridge. It was some sort of traditional Whitmead device.

So quickly had the Whitmead house and its routine become familiar to her, that now she talked to guests of 'our Whitmead device' and could hardly imagine a time when she had not regularly sat down to breakfast. Ninian would certainly worry if she didn't appear. Therefore, she washed her face, let herself be coaxed into the tawny grosgrain, brushed her hair, and put it into a lace cap, and went downstairs. Molly, who ate with the family, followed, in her usual respectable brown dress and clean white kerchief.

Ninian was already there in the sunny, spacious parlour, also dressed for the day, in a hip-length blue coat which was fashionable but also looked comfortable. He wouldn't have worn it otherwise. There was little of the peacock about Ninian and unlike Charles, he never asked anyone to admire his clothes. Nor did he show much interest in other people's, although he was keenly aware of their moods. As she came in, he searched her face and saw straight past the gown and the pretty cap to the sadness behind them.

'You're missing Charles, I can see.' Without getting up, he reached round the table and pushed out chairs for them. 'I knew you would, and no doubt you're thinking that a lame old man won't be much company.'

'Oh, no!' Louisa protested. She sat down and Dorothy, the maidservant, handed her the bread and poured the fresh chocolate. Dorothy was a tired-faced spinster in her late forties and Sarah and Joe Clifford, the cook and the manservant, were a married couple, similarly in middle age. None of the Whitmead servants were young. She had found it difficult, at first, to make any innovations in the running of the house because they were such creatures of habit.

'No good saying no,' said Ninian humorously. 'It would be strange if you didn't feel that. You may have got quite fond of your old father-in-law, but I'm not Charles. However, it won't be as bad as you think. I've some news for you.'

'News?'

'Indeed, yes.' He ate a roll thoughtfully, watching her with kind eyes. When Dorothy had left the room, he said: 'You have been more than welcome in this house. You've done much to brighten it, just by being here. You've also made Charles and me very comfortable by insisting on regular washdays and a little polish on the furniture. Bachelor households are apt to let these things go.'

'Oh!' Louisa always became shy when offered a compliment. 'I only do the things my mother taught me to do.'

'You've worked hard at them, though,' Ninian said. 'I think you should have a rest from housekeeping during the summer.' He gave Molly a smile. 'We have no secrets from you, Mrs Meade. As you know, Louisa's baby will be born in June but in the eyes of the world, it has no business to be born until August at the earliest. Before she was married,

'I promised her father that she should go to the country this summer and not return until the autumn; I trust with a baby, whose official birthday will be – August.'

'Yes. My father mentioned something about it to me,' said Louisa. Ninian had never been censorious about the circumstances of her marriage and she was grateful. 'But where am I to go?' she asked. 'My sisters both live in town and anyway, I haven't confided in them.'

'It's been a puzzle to me too,' Ninian confessed. 'But not now. Fate has taken a hand.' He felt in the pocket of the blue coat. 'A week or two ago, I had a letter. Here it is. You can read it.'

The letter, which was dog-eared but written in a very tidy hand and competently spelt, began with the words 'My dear cousin Ninian.' Louisa looked up. 'It calls you cousin,' she said. 'I did not know you had any other relatives.'

'Until I received that letter, I hadn't, in any practical sense,' said Ninian. 'At least, I had, but we were out of touch. However, that has now changed. Go on, read it aloud, so that Mrs Meade can hear.'

'My dear cousin Ninian,' read Louisa. 'It is many years since we have exchanged letters, for I fear that the disputatious times when Parliament was at war with the first King Charles divided our family as it did many others. I know that when my parents learned that you upheld the Royalist cause, they ceased to correspond with you, and I was then very young with no voice in the matter. I did indeed protest a little, but my father would not hear me.

'But that was many years ago. We are all united now under the second King Charles, and my parents are gone, which perhaps you did not know. Luke Whitmead my father died in the year 1660 and my mother Patience Whitmead followed him but a year later. I wish to mend the breach between our households and although perhaps my father and mother would not approve, still I cannot think it wrong to do so and hope you will not think so either.

'I have been married now these twelve years and although we have had our disappointments as many parents do, young children being so frail, still I have a son of nearly ten and a daughter soon to reach her third birthday, and another little daughter born one year since. I have four sisters, all well married (one is wed to a knight) and a good acquaintance in this county of Essex, where we have other kinsfolk of whom you may not know, but with whom we have kept contact and often make merry cheer at Christmas and other seasons.

'I and Charity my wife would gladly welcome you if ever you wish to visit us with your family, for we have ample space here in Whitmead House. Meanwhile, if you will write back to me and renew the friendship between our households as it was used to be, our hearts would be glad.

'Christmas Day, at Whitmead in Essex, from the hand of your affectionate cousin Samuel Whitmead.'

'Even with our modern postal service, a letter takes some time to get from Essex to London if it goes by way of Cornwall!' Ninian smiled. 'It was sent to the place where I was last heard of – Polmawgan, near

Land's End. But the people who bought Polmawgan from me are still there. They were introduced to me by a friend called Anthony Gubbes. Anthony died two years ago, but his son was able to give them my London address. Poor Anthony. He was an ardent Parliamentarian. When his son wrote to tell me of his death, he said that his father lost heart when all that Cromwell had done to make England godly began to slip away. I don't agree with that viewpoint, but I owed Anthony much, all the same, and I had known him all my life.'

'You must have left many friends behind when you left Cornwall,' Louisa offered. She laid the letter down on the table. Clearly they hadn't finished with it, but equally clearly, Ninian's mind had gone off at a tangent.

'Not so many,' he said. 'I left my servants, yes. They didn't want to leave Cornwall, but Jimmy Tonkin and the Bransons had been with me for many years and it was a wrench on both sides, parting. The Cliffords remind me of the Bransons a little though they're a little careless in their work – or were until you took them in hand. The Bransons were never that. Anyway, Jimmy's dead now and I pay a pension to the Bransons. As to personal friends . . . There was Anthony and the Deweys, but I had lost most of my friends, one way or another, before I came to London.'

'The Civil War must have changed everything,' Louisa said. 'In Cornwall just as it did here. It was dreadful here. Families were divided, neighbours quarrelled, especially when the King and Archbishop Laud were executed. My father cried the day King Charles was beheaded. And so many men went away to fight, and didn't return.'

'That's all too true,' said Molly with feeling. 'My husband was killed at Edgehill. I didn't even know he was dead until two months after. I was at home, waiting and waiting for news . . . Oh, well. It's over twenty years ago now.'

'But the scars remain.' Ninian emerged from his reverie. 'When I was a boy, there were four of us who went about together. We used to swim and climb rocks and generally get up to mischief. Anthony and I were two of them, and the others were Francis, who fled overseas to join Prince Charles as he was then, and died in exile and Christopher, who was killed in the last Royalist rising in Penzance. Believe me, there are times when I feel like a leftover. Do you know, I sometimes think that if I went back to Polmawgan Cove, I'd find us all there, fooling about, boys on the shore, just as we used to be. And but for the war, perhaps we would all still be together and alive. The war spoiled everything.'

He leant forward and took up the letter again. 'It divided me from my cousins, just as this says – Cornish ones as well as these – and it tore me and my friends apart: killed Christopher outright and the others slantwise, so to speak . . .'

To Louisa's horror, his voice faltered. 'I am so sorry,' she said, distressed.

Molly, in a calm, social voice, said: 'Do you miss Cornwall, Mr Whitmead? I have heard young Mr Whitmead speak of it but he says he was very small when he left it and can't remember it clearly.'

'Yes, I find it hard to imagine,' agreed Louisa, following Molly's lead and also pretending to have noticed nothing wrong. 'I've never seen the sea.'

'You'd find Polmawgan hard to imagine even if you had.' Ninian's voice had steadied again. 'The cliffs were so towering, the seas so powerful. When the big waves rolled in and broke on the rocks they crashed like thunder and the spume went up in white clouds and there were always seabirds calling, the wildest sound I know. On clear days, the light was incredible: so *lucid*. Miss it? Yes, I do. I loved it once. I loved my house. In fact, I loved Polmawgan so much that I was unwilling to leave and when finally I did flee, I'd left it too late and my wife died. It's strange. I had a great-aunt who loved her house more than she did any of the people round her and I always hoped I would never become like her. I understand her better now. But I've never been able to forgive myself. I was so ashamed after my wife died, and I turned against Polmawgan. I was thankful to leave Cornwall, thankful to leave the people who had hounded us; I thought I'd never want to see the place again But now – yes, it's extraordinary. I miss it after all.'

He fell silent again and neither Louisa nor Molly knew quite what to say to him. But presently, he looked once more at the letter and recalled himself to the present.

'I was glad to receive this, Louisa; you can't think how glad. After losing so many people, I'm very happy to get some cousins back. With luck, they may also provide somewhere for you to stay during the summer. They enclosed a memorandum giving details of how to reach Whitmead House. After giving it some thought, I've decided to write back to ask if you and I may visit them. We'll stay for about a month and then if all is well, I'll come home to attend to my business, and you can stay on, that is, if you're happy there. I won't leave you there unless I'm sure of that. But if all goes well, we'll be on our way to Essex in a week.'

The reply from Samuel was so welcoming that it bordered on the effusive. Nothing, it seemed, would please him and Charity, or his son Benjamin and his two little daughters, more than to receive Ninian and Louisa at Whitmead for a visit as prolonged as the visitors chose to make it. 'I hope they're as pleasant as they sound,' Ninian remarked.

'I'm sure they're kind,' said Louisa. 'I shall look forward to meeting them.'

She was growing heavy and in fact found the prospect of the journey rather daunting, yet she was glad of it. Charles' absence ached like a bad tooth. Even when technically at home, he was often out, on business connected with his ship or on mysterious male occasions about which he said little, which had once or twice upset her. But his presence was still in the house, in the form of clothes tossed here and there, his shaving kit on the washstand, his charts on the parlour table, an indefinable but thrilling disturbance in the air. Now all this was gone and ahead lay a vista of empty month on empty month. Whitmead would be a distraction.

The journey was easy after all. Ninian hired a boat for the first leg of the journey. They passed under London Bridge and Louisa regarded the houses with interest. 'How strange, to live on a bridge and look out of one's windows, straight down into the river,' she said.

They landed that evening on the Essex bank of the river and spent a night at an inn. Molly observed: 'Mr Whitmead, if your cousins have the same surname as you and live at Whitmead House, they may well be people of standing. They sound as though they've been there for generations.'

'They're sure to have standing. Didn't the first letter say that one of Samuel Whitmead's sisters is married to a knight?' said Louisa.

'Yes,' said Ninian. 'And Samuel certainly had a Puritan upbringing. We should be careful. Unless someone actually asks, don't say when you and Charles were married. As far as Whitmead is concerned, you are expecting your first child, Charles is at sea, London is too hot and I want you in the country for the birth. But if they do ask, you were married in September when the *Salisbury* came home. How much they know about my own marriage, I don't know, but . . . well, you both know that my wife came off a Courteen shipwreck. You were there when I told Louisa, Molly. But I don't want it mentioned, at least until I'm sure either that they know and it didn't raise their eyebrows, or that they don't, but it won't.'

'Such a romantic tale,' said Molly. 'But I agree; it would be best to be circumspect.'

'I will be careful,' said Louisa earnestly.

The land was flat and the view long and the house was in sight long before they reached it, perched on the only knoll for miles. Wide pastures surrounded it, threaded with glinting streams and patched here and there by clumps of woodland. A right-hand fork brought them at length to a small, arched gatehouse where, however, no porter was on duty. The gate stood invitingly wide, to admit them to a cobbled yard in front of a beautiful house, graciously designed in the fashion of the previous century; many-gabled, with rosy brickwork below, black timbers patterned on white plaster above, and dormer windows looking contentedly from the broad slope of a red-tiled roof. It had been grafted on to a smaller, older house which had no brickwork but only white plaster and plain timbers.

This now formed a separate wing to the left, and appeared at the moment to be the cause of some consternation. Workmen with picks and spades stood in an anxious huddle by its open door, except for one who had given up standing in favour of kneeling and appeared to be saying his prayers. Two maidservants and a woman in a cook's apron were also outside, staring at the door as though expecting a dragon to issue from it, and in the middle of the yard stood a supervisor, gesticulating with a rolled-up drawing and trying to explain something to a fox-haired man whose good black suit and tidy neckcloth proclaimed him as the employer.

'Are we really expected?' asked Louisa, peering timidly out of the coach window.

But they were. People were hurrying from the main door; two women, and then a young man and a boy, both of whom were as fox-haired as the man in the courtyard. The latter had turned at the sound of the coach and now, waving the supervisor impatiently back, he hurried towards it. Ninian, climbing out first, with the aid of his stick, put his weight awkwardly on his damaged leg and almost fell.

'Steady, now. Let me take your stick.' The young man, who was in his early twenties, came to his aid and the boy, who was about ten, offered an arm on the other side. Both were wiry and strong. Ninian straightened up, adjusting his weight gingerly. 'My thanks. Well! You're *Whitmeads*!'

'We are indeed.' The man who had been talking to the supervisor had now joined them. He was older, somewhere in his thirties, although at first glance he could have been taken for less, for his freckled face and broad grin gave him a boyish air. 'I am Samuel Whitmead and this young boy is my son Benjamin, and if Paul there has the surname of Browne, he nevertheless has a Whitmead in his ancestry, three generations back. And you, sir, must be Mr Ninian Whitmead. You must excuse the confusion in my courtyard. We are making some alterations to the east wing and have run into difficulties. The kitchen is in there and dinner may be late. Tell me, why the exclamation? Who else,' asked Samuel with amusement, 'would you expect to find at Whitmead House but Whitmeads?'

'Your hair,' said Ninian. 'My hair was that light red once and so was my father's. He used to say it ran in the family. My son is dark; he takes after his mother. But you three! I'd have known you anywhere as Whitmeads.'

'And you will say the same of my little girls. I call my children my fox-cubs.' The elder of the two women came forward, her hand held out. She wore clothes whose simplicity suggested Puritan parents, but she had not hidden her pinned-up brown hair and her settled, sensible face was pleasantly lined, with laughter creases round her blue eyes. 'I am Samuel's wife, Charity, and this is Lucy, Paul's wife. They were married only last year. They live in Quensted, which is quite nearby, and often visit us. Come, Lucy.'

Lucy was hanging back shyly but as Louisa descended from the coach, she let herself be drawn forward and suddenly took Louisa's hands. 'I didn't know! You are soon to have a child. How exciting!'

'Oh, *Lucy*! Will you never learn to watch your tongue? What a way to speak to a complete stranger!' Charity cried. But her tone was affectionate and if there had been any stiffness in this meeting, it was gone. Suddenly, amid their mutual laughter, it was as if the reunited families, far from being strangers, had known each other all their lives.

Even so, guests must observe certain rules concerning good manners.

Ninian, Louisa and Molly all longed to know what calamity in the kitchen wing had actually caused a workman to kneel down and pray, but the conversation over dinner – which wasn't particularly late – did not tend that way. Instead, Samuel set about filling in the gaps of knowledge between the sundered branches of the Whitmead families, marvelling over the astonishing fact that Ninian's father had been brother to Samuel's great-grandfather; and that Paul was the great-grandson of Ninian's first cousin Jane.

'But my side have all gone in for early marriages,' Paul Browne said and when the meal was over and the women had taken Louisa upstairs 'to lie down after your long journey and later you can meet the little girls in the nursery', Samuel fetched out a massive and ancient Bible, opened it on the dining table and showed Ninian the births and deaths and marriages recorded in a succession of hands on the flyleaf.

'There, as you see. Paul was married last year at the age of twenty-three and his father married at twenty-two and *his* father at twenty-one. Jane Whitmead wasn't quite twenty-one when she went to church to become the wife of Geoffrey Browne. And your father, Cousin Ninian, was of course many years younger than the brother from whom our side is descended.'

'I didn't marry until I was forty,' Ninian volunteered.

'What was your wife's family?' asked Samuel, his forefinger absently stroking the record of his eldest sister's marriage to a knight. 'Would we know the name? We have heard of all the main Cornish families – the Grenviles and the Arundells.'

Ninian shook his head, and then proceeded to explain Parvati in terms they would understand. 'My Penny came of no special family. She was gentle and beautiful but had no inheritance. My son and daughter-in-law,' he added, adroitly changing the subject, 'also married for love.'

Samuel noticed the lack of detail and was puzzled by it but tactfully changed the subject.

'I hope you'll enjoy staying with us. We haven't quite abandoned my parents' Puritan ways. I work on the farm with my own hands and so does Ben, and Charity is bringing up the girls to help in the house. There are no drones here. And we still go to church twice on the Sabbath – we have a very fine church only a mile away, in Whitmead village. But we make music of an evening and dress fashionably for holidays and we celebrate heartily at Christmas and on May Day. We work hard but we believe in laughter too.'

'I say amen to that. It's a brand new world and one can have a godly life, in my opinion,' said Paul, 'and still enjoy it. My mother came from a very stern Parliamentarian family but her grandfather was hanged for stealing sheep, if the truth be told. And the Lord alone knows what has gone on here in the distant past. The Whitmeads have been here since heaven knows when so they may well have been here when . . . well, Samuel? Shouldn't we show him what was found this morning? He must be wondering!'

'Something odd was clearly going on when we drove in,' said Ninian. 'What was it?'

Samuel closed the Bible. 'It was a shocking thing,' he said seriously. 'We went to see for ourselves while you were washing before dinner, and I daresay the wenches have told your womenfolk all about it by now. I think . . .' he glanced round the room '. . . Ben has slipped off somewhere; gone back for another stare, I expect. Come.'

He led the way out of the dining room, through the long, sunlit parlour which adjoined it, and through a low door at the far end. 'There are two steps down,' he said, mindful of Ninian's stick. 'This leads into the east wing. It was actually the original house. All the rest was built new by Theodore Whitmead, your grandfather, Cousin Ninian. He was employed at the court of Queen Bess, I believe, and he became quite wealthy. We use the east wing for the kitchen and servants' quarters now. I've been wanting to extend my wine cellar, which is under the later part of the house. There's a basement store-room beneath the kitchen, and I decided to enlarge that, make it deeper so that its floor is on a level with that of the wine cellar, and take out part of the wall in between them. This morning, the men were digging up the store-room floor. And, well . . .'

The low door had brought them into a square scullery where a manservant was polishing silver. A trapdoor in the floor was open and voices came from below. The manservant's face was pursed with disapproval.

'I know. My son's down there,' Samuel said to him, answering the unspoken remark. 'My thanks for seeing that we got our dinner, Fisher. You got the women back to their tasks very quickly.'

'Yes, sir, though not without difficulty. As it is, they're still whispering about it fit to burst in the kitchen.'

'Well, it's natural,' said Samuel, and ushered Ninian towards the trapdoor. 'Can you manage some steep steps?'

'I'm used to managing. Take my stick and I'll use my hands to help me.'

Carefully, Ninian descended, with Paul and Samuel following. The basement below was lit by two lamps and a branched candlestick. Half the floor had been dug up and flagstones were piled in a corner. Two workmen were continuing with trowels the work which picks and spades had started, taking care so that what had been found could be disinterred without damage. Benjamin, sitting on a barrel, was watching with enormous interest. The men rose and stood silently back to let their employer and his companions see why the cook and the maidservants had fled pell-mell from the kitchen and what had caused a workman to fall to his knees on the cobbles and recite the *Our Father*.

It was a human skeleton. It lay still partly embedded in the soil, but most of the skull and the ribs were exposed, as were the leg bones which lay close beside them.

'He was buried with his knees bent, sir,' one of the men said. 'Put in the ground huddled-up, like. It weren't no proper decent burial.'

'And look what else has been found!' Benjamin jumped off the barrel and showed them a heap beside the excavation. 'We don't know what it is, but it might be saddlery. It was probably put here with him.'

'You shouldn't be down here,' said Samuel, but went to look just the same. The others went with him.

'I think Ben is right. It's all hard and blackened but yes, I think it's leather. It used to be coloured, I should say.' Samuel held a piece up. It had a curious, scalloped edge and here and there flecks of dull red still showed. 'This is part of a rein, surely.'

Ninian stooped and picked up a piece of rusty metal, a short bar with a curved arch in the middle. 'And this was a bit, a curb. Were there any traces of clothing on the skeleton?'

'The soil's sort of different close round it,' one of the workmen said. 'That'd be where the clothes rotted, I daresay, but that's all.'

'I doubt we'll ever know the truth,' said Paul, 'but it looks like murder, long ago. I fancy that whoever killed him, buried his saddle and bridle with him, fearing that if they were found they would point to his killers. I wonder what they did with the horse?'

'He's probably been there for centuries, but as likely as not, it was a Whitmead that put him there, I'm sorry to say,' said Samuel.

'Medieval, from the shaping of that rein,' Ninian said. 'Poor devil, whoever he was. What will you do about him, Samuel?'

'Get him up, take him to the church and ask the minister to give him Christian burial.'

'If he died in the Middle Ages, he was probably a Papist,' Ninian observed.

'Well, Papist rites he'll have to do without,' said Samuel. 'But a decent service read over him and a grave in hallowed ground; those he shall have. If a Whitmead was responsible, I'll put it right as best I can. We never know what kind of people our forebears were.'

'Will you tell them now about the shipwreck?' Louisa asked, when Ninian had returned to the open air and sought her out in order to tell her about the discovery.

'I'm not sure. It certainly looks as if the family has a worse skeleton in its past – literally – than a foreign castaway, but still . . . no, we'll wait.'

He had lost Parvati seventeen years ago but she lived on still in a secret place in his mind. He had told Charles the full truth, because Charles was her son, and with Louisa and her family he had shared some of it, because Louisa was carrying Parvati's grandchild. But from the rest of the world, even from these pleasant cousins, instinct still said to Ninian: defend her.

The nameless bones were laid to rest in the churchyard of St Mary's in Whitmead village, at a service attended by all the adult Whitmeads, and performed with scrupulous propriety by the vicar of Whitmead, even though he could only refer to the deceased as 'our brother'.

Samuel, however, paid for a headstone with *Requiescat in pace* carved on it, saying that this was no more than his duty, since he owned the village and his grandfather had dedicated the church. The village, he told Ninian, had arisen in the previous century, beginning from a cluster of cottages which housed the Whitmead farm labourers.

'It's grown since then,' Samuel said with pride. 'We have our own weekly market now.'

The Whitmead family altogether struck Ninian as fine and thriving. They were very willing to look after Louisa through the birth of her baby. 'Are you agreeable to staying with them?' Ninian asked his daughter-in-law. He was secretly longing to go home, not only to attend to business but also to get back to the books of plays and verse which occupied the bookshelves in his study.

'I shall miss you. But yes, I'm happy to stay. Your cousins are very kind.'

'They seem to be,' Ninian agreed. 'I wish I knew them better. I brought you here with the idea of leaving you with them for a while but now that we're here, I find I keep wondering . . . this and that.'

'But why?' Louisa was surprised and so too was Molly.

'I can't say,' Ninian told her. 'I'll have a talk with Samuel. If I feel I should, I'll stay with you. I can delegate someone in London to see to my business affairs.'

He left them stitching baby clothes in Charity's parlour and went out to find Samuel, whom he had glimpsed from a distance walking through the sunlit afternoon towards a cornfield. Samuel, examining the young wheat, greeted him with pleasure. 'Ah, Ninian. The crop has begun well although I could wish for more rain. Did you want something in particular? You've come a long way, with that limp.'

'Sometimes I need to walk, even if it's painful. I saw you and thought I'd join you. The corn looks healthy.' Ninian frowned, wondering how to bring the conversation round to the point he wanted. 'I've always said that it's damp weather that breeds trouble. In Cornwall, people were apt to ascribe crop diseases to witchcraft, but I thought that was nonsense. Do you believe in witchcraft, Samuel?'

'I'm not sure. It's not fashionable to believe in it nowadays, but it's attested in the Bible,' Samuel said. 'How can you go against that? But there have been no cases of witchcraft round here in my lifetime for which I thank God. I've no experience of it, I'm glad to say.'

And that, thought Ninian, as he pulled up a weed or two and threw them aside, fairly summed up his own feelings about his cousins. Secure in their quiet family life in this country place, rooted in their beliefs, they had goodwill but lacked experience and their untroubled faces were proof of it. He would never risk telling them about Parvati, and he would remind Louisa and Molly not to speak even of the little they knew. But it should be possible to leave Louisa with them. She would have Molly, after all, and she could come home once the summer was over.

But in the end the decision was taken out of his hands. The day before Ninian meant to leave, Barnabas Lagrange presented himself at Whitmead to announce that plague had broken out in London.

'It's bad,' Barnabas said, conducting the interview with Ninian out in the open air, having accosted a groom and asked for Ninian to come out to him. 'Your maidservant Dorothy came to tell me. The Cliffords fell ill and died within two days and, well, there she was, alone in the house with two dead bodies, and you know what the law is. As soon as the authorities got to hear of it, they'd have been round to take the corpses away, but they'd have nailed up the door and shut her in for the next thirty days. She ran away and came to me. I sent her to her home – hard on her family if she sickens but I have to put mine first – and set out at once to warn you not to come back. Luckily you left your direction with me.

'I'm not going to ask to come in, just in case I'm carrying it, and I'll go away without seeing Louisa. I'd be glad of permission to sleep in an outhouse. It won't be any hardship in this hot weather. It's too hot if you ask me: plague thrives in heat. If you can bring me out some food, I'll be content.

'I've reported the bodies in your house and they'll have been cleared out by now, but you shouldn't go home until the outbreak's over, and certainly Louisa shouldn't. I've sent most of my servants away on full pay and I've packed Clemency off to my sister Faith in Taunton. I've a living to earn, so I'll return to my work, but I won't risk anyone else.'

'If you're going back to London,' said Ninian, 'will you take some letters with you? I've business to transact from a distance, and I'll need to leave word at Charles' shipping office so that when the *Salisbury* anchors, he knows that he should come straight here and not go home. If the plague's got a hold, it won't abate until the autumn. It never does.'

Samuel was relieved that he was not expected to let Barnabas into his house, but sent out bedding and food and offered the use of an empty barn for the night and Louisa was allowed to talk to her father from an upper window. Charity and Samuel agreed wholeheartedly that Ninian must remain at Whitmead.

Therefore he was in the house on the day when Louisa, who had by this time become not merely large but enormous, was taken with pains one morning at breakfast, and was whisked off by Charity to the lying-in chamber which had been in readiness for the past week, while the head groom was dispatched at a gallop on Samuel's fastest horse to fetch the midwife from the village.

Remembering Parvati's agony when Charles was born, and worried by Louisa's size, which seemed to suggest a very big baby, Ninian fretted wretchedly, limping from room to room on his stick, and refusing to be distracted by Samuel's offer of an expedition to the nearby marshes, where they might paddle a boat along the waterways and perhaps shoot some wildfowl.

But after all, it was only a few hours later that Ninian heard the sound of a baby's cry. He was standing at the foot of the stairs, head cocked, when Charity came down, smiling, to announce that he now had a grandson. 'Not very big after all, which is odd considering how huge Louisa was, but perfectly healthy as you can hear. In a short time you can come up and see him, and his mother.'

'A grandson! Charles will be pleased. I believe he and Louisa have chosen the name Matthew for a boy,' Ninian said and then stiffened. 'Listen! That's Louisa!'

Upstairs, Louisa had cried out. Now her voice became mingled with clearly audible staccato orders and expressions of amazement from the midwife. '. . . Lord, who'd have thought it? Grip this . . . push . . . Well, who'd have supposed . . .?'

Charity whirled round, picked up her skirts and tore upstairs. Ninian sank down on to a settle nearby and waited, alarmed but a little comforted by the fact that the distant female voices – fainter now that Charity had shut the door, but not quite out of hearing – sounded more exhilarated than dismayed. Half an hour later, Charity, beaming more broadly than ever, once more came in search of him.

'You can come up now and admire them. You are a grandfather twice over.'

'Twice?'

'Indeed yes. It's twins. *That's* why she was so big. But she had them with no trouble. Your daughter-in-law is very well and very pleased, and you have a granddaughter as well as a grandson.'

He had a sense of awe as he approached the single cradle which these two new people were of necessity sharing. These were Charles' children and therefore the descendants of Parvati and he was the more aware of it because one of them was a girl. They were both small, but quite perfect and very alike: two little heads with a scattering of dark down, two pairs of tiny hands whose fine detail of finger-joint and gleaming nails might have been put there by some cosmic master-craftsman; two sleeping faces . . .

Were they dreaming? Ninian wondered, gazing at the curve of their closed eyes and the answering angle of the exquisitely moulded ears, and the dusky bloom on the baby skins. If so, he thought, the dreams behind those curiously secretive, un-English eyelids were not of green fields and cool patchwork skies, of the dazzling skies and dusty plains, the brown faces and the bright fabrics of the east. Even at birth, they were so like her, so unbelievably like her.

Charity, who was standing beside him, remarked: 'They're going to be very dark.'

'They take after Charles,' said Ninian. 'His mother was . . . dark.'

When William Beresford-Higham became suddenly feverish, he knew at once what he must do. 'Send the servants away at once, Mary. If this is plague, I won't have them trapped here. Then you and I must call the Watch, let them nail up the door, and take our chance.'

Mary trembled but did not argue. She already had a splitting headache and a rash on her forehead, and she had sneezed several times that morning. She also knew that the disease had been confirmed in the house next door only yesterday. She fetched the things they would need and placed them in the bedchamber. Water they must have and she filled every pail and basin and jug in the house. She collected bread, some cooked ham and some dried fruit; set a chamberpot on each side of

225

the bed, some clean clothes on a chair. 'For when we're better,' she said with an attempt at valour.

She was braver than she used to be. Beresford-Higham had done that for her, simply by being an attentive husband and giving her children. Neither of their little boys had lived long but in conceiving and bearing them; caring for them and mourning them, Mary had at last made contact with her own hitherto unused depths and found maturity. She had survived the suffering, because her husband desired her and her children needed her; she was no longer despised.

'People do recover,' Beresford-Higham agreed, his voice noticeably and suddenly very hoarse. 'And we're healthy as a rule.'

She lay down beside him and they held each other for a while. Mary was thinking about the beginnings of their marriage; how Beresford-Higham the Puritan had mellowed while he was living at Rosnance, even before she had learned she was a widow and therefore free to marry; how astonished and how glad she had been when, not long after the news came of Francis' death, he had asked her to be his wife; and how they had laughed when he told her that he had wanted her from the beginning.

'You were always afraid I would make you chop up your precious bits of furniture, your painted writing table and your rosewood chest, and in those days, I'd have thought it right to chop them up. I thought they were too decorative and that you loved them too much. But just because you loved them – I couldn't bring myself to harm them.'

'If we marry, can I keep them?'

'Is that a condition of our marriage?'

'No. Oh no!'

'Keep them,' said Beresford-Higham with amusement, 'with my blessing.'

She had brought the pieces with her to this London house when at last her husband left the army and returned home to be once more the respectable civil servant he had been as a young man. They had been much admired when, after a time, Beresford-Higham abandoned his Puritan ways and took to entertaining fashionable company. She wondered who would have them when she wasn't here any more.

Because she wouldn't be here for long, and nor would William. She already knew it and soon, she felt too ill to care. She pulled some of the water vessels near to the bed and put beakers to hand so that they could dip drinks without getting up. She didn't think they'd need the food.

They lasted, the two of them, for another forty-eight hours. Beresford-Higham sank into a muttering coma first and then Mary lay, drifting between delirium and painful consciousness, listening to the sounds from next door where six people had been immured with a plague-ridden seventh and where the disease was now swiftly overtaking them all.

The wall between the houses wasn't thick and the captive six had begun their imprisonment, as Mary could clearly hear, by carousing. There had been drunken singing, the sound of a fiddle, and what was surely a fierce and breathless coupling.

226

Then the fiddle was heard no more and someone on the other side of the wall was vomiting, and although there was still intermittent singing, it was further off, as if the revellers had gone into another room. Presently that stopped too, and she heard someone crying and saying the Lord's prayer, very fast, over and over, and someone else pleading huskily for water. Then she lost interest in the sounds for she was beyond it. She was even beyond fear.

The fear returned for a while when one of her spasmodic drifts back to awareness brought her into a fetid room where day was breaking and by its pale light she saw that the man at her side was dead, his skin covered with dark spots like blackening bruises and his lips drawn back from his teeth.

Terrified, she tried to get out of the bed, to get away from him. But her legs wouldn't bear her and her head felt like a huge, throbbing ball about to split and the attempt at movement would have made her scream, except that her larynx was too sore and stiff to utter more than a moan. Then she saw the dark spots burgeoning in her own arms.

She flopped back on to the bed and shut her eyes and prayed silently to die too. After an agonising hour or two, her prayer was answered.

Chapter Seventeen
Reminders of Yesterday

'Leave word at Charles' shipping office so that when the *Salisbury* anchors, he knows that he should come straight here,' Ninian had said, responding by instinct to the crisis of the plague.

'I must be getting old,' he said to Louisa afterwards. 'It never occurred to me to warn Samuel and Charity what he was like. I suppose that to me he's just my son Charles. But to them . . . !'

For Charles, browned by a West Indian sun and by weeks at sea, and with maturity settling more and more into an Indian cast of face, so startled the manservant Fisher when he appeared at the front door, that instead of announcing him in his usual fashion, Fisher left him standing in the hall, went into the study where Samuel was talking to his bailiff, and whispered into his master's ear: 'There's a gentleman to see you, sir, who says his name's Charles Whitmead but he looks to me just like a Moor.'

Ninian, hastily called in from the garden where he was sitting in the afternoon sunshine, identified his visibly irritated son; and Charity, emerging from the task of preserving plums, led the guest upstairs to where Louisa was feeding the twins, to reunite him with his wife and introduce him to his children. But when she came down again, she and Samuel gently but inexorably surrounded Ninian.

'You never told us,' said Samuel, 'But was your wife English, Cousin? Because Charles . . . well . . . he doesn't look very English. He looks more like . . . like . . .'

'You said her name was Penny,' said Charity, puzzled.

'Her baptismal name was Penelope,' Ninian told them. 'But she was Indian. She was on a ship that was wrecked at Polmawgan. I took her in and looked after her and later on, well, we came to love each other and I married her. Her original name was Parvati.'

'You mean,' said Charity, lowering her voice, 'that she was . . . was a Moor?'

'No, she wasn't Moorish. I said: she was Indian.'

'But – she must have been very dark,' said Charity.

'And born a heathen.' Samuel's voice too was hushed.

'That's true. But she took the Anglican faith and the name of Penelope, and became as good a Christian as any of us, I promise you,' said Ninian. 'As for being dark – I hardly noticed. She was beautiful.'

'But, all the same . . .'

Inexperienced. Exactly. In this quiet corner of Essex even a

Frenchman or a Scot was thought exotic. Samuel and Charity could not imagine the world outside Europe at all, couldn't conceive of lives which didn't revolve round the Christian religion. The skeleton found under their store-room floor had been unquestioningly buried according to the familiar Christian rites. Parvati's brown skin and the strange gods of her youth were beyond their comprehension.

'Well,' said Samuel, struggling to understand, 'I know my parents were shocked when you married, Ninian. That would be why, I suppose. I take it that they knew? But still, if you were happy together and your wife received the message of salvation . . .'

'She did,' Ninian assured him, repressing all memory of uninhibited drawings of Shiva, and sensuous dancing and the musical jingle of his wife's bangles, and the oneness with Parvati which had been at least partly based on the mutual deception they were practising on the Puritan world all round them. Those of Parvati's trinkets which he had kept were with him now, in their sandalwood box, which he had had fitted with a lock so that no servant should ever pry into it. His memories were in that box but they were clearly not memories he could risk sharing with his cousins.

'Are you talking about my mother?' Charles, washed and tidied, sauntered into the parlour. Ninian took one look at him and with sudden misgiving, saw that, judging from the glint in Charles' eyes, and the way his smile revealed his teeth, he was abrim with mischief, and also with the desire to be avenged for having his identity questioned.

'Charles!' said Ninian warningly.

Charles relaxed on to a settle, crossed his legs, and paid no heed. 'The ship from which my mother came,' he said, 'was actually, more or less, a pirate vessel. My mother was the slave – again more or less – of its captain. She had a lot to put up with in England, from people who blamed her for what she couldn't help, such as being brown, and being born a heathen, and made a slave. Has anyone told you how she died?'

'Charles, be quiet,' Ninian snapped. He turned to his cousins. 'I was in a Royalist rising at Penzance. It failed and my wife and I were trying to escape from Cornwall by boat when . . .'

'You were also trying to escape because ignorant people had accused my mother, on account of her foreign origin, of witchcraft.'

'*Charles!*'

'You never talk of that, except to me,' Charles said. 'You say people wouldn't understand. It strikes me that it's high time a few of them were made to understand. It's not a crime to be foreign, or even heathen.' He turned to Samuel and Charity, who were staring at him in amazed horror. 'My mother threw herself into the sea to escape arrest and perhaps burning, and my father held the enemy off with his sword so that they shouldn't drag her back. Because of that, he is now a local legend. Yes, you are, Father! The *Salisbury* called at Penzance on the way home and I went to see my mother's grave. I also went into a Penzance tavern and when I let out who I was, quite a crowd gathered round to talk to me. You are now upheld, Father, throughout Penwith as an example of a great lover and a great swordsman.'

'What?' said Ninian. 'Me? A great . . . ? I never heard of anything so absurd, or embarrassing . . . !'

'*Witchcraft?*' said Samuel and Charity in horrified voices, simultaneously finding their tongues.

Charles gave them a buccaneer's grin, bold and unpredictable. 'She wasn't guilty,' he said. 'And I regret it. I should like to think I was a witch's son.'

'You infuriate me,' said Ninian, when Samuel, recognising Ninian's desire to be alone with his son and evidently also wishing to be alone with his wife, had taken Charity away. 'How could you? To our cousins, of all people. All these years, I've protected your mother's memory and in five minutes, in a fit of pique, you throw it all away!'

'Aren't you proud of being a legend?' asked Charles, unrepentantly.

'No, I'm not! A great lover? I've grieved for years because if I'd been wiser I might still have saved your mother's life. *Great lover?* I'd like to have five minutes with the nitwit who thought up that one.'

'I don't understand you, you know.' Charles was still sitting at ease on the settle. 'For years I've accepted that what happened to my mother was unmentionable, but after calling at Penzance, and then seeing the reception these cousins gave me, I suddenly found myself wondering why. You loved my mother. You know she was innocent. So why hide the truth? It's as if in spite of all that, you're somehow ashamed of her. Well, I'm not!'

'It has nothing to do with being ashamed. It's more to do with living a quiet life and not upsetting people. Samuel and Charity are decent and honest but they're limited in their minds. The word witchcraft frightens them. They can't help it.'

'They're fools. I was coming to this room,' said Charles, 'and I was just outside the door when I heard them talking in hushed voices about being *dark* and a *heathen*. I actually stood still for a moment to hear better and I gathered that they meant my mother. Their stupid manservant had insulted me, leaving me to stand in the hall because I haven't got a bucolic English face, all red and crude like a side of beef, and now they were insulting my mother. I'll give them something to whisper about, I thought. Damn fool superstition!'

'What you have done, Charles, is to smear your mother's name, because the world can't tell the difference between a slave and a whore, or grasp the distinction between being accused of witchcraft, and being guilty of it. Have you ever told Louisa the full story, by the way?'

'No.'

'So you do understand that what you have said is a smear, even if you won't admit it. I had better go after Samuel and make sure he and Charity don't tell her, either. I only hope they don't ask us all to leave tomorrow morning.'

'Of course we don't want you to leave. We wouldn't send anyone back to a plague-infested city, least of all our own kinsfolk,' said Samuel, and

231

on the surface the atmosphere remained pleasant and hospitable. Indeed, both Samuel and Charity showed particular kindness to Louisa, Molly and the twins.

'I think they're sorry for them, being entangled with us. I won't ask you if you now regret what you've done,' said Ninian acidly to his son.

'I don't. It was like scratching an itch,' said Charles.

After a few days, however, he commented that he was tired of being addressed from a safe distance as though he were a questionable piece of artillery which might explode at any moment, and announced that he had work to do connected with the *Salisbury* and was going back to London.

He had already visited the house in Wych Street before coming to Whitmead, despite Ninian's instructions that he should come straight to Essex. He had also been able to reassure Louisa that her parents were safe, Barnabas living alone in his house while her mother remained in Taunton. The maidservant Dorothy had gone to her brother, an Essex smallholder, and was also well. He had called on her on the way to Whitmead.

'I'm not too worried about the plague. There are fevers in the Caribbean but I never seem to get them. Some people don't. Remember that old soak Piper MacPherson that plays his bagpipes on the corner? He's been carried off twice by the plague cart because they took him for a corpse, but he wasn't dead, only dead drunk, and he's none the worse even after being dumped on top of the plague victims. I should think the outbreak is nearly over by now. Every other house in London is closed and there's so little traffic that the grass is growing up between the cobbles in the Strand. There's no one about to catch the disease from!'

'Frankly, I think it might be better if you did go,' said Ninian candidly. 'If you intend going back by the same route, tell Dorothy that we're likely to come home in a month or so, and will collect her on our way. And you might see that our house is fumigated and ready for us. Make yourself useful, in fact. We'll be following you as soon as it's really safe. I fancy my cousins will be glad to be rid of me, at least. Thanks to you.'

'I liked them, you know,' said Charity, after Ninian and his family had gone. 'I really did. But how *could* Cousin Ninian have married a . . . well, if she wasn't a Moor exactly, she was the next thing to it. What an extraordinary married life he must have had!'

'But we must be ready to welcome them again,' said Samuel. 'After all, they are family, though they're distant. Ninian and Louisa have never done anything to offend us, and the little ones could hardly be more innocent. We saw Matthew and Henrietta baptised in our own church. Indeed, I feel we should do all we can to offer those twins the opportunity, as they grow up, to experience our simple Christian family life here.'

Charity nodded her smooth head and smiled. 'Our Benjamin says that he thinks Henrietta will be pretty, one day. We shall have to find him a dark-haired bride! But . . .' her face became serious again, '. . . I would prefer it if Charles himself didn't come too often, if at all, and not just on account of his mother, either. You've more or less said that he won't offer his children much in the way of Christian family life. You know, Samuel,' said Charity thoughtfully, 'I call myself unworldly. But sometimes people who have cultivated simplicity in themselves are good at sensing the lack of it in others. One sees most clearly through a clean window, after all. Charles looks like a Moorish pirate and probably thinks like one. But Louisa has simplicity, and I fear, poor girl, that she will not have an easy marriage.'

Molly Meade had grieved deeply for her own husband and had sympathy for her young mistress when Louisa pined for Charles. But Charles himself annoyed her. He had been away at sea for half the year; he might at least, she thought, try to give his wife some companionship during the other half. But even now, when they were all back in London and whatever business he had to transact was close at hand, Charles was hardly ever at home.

He seemed to look on Louisa and the twins more as possessions than people. He was proud of them, would show them off to the friends he occasionally brought to the house, and was willing to spend money on good clothes for them. But he saw no reason why he shouldn't absent himself without explanation whenever he felt like it, and even, on occasion, for several days and nights at a time. Louisa did not complain but Molly saw the strain on her face, and watched her joyous greetings when he reappeared. Charles would receive them with a lordly air as one who accepts a just tribute, and presently announce casually, often within forty-eight hours of his return, that he was going off again on business for another week or so, and she should expect him when she saw him. 'Mind you stay faithful to me, my chatterbox,' was his usual jocular remark on these occasions, and Louisa, bravely, would try to smile.

Molly could not let her annoyance show, for it was not her business to make trouble, but to support Louisa. 'You see, Madam, men please themselves,' she said when Louisa wondered aloud when Charles would come home. 'Just make the best of him when he's here.'

'He went off sometimes last year, when we were first married,' said Louisa. 'But not as much as this.'

'Ah, well. The honeymoon's past now,' said Molly, and added: 'It's always best to show him a smiling face,' not because she believed this was fair but because she believed that protest would be useless.

But by the time February had arrived, Louisa was finding it almost impossible to hide her despondency.

'I don't want to go to this party,' she said, sitting unhappily in front of her mirror, while Molly curled her hair. 'I'd rather stay at home and play with the twins.'

'That was all right while you were feeding them,' Molly said. 'But they're weaned now and thriving, and there's your husband eager to escort you. I'm sure you'll have a lovely time.'

'I never have a lovely time at Alexander Morris' parties. I don't like him or the sister who always plays hostess. They always look at me as though they're laughing at me.'

'Envy, I expect,' said Molly firmly. 'You'll be one of the most beautiful ladies there and that's not flattery. And you'll be with your husband, as I said.'

'Yes, but will I? You don't know, Molly, because you don't see these things. You never come with me on these occasions.'

'Madam?' said Molly uncertainly.

The afternoon was fading and there was more candle-light than daylight in the room. Candle-light was kind to the complexion, but now it could not hide the pinched look on Louisa's face. 'I mean,' said Louisa harshly, 'that once we're there, he'll vanish. He always does. I probably won't see him again until it's time to come home. I don't have his company even when I'm *with* him, Molly. Yet you always tell me to smile.' She twisted round, jerking her ringlets out of her maid's hands, and glared at Molly, face to face, as if meeting her eyes in the mirror didn't count. 'Why must I always smile? Why must I always hide my feelings and lie and pretend? He doesn't! Take those curlers away. I'm not going to that party!'

'Madam,' said Molly after a shaken pause, 'you must. You really must.'

'I won't. I shall say I have a headache.'

'Mrs Whitmead, please don't. It's unwise. Your husband expects you to accompany him and . . . and . . .'

'Yes, Molly? And?'

'You miss him when he's away. If you refuse to go about with him when you have the chance, well, what if he stopped giving you any chances?'

'Then what *am* I to do?' cried Louisa in exasperation. 'Have I no weapons at all?'

'Well, yes, madam, of course you have.'

'I'd like to know what they are!'

'You go with him to that party,' said Molly, gently turning her mistress' shoulders so that Louisa once more faced the mirror, 'and enjoy every single moment or at least make out that you do, and on the way home, talk about how much you've enjoyed yourself and repeat every compliment you've been paid. You'll be paid a few; I'll see to that. Your hair's never looked so nice and your dress is beautiful. This corn-coloured satin suits you. You'll dazzle them all.'

'You mean, make him jealous?'

'I don't mean do anything you shouldn't. But make him look at you twice, yes,' said Molly.

Since their marriage, Charles had several times taken her back to Alexander Morris' house and she detested it. They always went by water, just as on that first occasion, and the sight of the observatory tower always made her uncomfortable. Up there, the twins had been conceived, in that unromantic union on top of a star-chart. She loved

Charles and hated knowing that but for her pregnancy and the insistence of both Barnabas and Ninian, he would probably never have married her. She avoided thinking about it. But the knowledge was there, deep in her mind like a buried splinter. At the sight of the tower, the splinter moved, and hurt.

This occasion was no better than any which had gone before. Ninian, who was with them and knew that Louisa was not at ease here, gave her an encouraging smile as they went inside, and as Alexander Morris and the Davisons greeted them, attempted to amuse them all by paying Christabella a backhanded compliment. 'You are in wonderful looks, Mrs Davison, but is the tendril of hair on your left temple the latest fashion or a mistake?'

'It is intentional, Mr Whitmead. It is correct just now to say that perfection is not for human beings.'

'So Christabella outwits the gods with divine asymmetry!' said Charles gallantly, and the jarring note she had dreaded had been struck. Louisa, who had done her best to avoid the slightest imperfection or asymmetry, greeted Mr Davison a little too effusively. When she looked round again, Charles had disappeared. She had known he would, and yet hoped so much that for once things would be different.

She should have had that headache after all. But Alexander Morris was now bowing over her hand and saying that her corn-coloured dress had brought a touch of summer into the house, and Molly had after all told her to put on a show of enjoyment. She burst into bright, inane speech.

'It reminds you of summer? What a pretty compliment, and in the midst of winter, too. It was so chilly on the river, although of course, what can one expect in February?'

'You are cold?' inquired Christabella, who obviously wasn't, despite the filminess of the scarves round the low neck of her pale-blue silk. 'Alexander, show Mrs Whitmead into the parlour and find her a seat by the fire.'

She found herself being led away, through a sea of rippling periwigs and floating scarves, velvet coats and silken skirts, to a double seat beside a fire of glowing logs, where, disconcertingly, Morris sat down beside her, remarking that there would be dancing later, and enquiring after her children. 'You have twins, have you not? Amazing! What are their names, now? Matthew and . . . ?'

'Henrietta. Yes, indeed I have twins and they are flourishing. The name Henrietta is becoming popular again; it is such a musical-sounding name. I've always liked it.'

She had an uncomfortable feeling that Morris, smiling down at her from the height which was noticeable even when he was seated, was aware of her brittle sprightliness and might even have guessed the cause. But he answered soberly.

'People have short memories. The queen who bore that name did England no good. But for her Popish influence on the first King Charles, we might never have had a civil war. Though the name is melodious enough, I grant you that.' He regarded her with kindly amusement. 'No doubt that's what you ladies judge by. Are you warmer, now? Where has your husband got to, I wonder?'

'Charles knows so many people.' Louisa's tone was studiously indulgent. 'He will take half the evening to greet all his friends.'

'Very ungallant of him to wander from your side so soon. He should have let his friends come to him instead. They soon would – for the sake of exchanging a word or two with his lovely companion at the same time.'

'You're too kind, Mr Morris,' said Louisa politely and then, because his gaze had become so intent that it embarrassed her, looked away from him. When she turned round again, he was nodding to a man across the room. A moment later, he rose, bowed, and left her.

She was supposed to look as though she were enjoying herself. She saw two ladies she recognised and went quickly to join them. The one thing she mustn't do was sit alone.

The effort of being bright grew easier as the evening wore on. Someone obtained a glass of wine for her and then another and the wine cheered her up. Dancing began and Alexander Morris reappeared to lead her out, and she found herself making quite sparkling conversation with him. A succession of other partners followed, and the yellow dress was certainly a success for they all paid her compliments. Her ploy was working. She only hoped that Charles, of whom she had caught only fleeting glimpses, had noticed. She managed, once, to wave casually to him across the room, and it felt like a triumph. On the strength of it, she drank some more wine.

Afterwards, she couldn't quite remember how it was that she let herself be swept up into the party which, as on that first momentous evening in this house, was bound for the tower observatory with Alexander Morris to look through his telescope. She hardly realised where she was going until she was halfway up the steps, and by then it was too late to turn back. The steps were narrow and three people were climbing them behind her.

The octagonal room looked just as it had done then except that tonight, no moonlight came through the windows. Candle-light showed the telescope on its wheeled stand, the table and the star-charts, at the sight of which, Louisa blenched inwardly. Her behaviour that night had been shameful and if Charles were neglecting her now, perhaps it was because no man could respect a girl who gave herself in such a way. She had got the twins out of it, and they had been born in wedlock; what more could she hope for? She took a hold of herself and tried, through a fog of wine and uneasy memories, to attend to Alexander Morris on the subject of the dog-star, Sirius, and to look eager when invited to gaze once more through the telescope.

Sirius, in fact, was well worth looking at – a scintillating and rainbow-shot wonder – and when one of the other guests murmured something about the influence of the stars on destiny, Morris' cool refutation of the whole theory of astrology was well worth listening to. He and Sirius between them actually pierced through the fog.

'In the Royal Society,' said Morris in measured tones, 'it is considered that all the wonders of the universe can be explained by the study of motion, substance and the mathematical laws that govern them. Laws, ladies and gentlemen, which can be learned, understood and applied. Science has no more to do with the occult than a set of bankers' accounts!'

Louisa, who had thought of herself as being well-educated – she could read, write, do accounts, speak French, dance, embroider, play the lute, find the West Indies on a globe and make first-class quince marmalade – suddenly wondered what it would be like to study science, really study it. Barnabas was inclined to be scathing about it, but that was because he associated it with astrology and alchemy. 'A few little stars shining away up there can't decide my destiny for me; only God can do that.' 'A man who spends his time leafing through old books and boiling up smelly concoctions in the hope that he'll find out how to turn lead into gold ought to take some physic for his brain.'

But according to Alexander Morris, science wasn't like that at all. For a moment, her distressing associations with the observatory tower dwindled, became unimportant, and the domestic, feminine world in which she had grown up seemed unbearably circumscribed and trivial. Morris had now shifted the telescope and was inviting them all to examine the planet Jupiter, which, he said, had been proved to be over three hundred and sixty million miles away at its nearest approach to the earth. Such distances simultaneously made her mind reel and her spirit soar. She took her turn at viewing Jupiter, gasping as what had been just a vivid star turned into a luminous disc with a strange spot on its face.

Stepping back, she looked at Alexander Morris, not knowing that in the candle-light her eyes shone more brightly than either Sirius or Jupiter, and said: 'It's all *wonderful!*'

'I'm glad you think so,' Morris said. 'I hoped you would. Would you like to look again?' And somehow, when everyone was once more making for the steps, he had manoeuvred her into being the last to turn away from the telescope, so that she was once more alone in the observatory with a man; not Charles this time, but Alexander.

Who should have been snuffing candles but instead was advancing on her with a terrifying smile and the obvious intention of embracing her.

'Mr Morris, what are you doing?' His arms came round her like steel hoops. She pushed at them vainly, turning her head aside so that his mouth would descend on her ear instead of her lips, and discovered to her horror that he was pushing her backwards into the table and that in a moment – oh God, no! – she would be once more flat on her back on top of a star-chart. She stamped on his instep, with her full weight on her high-heeled shoe. He uttered a muffled yelp and released her, quickly and indignantly.

'What in the world is the matter? Weren't you expecting that?'

'No, I was *not!*'

'So it has to be Charles, then?'

'Well, it . . . of course it has to be Charles! Charles is my husband! Mr Morris, please can we go downstairs, at once?'

'By all means,' said Morris huffily. 'If that is your wish, my dear Mrs Whitmead. But I believe you weren't so nice when you visited my observatory before. And Charles wasn't your husband then.'

'Well, he is now and if he were to hear of this, he'd . . . he'd call you out!' Still backed against the table, Louisa glared at her host.

'Oh, I'm not afraid of you telling him,' said Morris tranquilly. 'He might indeed call me out but what might he do to you, for encouraging me?'

'I didn't encourage you!'

'No? *You're too kind, Mr Morris*, and a coquettish glance away from me; cascades of laughter while we're dancing; beautiful eyes sending messages to me while you're telling me outright that I'm wonderful . . . What do you call all that?'

'I didn't say you were wonderful. I said *it* was: this place, looking at Sirius and Jupiter and hearing about them. It *was* wonderful, and you've spoilt it!'

'Oh, my dear Louisa. You sound like a child whose toy has been broken.'

'Is your observatory just a toy to you, then? If so, you're not worthy of it!' Louisa snapped.

Morris' eyebrows went up almost into his wig. 'A fine retort, that; you have a pretty wit, my dear. I'm sorry you won't allow me to enjoy you to the full. May I know whether it's because you prefer Charles or because you don't like me?'

'I am Charles' wife and . . . and whatever I did when I was a girl and . . . and ignorant . . . I love Charles very much and I shall always be faithful to him. Always.'

'Even though,' said Alexander Morris smoothly, 'he isn't faithful to you?'

Well, she had asked Molly to suggest a weapon. As she lived through the disagreeable blur which formed the rest of the evening, the unfeminine alter ego which Louisa had discovered in herself as she peered at the universe through Morris' telescope commented grimly that Molly had handed her a gun which not only hit the wrong target but kicked its user flat.

Meanwhile, she must keep her countenance. Having rejoined the gathering, she drank more wine, talked, ate, danced, was reclaimed by Charles at the end of the evening, went home with him by boat, and even, because Molly's instructions still seemed to her the only alternative to a stunned silence, talked brightly to him of the entertainment, boasting a little of the compliments she and her dress had been paid, and marvelling at the splendours of Sirius and Jupiter.

'I've seen them from the deck of a ship,' said Charles, amused. 'They are indeed magnificent. But don't become too scientifically minded, will you? It doesn't suit a woman.'

Dampened, Louisa fell silent. When they got home and went to bed, however, he turned to her at once and took hold of her possessively.

'You've had them all looking at you tonight, but I'm the one you belong to. You'd better not forget it.'

His arms tightened. It was some time before he was able to make love to her, however. Lying against him, waiting, Louisa wondered why. Had he spent himself elsewhere in the course of the evening, and if so, with whom?

The idea was horrible, an almost physical thing like a cold worm coiled in her stomach, and simply because it was horrible, she dared not ask. Charles was perfectly capable of admitting it.

If he did, she couldn't bear it. She couldn't seek revenge by infidelities of her own. She didn't want Morris, whose bony shape and too-subtle tongue aroused in her not the slightest desire to investigate either his body or his mind; and there was no one else she wanted. And besides . . .

Lying in the dark, waiting for Charles to become aroused, she thought again of the marvels she had viewed through the telescope. Charles might not want her to talk about them, but she could think about them secretly and needed to think about them, for they had vouchsafed something to her.

Looking at Sirius and Jupiter, she had understood that she was nothing at all compared to the rest of this universe, so that in one way, it didn't matter what she did, or what Charles did. And yet, in another way, all that hugeness and significance were a reason for trying to live as though one did matter. Such a universe required some kind of tribute. She would choose to go on loving Charles and being loyal to him because she would feel not only guilty but diminished if she did not.

Charles was nuzzling her, warming to her, sliding himself over her. She yielded to him. She could live with his unfaithfulness, she thought, as long as she did not let it tarnish her, as long as she stayed faithful herself.

And as long as she never knew any details, she could hold on to the fact that he was her husband, and was jealous of her, and so would always come back, in the end, to her.

Chapter Eighteen
Out on the Tide

Ninian stood at his study window in Polmawgan and watched as the mysterious crenellated ship moved out of Polmawgan Cove across a moonlit sea. He was acutely aware that people he loved were aboard it and that they were going away for ever. Parvati was there, and Francis and Christopher and Anthony. And then he was awake, lying in bed in the Wych Street house. The bedcurtains were drawn back because of the heat and there was moonlight on his face, but what had roused him was the rumble of the plague cart. The pestilence had returned for the second year running, and the plague cart came through the street every few nights, manned by a succession of men who had taken the job because they were themselves so eaten with disease and dirt and degeneracy that they could get no other. Ninian sometimes imagined his own body, or those of Louisa or the twins on that cart. It was unbearable.

The curious internal clock which kept count of time even while one slept told him that midnight was long past. It was the second of September now and soon, by rights, pestilence must abate. No one had ever learned its cause. Ministers led congregations in prayer against it; every quack and beldame had a list of allegedly infallible remedies; and the number of people who tried to ward off disaster by chalking *Lord have mercy on us* on their doors was at least equalled by those who painted cabalistic signs against the evil eye. There had been at least one case of the ritual sacrifice of a black cock in order to daub a door with its blood.

But one thing was certain: plague flourished in hot weather, and this summer had been hot, like the one before. Samuel and Charity, despite their mixed feelings about Charles, had offered Louisa and the twins a refuge but had to withdraw the invitation at the last moment, because, as Samuel said apologetically in his letter, Charity was very ill after a stillbirth and the household was too disrupted for guests. 'It seems,' Ninian said, 'that Lucy Browne has just had a healthy little son and this has made Charity worse. She lies abed all day with the curtains drawn.'

'Poor Charity,' said Louisa sympathetically.

'They've got three children!' said Ninian with a snort. 'Benjamin's a fine lad and they have Cherry and Frances. Charity should pull herself together. Perhaps you and the twins could go to your aunt in Taunton. Barnabas has sent your mother there; you'd have her company.'

241

But Aunt Faith, when asked, wrote back that she was already sheltering several friends who had fled from London and had no room. They must commit themselves to God and pray to Him to preserve them, said her letter piously.

Well, so far, He had. Ninian often marvelled at his own immunity. Louisa and the twins were young, while the only two servants, Molly and Dorothy, though middle-aged, had sound health. But he was ageing and was now very lame, for the muscles of his damaged leg were wasted and, without their support, the bones of his hip had begun to wear. He might feel homesick still for Polmawgan, but if he were there, he wouldn't be able to get up and down the path to the village; the short path would be too steep and the easy track too long. And yet, lurching crock though he was, the plague still ignored him.

Well, there it was. No one in his house had succumbed this year, although many friends and neighbours had died. One of Louisa's sisters had perished, together with her husband and child; Alexander Morris and Edward Davison too were gone. Christabella Davison had reportedly had the disease but recovered, although she was said to be distraught.

Perhaps the Whitmead household owed its survival to Louisa, who had learned of a recipe which was supposed to be a protection, and every evening since, had with her own hands brewed up a daily potion of ginger, nutmeg, sage and rue boiled in wine and angelica water, and dosed the entire household with it after supper.

He was anxious about Louisa, however. Her new baby was due in November, and though physically well, she was fretting for Charles. She had said repeatedly that she was praying for the *Salisbury* to come home soon. She was proud of Charles because he hoped to become a captain next year, but she was worried in case his ship fell foul of the Dutch, with whom the trade war, now being masterminded by the King's illegitimate son the Duke of Monmouth, still dragged on, and even more worried by something Charles had told her, quite casually, before he sailed.

'I wonder if he really means to transfer to the East India Company as he said? I can understand that he might want to see his mother's land, but he would be at sea for even longer than he is now. I'd hardly ever see him,' she observed anxiously.

Once, she had said forlornly to Ninian that she felt as if she had spent most of her married life waiting on the quay for Charles. Although, she added with gallantry, she was glad to have him to wait for. Ninian sometimes had the impression that the sheer strength of Louisa's feelings for Charles was the source of her own strength, her shield against disease.

And he knew something that Louisa didn't. Rowing the *Penelope* down to the City two days ago, he had come across the *Salisbury*, already in and anchored. It had taken a single inquiry at the appropriate shipping office to ascertain that Charles was on board, alive and in good health. But he had not yet chosen to come home or send any word to his family. If I were not such a cripple, Ninian thought as the plague cart clip-clopped and creaked away down the street, I would half kill him. He should be here, damn him.

If Charles didn't announce his return very soon, Ninian decided, he'd have to send for him. Meanwhile, the plague cart was receding. He could go back to sleep. He closed his eyes but opened them again almost instantly and sat up at the sound of running feet outside, accompanied by frightened cries. Somewhere in the distance was a faint but familiar skirling.

Heaving himself out of bed, he flung the window open and leant out. 'What's all this noise? What the devil's the matter?' Three shadowy, fleeing figures halted, clutching each other and peering over their shoulders along the moonlit street, and three gaunt and pockmarked faces were turned up to him. 'It's the devil that's the matter, right enough! He was on our cart among the corpses, come to take the souls of the dead, old Satan himself . . . !'

'And he sat up, and he made such noises as 'ud call the very imps of hell . . .'

'Ow! Listen, he's coming after us . . .'

Other windows were opening and nightcapped heads were peering out. The distant skirling was indeed coming nearer. 'That's not the devil; don't you know bagpipes when you hear them, you fools!' Ninian shouted. 'You've picked up Piper MacPherson again! He keeps his pipes tied to him. Are you new on this round? The ones before you learned to leave him be when they found him drunk in the gutter!'

'That's right! They're nothing but rogues and cretins. Taking Piper MacPherson for the devil, indeed, and waking us up with all this to-do!' A voice from a neighbouring house joined in indignantly.

And then, as Piper MacPherson's inebriated version of a Scottish lament came round the corner and the cart-keepers, not convinced, took to their heels once more, the same voice added, in a dry tone: 'Though it looks as if something's opened the gates of hell tonight. Either that or there's an almighty fire in the City.'

Ninian raised his eyes, aware that for some moments he had been conscious of a flickering redness in the sky to the east, which wasn't moonlight and couldn't possibly be dawn, not yet. His neighbour was right. Something over there was decidedly on fire.

But it seemed a long way off; probably as far as London Bridge, which was not far short of two miles. He went back to bed.

They woke in the morning to what should have been a quiet Sunday, with a visit to church and a good roast dinner; to find dark smoke streaming overhead, borne by a strong wind, an acrid tang in the air, and excited reports from people who had risen early and gone to see what was happening. A big fire had started near the City end of London Bridge. The people living near it were leaving their houses in a hurry. But it was being controlled; there was no cause for alarm this far away, only it was quite a sight to see.

'I daresay, but I'm sorry for the people in those wooden houses on

London Bridge,' Ninian said. 'What with this dry weather and that strong wind, it could easily spread there. That would be a great disaster, and not only for them. It would block the traffic in and out of the City to the south. London could come to a halt.'

When they set out for church, later in the morning, they met the neighbour who had caught sight of the reddened sky last night. He had been to the scene and was eagerly describing it to everyone he met. The fire had actually begun at a baker's in Pudding Lane, which was very close to London Bridge indeed, and it most certainly was spreading. He glanced back as he spoke, as though he feared the flames might be galloping up the street behind him. The dwellers on the bridge had already evacuated their houses, and a bucket chain had been organised to take water from the river, but: 'They might as well just spit on the fire, for all the good that's going to do.'

'I'm sorry,' said Louisa. 'But I feel faint. I can't go to church. Please, Molly, take me home.'

'We'll all go home,' said Ninian.

Dorothy went venturesomely out in the late afternoon and came back looking scared.

'I got as far as Watling Street,' she told them. 'I couldn't get no further, for all the people coming the other way with their goods, getting them out of the fire's reach. There was donkeys and ponies dragging carts so piled up with bedsteads and tables and the Lord knows what, that the poor things could hardly haul them along; and there was whole families heaving handcarts along, and I saw two or three sick people being carried on their beds . . .'

'What's being done to put the fire out?' demanded Ninian.

'Well, like our neighbour said this morning: they're dipping water from the river. But it's no use.'

Louisa, very big again at not quite seven months, sat with her shawl wrapped round her, her face frightened. 'Could it reach us? Could it come so far?'

'I shouldn't think so,' said Ninian reassuringly. 'And even if it did, we've plenty of time to get away. We could go to your father. Now, don't worry.'

'I can't help it. I can . . . I can smell it in the air,' said Louisa. 'I shan't sleep tonight.'

'Yes, you will. I'll sit up and keep watch,' said Ninian.

'I'll take turn and turn about with you, sir,' Molly agreed. She moved to the window and peered out. 'If only that wind would drop. But you need not fear, Mrs Whitmead. You can sleep soundly, knowing that we're on guard and will call you if necessary.'

'I wish Charles were here.'

'I'm sure you do,' said Ninian grimly.

They were further alarmed, shortly afterwards, by the sound of distant explosions. Then came a vigorous knocking at the door, which when opened revealed Barnabas.

'I came by boat; there are such rumours flying that I wanted to know what was happening and if you were in danger. Thank God you're not,'

Barnabas said, as they drew him in. 'What a thing! What a calamity! I hear the King's given orders to the Lord Mayor to pull down houses in the path of the fire, but it's moving faster than they can work. I've been to see. It's pitiful. There are people being ordered out of the houses that are to be destroyed and they don't all understand the need. Some are having to be dragged out and I saw a woman just standing there, crying her heart out as the soldiers went through her house smashing it with axes and sledgehammers. Hammers!' he added in tones of practical exasperation. 'If they're going to wreck houses at all, they ought to use gunpowder and speed things up.'

'Perhaps they already are,' Molly said. 'We have heard explosions.'

'No, those were warehouses,' Barnabas told her. 'Ones with oil and wine in them and things of that nature. When they catch fire, they blow up. I'm fortunate to be so far out to the west. I must write to Clemency tomorrow about all this. Your mother is coming back from Taunton, Louisa, in good time for your confinement.'

'I do hope Charles comes in good time for it,' said Louisa.

'Barnabas,' said Ninian, 'will you stay here with the womenfolk? I want to take the *Penelope* and see this fire for myself.'

Lame and in a hurry, Ninian wasted no time trying to descend Temple Stairs in the ordinary fashion but sat down and bumped himself from step to step, doing damage to his breeches but saving his hip a good deal of pain.

The *Penelope*, which he had used less this year simply because of his hip, was moored at a small jetty. She was sinking gently on the ebbtide so that to reach her he must descend some more steep steps, wet ones this time. Ignoring the damp, Ninian again sat down and slithered.

Once aboard, he unshipped the oars thankfully and manoeuvred the boat out into the river, at home as always when he was on the water, and glad to transfer the strain of moving about from his dubious legs to his muscular arms. The wind was against him but the tide was not. Oars would do better than sail and the journey shouldn't take long.

But the Thames, usually as familiar to him as his own dining room, had undergone strange changes. The strong south-east wind, which would normally have borne a faint tang of estuary salt, tonight smelt of ash and burning. Billows of dark smoke rolled across the sky, bringing a premature twilight, and the air beneath was hazy. To the east, from where the smoke was rising, there was a flickering glow.

The river itself was more congested than he had ever seen it before. The inhabitants of the City had taken to it in a frightened exodus, seeking the sanctuary of water, and the straightest route away from danger. Craft of all patterns – flat-bottomed lighters, rowing boats, ferry-boats, private barges, sailing vessels of every size from dinghy to merchantman – were crammed on to the water, some anchored in midstream to wait for the tide, but many struggling with sail and oar to use the wind and make headway upstream against the current.

There was a background of sound: people shouting warnings as they tried to avoid collisions; voices exclaiming, comforting, weeping. Most of the vessels were crowded with people and many were so heavily laden, not with the sacks and crates of conventional cargo, but with haphazard piles of household goods, that they rode alarmingly low. Fear and urgency hung over them like another kind of smoke. Ninian, glancing warily over his shoulder, made good use of the skill acquired from sailing in the rocky Cornish seas, as he evaded first a small boat laden with furniture, kitchen pots and a pair of virginals; and then a wallowing lighter burdened with what looked like the contents of an ironmonger's shop. A furiously poled barge went by, with a wash which set him bouncing and which slopped over the lighter, sweeping trays and shovels and fire-irons into the water, amid outraged shouts from their owner.

He rowed on gingerly, encountering new perils, for as he went downstream, the river became strewn with bobbing objects which had fallen into it. He used his oars to fend off a floating mattress and a bucket and a little flotilla of waterlogged ledgers: somebody's account books, presumably. When he looked round him again, he was within sight of London Bridge.

It was an arch of fire.

The sight was spectacular enough and horrible enough to make him rest his oars and sit there, half-turned, staring. In the dusk, the fire seemed to be gathering power. He could see houses and spires outlined against a mass of blood-red flame which rushed up into the sky from where the City should have been. The bridge was a murderous tentacle reaching over the river as if to claw at the southern bank. Its houses were all ablaze, and burning timbers falling from them splashed and steamed as they hit the water.

Wails of distress came over the water from the other vessels although on the south bank, Ninian could see the lights of taverns, and groups of sightseers standing outside to drink their ale and gape. Fiery flakes drifted in the air above him; and fresh tongues of fire constantly leapt up from buildings newly kindled. Heat wafted on the wind together with the smell of burning and as fear spread along the north bank of the river, more and more people were loading themselves and their goods into whatever craft they could find. He was still at a safe distance, but nevertheless he could hear the roar and crackle of the fire.

'Hell!' said Ninian aloud, and wasn't sure if it was a mere expletive or a description.

But his destination was in sight. He had been worriedly scanning the river in case the *Salisbury* had left her moorings and was one of the ships now moving in midstream. In the failing light, where dusk had now been added to the smoke, he was afraid of missing her. But she was still where he had last seen her. He pulled for the north bank, the only vessel moving towards the land instead of away from it. A man poling a barge bawled: 'Forget something?' at him, and a frantic individual, trying inexpertly to row his family and a wobbling tower of belongings out from the shore, swore at him for getting in the way. He got clear of them eventually, as he drew in towards the quay where the *Salisbury* was moored, and came under her stern. He could just make out her name.

Ninian stood up, banged with an oar on the ship's hull and shouted at the top of his lungs.

Not one but six seamen instantly appeared above him, every one of them grasping a belaying pin. A voice from among them, booming through the background of noise from the bank, recommended Ninian to piss off and shift for himself like everyone else.

'Is Charles Whitmead aboard?' Ninian called.

'You're not boarding this ship! This here ain't a ferry service!'

'I don't want a ferry service! I said is *Charles Whitmead aboard*? Are you deaf?' Ninian shouted.

This penetrated. 'You want Charles Whitmead?' said the voice from above.

'Yes!'

'And who might you be?'

'I'm his father! And as I can't climb rope-ladders and therefore couldn't come aboard if I wanted to, will you kindly find him and tell him I'm here!'

High above him, there was a muttered discussion. But a few minutes later, a rope-ladder flopped down and Charles descended it, stepping neatly into the boat and seating himself on a thwart. 'Father? What is it? The fire's not reached Wych Street, surely?'

'Thank God. I was afraid those oafs of seamen wouldn't tell you I'd come. But would you mind telling me why I needed to? You've been docked for days and not one word have we had from you. I only knew you were here because I'd seen the *Salisbury* from the river – and I inquired to make sure you hadn't fallen overboard on the voyage. Why didn't you send us a message?'

'Because there are a thousand and one things to do before I can take any leave and because I knew that Louisa would be disappointed if she knew I was in London and yet not with her. I was going to come in a couple of days' time, and stay.'

'I see. Well, I've come to say that I want to tell Louisa you're here. The fire's upsetting her and she keeps wishing you'd come home. You must remember she's pregnant. But I can't tell her you're back unless I can tell her when to expect you. You have been remiss, Charles.'

'I'm sorry, Father. Tell her I'm here, by all means, but you must also explain that I can't come home at once.'

The sun had set, but the night was grimly firelit. The glow was reflected from Charles's bronzed cheekbones and glinted redly in his eyes. 'We're preparing to move the ship,' he said. 'She could be in danger, anchored on this bank. We've already had people trying to board us. Panic can turn the most respectable men into pirates! I'm the second in command, and I can't leave her, any more than the Captain can, until she's safe. I wouldn't get permission even if I asked for it and I don't propose to ask.'

Reared among seafaring Cornishmen, Ninian saw the point. 'When will you move her?'

'At dawn, probably, when the river's emptied a bit, unless the fire forces us to act sooner.' Charles looked up at the flying sparks above the

City. 'Which it might. This wind won't drop yetawhile, or I know nothing about weather. Rain would help but we're not going to get that, either. I will come as soon as I can, Father. Meanwhile, I think you should take Louisa and the twins to Barnabas, just in case. I can't believe that the fire will ever reach that far west but now I think about it, I'm not so sure about Wych Street.'

'Barnabas is at my house now, or I wouldn't have been able to get here. I wouldn't have left Louisa. Very well. But Charles . . .'

'Father?'

'Come as soon as you are able, if only for an hour. Come to Barnabas' house. I'll look after your wife as best I can, but she needs you.'

'Very well.' Charles stood up, and then paused, peering at Ninian in the uneasy light. 'The tide's on the turn, but I can see you're tired, Father. I reckon we can spare a cabin boy to row you home. He can make his own way back. Also, I have a little pull, here and there. You'll want to get your belongings away as well as yourselves. You'll find a lighter waiting for you at Temple Stairs, first thing in the morning, and two lightermen to help you load it.'

'I hope that won't be necessary.'

'Do it, Father, whether it seems necessary or not. Then you won't have to do it at short notice. Louisa values her furnishings.'

'Very well. Thank you, Charles,' said Ninian.

The fire was still far away from Wych Street. There was no immediate danger. But they could all sense fear and disturbance, through the very pores of their skin. Supper was a makeshift affair of some cold mutton and a warmed-up dish of cauliflower which happened to be in the larder, and for the first time ever in the Wych Street house, Louisa ate a meal from a bare table, because Ninian's precious table-linen with the Whitmead motif had already been put into a chest ready for tomorrow's journey.

Afterwards, Louisa was sent to bed while the others went on packing household goods and Ninian's books, and attempted, each in turn, to lie down.

But in the morning, five white, tired faces looked at each other across the rolls and butter and the hot chocolate which Dorothy had wearily made, and the question: 'Did you sleep?' was pointless.

'I dozed,' said Barnabas. 'But I kept dreaming the house was afire, and waking up again in a fright.'

'I know. I could smell the smoke all night,' said Louisa. 'I did sleep once, just before daybreak, but I dreamed I was searching for Charles. There were houses and great churches, all blazing and burning and timbers crashing down, and I was running through the streets and I couldn't find him. Then I was awake again and it was daylight. I feel so tired but I can't rest till we get away from here.'

'There should be a vessel waiting for us now,' said Ninian. 'Barnabas, will you go down to Temple Stairs to see?'

Barnabas nodded, but he drew Ninian out of the room with him as he went, for a moment of worried private speech.

'Louisa looks ill. If the lighter isn't there . . .'

'I'll take her and the twins at once, in the *Penelope*. She'll be safe in bed in your house before the morning's out. I promise.'

The lighter was there. The lightermen with it looked somewhat villainous but were helpful. If they got on promptly with loading, they told Barnabas, they would catch the tide nicely for travelling upstream. Aboard their vessel they had a handcart and some tackle with which to hoist it up the Stairs. 'Just give your orders, sir. We'll see to it all.'

They kept their word. Barnabas and Ninian had little to do beyond issuing instructions. 'The larger pieces of furniture must be left,' Ninian said when the cart arrived at the house. 'But all the linen and curtains are ready to go, all the books and plate, most of the earthenware and the cooking gear. Two journeys will do it.'

'Dorothy and I will carry your money chest,' said Barnabas, distrustful of the lightermen.

They had to negotiate the crowds of people and carts fleeing from the City, and Ninian was not the only inhabitant of Wych Street to be moving out. One good-natured neighbour, catching sight of Piper MacPherson nodding seraphically in the gutter, had picked him up and dumped him on a pony cart, on top of a kitchen table. Fortunately, the distance to the steps was less than half a mile. Louisa turned sick with nerves and impatience while she was waiting to leave the house, but once on her way, with Molly's arm round her and the twins perched on top of the final cartload, she revived and walked steadily.

They had locked the house up behind them and were safely on the lighter with their belongings, including the money chest, while the water was still slack. The *Penelope* had been hoisted aboard along with the rest of the goods and Molly had brought some rugs and loose cushions with which to settle the twins and Louisa comfortably. 'There we are, now. You're not cold, Mrs Whitmead?'

'No. I feel safer now. I might even fall asleep.' Louisa gazed in the direction of the fire. 'It's still a long way off. Perhaps it's been halted.'

'Not it,' said one of the lightermen. 'St Paul's will have gone by the end of today unless there's a cloudburst, and then the blaze will start up Fleet Street; I'd put a wager on it.' He glanced at the water. Beneath the wind ripples, a deeper, stronger movement had begun, and the surface was ruched on the downstream side of the jetty's wooden legs. 'Here comes the tide. Cast off!'

As before, the river was dotted with craft, moving with the wind, away from the belching clouds of smoke to the east. Another lighter, which had been anchored in midstream to wait for the tide, was just setting forth, getting in the way of a small sailing boat with red sails, and causing the skippers to exchange abuse. The twins, among their rugs, were squeaking with excitement. 'It's quite a show,' Molly said, awed. 'I doubt if we'll ever see a sight like this in all our lives again.'

'Let us hope not!' said Louisa with some asperity. She sat up a little, however, and showed some interest in the scene.

The wind had put a little colour into her face, Ninian thought, looking at her. A few hours' rest under her father's roof would be a sure cure for her exhaustion. He was still looking at her as they came close enough to the other lighter to see who was aboard it. He saw the blood drain from her face, leaving it waxy yellow, saw her eyes widen and darken and her hand go to her mouth, and then he glanced at the other vessel, and understood.

Whoever had hired the second lighter had decided, unlike Ninian, not to let their larger items of furniture take their chance. It carried, among much else, a huge walnut sideboard and a complete fourposter bed with carved uprights and blue velvet hangings. Sitting on the bed was Christabella Davison, and beside her, his arm round her shoulders, was Charles.

Ninian had never been a cruel man. He had given Charles a beating or two when Charles was a boy, but it was a task he hated. This implacable anger, this ruthless desire to do his son real and lasting hurt, was something hitherto beyond his experience. But so was the spectacle of Barnabas, changed overnight from a bonhomous, card-playing Master Woodworker with a plump waistline, to a shrunken, hollow-eyed shadow. And so, above all, was the tragedy in the pretty bedchamber which had been Louisa's room when she had lived with her parents.

'You have come, I suppose,' he said, facing Charles in Barnabas' hallway, 'to see Louisa?'

'Yes, Father. And to – set things right, as far as I can. I'm talking about Christabella, of course. She is virtually alone in the world. She lost her parents long ago and I don't know if you know, but Alexander Morris and Edward Davison died of the plague this summer. Even her sister-in-law, Morris' wife, died last year. She has no one.'

'I did know, about Davison and Alexander Morris, anyway. But how did you find out, unless you went in search of Christabella as soon as you reached England? You sought her out, but not your own wife. She saw you, Charles, as you have obviously realised, aboard that lighter with Christabella.'

'Christabella needed my help. I never thought that you might see us with all that confusion on the river. I don't expect you to understand. I knew her long before I set eyes on Louisa and she has a claim on me. I used her, you know, to meet Louisa and I owed her something for that. But I've sought my own wife out now, Father. Where is she?'

'Upstairs.' Ninian stood aside. 'Go up, Charles. The room is the first door to your left at the top. You will find Louisa there, with your newborn son.'

'My . . . ? But the child wasn't due until November!'

'Quite. Go on, Charles. Go up. You will find me in the parlour when you come down.'

'Are they dead?'

'Go and see.'

'They *are* dead. I can tell from your face. Oh, God.'

'Leave God out of this, Charles. The fault is yours, not the Almighty's. Louisa didn't understand faithlessness. While she was . . .

250

giving birth . . . she said as much to Molly. She said she knew you were unfaithful and it bewildered her, but she could live with it as long as you didn't flaunt it at her, as long as you didn't fail her when it mattered. And you – you had to do precisely those things, didn't you? *Go up and see them. Go.*'

Halfway up the stairs, however, Charles paused and looked down at his father. 'I did send you that lighter, you know. But for that, this would never have happened.'

PART IV
Henrietta:
Uneasy Waters
1684

Can you force love into a scornful breast?

The Indian Queen, *John Dryden*

Chapter Nineteen
The Betrayal

'I daresay the news is a disappointment,' said Charles Whitmead, in serious tones which fitted not at all with his white smile, his bold, dark eyes and his weather-browned adventurer's face. 'I realise that you and your cousin Benjamin have been friends since childhood. I was never in favour, frankly, of my children spending so much time at Whitmead – nearly every summer! – but my father overrode me and with your mother being dead . . .'

And Christabella quite indifferent even to her own child, let alone her stepchildren. The words floated in the air and both father and daughter were well aware of them. They did not, however, choose to utter them.

'Samuel Whitmead and his wife were most generous with their hospitality towards you,' Charles said. 'With the result that you and Benjamin were thrown much together. I can believe that he was kind to you. But you refined on it too much.'

'No!' Henrietta sat opposite her father in the Wych Street parlour. It had been a light, uncluttered room once but Christabella hated draughts and liked buying furniture and now the room was darkened and crowded by heavy curtains, two massive cabinets and an elaborate escritoire in walnut. Neither Charles, with his sash and sword, his jet-black sailor's queue and his aura of sloping decks and seaspray, nor Henrietta, whose dusky, fine-boned looks cried out for sunlight and bright silks, looked in the least at home there.

Charles, in any case, regarded his ship as his principal home. His rare descents on Wych Street were to him interruptions in his real life. The daughter who bore such a marked resemblance to himself was someone he scarcely knew.

Henrietta on her side hardly knew how to address the man who was her father. She had changed from child to woman in the years since their last meeting. She was keenly aware that her unhappiness meant very little to him; that he did not care that she had been jilted by someone on whose fidelity she would have staked everything she owned; and that he didn't want to listen to her protestations that Benjamin could not possibly have behaved like this. She had an obscure urge to blame her father for it instead of Benjamin.

'I didn't refine on *anything*.' Charles' face was disbelieving but she pressed on. 'Benjamin and I talked most seriously of our future. We looked on ourselves as betrothed. We parted only last September and when I said goodbye to him, he said: "When your father comes home, I

255

shall send to ask if I may marry you." He would have asked before, only you were not here. It takes so long, going back and forth to India. I have been waiting, longing, for the *Restoration* to come home. And I thought, when you said you were going to meet Benjamin's father, that . . . that Benjamin had asked . . .'

Charles shook his head. 'Samuel Whitmead asked to meet me in a London coffee-house. Had he been bearing a proposal, he would have come here. Must I say it all again? He and his wife knew of your hopes and he wished to inform me that Benjamin has engaged himself to marry someone else, so that I as your father could, in turn, break the news to you gently. He stressed that I should be gentle although he said – and I agree – that it was most wrong of you to entertain the idea even of an unofficial betrothal without my sanction. Come, no need to be so downcast. You are not yet nineteen and you are well dowered. I have good portions set aside for both you and Caroline. You'll be well married, never fear.'

'I don't want any other husband but Benjamin! He had waited for me; he told me so. He knew when I was only twelve that he loved me. He was already twenty-two then, but he waited so that I could grow up. When I was sixteen, he asked if I thought I could ever love him.' It had been just before harvest, as they'd been walking by a cornfield, at twilight. Remembering it, the haunting sweetness of it, with a huge full moon just beginning to grow luminous and the call of the first barn owl abroad that evening, quivering softly across the meadows, Henrietta found her voice shaking. Benjamin had kissed her then, for the first time. 'You were away, bound for India. I told him I'd loved him ever since I could remember. We plighted ourselves to each other and promised to be faithful always and since then we've waited, waited, for you to come home so that . . .'

'Life,' said Charles, 'isn't a matter of childhood sweethearts. People grow up, and alter, as Benjamin has evidently found out. Samuel told me that Benjamin now realised that he loved you only as a sister, and was sorry to hurt you, but hoped that perhaps you too had reached the same conclusion. According to Samuel,' Charles added sternly, 'Benjamin also recognises what you apparently do not, that without your parents' consent, neither of you had the right to bind yourselves.'

'But we were waiting to *ask* your consent!' cried Henrietta. 'I don't believe Benjamin would wait so long and then abandon me at the last moment and if he did, he'd come and tell me so himself. Who is she, this other girl he's supposed to want to marry?'

'Samuel didn't say,' said Charles, becoming bored. 'I gained the impression that she lives near Whitmead. What of it? The fact is, Henrietta: you have behaved very ill and this is no more than you deserve. Your only excuse is your youth. To Benjamin, I daresay it was half a game. Perhaps he partly meant it then, but he has grown older and he has changed.'

'No!' Henrietta's dark eyes were brilliant with anger and tears. 'He can't have. He wouldn't. I don't believe in this other girl! It isn't *true*!'

'Oh, but it is,' said Charles.

The fire died out of the dark eyes and Henrietta's head drooped, as though her fashionable flowing curls were too heavy for it. Addressing that bent head, Charles observed: 'In any case, I have already formed other plans for you. They are not yet final, but I must ask you to hold yourself in readiness to do my bidding. Your feelings are too strong, Henrietta. Women shouldn't have strong feelings. Your business in life will be to study the happiness of the husband that I select for you, and find your own happiness through his. I daresay that now you want to cry. Well, go to your room and get it over. And don't push yourself up from the arms of your chair like that as if you were nearly ninety instead of nearly nineteen. Leave the arranging of your future to me. I shall have your best interests at heart.'

'Yes, Father,' said Henrietta, because this was what he expected her to say, and bobbed the curtsy which was also expected.

Charles fished in his coat for a wad of tobacco to chew, and listened irritably as his daughter's feet retreated up the stairs. No doubt she'd be shut in her room for hours. His wife Christabella was also in her room, as was usual these days, and his father Ninian was in his. His younger daughter was probably in the schoolroom with Molly Meade, who had stayed on to be his daughters' governess.

Sometimes it seemed to him that his entire household consisted of people skulking in private cells like a lot of damned hermits. His son ought to have been a companion to him but Matthew was the worst disappointment of his life. Matthew hated ships, was capable of being seasick on the Thames in a dead calm at ebbtide, and was now away at university studying to be a lawyer, of all things.

With all his heart, Charles longed for his vessel the East Indiaman *Restoration*, for the murmur of the sea under her forefoot and the moan of the wind in her rigging; to be setting forth on the long voyage to India, southwards down the Atlantic and across to Brazil to pick up the trade wind for the voyage round the Cape of Good Hope, and then northwards again through the stormy Indian Ocean. She would be sailing with a hold full of European goods for sale not only on arrival at the East India Company's base in Fort St George, Madras, but also to the passengers travelling thither with him. The captain of a Company ship made money all the way.

Not that one couldn't always do with more, of course. And for what other purpose had God invented daughters, except to marry money for their fathers' use?

'I daresay that now you want to cry,' her father had said, dismissing her misery as though it could be dispelled by a little ritual expenditure of salt water.

But Henrietta, lying on the bed she shared at night with her half-sister Caroline and staring up at the ceiling beams above her, learned that afternoon that some kinds of pain are beyond tears. She was in a black void, where once there had been Benjamin, and the size of her loss had left her dry-eyed and numb.

She had been engaged to Benjamin for three years. Every spring

257

when she went to Whitmead, his eyes had lit at the sight of her; and in each of the last three Septembers, when she went away, he had said: 'One day, you'll come for good.' One winter he had come to London on an errand for his father and stayed in this house for a month, while they shared secret love-talk and snatched kisses and last winter, the coldest in living memory, he had written complaining that the snow had kept him from coming again. He loved her. How could he without warning just change his mind?

But apparently he had, and with that, the tears welled up after all. Henrietta rolled over to lie face down, weeping while her fists pounded the bed in rage, as though it were Benjamin's hateful, beloved, treacherous face.

It was Caroline, released from studying geography with Molly Meade, who found her first. 'Rietta! Oh, Rietta, what is it, what's wrong?' She sat on the edge of the bed and put a gentle hand on Henrietta's shoulders. 'Are you ill?'

'No! Go *away!*'

'I can't leave you like this,' said Caroline reasonably. Caroline, at sixteen, was already more solid of body and more stolid of temperament than Henrietta. 'Please tell me what's wrong. I'll help if I can.'

'You can't. You mean well but you won't understand this; it hasn't happened to you.'

'What hasn't happened?' said Caroline. 'Oh, Rietta, do talk to me.'

Henrietta sat up slowly and looked at her. Caroline was Christabella's daughter, which showed in her appearance, for her skin was much fairer than Henrietta's, and her hair not black but a pleasant light brown. She had Christabella's pansy-brown eyes, too. But Caroline's eyes were softer.

'Love,' said Henrietta unwillingly. 'And that's all I'm going to say. Go away, Caro. Go and be Father's good girl and finish embroidering the Whitmead device on all our kerchiefs and napkins; you'll enjoy that and it will keep Father in a good temper. He loves to see us sitting quietly about smiling sweetly and stitching. He can't bear the sight of tears or anger no matter how justified they are!'

'If I can't help,' said Caroline, ignoring this, 'could Mrs Meade?'

'No. I wish Matthew were here.'

Caroline regarded her sister worriedly. They had always been friends as well as sisters; more than friends, allies together with Matthew, depending on each other because their father was hardly ever there and because Christabella was equally indifferent to all three of them.

At times when they needed help but couldn't provide it for each other, they had turned to Molly Meade or . . .

'I can't just wander off and embroider napkins while you're in this state,' said Caroline. 'Matthew's in Oxford and you don't want Mrs Meade. All right. That leaves Grandfather. I'm going to get him.'

She went briskly out of the room. Henrietta, left alone, curled into a ball. Her tears had stopped but the black void seemed now to be inside her instead of around her, a huge, aching pit in the centre of her stomach. She couldn't remember a time when Benjamin wasn't there.

He had been her life. Let Caroline fetch Grandfather if she liked. She had lost her life and all the grandfathers in the world couldn't help her now.

Outside the door was an awkwardly shaped landing, created when Christabella had the house modernised, so that people could get to their bedrooms without having to pass through anyone else's. Henrietta heard the wheels of her grandfather's chair squeak as Caroline brought him out of his room opposite, and then he was being pushed into the room and up to the bed. Caroline left him there, closing the door softly as she went out.

'Well, well,' said Ninian. 'What's all this, Henrietta? Caroline says you're in great distress but won't tell her why. She seems to think you might tell me. Will you?'

'Oh, Grandfather!' said Henrietta, and although it was no use, and he couldn't possibly help her, she turned to him, slipping off the bed to kneel beside the wheeled chair and put her arms round him.

'There, there.' Ninian stroked her head. Even the hot tongs which renewed her curls each morning couldn't destroy the texture of Henrietta's blue-black hair. It was just like Parvati's. Though Louisa had been dark as well, it wasn't in the same way. He never saw Henrietta's hair, still less touched it, without thinking of Parvati. There had been a time when her memory had faded a little, but lately it had come back to him, troubling his dreams, and springing into his head and his heart at the least reminder, as though Parvati's shade were impatient for him to join her and wondered why he tarried.

He frequently wondered the same thing. For ten years now he had been unable to walk except with great pain, and spent most of his life in his room, either in bed or in this chair which Paul Browne had made for him, the very last time Ninian ever managed to visit Whitmead. By rights, Ninian thought, his immobilised hulk should have admitted defeat and died long ago. His excellent health was his worst enemy.

'What is it, my child?' he said.

Henrietta looked up. His granddaughter's face, too, was heartstoppingly reminiscent of Parvati. She had the same smile, both sweet and valiant; the same dark brown, almond-shaped eyes; a skin fairer than Parvati's yet tinged with the same ivory; high cheekbones curved just so, like a perfect reflection from the past. It was Matthew, not Henrietta, who resembled their mother.

'Benjamin Whitmead and I were engaged to marry,' Henrietta said. 'I told you about it, Grandfather, do you remember? When I was sixteen?'

'Yes, you did. I always liked Benjamin. I was pleased.' He hadn't been so sure that Benjamin's parents would be pleased. True, they had been kind to his grandchildren, taking them every summer, ostensibly to protect them from the risk of plague in London, even after it became clear that the great fire had somehow burned the plague away. But Ninian suspected that they were acting out of a sense of Christian duty and were really trying to protect them from what they saw as unsatisfactory influences at home. He also suspected that they had never really changed their opinion that his grandchildren were somehow tainted by their ancestry. They had certainly kept their distance from Charles.

Probably they had assumed that because the two households were related, the young people would think of each other only as siblings. But the cousinship was distant and Benjamin was a handsome, good-natured, likeable boy and Henrietta as sweet and exotically pretty as an orchid. What was more natural than for them to fall in love?

'You said you *were* engaged to Benjamin?' he asked tentatively. 'Past tense? Have you changed your mind?'

'No! *He* has,' said Henrietta, and broke down again. For some time he could only hold her in the crook of an arm and murmur soothingly. Until at last she was able to repeat to him what her father had told her.

When the story was told, she fixed piteous eyes on his face. 'What am I to do, Grandfather? If Benjamin's gone, what is there for me?'

'Sit up, on the bed. That's it.' He did not make Charles' mistake of underestimating her feelings. Henrietta had matured physically at twelve and her emotions were in step with her body. But still, it was a fact that she was young in years. 'Don't say that, Henrietta, please don't say that, or think it. There's a great deal ahead for you. If Benjamin has failed you, well, perhaps he wasn't what you thought him and you'll do better, one day, with a more trustworthy man.'

'But don't you see?' Henrietta cried out. 'If Benjamin can fail me, anyone can! I can never trust anyone again. I wanted to trust Benjamin. Oh, *Grandfather!*' It wasn't an appeal for help this time, just a cry of despair. Once again, he could do nothing but hold her and murmur useless phrases of comfort, bitterly aware that he was eighty-four and crippled, and that to help her was beyond him.

Though he tried. When at last Henrietta was calmer and had consented to seek Molly Meade's company, he called Caroline to wheel him back to his room and dispatched her in search of his son.

Charles arrived a few moments later, punctiliously bowing to his father on the threshold, before coming into the room with inquiries as to how Ninian found himself today.

'I see your manservant isn't here, Father. I hope he's proving satisfactory? I want you to be properly attended and I'll replace him if necessary.'

'It's Harrison's afternoon off. Even menservants are entitled to an occasional break. I don't slave-drive my employees the way you drive your crew, Charles. What's all this about young Benjamin jilting Henrietta? Sit down there where the light falls on your face, and tell me.'

Ninian's windows looked east and west, so that they received the morning and evening sun. The April day was wearing on now and growing chill and the sunlight which slanted on to his bookshelves and the sofa he kept for visitors was tinged with orange. His fire was lit and his chair was in its usual position, where all his books were within arm's length, and on the table beside him was his candle and the decanter of port from which he drank after supper. Charles sat down where Ninian pointed, on the end of the sofa where the light fell.

'You knew of Henrietta's so-called engagement, then?' Charles said.

'I had an idea of it, yes.'

'She's always talked to you,' said Charles in a dissatisfied tone. 'Well, shortly after I came home, I received a letter from Samuel Whitmead asking me to meet him at a coffee-house. He had apparently arranged to be told when the *Restoration* was in, and had come to London. When we met, he informed me that Henrietta and young Benjamin had been doing some childish sweethearting and that Benjamin had now changed his mind and wished to release himself without causing Henrietta too much pain. The idea was that I should break the news to my daughter and, well, soften it for her as best I could.'

'I see,' said Ninian.

He saw a good deal more than Charles knew. He had learned, long ago, that when Charles' grin was as confident and open as that, and when he met one's eyes so very directly, with quite so much amusement in his own, he was probably lying his stockings off.

Christabella had learned that, too. Ninian had detested his second daughter-in-law when Charles first married her. Later, he had become very sorry for her.

'There's nothing you can do, you know,' said Charles gently.

'Is there not? I can write to Benjamin himself for an explanation. And make sure my man Harrison dispatches the letter in person, furthermore.'

'It might be better not to interfere,' said Charles. 'You'll hardly want to force Benjamin to marry the girl against his will.'

'If it is against his will. I'm eighty-four,' said Ninian furiously, 'and I can't get out of this house. I can hardly get out of this room! Or I'd go to Whitmead myself and see Benjamin face to face. This is not like the Benjamin I remember.'

'You haven't seen him since the winter before last, when he spent a few weeks here. He's altered.'

'Has he? So much, so quickly? I hadn't seen him for years before that winter, but while he was here, I got to know him well. He had a taste for poetry and plays and not much chance to indulge them, at home. We did some reading together and we discussed some of the plots and emotions in Shakespeare and Dryden. Nothing tells you how someone's mind works better than that. I say that this is out of character. I mean to get to the bottom of this. And your smile, my boy, would look well on the face of a pirate.'

Charles stopped smiling. 'There is something you should know. I have my own plans for Henrietta and they don't include Benjamin. I would not consent to the marriage even if he came here in person and knelt at my feet. It would be much kinder to Henrietta to let things be. I think myself,' said Charles coolly, 'that a complete change of scene might be of benefit to her. I would agree that Benjamin's picture should be allowed to fade from her mind before I require her to replace it with somebody else's. Also, I suspect that she's going to mope, and I'd prefer her not to do it all over my house. If you want to help her, perhaps you could suggest somewhere for her to go.'

Ninian, tiredly, recognised defeat. 'You and Samuel dislike each other,' he said. 'I know that if you'd been at home while the children were growing up, they wouldn't have been allowed to visit Whitmead. What did you and he say to one another in that coffee-house?'

'I have always rather resented the way you took it upon yourself to let my children stay with Samuel in my absence, even though you knew very well what Samuel and I think of each other.' Charles' voice was cooler than ever. 'I prefer to keep my conversation with Samuel confidential. Now. About Henrietta. She can't go to Essex. Where else is there?'

'It would certainly be a good idea for her to go away for a time,' said Ninian grimly. 'On that head, I agree with you. Where? It's a pity Louisa's sisters are both dead. Neither left any children; Henrietta hasn't even got any first cousins. But Louisa had some other relatives in Somerset – at Taunton. Perhaps they're still there. Ask Clemency.'

'Thank you. I think I will. Will that be all, Father?'

'Oh, get out,' said Ninian.

Charles smiled his pirate's smile again, bowed and departed. Ninian turned his chair to face the eastward window, beyond which the new City of London was rising stone by stone from the ashes of its burned and plague-ridden predecessor. The man called Christopher Wren, who had once refused to be turned from an astronomer into an architect, had at last been tempted from his Chair of Astronomy at Oxford, by the wondrous prospect of reconstructing London, with the King's goodwill and the royal purse behind him. He was the new City's designer and the King's Surveyor of the Works. His plans were said to be quite extraordinary. Wren's version of St Paul's Cathedral was going to be a notable addition to London's skyline if all that Ninian had heard were true. It was going to have a dome instead of an ordinary steeple. Ninian had seen a picture of a domed mosque and both Parvati and Charles had seen such things in reality, in the east, and told him about them.

It was very difficult to imagine such a thing here in London, but he would have to be content with imagination for he would never see it in reality. It would take years to complete and by then he would be dead and buried.

He swung round to look the other way, towards the west, where the orange sun was going down behind the neighbouring roofs. Gulls took refuge inland during the winter, seeking the easy pickings of the town, and some of them were still here. He could see one drifting on the air currents above the chimneys and hear its mewing cry. It reminded him of Cornwall.

Gulls cried all the time at Polmawgan and the sun, there, rose out of the sea and went down behind the smooth hills of the Cornish peninsula.

He'd never see Cornwall again. He had left it thankfully, never expecting to miss it, only to surprise himself by becoming homesick for

262

it. Now the homesickness was a gnawing fury and he cursed the ruined body which would not let him either help his granddaughter or journey once more to Polmawgan.

He had lived to see an intriguing new world come into being. He wished that the surge of interest in science and mathematics and astronomy which had followed King Charles' restoration had come about when he was young. It was a cleaner, healthier air than the overheated religious miasma of his youth, which had bred superstition as the old City of London's filthy streets bred plague, and so killed his Parvati.

He missed her still, and he was too old now to study science. What was worse, even the poetry he had once enjoyed so much seemed stale, as though he had sucked it dry. He would be glad to go, to be rid of the burden of his crippled body and tired mind, and free at last of love and yearning. It wouldn't be long now. Henrietta, poor child, must live her life as best she could without him. Charles was her father, and if Charles had set his face against a marriage with Benjamin, it would indeed be wiser not to interfere. But he grieved for her, all the same.

Harrison came into the room with his brisk, quiet step. 'Good evening, sir. My, it's getting shadowy in here, and turning cold, too. Let me light your candles and build up the fire. What shall I fetch you for supper?'

'You can start,' said Ninian, 'by pouring me a very large port.'

In Whitmead, Charity came from the kitchen where she and her daughters were helping to prepare supper, and found that Samuel had returned from riding round the fields, and was settled in a chair with his evening ale beside him. 'Where's Benjamin?' she asked.

'Still out and about on the home farm.'

'He's a good hard-working boy,' Charity said approvingly but very seriously. She was sterner than she used to be. The change had come with the stillborn child from which she had recovered so slowly and it had never reversed. 'I think things have turned out for the best, don't you?' she remarked.

'Very much so. God has answered our prayers in every direction. We lost scarcely any stock last winter, in spite of the weather – what a freeze! I thought it would never end – and now we have an excellent marriage in prospect for Benjamin. Have Mr and Mrs Saunders accepted our invitation to bring Beatrice over from Quensted on Sunday?'

'Indeed they have. Beatrice is such a thoroughly nice girl. Benjamin really does like her, you know. I think the marriage should prosper very well.'

Chapter Twenty
Eleanor

One's heart might be broken, but daily life had to go on, and from time to time, Henrietta discovered, this meant making small-talk. One could not remain permanently silent. 'Somerset is much more hilly than Essex,' she remarked, peering from the windows of Charles' coach as it bumped and rattled slowly down a steep, rutted slope between walls of red-tinged earth and pinkish stone, topped with grass. Outside, on his box, the coachman's voice rumbled out a stream of reassurance and encouragement to the horses. The sun was out and the inside of the coach was hot. 'The roads are rougher, too. I didn't think it would be so different.'

'Things rarely turn out as we expect. I never expected to get fat,' said Christabella.

This was irrelevant, self-centred and perfectly true. Christabella took up so much of the forward-facing seat that her maid Nan had to share the backward-facing one with Henrietta, and the satins and ribbons and bits of lace which adorned her bulging form made her look like a bedizened pig. A pig past its prime, at that. The hair which Nan still curled each morning was grey now instead of butter-coloured. Henrietta judged it more tactful not to reply directly.

'It was kind of you to accompany me, Stepmother,' she said.

Christabella snorted. 'It makes a change of scene.' After a pause, she added: 'I haven't said this before, but I'm sorry for your disappointment. Still, you may as well learn. Life is mostly disappointment, especially where men are concerned. Benjamin wouldn't have been any different from the rest, take it from me.'

'But . . .' Henrietta was taken by surprise. Christabella rarely showed much sympathy for other people. Ninian had said once: 'Bear with her, Henrietta. She's unhappy.'

'Surely,' said Henrietta, 'everyone isn't disappointed?'

'Most are,' Christabella assured her. 'The earlier you realise it, the better.'

Her own disappointment had begun at the age of fifteen, when her parents arranged her marriage to Edward Davison. She hadn't been reared to expect romance, but she was a warm-blooded young female with a sharp mind; she had expected sexual satisfaction and the fun of having someone to talk to as an adult.

She found herself tied instead to a dull man who expected his wife to look ornamental and entertain well, but had hardly a word to say to her in private, and only made love to her once a week, as a duty.

As Mrs Davison she had learned to find her satisfactions elsewhere; in repartee with her guests and in bed with other men. Especially Charles. Under Charles' spell, she had become like a naive fifteen-year-old all over again. She had raged and wept like a hurt child when he told her he was going to marry Louisa, but had to do most of it in secret for fear of offending husband and lover alike.

And when, a year after the deaths of both Edward and Louisa, Charles asked her to marry him, she had been fool enough to think that the sun had just risen on Paradise.

It had taken just a few weeks to realise that to be Charles' wife wasn't at all the same thing as being his mistress. She still shrivelled inside at the memory of that first matrimonial quarrel, when he came home after being inexplicably absent all night and answered her demand to know why by telling her shortly that it was none of her business. When she persisted, he had snapped that her proper business as his wife was to run his house, look after his children instead of being so obviously bored by them, and provide him with some more sons. 'No need for sponges soaked in vinegar now, my lady. So where are the healthy boys a man should have to follow him?' He added that Louisa had never questioned him like this, and then slapped her.

That time, she hit him back, threw things at him – a silver-backed brush, a pair of curling tongs and a pot of ointment – and finally, because the contest was so uneven, fled screaming from the room to seek protection from Molly Meade who kindly locked Charles out of her room until he had got his temper back.

Peace terms were finally negotiated through the keyhole. But she was afraid thereafter of direct confrontation and found herself relieved when he went to sea. He came back to discover that he was a father once more but to a daughter, Caroline, and not the son he wanted.

After that, Charles stayed out at night more and more often and Christabella, after trying such varied ploys as tears; stony silences; a façade of gaiety during which she spent immense sums on fashionable clothes and held endless elegant dinner parties which caused two cooks in succession to give notice; took to refusing sex to him. Charles responded by scarcely ever sleeping at home at all.

On his return from his next voyage, he found that Christabella had a lover. The lover was a seaman, as Charles was informed by a busybody of a clerk in his own shipping office. He arrived home in such a towering fury that Christabella had thought ever since that he might have killed her, except that he began shouting threats as soon as he was in the house, giving her time to run once more to Molly's room and bolt herself inside.

Ninian negotiated the peace that time. Christabella swore on a Bible never to leave the house without a maid in attendance again, and Nan swore never to conspire with her mistress against Charles. Charles sent a couple of friends round to the lover with a challenge, but the lover had been warned and had disappeared, probably aboard some vessel bound on a lengthy voyage. He was not heard of again.

Since then, Christabella had sunk into bored indolence, taking her pleasures in food and occasional playgoing and gossip with a few women friends, indifferent alike to Charles, her daughter and her stepchildren. Molly Meade ran the house and taught the two little girls; Charles came and went as he pleased and slept in a separate room. He showed a degree of interest in his offspring, but Matthew wasn't the kind of son he had hoped for and the girls were to him 'only daughters', although as they grew he became fond of them in a fashion.

The entire household was happier when he was at sea. And Christabella, as the years went on, had grown fat.

One thing I'll never do, said Henrietta silently to herself, is let myself become fat. Aloud, she said: 'We've made good time. We were only twenty miles from Taunton this morning, the coachman said. We must be nearly there.'

'God knows what sort of household it'll be,' said Christabella. 'I gather that your grandmother Clemency hasn't been to Taunton now for years, and doesn't know what things are like there, but that your Great-Aunt Faith is probably still living in spirit in Cromwell's day.'

'Yes. Grandfather let me see her letter. She said she hoped I was a godly girl reared in ways of righteousness,' said Henrietta. 'But Cousin Ruth wrote back to us as well as my great-aunt, and she sounded very amiable though the letter was rather wordy.'

'I shall be leaving for London again after you're settled. But if you're unhappy, just write. You can come home whenever you like,' Christabella said.

Henrietta glanced at her stepmother, frowning a little. 'It's an odd thing. But do you know, Stepmother, I don't believe I've ever talked to you freely before. This is the very first time.'

'You've thought of yourself as a child before,' said Christabella. 'I thought of you as a child, too, and I've never cared for children. But now, all of a sudden, you're a woman, talking to another woman. It makes a difference. I wish you well, my girl, and better luck than I've had.'

They arrived half an hour later, clattering into the outskirts of a town where houses of various patterns stood dotted along either side of the road, and drawing up before one of them.

Henrietta descended, accepting a hand from the coachman. The air smelt sweet, quite different from the reek of London or the tang of salt and marshland which meant Whitmead. The day was clear and she could see hills in the distance. The house in front of her was friendly, built of pink stone and dark timber, snugly thatched, opening directly on to the road, but flanked to either side by a garden which was responsible for some of the warm scents all round her. She could see lemon verbena, lavender, mint. The words Peace-Through-Praise were painted on a board over the front door, and the door was now being pulled open. A small, bent-backed woman in grey, with an old-fashioned white linen head-dress, scurried out to meet them.

'Oh, you're here, safely here. How good to see you. You'll be Henrietta, and this will be Mrs Whitmead, your mother, no, not your mother, no, of course not; do excuse me, but our families are that out of touch. I'm Ruth Clarke, your mother's first cousin, whatever that makes me to you. Mr Clarke's been dead and gone these two years; such a shame he couldn't be here to greet you; but there, we all drifted apart after my uncle Barnabas died. Oh, and this is my sister Becky. Becky, you'd best explain to the men where the stableyard entrance is . . . Here's Graves; Graves, bring the baggage in and take it to the east gable room. You'll be the maid, won't you, dear? What's your name? Nan? Now that's a pretty name. You'll be in with the other two maids; nice girls they are; I hope you'll all get on . . .'

On a tide of murmurous talk, all in a soft accent new to Henrietta, Ruth hurried them indoors. Becky, who was much like Ruth to look at but was straighter in the back and not nearly so talkative, had waited in visible patience for Ruth to run out of breath or go away, before beginning to explain to the coachman and groom where they should take their vehicle. As they went inside, Ruth stopped to prop the door open with a lump of stone, so that Becky could follow and the manservant Graves could bring in the baggage. The house seemed cool and dark after the sunlit outdoors. Somewhere, somebody was reading a psalm aloud.

'Mother said bring you straight to her, my dears,' Ruth said. 'You won't mind me calling you my dears? It's just the way we talk, down here, but London's maybe different. Mother's in the parlour having the Bible read to her as she always is this time of day. Usually we'd be with her but getting ready for you broke the routine a bit. When there's bedding to air and rooms to be swept, it cuts down the time you can spare for prayers and readings and whatnot.'

And suddenly, the thin, middle-aged face within the frame of white linen broke into a smile of astonishing charm, full of an innocent mischief which made Henrietta laugh, much to her own surprise. She hadn't laughed since she heard of Benjamin's defection. She thought she had forgotten how.

'We shall have to attend prayers before supper, however.' Ruth had become serious again. 'You've brought something plain and dark to wear, have you? Mother doesn't like bright colours. I hope you'll be comfortable in the east gable; it would have been the west gable which has a better outlook, but there, my daughter Eleanor came home unexpected-like a month ago – lost her husband, poor thing – and that was her old room . . .'

In the depths of the house, the psalm-reading stopped. *'Ruth!'* The voice was female but sounded as commanding as that of a general. 'Stop that idle gossiping and bring our guests here at once!'

'Coming, Mother!'

Ruth led them through a small, dark parlour full of bleak-looking oaken furniture with no cushions, then through a low door and down two steps and into a second parlour, bigger, but just as dark and just as plain. An elderly woman dressed in black except for a white cap and shawl sat by the unlit hearth and beside her was a younger woman, also wearing black, with a book in her hands. Presumably it was she who had been reading aloud.

'Mother,' said Ruth, 'this is Mrs Christabella Whitmead and this is Cousin Henrietta. My dears, this is my mother, Mrs Faith Ross, and this is my daughter, Eleanor Henderson . . .'

Henrietta looked curiously at Eleanor, who was only a little older than herself. It was clear that her black gown represented deep mourning, but the face that looked out at Henrietta from the midst of the dark veil had nothing withdrawn about it.

Henrietta took in the strong features: the definite nose, prominent cheekbones not in perfect symmetry; the natural pallor as intense as white flame; and blue eyes which burned into hers before they softened in a smile. In a low, beautiful voice, Eleanor said: 'Mrs Whitmead, Cousin Henrietta: I am delighted to make your acquaintance.'

'Lord, how long shall the wicked, how long shall the wicked triumph? How long shall they utter and speak hard things and all the workers of iniquity boast themselves?'
Eleanor was embarking on yet another psalm. It was a hot afternoon. A wasp buzzed on the window-pane and Henrietta, who hated them, kept a wary eye on it but sat still, because a guest must keep the rules of the house. Great-Aunt Faith wanted Eleanor to read the ninety-fourth psalm and they'd all have to listen to the end.

'They break in pieces thy people, Oh Lord, and afflict thine heritage. They slay the widow and the stranger, and murder the fatherless . . .'
Across the room, Eleanor glanced up from the Bible just long enough to catch Henrietta's eye and Henrietta lowered her own to hide a flicker of laughter. Becky and Ruth were murmuring the words of the psalm along with Eleanor, from memory. They knew it by heart because, as Ruth had told Henrietta, Great-Aunt Faith had been having it read to her at least once a week all that year.

'She always hoped that King Charles would have a son and cut that Catholic brother of his out of the succession,' Ruth said. Ruth looked and talked like a garrulous countrywoman whose concerns were purely domestic and Becky like a less talkative version of the same thing, but it was deceptive. They had grown up in a house where matters of politics and religion were everyday conversational currency; where every detail of Cromwell's campaign and rule were known; where the fortunes of the anti-Catholic Whig party were followed with passion; and in which James Duke of York was loathed for not only being a Catholic, but also for marrying one, and James Scott Duke of Monmouth was regarded with surprising tolerance even by Great-Aunt Faith. It was shocking that he was illegitimate, but that was his parents' fault, not his, and he *was* King Charles' son and furthermore, a Protestant.

'At the very least,' Ruth explained, 'my mother has prayed that the Whig attempts to get the Duke of York cut out of the succession would succeed. She even thought Titus Oates was inspired by God.'

This conversation had taken place before Christabella went back to London. 'Oates?' said Christabella in a scandalised voice. At home, she had never been heard to pass a remark on any political matter, but she now turned out to be as well-informed as anyone. 'But all the Catholic plots he claimed he'd discovered were lies. He is quite discredited.'

'Mother feels that he sinned in a righteous cause,' said Becky, quite seriously. 'Mother grieves very much for the days of Cromwell. It horrifies her that the clock might be turned back and a Catholic monarch sit on the throne once more. She would have accepted it if King Charles had declared Monmouth his heir. But instead . . .'

Ruth cut in. 'Instead, there were all those plots last year against both the King and his brother; seemingly there's some that go further than not wanting a Catholic monarch. Want the republic back like in Cromwell's day, they do. Seems that the King don't believe Monmouth had anything to do with any plots, but Monmouth's had to go away to Holland and the Duke of York is at the King's side and to Mother, why, it's as if the heir to England is anti-Christ in person.'

'Will you mind being left here?' Christabella asked her step-daughter, later that same day. 'You need not stay if you would rather come back with me. This place is hardly what you're used to. What a name to give a house!' she added, with something of the sophisticated disdain of the old Christabella, who had been the hostess at elegant London parties. 'Peace-Through-Praise!'

'No, it's not what I'm used to,' Henrietta agreed. 'But it doesn't matter. I'm best away from home for a while and nothing will ever again be like . . . like Whitmead. This will do. I'm already fond of Ruth and Becky.'

She could have added that she was amused by them. Her two middle-aged cousins, Ruth a widow and Becky a spinster, lived to outward appearances under the iron control of their mother, Henrietta's Great-Aunt Faith. In reality, they gave the apparently solemn regime of Peace-Through-Praise considerable spice by conducting a secret running warfare against their mother's rules.

'Mother does not like us to cultivate flowers in the garden,' Becky explained. 'She considers them to be wasteful fripperies and their perfume to be an indulgence of the senses.'

'But we must have lavender and lemon verbena to keep linen fresh and free from moth and we must grow mint and thyme for the kitchen. Meat can taste that funny in hot weather, metallic-like unless there's herbs with it,' Ruth added gravely. 'And trees that bear nice practical fruit also blossom in spring.'

They frequently evaded their mother's Bible readings and prayer meetings on the plea of domestic duties. Windows were cleaned, clothes washed, furniture polished, with astounding frequency in Peace-Through-Praise, but all with a secret undercurrent of merriment; and every chance of an expedition was seized upon eagerly. Henrietta was constantly accompanying them to the houses of friends, to drink chocolate, and chatter about small everyday matters and 'be comfortable', as Ruth put it, on upholstered sofas of the kind forbidden under Great-Aunt Faith's roof. Ruth and Becky did the marketing oftener than the maids did and took their time over it, chatting to acquaintances and stopping for hot pies and ale before they came home.

While Henrietta would never forget how, on the morning after Christabella had gone, Ruth and Becky had called her early and they all went into the nearby fields to pick mushrooms and also, once out of hearing of the house, to sing country songs, and caper, actually caper, in the dew. Becky, aged forty-six, scampered across the meadow and laughed to see the green trail that her feet left in the silvered grass.

And then, of course, there was Eleanor.

Eleanor, newly widowed after less than two years of marriage and therefore restricted by mourning, did not join them for any of the outings. Great-Aunt Faith was determined about that. But Eleanor had her own secret ways of rebellion: a melodious, ironic inflection in her voice as she read the afternoon psalm; a too-marked solemnity when Great-Aunt Faith – as happened fairly often – spoke of her bereavement and besought her to remember that the ways of the Lord were mysterious; a fugitive waft of lemon verbena from her black clothing; a glance from her blue eyes at Henrietta in a wordless invitation to share a secret jest.

Henrietta had quickly grown fond of Ruth and Becky, but by Eleanor she was fascinated. So far, in this first month, the two of them had talked often, but only in a superficial fashion. Eleanor was not one to offer too much friendship too soon and Henrietta could not make the first approach. The daughter of the house, a grown woman who had experienced marriage, was above Henrietta in the subtle domestic hierarchy.

The ninety-fourth psalm neared its end and the wasp zoomed back and forth from the window with increasing fury. Recalling Eleanor's secret glance, Henrietta knew that the moment would come when they would become friends, and then surely Eleanor who had known bereavement would understand what the loss of Benjamin was like.

The psalm ended. They all waited, hoping that Great-Aunt Faith would say that that was enough for the afternoon. Alternatively, she might say that she wanted another psalm, or a reading from a sermon. Silence fell, even from the wasp. Eleanor's eyes remained studiously on the page in front of her. Great-Aunt Faith's gaze turned, annoyingly, to the shelf of sermons beside her and her left forefinger tapped a small, thoughtful tattoo on the wooden arm of her chair. Then Becky snatched Eleanor's Bible from her and hit her mother's left wrist extremely hard. But not quite fast enough, for Faith cried out before the descending Bible squashed the wasp which had just stung her.

In the confusion which followed, while Becky seized their mother's wrist and peered at it, and Ruth kicked disgustedly at the black and yellow corpse which had fallen by her feet, and Faith tried at one and the same time to complain that the wasp had stung her without cause, accuse Becky of having gone mad and be outraged because the reading of Holy Writ had been interrupted for such a mundane reason, Eleanor caught Henrietta's eye and signalled with a jerk of her chin. The two of them slipped out of the parlour and made their way into the back garden.

'We can be looking for something to bathe it with. Dock leaves, perhaps,' said Eleanor.

'They're for nettle stings.'

'Well, they might work on wasp stings. Why not?'

Eleanor steered them deftly behind a screen of apple and cherry trees to a little patch of wilderness at the end of the garden with plenty of nettles and dock leaves, and also a few bushes, behind which she sank down on to the grass, pulling Henrietta with her. They looked at each other and burst out laughing.

'We've escaped!' Shaking with amusement, Eleanor threw herself backwards and clasped her hands behind her head. 'She was going to inflict a sermon on us as well. God must have sent that wasp to rescue us!'

'I expect Great-Aunt Faith would say the devil had sent it,' said Henrietta with a giggle.

Eleanor sat up. 'I knew we should laugh at the same things. I knew it the moment I saw you. Oh, my mother and Aunt Becky are dears, but when *you* came into the house, it was as if someone had opened all the doors and let a fresh wind blow in. I've been longing to talk to you, really talk to you, I mean. But I've been half afraid to in case I was wrong about you, in case you were . . . oh, just ordinary after all. You were so quiet, so well-behaved. But you're not just ordinary, are you?'

'Well . . . oh dear, I'm going to disappoint you. I'm very ordinary, really. No one has ever called me a fresh wind before. Except that Benjamin once said I refreshed him . . .' Henrietta stopped, biting her lip.

'Benjamin?' said Eleanor.

'He's why I'm here. Why I'm so quiet, I suppose. He's a distant cousin of mine, but that isn't what matters. We were betrothed, you see. And then he let me know – he didn't even tell me himself – that he wanted to end the engagement. I believe he wants to marry someone else. I was sent here for a change of scene, to get over it. Father says he'll have plans of his own for me later, but I don't know what they are. I don't want to think about them yet.'

'This Benjamin jilted you? He must be a complete fool.' Eleanor turned her head to study Henrietta's face. 'You're enchanting. Where did you get those gipsy looks?'

'Oh, no. Not gipsy looks, surely. Mrs Meade – she was my governess – always said I should stay out of the sun and when I'd been visiting Whitmead – that's where Benjamin lives; it's a farm – she would click her tongue because I'd become so brown. I had an Indian grandmother, you see.'

'A treacherous lover called Benjamin who lives on a farm, an Indian grandmother . . . I can see you have a thousand tales to tell me.'

'I'd like to. I was shy of speaking to *you*,' said Henrietta.

'Shy? Oh, surely not. Why?'

272

'Well, you . . . you've had a husband and lost him. I couldn't imagine what that must have been like. I was so sorry, but I couldn't think of how to say it without sounding presumptuous.'

'You mean you thought of me as pining, grieving?'

'Well . . . yes.'

'I suppose you would,' Eleanor said slowly. 'It's the natural assumption. The conventional one.'

'You mean it isn't true?'

'It's anything but true. Pining? Grieving? For Jacob Henderson? My dear girl, I never wanted to marry him in the first place. It was arranged by Grandmother Faith and my father. I tried to object but my father was dying at the time and we all knew it. I don't think my mother and Aunt Becky cared for Jacob much either, but they put Father first. It was: "Nell, dear, you can't upset your father now," and "Eleanor, your father only wants the happiness of seeing you settled in life before he goes" and "You know, child, that the Fifth Commandment bids you honour your father and mother and that means obeying them . . ."'

'That was Great-Aunt Faith.'

'Yes, it was. And Aunt Becky took me aside and whispered that it was a dreadful thing to be left unmarried as she well knew and in the end . . .' Eleanor shrugged. 'In the end, I became Mrs Henderson.'

'And . . . you weren't happy?'

'Happy? He was twenty years older than I was. He was born in 1640 and brought up as a Puritan and he was still one. A rabid one! His household was far worse than this. Here, well, you may have noticed that we are not all *quite* as much under Grandmother Faith's thumb as she likes to imagine?'

'Yes,' said Henrietta. 'I had noticed it as a matter of fact. It reminded me of some of the stories my grandfather at home has told me; how he and my grandmother used to play music and dance in secret during the Puritan days. Were you and your mother and aunt and grandmother all living together in your father's lifetime?'

'Yes. This was his house. Grandmother Faith came to live here when she began to feel her age, as she put it, though if you ask me she's the healthiest one of us all. She really just missed having a family round her to bully! She didn't find Aunt Becky stimulating enough. She brought Aunt Becky with her, you understand, and started trying to rule us all. It was my father who started all this business of evading the rules. But when he was ill, he changed. He became afraid of hellfire and he got it into his head that I should be safely married to a well-off, godly man who would care for me in body and soul.

'So he sent for Jacob. They knew each other; they were both cloth merchants. Jacob was a widower. I should think his first wife died of boredom. I married him not liking him much; before a week was out, I knew I was wretched. Everything I did was wrong. It was wrong to play the lute, to sing about the house; wrong to smile on a Sunday, to wear anything but grey or black; wrong to read or even sew for amusement; or even to enjoy one's food. I was always being gravely reproved, with solemn shakings of the head, and then I wouldn't be spoken to for days

on end, or else I'd be shut in my room and told to meditate on my sins.'
Eleanor sat up, her blue eyes suddenly flashing. 'I *hated* the sod! He
died of natural causes; I didn't feed him arsenic. But, by God, I
sometimes wonder why not! I spent three years of hell with him and I
hope he's spending the rest of eternity in it.'

'Oh,' said Henrietta inadequately. 'How . . . how dreadful. But it's
over now. You're free.'

Eleanor lay back once more. She picked a grass stalk and nibbled it.
'Yes, and I don't intend ever to let myself be shackled to any man again.
Well! That's the story of my life. And now, Henrietta my love, tell me
yours, in order, from the beginning. Or preferably, from before your
beginning. How do you come to have an Indian grandmother?'

The deed was done. Benjamin Whitmead was a married man.

And everyone was pleased about it. Circulating among the guests at
his wedding feast in the home of the bride's parents at Asleigh Acres
near the village of Quensted, he was in the midst of joviality and
approval.

'. . . Samuel and Charity must be well pleased. I don't mind
admitting I'd have liked Beatrice for my lad. She's good sound stock
and there's a penny or two to go with her . . .'

'. . . you've everything in your favour, my boy: youth, good health,
a few worldly goods and a comely young wife with her feet on the
ground. This is a happy day.'

'. . . they make such a handsome couple. Proper young Whitmead
that lad is, with that light red hair and those dark brown eyes, and
didn't Beatrice look a beauty in her wedding gown?'

'. . . *and* she can make a loaf rise and get the butter to come as well as
any wench that works in the dairy for her living. All you need now, my
lad, is a son for Whitmead, and you can set about that as soon as the sun
goes down, lad, and good luck to you.'

'Good luck to you in life, my son. You've everything in your
favour . . .'

Everything in your favour. Everything in your favour. The words
hammered in his brain all through the rest of the feast, all through the
noise and the friendly, earthy jokes as he and Beatrice, who had been
Beatrice Saunders and was now Mrs Benjamin Whitmead, were
escorted to the fourposter bed upstairs, the bed where Beatrice's
parents usually slept, and had the curtains drawn round them.

There was nothing wrong with Beatrice. He had known her, on and
off, for most of his life, as the daughter of his parents' friends. She was
solid, good-humoured, sensible, and nice to look at with her clear skin
and her glossy, waving brown hair. She had an open smile and a
pleasant voice and she had been genuinely pleased when he presented
himself, hat in hand, to ask her to marry him.

And now it was done. They had been pronounced man and wife in
front of a church altar, had danced at their wedding feast, been
congratulated by half Essex, been officially and legally bedded.

And he felt as though he were lying beside a complete stranger, who, for some reason, was behaving as though they were the best and oldest of friends.

'I must say I've enjoyed today, Ben. Have you?'

'Of course I have. But you must be very tired. If you would like just to go to sleep, I promise not to . . .'

'Now, don't you be a silly. Why should I be tired? I get up most mornings at dawn to see to the hens and my special cow, and I work till sunset, in the house or the dairy. You don't need to pamper me.'

Oh God, she was being arch. What was he doing here? How had it happened? What had he done?

'Today's been easier than most because my mam made me have my breakfast in bed. No, I'm not tired,' said Beatrice, stretching her arms above her head and letting the coverlet slip down. The days were still long and even in the shadowy bed, there was light enough to see and recognise the unspoken invitation.

The deed was done. He'd got to go through with the rest of it. He'd been getting more and more worried about it, all through the last week or two, as the day came inexorably nearer. He wouldn't have been afraid with Henrietta. With Henrietta, mind and body would have worked together in natural harmony. But Beatrice . . .

He took her in his arms. If only he could close his eyes and pretend that she was Henrietta. But although Beatrice's body was smooth and sweet-smelling, she was big and firmly padded, her globular breasts nothing at all like Henrietta's. He remembered the slender bones and lithe contours which he had felt only through clothing when they had held each other in the chaste embrace suitable to a couple who were only engaged; and longed for them, and for Henrietta's blue-black hair and dark eyes and her gallant, entrancing smile.

But never, now, would he lie in bed with Henrietta and hold her. He was tied for life to Beatrice and now it seemed that he couldn't even . . .

Yes, he could. Nature was working at last. Thank God for that. He would at least not disgrace himself on his wedding night and not be confronted next day with a disappointed bride. He'd got to treat Beatrice properly; it wasn't her fault that she wasn't Henrietta.

Where are you, Henrietta? How I wish that you were with me here. Oh, Henrietta, why?

'I shall miss you when we part,' Eleanor said, as she and Henrietta moved about the garden with baskets on their arms, gathering herbs and vegetables for the day. 'How long are you to stay?'

'For the summer, I suppose, as I used to do at Whitmead. My father hinted in his last letter that he expected to see me in September. I don't know what news he'll bring. I rather dread it. It will be to do with marriage and I don't want to think about such a thing, not yet, not for a long time.'

'He isn't at sea this summer, then?'

'No. He doesn't depend entirely on being an East India captain. He has shares in shipping, too; at least, my grandfather has, but Father has to see to it all now.'

'September,' said Eleanor thoughtfully, plucking mint. 'Not long. July's almost out.'

'Yes. I wish Matthew would come to see me. He writes, but it isn't the same thing. He must be free of the university by now.'

'You're always wishing for Matthew,' said Eleanor, with mild impatience. 'I think,' she added, 'that I'll stay here as long as you do.'

'Are you going away as well, then? I thought you had come home to live.'

'*They* think so,' said Eleanor, nodding towards the house and presumably referring to her mother, grandmother and aunt. 'They took it for granted. No one ever actually asked me what I wanted to do. They came for the funeral and just assumed that I'd come back here with them, which I did, because at that time I had nowhere else to go. My husband's house and business went to his son by his first marriage. He left me nothing but a small income. He decided quite soon after the wedding that it had been a horrible mistake and that he didn't like me any more than I liked him. However . . .' She picked some rosemary and stood twirling it in her fingers, her eyes dancing. 'I am not without means.'

'But if your husband left you so little . . . ?'

'My father apparently had his doubts about my marriage after all.' There were no seats in the garden but Eleanor sat down on a tree-stump, and Henrietta, setting her basket at her feet, perched on the low wall which divided their garden from the next. 'He was so anxious for me to accept Jacob,' Eleanor said, 'and seemed so sure that he was doing the right thing, and yet at the same time, he took steps to protect me if Jacob failed me. He gave me a marriage portion, of course, which has been invested for me. A lawyer in Taunton manages it for me. But my father also left instructions in his will for a small house to be bought and maintained for my use if I were ever in need of a home, and for some funds to be set aside to provide me with extra income if I ever found myself widowed or without support from Jacob. I have somewhere to go and the wherewithal to keep myself, in fact. Well, I intend to make use of them.'

'You mean to live alone?'

'Well, I'll have to get a companion. But live independently, yes. I made up my mind about that after my first week here. Circumventing my grandmother was funny for a while. But years and years of it? Unbearable! My house is in the Quantocks, out to the north of Taunton. It's been let, of course. But I gave the tenants notice some time ago and yesterday I heard that they had found another place and were moving out this week. I am already receiving the income from Father's fund, and I've been in touch with a couple of the servants I had when I was married. There's a groom who is willing to come to me and a woman who will cook. There's nothing to keep me here.'

'But – they must know about your father's will.' Henrietta also nodded towards the house. 'Surely they are expecting you to go.'

'I don't think they are. They've never mentioned it. And I haven't told them that I've given my tenants notice. I think it's never occurred to them that I might choose to live my own life. My grandmother has spoken to me about the money. She said she would expect me to pay my share of the household expenses! But, as I said, I shan't leave until you do. I don't want to miss a moment of your company. Let's be *very* wicked this afternoon, shall we, and not be here when it's time to read psalms to my grandmother. Let's go to a neighbour who has a lute or a harpsichord and will let us practise some music.'

The back door of the house opened. 'Nell! Henrietta! What on earth are you doing? Here's us wanting the things for dinner and you two just sitting about in the sun and idly chattering!' called Ruth. 'And there's a visitor here for Henrietta; her brother's come to see her!'

'Matthew!' squealed Henrietta in delight, and catching up her basket, ran at once for the house.

He was waiting politely in the parlour. 'Oh, you should have come straight out to the garden. Why so formal?' Henrietta cried, flinging herself into his arms.

'Because the door was opened to me by Great-Aunt Faith, that's why. Except that I didn't know she was our great-aunt then, of course. I thought she was a Spectre,' said Matthew, dropping his voice to a sepulchral note and giving the word an audible capital S. 'She told me to wait here so I did. I wouldn't have dared do anything else. How have you lived with her all this time? I know you said in your letters that she was intimidating, but really!'

'Oh, Ruth and Becky are human enough and wait till you meet Eleanor. I've written to you about her but I don't expect I did her justice, either.' A scheme had sprung into Henrietta's head from nowhere. If Matthew and Eleanor took to each other, something might come of it, once Eleanor's mourning was over. Then she could have Eleanor as a sister, for ever and ever. 'How are you, Matt? It's so long since I've seen you.'

'I'm very well and I must say you look well.' Matthew's kindly grey eyes scanned his sister earnestly. 'I'm glad. I'd feared to find you wan and pale and still remembering.'

'You mean remembering Benjamin? I'd like to forget him, but one can't forget to order. I do my best. One has to go on living. I've had Eleanor to make me laugh and she keeps me from brooding.'

'I'm glad to hear it. I wanted to go to Whitmead and ask Benjamin what kind of game he thought he was playing,' Matthew told her. 'But I was in Oxford at the time and I didn't know what had happened until you wrote yourself to tell me. I wrote to Father asking if he'd been to Essex and saying that I'd like to have a few words with dear cousin Benjamin in person, and I got a sharp letter back telling me that I was to mind my own business.'

'It was best,' Henrietta said. 'I don't want a man who doesn't want me. I have my pride. Oh, Matt, how good it is to see you. Let me get you some refreshments.'

She hurried from the room and came back with a tray. 'Cakes and cider. Eleanor made the cakes. Try one.'

'Henny,' said her twin, as he accepted, 'I'm not here just because I wanted to see you, although I did. I was planning to come. But then I had a letter from Father saying I was to visit you at once, to give you a message from him. He's on his way here, now, but before he arrives, he wanted me to give you some news and to prepare your mind for something.'

Henrietta sat down in the nearest chair. She became very still. 'Yes?'

'Well, first of all . . .' Matthew stared into his cider and then looked up, into his sister's worried eyes. 'I'm afraid this will upset you, but you need to know. Benjamin is married. He married Beatrice Saunders, from Quensted. I remember her, I think. The Saunders family sometimes came to Whitmead when we were there.'

'Yes. Yes, I recall.' Henrietta's hands clasped each other and gripped hard. 'I knew he wanted to marry someone else,' she said after a moment. 'But to know it's done, and the name of the girl . . . just give me a moment. And don't say I'm well rid of such a faithless lover. I know that, and it doesn't help.'

Matthew finished his cake and cider in silence, while Henrietta gazed out of the window. Then she said: 'All right. Now tell me the rest. You're to prepare my mind for something? What is it?'

'Father is bringing someone with him, a Mr Gale. He's a ship-owner.'

'Yes?' Once more, Henrietta's hands gripped each other tightly.

'Henny, can't you guess?'

'He wants me to consider marrying this man?'

'Yes. Well, not consider. He said I was to tell you that it's all settled. But . . .'

'It's *settled*?'

'Yes, but . . .'

Eleanor swept into the parlour, carrying a spray of meadowsweet and foxgloves in a tumbler. 'I found these growing in the wild patch at the end of the garden and I'm going to put them in here no matter what anyone says. If God could go to the trouble of creating flowers, I don't see why my grandmother should object to them. Is this your twin brother, Henrietta?'

'Yes, oh yes. Matthew, this is Eleanor.'

'I'm so glad you've come,' said Eleanor. 'Henrietta has been positively pining for you.'

'So you're Eleanor. Henrietta's letters have been full of you.'

'Really?'

'Yes. But if you'll excuse us,' said Matthew in definite tones, 'when you came in, I was breaking some rather private news to my sister.'

'Oh, I've no secrets from Eleanor,' Henrietta said. 'Eleanor, my father is on his way here with a man he intends me to marry. Well, I knew that he had something like that in mind. But Matt says it's all settled; which I suppose means I am to have no choice – is that what it means, Matt?'

'Well, yes, Henny. I think so.'

'And,' said Henrietta fiercely, 'it's someone I've never seen, never even heard of before!'

278

'Good God!' Eleanor stood there horrified, the tumbler of flowers still in her hand. 'You poor thing.'

'It's too soon, anyway. It's too soon!' Henrietta cried. 'Oh, why couldn't Father leave me alone for a while?'

'You may like Mr Gale when you see him,' said Matthew awkwardly. 'Father said I was to tell you that it's a good match, that Andrew Gale is both wealthy and healthy . . . Oh, Henny, don't upset yourself and don't be angry with me. I had to give you the message, you know. But wait till you see Mr Gale before you decide what you feel.'

'Does it matter what I feel?' asked Henrietta bitterly. 'Will Father care? He just thinks his daughters ought to smile nicely and do as we're told.'

'My husband was like that,' said Eleanor. 'Except that he preferred one not even to smile. I'm against marriage now on principle.'

'It's just as well everyone doesn't share your principles,' said Matthew. 'Or the human race would disappear.'

Looking at her cousin and her brother, Henrietta saw, dejectedly, that her dream of a marriage between them was doomed to remain only a dream. They had disliked one another on sight and it was real dislike, not mere sparring.

Not that it really mattered. She had more important things to worry about. 'Excuse me,' said Henrietta abruptly, 'I want to go to my room. There's no question now of an outing this afternoon, Eleanor. Father may appear at any moment and I need to be alone while I can.'

Charles and Mr Gale arrived that very evening. It was true that Andrew Gale was both wealthy and healthy. His clothes were in the height of fashion, adorned with bunches of ribbon and topped off by a flowing mane of a wig. His posture was straight and his manners gracious. The face framed by the black, curly mane was as wrinkled as a prune and the faint stubble on the jaws which hadn't been shaved since dawn was white. The hand that took Henrietta's was a gnarled claw. He was seventy if he was a day.

Chapter Twenty-One
The Casting-Off

The senior staff at Peace-Through-Praise were Joshua Graves the man-servant and his wife, Judith, the cook. The youngest was a maidservant called Dotty, who was fourteen, skinny, hardworking and incurably interested in the 'goings on' as she called them, of those whom Mr and Mrs Graves referred to as 'our betters'. At the moment, Joshua and Judith were hard put to it to keep Dotty's curiosity within bounds.

'But *listen* to them!' Dotty exclaimed, pausing open-mouthed, her arms full of firewood, as the two noisy arguments in progress in the parlour and the main bedchamber respectively both crescendoed at the same time.

'Better not. No good ever came of taking too much interest in what happens among our betters,' Joshua said, but flinched all the same as the parlour door slammed violently.

'That there's Mistress Eleanor,' said Dotty. 'She's suddenly taken it into her head to go and live in some cottage or other on her own, that's what it's about. I never heard of a lady doing a thing like that, not even a widowed lady; did you, Mrs Graves?'

'Dotty, *will* you put that wood into the oven or do I have to take the flat of my hand to you?'

'An' that's Mr Whitmead shouting. Lord, he do sound that angry. When I were brushing the stairs, I heard Mistress Henrietta crying fit to break her heart. I don't blame her, either.' Judith made a menacing movement and Dotty hastily fed the fire. 'But I *don't* blame her,' she said defiantly over her shoulder. 'That awful old man; nigh on a hundred, he is, by the look of 'un. Where's he gone now?'

'Out, along with Mr Matthew. I reckon Mr Whitmead arranged it to get them out of the way. And Mr Matthew didn't like it, I could see that, and not just because any fool could see it was going to rain and rain always turns the roads round here into soft cheese. Oh, lord,' said Graves. 'I can hear wheels. They're coming back. Now there'll be trouble!'

'*Will* be trouble?' queried Judith. 'What do you call this, then?'

Charles Whitmead was in the habit of having his own way. As a child, he had wrung it ruthlessly from the adult world, learning early that sheer determination could sometimes outweigh both authority and superior muscle power. As a man he had learned how to get his way with women; as a seaman he had taken orders merely as a means to ending up as a captain and once a captain, had no difficulty whatsoever in keeping his crew under control.

That a mere daughter, a creature intended by nature to be soft of voice and foot and submissive to a father's will, should actually dare to defy him, seemed to him incredible. It was like being challenged by a cabin boy.

'I tell you again, Henrietta: I can't believe my ears.' He stood in front of the hearth in his daughter's room, staring with amazement at Henrietta, whose face was streaked with tears, but whose mouth was obstinately folded. 'The matter is settled. And in your best interests at that. How many more times?'

'But he's *old*! I keep saying it but you won't listen. Father, how can you expect me to marry an old man?'

There had, of course, been indications before that this daughter of his had a hidden will of her own. There had been that outrageous, unsanctioned engagement to her cousin Benjamin. And then, last night, she had fled to her room five minutes after meeting Andrew Gale and reappeared just before supper, to pluck his sleeve and whisper: 'Father, I can't marry him!' which was most embarrassing because Gale himself was at the other end of the same room.

Matthew had already drawn him aside and tried to protest about the marriage but he had overborne Matthew with a curt order to be silent, accompanied by the intent stare with which he terrorised his crew on the *Restoration*. It had never occurred to him that Henrietta might be harder to deal with than her brother. She looked frightened; she was obviously well aware of his parental authority. But she still persisted in arguing.

He wasn't going to have it.

'You are being silly and childish, Henrietta. I will go through it once more. Andrew Gale is well-off enough to keep you in the kind of luxury most girls only dream of and he's also offering me, your father, a share in his ship-owning business which will do wonders for my income and your brother's inheritance.'

'But he's *old*,' said Henrietta desperately, again.

'His age is to your advantage. There's not much amiss with him now,' said Charles coolly, 'but in the course of nature he ought to die in the next ten years or so, which will leave you as a widow, probably still under thirty, and then you can marry anyone you like and with the money and property he'll leave you, you'll have plenty of choice.'

'I can't bear it. The very thought nauseates me!'

'You'll soon get over that when you see the kind of home he's prepared to offer you. He's out this very morning looking at a fine country house he may buy as a wedding gift for you . . .'

'I don't want a country house.'

'Don't be petulant. And if you're still pining for Benjamin, let me tell you that marriage is the fastest way to drive him out of your head.'

Henrietta was exhausted. She had scarcely eaten anything at either supper or breakfast, and had not slept in between. 'I will talk to you in your room at ten o'clock tomorrow morning,' her father had said, unplucking her hand from his arm when she tried to accost him the evening before. The hours between had seemed a century long. Charles saw the exhaustion and as she moved to rest her shaky legs by sitting down on the bed, snapped: 'Remain standing and listen to me. You are going to marry Andrew Gale and that is that. Oh, no doubt you would be better pleased if he were twenty-five and good-looking, but unfortunately, young men often have their way to make. I wish you to have a comfortable life. And, yes, I also want a share in a lucrative business. To help their families by making advantageous marriages is what girls are for. They're precious little use otherwise.'

'But . . . !'

'I don't want to hear that word again.' Charles allowed his voice to deepen to a grief-stricken level. 'I am very shocked, Henrietta. You appear to harbour secret thoughts and selfish wishes in a thoroughly shameful way.'

Oddly enough, he could understand it if she did. Sometimes, he recognised himself in Henrietta. He had enjoyed secretly seducing her mother, and he had never felt any regret for continuing his clandestine affair with Christabella. It was a pity Louisa had died like that, but she should have been more willing to accept his nature. He also knew, because Ninian had told him, that his parents had enjoyed going to church dressed in black and then indulging behind locked doors in bright silks and frivolous music, and no doubt in other things which Ninian had politely not mentioned. A love of secrecy probably ran in the family. But in Henrietta, it couldn't be allowed to flourish. He had too much at stake.

'Enough of that. You will marry Mr Gale and that's the end of it. There is no more for you to say except to thank me for my efforts on your behalf, and to accept Mr Gale graciously when he speaks to you.'

'If I were a man of his age, I wouldn't force myself on a young girl!' said Henrietta in a flash of bitterness, and then stumbled back with a cry as Charles slapped her.

'Did Mrs Meade and your besotted grandfather never tell you not to insult your elders?' If she said that to Gale's face, Charles could see his hopes of a new fortune vanishing over the horizon along with Gale himself, aboard a ship called the *Mortally Offended*. 'Mr Gale knows his worth. You are a silly but very fortunate young girl.'

Henrietta sank on to the bed, her face in her hands. She was so alone. Even Matthew was out of the house. He was as horrified by Gale as she was but he couldn't withstand their father. Charles had sent him out to look at houses with Gale and Matthew had had too stern a training in obedience to his father to refuse. Nor could her cousins help her. They were down in the parlour involved in some mysterious uproar of their own. Every now and then, distractingly, their raised voices penetrated to her room. She could hear Aunt Faith intoning what were probably quotations from Holy Writ, Becky and Ruth expostulating, and

Eleanor shouting back. She must fight her father alone and he was entitled to beat her or lock her up on a prison diet until she did as she was told and no one could prevent him.

Downstairs, the altercation suddenly ended with the violent slam of a door. She heard angry feet and the swish of a skirt as someone, probably Eleanor, came upstairs; heard Becky crying. And was that the rumble of a coach outside?

Charles cursed under his breath. Henrietta looked so very pathetic that he felt sorry for hitting her and didn't want to do so again. But he had more than once persuaded a reluctant girl into his bed with kindness and caresses. Perhaps he could persuade Henrietta into Mr Gale's bed by the same means. He sat down beside her, put an arm about her and found a napkin with which to wipe her face.

'I'm sorry, my dear. You shouldn't have been rude, but still, I'm sorry. There, now. I didn't hurt you very much, did I?'

'Oh *Father*!'

It was a protest at his harshness and an appeal for his understanding all in one but Charles shook his head at it. 'My dear, there's a fortune for me in this marriage and you'll benefit from that too, you know. I think Mr Gale has returned. Wash your face and tidy your hair. Then I want you to receive him in whatever room we can find in this house which isn't full of people quarrelling, and accept his proposal with a smile.'

Henrietta looked up into his face and said bravely: 'Would Mr Gale want me if he knows I'm unwilling?'

'For the love of God, Henrietta!' Charles was angered anew. He stood up, withdrawing himself. 'Andrew Gale is as capable as I am of recognising schoolgirl nonsense. He will discount it. You'll come round once you're married. If you continue to argue with me, however . . .'

Henrietta was mute, waiting.

'I don't want to hit you again,' said Charles. 'As your father, I have the right but I don't wish to use it.' There were other sanctions, anyway. He grinned suddenly, having had an inspiration. He couldn't see Henrietta withstanding this one, and he wouldn't have to lay a finger on her. 'Hear this, Henrietta. Unless you become Mr Gale's wife, you will cease to be my daughter. I shall cast you off. There will be no room under my roof for you, no money for your upkeep, no dowry for your marriage. You can stay here if your cousins will have you, or take refuge with any other relative who is willing, or hire yourself out as a maidservant or a whore. I shall forget you ever existed. Do I make myself clear?'

Henrietta stared at him, her face stricken. Slowly, she took in the meaning of his words. He waited, letting her absorb them. Slowly, miserably, she nodded.

Charles let out a sigh of relief. 'Good. I thought the prospect of having no home would change your mind. Now, if you will be good enough to tidy yourself . . .'

There was a knock at the door and then Eleanor, tall in her black draperies, stalked in without waiting to be summoned. Charles looked at her with raised brows. 'Did I give you permission to enter?'

'It is not your room, Mr Whitmead. It is Henrietta's and I feared she might be too upset to answer my knock. I have been doing worse than walk in without an invitation. I've been listening outside the door. Henrietta, I have come to say that you need never be homeless. I am leaving in the morning for my cottage in the Quantocks. I'm afraid my mother and grandmother and poor Aunt Becky don't approve but I am of age and there is nothing they can do to stop me. However, I need a woman to bear me company. If you will join me, I would be very grateful; so much so that I am willing to make over part of my private income to you. I have gone into the matter and it seems that the income is larger than I expected, so it will be no sacrifice, and you will not be my pensioner. I announced my plans today on purpose to give you a chance to come with me. What do you say? Will you take your father at his word?'

'They've gone, have they? I thought I heard horses.' Charles, exotically wrapped in a crimson dressing robe, descended from his room, having breakfasted in bed, from a tray brought by a disapproving Judith Graves. Ruth, her eyes red-rimmed and lacklustre, looked up as he sauntered into the parlour.

'Yes, they've gone. I can hardly bear it. My own daughter doesn't want to take shelter with me. To live apart with only a girl, younger than herself, for company: what are times coming to?'

'She's clever, is Eleanor.' Becky was standing sadly by the window, gazing out in the direction which Eleanor and Henrietta had taken. 'She's taken back a groom who used to work for Jacob, and got him to hire horses and a baggage cart. He fetched them and their baggage away half an hour since. My mother's still in her room, reading. She wouldn't come down to watch two young women ride away to perdition, she said. But there's more than perdition to worry about. Will they be safe, on their own like that? Oh, dear!' Becky, overcome, fled from the room.

'I'm usually the talkative one but I've no more words, and that's a fact. That I should see this day,' Ruth lamented.

The house was very quiet, in contrast to the last two days, during which Peace-Through-Praise had been anything but peaceful. They were all exhausted now after the endless pleading and arguing, the tears, the wrung hands and the menacing prophecies of divine wrath on the obstinate sinner. Andrew Gale had packed his bags and left on the first day, at which point Charles said to Henrietta: 'You seem to have made your choice,' after which he had ignored her existence. Matthew attempted to speak up for her once, unsuccessfully, because Charles simply turned his back and would not answer. But the storm raised by Eleanor had raged unabated until the very moment of her departure with Henrietta.

'Where's my son?' Charles inquired abruptly.

'In his room, I think. He's not been down this morning. I think he said goodbye to Henrietta upstairs,' Ruth told him.

'Said goodbye to her, did he? Then I've a few words to say to *him*,' said Charles, and also strode out of the parlour.

285

He found Matthew in his room, gazing from the window much as Becky had done. He turned his head as his father came in but omitted to rise respectfully to his feet. He raised questioning eyebrows.

'She's gone, as you plainly realise,' said Charles. 'And good riddance. Andrew Gale's last remark to me was that I had apparently brought him here only to be insulted. I shall have to make a massive investment in his ships to prevent him from blackening my name in every port from Penzance to London. As far as I am concerned, Caroline is now my only daughter. And that goes for you, Matthew. You hear me? You are not to communicate with Henrietta in any way. You are to forget that she was ever born.'

'Yes, sir.'

'Stand up!'

Matthew obligingly did so. His son was somehow, Charles thought with exasperation, a lesser being in every way. It wasn't just that he didn't like ships. Compared to his father, he was less swarthy, his hair less black, his eyes not dark but a good-humoured grey, his smile nothing at all like that of a pirate. Matthew was also three inches shorter and had to look upwards to meet his father's gaze.

'I want your promise,' said Charles. 'You will not write to Henrietta, or send messages to her by word of mouth, or visit her, or utter her name. What do you say?'

'I promise,' said Matthew.

Charles glared at him, disconcerted. Was his son quite such a lesser being after all? During his recent absence at university, he seemed to have matured in some subtle way.

'My God,' said Charles. 'You liar! You're going to communicate with her behind my back. *Aren't you?*'

'Possibly, sir,' said Matthew calmly. 'She is my sister after all, my twin sister at that. I am fond of her and I can't kill affection like wringing a chicken's neck. And why should I? Andrew Gale was quite unsuitable for her. Why can't you see that? Why wouldn't you listen when I tried to defend her? Sooner than admit you're wrong, you've let her go off with Eleanor, whom I, frankly, distrust. I'm afraid for Henny. What sort of father are you?'

Charles choked and half-raised a hand but Matthew stood his ground. 'I'm smaller than you, sir, but I'm younger and quite strong. If you hit me, I shall retaliate and it will all be most undignified and you might not win.'

'You . . . what if I cast you off as I have your sister?'

Matthew went pale, but said steadily: 'Ever since Mr Gale set foot in this house, I've been afraid of something like this. It's been difficult to speak out. I even went out with Gale in that coach, and sat there almost strangling myself with the effort of being polite. But now – well I've lain awake, learning to face the worst. I must risk being cast off, I suppose. I imagine Grandfather might help me until I could establish myself financially.

'You . . .!'

'But I am your only son, sir. Would you really wipe me out of your life, as well as my sister? I can't really believe that you want to abandon her entirely, you know.'

'I intend to do precisely that,' Charles assured him. 'Make no mistake about it. Oh, do as you like! Gad off to the Quantocks if you want. But don't mention your sister to me – ever!'

PART V

Henrietta:
Storms and Doldrums
1684–1710

Oh no, they die not for their parents' sake
But for the poisonous seed which they partake.

The Indian Queen, *John Dryden*

Chapter Twenty-Two
Broom Cottage

Eleanor's house in the Quantocks was called Broom Cottage. Built of stout stone, thatched and gabled and surrounded by a small garden, it stood on a south-facing hillside covered with grass and yellow-flowering wild broom.'

At the foot of the hill was a valley with a village and a church; to the north and east, the Quantocks rose, keeping off cold winds, and to the west was a sweeping view towards a dim skyline which Eleanor said was the Brendon Hills, beyond which lay Exmoor, twenty-five miles away.

The cottage itself was sizeable, with three good bedrooms on the first floor and two attic rooms where Mrs Johns, the cook, could sleep, 'and so can our maidservant when we find one,' said Eleanor. On the ground floor it had a big square kitchen, a scullery and a large pantry, a wide, sunny parlour the size of both the parlours at Peace-Through-Praise put together, and a dining room capable of accommodating a party of a dozen, with a squeeze.

The garden was a tangled affair with a bite taken out of it at one side to provide a small walled yard containing a cart shed and stabling for six horses, with a loft over it which could accommodate the groom, Ricky.

'When we hold large parties,' said Eleanor, 'guests' horses can overflow into the cart shed. I don't propose to keep a cart. Everyone rides in this part of the world because the roads are so hilly and get so mired.'

'Are we going to hold large parties?' inquired Henrietta.

'I certainly hope so. We're not that far from Taunton and the house where I lived with Jacob was between Taunton and here. I've quite a wide acquaintance that my mother knows little about because of course everyone has respected my seclusion since I was widowed. I can arrange for us to see some company, whenever I'm ready.'

'In that case,' said Henrietta, 'Mrs Johns will certainly need some help so we ought to set about finding that maidservant. We shall also need a dining table. Not to mention some chairs and occasional tables for the parlour. Possibly even some extra beds!'

'I know.' Eleanor looked ruefully round the bare parlour. Dust motes danced merrily in shafts of sunlight which streamed in, hindered only by the leadwork of the diamond-paned windows. 'I didn't know,' said Eleanor, 'that my tenants had owned most of the furniture and were going to take it with them. Somehow I thought that the bit in my father's will about maintaining the house meant that it would be furnished. It's as well we brought our own linen and pots and pans, and thank heaven I sent Ricky and Mrs Johns here in advance. They did at least have the sense to borrow some of the other essentials from friends. Mrs Johns actually comes from the village down there and her sister lent us the table and our two beds.'

'Or got rid of them,' said Henrietta. 'The beds both sag and the table has one leg shorter than the rest; it's broken off near the foot.'

'Is it? But we've eaten one meal off it already and I didn't notice.'

'I daresay. I saw it the moment we got here and pushed a book under the short leg to even things up.'

'How resourceful of you. What book was it? Not your beautiful Shakespeare that your grandfather gave you?'

'No,' said Henrietta. 'It's that volume of sermons that Great-Aunt Faith gave me.'

Eleanor burst out laughing. 'Oh, Henrietta, how glad I am to have you here with me! I'm sure this isn't what my father envisaged when he made his will. If he ever imagined me in my own house he thought I'd be in middle life, or else chaperoned like a schoolgirl by some grave and elderly dame. Instead, I'm young and free and I've got you. And we're going to enjoy making Broom Cottage into our home. We can decide everything ourselves; think of it! Jacob chose all our furnishings and we had a housekeeper – Lord, she was such a black crow of a woman – who hired the servants. I was considered too frivolous to have good judgement. Now I can please myself and there's enough money, Lord be praised. Not for extravagance, but for reasonable comfort. We'll go to Taunton tomorrow and set about it.'

'We might find a girl in the village,' suggested Henrietta. 'Couldn't Mrs Johns help us there, if she comes from the place? What is it called, by the way?'

Eleanor put an arm round her friend's shoulders. Her blue eyes sparkled. 'You're not going to believe this.'

'Why not? Is it a comical name?'

'You could say that,' said Eleanor with a chuckle.

'Well, what is it?'

'You're *not* going to believe me.'

'Oh, Eleanor, do tell me.'

'It's called Chugg's Fiddle,' said Eleanor and then the dusty, sunny, empty parlour rang to their peals of laughter.

'We do have to have guests,' Eleanor said seriously, as, a week later, they toured a domain which was now more or less furnished, although some items were still in the making. 'It's important, Hen.'

'Well, I'd like it. Imagine us, being hostesses in our own home! But why is it important?'

'Our reputations. What we're doing is very unconventional and the world is censorious. Tongues will wag. You know! Two young women living alone together and who's to know who's visiting them; and then we give a drink of ale and directions for the road to a couple of passing travellers and some old biddy from Chugg's sees them come out of our gate and goes round whispering to all the other old biddies that we've had men calling on us. You must have noticed that we got a strange look from that furniture-maker in Taunton when we ordered the writing desk and you let out that we were setting up home together. Ricky is in his fifties but I wouldn't put it past them to talk about *him*.'

'Is that why you insisted that we employ such an aged gardener?'

'It is. The garden has been shamefully neglected,' said Eleanor bitterly. 'I don't believe my ex-tenants would have known a hoe if they'd fallen over it. But I've hired a man who's almost too old and rheumatic to pull up a dandelion, just so that no one can gossip about him. Now do you see? We must cultivate respectable people, so that they visit us and we visit them. Even though I'm still in mourning, we can accept quiet invitations, and issue them. Gradually, we shall get known as being respectable ourselves: eccentric, perhaps, but nothing worse. Later, we can have the large parties I mentioned. Now, I've made out a list for a first small gathering.' Eleanor closed the last bedchamber door and led the way down to the parlour. 'I thought,' she said, taking up a sheet of paper from the window-seat, 'that we could start by inviting just six people.' Her eyes sparkled again. 'I've gone in for the very best respectable quality.'

'As though you were buying serviceable material for winter dresses?'

'More or less. Some of them will be dull, I'm afraid. I think we should ask the vicar from Chugg's and his wife and Mrs Dyer is dreadfully dull. They have seven children and she never talks about anything but their spots and their latest comical sayings or pieces of destructive mischief. But nothing could be more respectable than a vicar, and William Dyer is quite well-informed on political matters. They're old acquaintances; Jacob had them both to dinner occasionally. I've also got Sir John and Lady Handley down; they live about nine miles away, near a place called Washford. Jacob knew them, too. The Handleys are quite pleasant. They hunt and keep dogs. The last two guests are schoolmistresses.'

'Schoolmistresses?'

'Yes. Mary Blake is the headmistress of the school I went to in Taunton – Sir John Handley's daughter was a pupil as well – and Susanna Musgrave is her assistant. Susanna is quite young; she came to the school first as a pupil herself. I've always kept in touch with Miss Blake.' Eleanor's voice softened. 'Taking a cup of coffee with Miss Blake now and then was one of life's great pleasures when I was married to Jacob. He approved of her, you see. She was a teacher, a dignified calling, even for a woman, and she comes of good Parliamentarian stock. She's quite well-connected, as a matter of fact – the Handleys are used to mixing with her socially. She's distantly related to Admiral Robert Blake, who was a Captain of Dragoons in the Parliamentary army during the Civil War and very active in the West Country. Some of her relatives went to America sooner than stay in England under the Restoration. Jacob thought she could only be an influence for good. But what he didn't know was that she actually likes me. Going to see Miss Blake was an escape. You have no idea, Hen, what a relief it is, when you spend all your days being chided and disapproved of, to pass just an hour or two with somebody who *likes* you.'

So here I am, thought Henrietta, astonished at herself, co-hostess with Eleanor Henderson, dispensing chicken fricassée and venison roasted with cloves and split peas with saffron across our very own table in Broom Cottage. All I have of my own family now are occasional letters from Matthew. Eleanor seems almost jealous of them – I suppose she's afraid I'll change my mind and leave her on her own. But she needn't be afraid because I'm happy. I can hardly believe it, but I'm happy!

It was of necessity a quiet party. Henrietta had put on a smart gown of amber velvet but in deference to her cousin's mourning state wore no jewellery, and Eleanor herself was in modestly cut dove-grey brocade. Eleanor had couched the invitations simply in terms of wishing to see old friends. There would be no entertainment other than a good dinner and pleasant conversation. But the guests were clearly enjoying the food provided in such excellent quantity by Mrs Johns and Dotty, whom Ruth, touchingly anxious to maintain kindness between herself and her daughter, had dispatched from Peace-Through-Praise to fill the post of maidservant. Conversation, so far, had been a little wary as the Handleys and the Dyers and the two schoolmistresses took careful stock of this unusual household. The Dyer children, in fact, were proving a useful solvent. Whenever the talk ran dry, Mrs Dyer rushed into the gap with them. She was doing it now.

'. . . I must say, Mrs Henderson, that you have made the inside of your cottage quite charming, although it would be no place, I fear, for my lively brood. In the vicarage we lock all our plates and cups and glassware in cupboards. But there, children will be children. It is such a pity, Mrs Henderson, that you had no offspring.'

'But you paint such a discouraging picture of life with children,' said Eleanor, and Sir John Handley let out a snort of laughter. Eleanor smiled, and pushed the chicken fricassée along the table.

Both Mrs Dyer and Miss Mary Blake plunged their fingers willingly into the dish. Mrs Dyer's fingers were reddened with kitchen work but also plump; she was a stout little woman with stubby arms and legs. Mary Blake's fingers were also those of a working woman, but a different kind of work had hardened them. There was a pen callus on the middle finger of her right hand and traces of ingrained ink on her fingertips, and she was not stout, but angular and lean, with an austere face, dominated by a long chin and a curving beak of a nose.

The austere air, however, was misleading, for Mary had a softer side. 'I am sure Eleanor would love to have children but perhaps we shouldn't remind her of that now.'

'Oh, dear, I'm so sorry. I quite forgot. And of course, they *can* try one's patience. Only yesterday, Robbie . . .'

'I sometimes regret not being married,' said Mary, deftly deflecting her. 'But there, wedded bliss doesn't come to us all, least of all when a civil war has killed so many men. I can scarcely complain that I lack young company. We have twenty-seven pupils in the school now.'

'Children need not always be naughty.' Susanna Musgrave was sharp of feature and elbow, with a sallow skin and eyes of an unremarkable grey, and a forthright personality. The quiet shades which she and Mary Blake both wore did not suit either the complexion or the forthrightness. 'We manage to instil good conduct into our pupils, on the whole.'

'Indeed,' Mary agreed. 'Some were wild and ill-mannered when they came but they quickly improve with guidance. One must be kind, but firm, and make the effort to interest them in their studies. Even you were a little wild as a girl, Susanna.'

'Where do you come from, Susanna?' Henrietta asked. 'Is your family in Taunton?'

Susanna shook her head. 'Not now. My parents brought me to Taunton when I was a child but they died soon after. My grandparents live on Exmoor, in Dulverton, and I visit them sometimes, and I've an uncle who's a sailor and lives somewhere on the coast but I haven't seen him in years.'

'Susanna had just become one of my pupils when she lost her parents,' said Mary Blake. 'Her father left money for her education and her grandparents thought she had better remain with me. Mr Musgrave dealt in dyes – Taunton is a cloth town, Miss Whitmead. Many of my girls come from merchant families in the cloth trade.'

'Of course, girls are more manageable than boys.' Mrs Dyer's mind could never be really detached from its favourite preoccupation. 'Now, Robbie and Will – and Philip when he was younger . . .'

'Even though your vicarage is large, you must be quite crowded there,' Eleanor said mildly. 'That was the reason why I decided to set up house here. My mother's home is too full. My aunt and grandmother are both there, you know, and really there was no space for me. Besides which, I have grown used to being mistress of my own home.'

Henrietta, recalling what Eleanor had said about her lack of authority in her married home, kept a poker-face with difficulty and added: 'It was most kind of Eleanor to offer me a home with her.'

'Henrietta's father wished her to marry a man of seventy. Daughters should obey their parents but this was not reasonable. Truly it wasn't,' said Eleanor. 'I am giving Henrietta a refuge and I can't believe I'm doing wrong.'

William Dyer suddenly smiled. The vicar had pronounced Grace but since then been very quiet and Henrietta thought that he was decidedly doubtful about the Broom Cottage household. But one of Eleanor's purposes in arranging this gathering had been to explain their establishment and now she had done so. Mr Dyer was responding.

'I am not myself in favour of young people being forced against their wishes and certainly I would not approve a union between a young woman such as Miss Whitmead here, and a man so advanced in years. But I hope that your family breach may be healed, Miss Whitmead, and that you will soon hear from your father that he has found you a more suitable match. And Eleanor too is still young, of course. Who knows what the future will bring?'

'Who indeed?' said Eleanor and then skilfully turned the conversation. 'That could apply to great affairs as well as little ones. In Taunton the other day, I heard some disquieting talk about the King's health. There was mention of gout, and a sore on his leg. Does anyone know if the report is true?'

'I believe so,' said Sir John, and Lady Handley nodded in agreement. She was a splendid figure in crimson, with her hair dressed high and her rather hard face expertly painted to hide the marks of advancing middle age. 'I have heard the same report,' she said.

'What on earth will happen, one wonders, when the King dies?' said Eleanor. 'There is no likelihood now of his queen producing a direct heir and the Duke of York . . . well . . .'

'Is a Catholic, as we all know,' said Dyer gloomily.

'And we *can't* have a Catholic on the throne. It's unthinkable,' exclaimed Susanna.

'Well, I doubt if we shall have much alternative,' said Sir John. He was a short, tough man with a weather-reddened face. 'Unless young Monmouth lands with an army, which raises the question of whether our Constitution would come to more harm if an illegitimate son accedes than if a Catholic does.'

'Nothing could do more harm than a Catholic!' Pink spots of passion appeared on Susanna's sallow face. 'England returned to the Papists, under the thumb of the Pope in Rome? I would want to help Monmouth!'

'There would have been an alternative if only the House of Commons had agreed to pass over James and make his daughters by his first wife the heirs instead,' said Dyer with regret. 'That would have kept the inheritance in the direct legitimate line but given us good Protestant heirs. The elder princess, Mary, is married to William of Orange and you can't get much more Protestant than he is. That Dutch marriage was wise. A good deal wiser than the Duke's second marriage,' he added. 'What can have possessed James to pick Mary of Modena – an Italian Catholic? I used to call myself moderate, but I turned Whig when I heard that marriage was in the wind, back in '73. Of all the stupid things for a prospective English king to do!'

'She's said to be very beautiful,' said Mary Blake, with the wistfulness of one who had never even been pretty. 'People say she didn't want to marry James at first but that they are much in love now.'

'She may be as beautiful as an angel,' said Susanna, showing no disposition to be wistful about her own plain features. 'And they may be as much in love as Romeo and Juliet but what of it? What people think and believe matters more than how they look, and it isn't the business of princes to marry for love. They marry for the benefit of their people. The Princess Mary Beatrice was the wrong choice.'

'I think,' said Sir John, 'that if King Charles were to die, there would be a risk of another civil war. There would be factions for the Duke, for Monmouth, perhaps even for William and Mary. Much would depend on how much James respected the Anglican church. If he threatened it in any way . . .' he shrugged ominously. 'Anything could happen.'

'The idea of another civil war is horrible,' said Mary Blake. 'I'm in my forties. I can remember something of the last one. Yet a Papist on the throne could well be more horrible still.'

'For all we know, there already is one,' said Sir John. 'There have been whispers that the King himself is secretly attracted to Catholicism.'

'At least he's keeping it secret. But an openly Catholic king! Would there be persecutions of heretics again? Fires at Smithfield?' demanded Susanna.

'That is what we would all fear,' said Sir John grimly, and Dyer nodded agreement.

'If Monmouth had strong enough support,' said Susanna, 'and moved quickly enough, there would be no civil war. He would just seize England, as King Henry the Seventh did at Bosworth in the fifteenth century. One battle would do it, if he had the backing.'

Mrs Dyer said anxiously: 'I hope it doesn't come to such a thing, indeed I do. My eldest boy Philip is turned sixteen now and for sure he'd be off to join any war against the Catholics and I'd never sleep in peace in my bed until he was safe home again. Oh dear, I feel quite upset.'

'Well, King Charles is still with us just now and not persecuting anybody,' said her husband comfortingly and Eleanor said: 'Take some more wine, Mrs Dyer, and let us talk of more cheerful things. Tell us what you think we could do to improve our home still further. We are barely settled in, you know.'

'We are thinking,' said Henrietta, 'of having a little household device. We can amuse ourselves by embroidering it on to linen and so forth, during the winter. My family actually has such a device, a very simple affair of curved lines arched over wavy ones, like a sketch of a bridge above a sketch of a river. Eleanor has suggested that we work it up into a proper picture of a river and a bridge, with brickwork on the bridge – we could embroider it in musty pink like Somerset stone – and have the river in blue. Do you think that would be a good idea?'

'Oh yes. I am so glad you are keeping up your embroidery, Eleanor,' said Mary Blake. 'I am proud of the instruction we give our girls in the art. Embroidery is a pleasure for life, as well as being useful.'

'I have never been very gifted at it,' said Lady Handley. 'But I have an excellent new maid who has done remarkable things with my wardrobe. I am very pleased with Sapphira.'

'Sapphira?' Eleanor queried.

'Yes, she's of Spanish descent. No, no, she's not a Papist. She comes to the Anglican church with us just like all the other servants.' Lady Handley did not go in for laughing because she considered that it encouraged wrinkles, but now she smiled and for a moment, Henrietta saw in her eyes the lighthearted young girl she had once been. 'She's a good respectful girl enough, but when our butler, Robbins, suggested she might be a Papist, the histrionics had all the servants' hall in an uproar. She was an actress once but not a very successful one. She's better as a maid. She truly enjoys embroidery and will even work by candle-light although I think it best to discourage that.'

'Oh, indeed. Fine needlework should only be done in clear daylight, or you can strain your eyes,' said Mrs Dyer.

The conversation settled down into mundane channels, leaving politics and religion behind.

'I think our first dinner-party was a great success, don't you?' said Eleanor as they waved their guests goodbye. 'But as time goes on, we'll do still better. In time to come, cards and dancing!'

'Eleanor,' said Henrietta, when the two of them, having helped Mrs Johns and Dotty with the washing up, had shed their aprons and withdrawn to the parlour to sit by one of the first fires of the season, with the curtains closed and the candles lit, 'Eleanor, did you want children?'

'Not particularly. And certainly not Jacob's.'

'Might you have liked being married if Jacob had been different?'

'Perhaps. With Jacob, marriage was just a task, in bed or out of it. You're thinking of your Benjamin, aren't you?'

'A little.'

Earlier, round the dinner table, she had been happy. But from the moment she and Eleanor arrived at Broom Cottage, they had lived in a state of hectic activity: buying things, making things, gardening, cooking, forming a routine, preparing for tonight's dinner. Now quietness had descended. And she had remembered that it was September.

She had said farewell to Benjamin just a year ago. Then, just as on that evening three years before, when they first betrothed themselves, they had walked beside a cornfield as a full moon was rising, and kissed and that had been the moment when Henrietta's maturing mind and body had understood for the first time the true nature of desire.

There was another full September moon tonight. She had paused to look at it before drawing the curtains. Now, without warning, that yawning ache in the depths of her had come back and she did not know what to do about it. She longed for Benjamin, and he had married someone else.

Eleanor came to perch on the arm of her chair, resting a hand on her shoulder. 'I understand. If only Jacob had been a different kind of man . . .' She put her arm round Henrietta. 'Mr Dyer said he hoped you would soon hear from your father and that he would find you a better match than Gale. Do you think it likely?'

'No. My father has cast me off and I think he meant it. I don't mean very much to him,' said Henrietta. 'In fact, we scarcely know each other. He has always spent so much time at sea and when he's home he never takes much notice of his daughters. He thinks of us – and of my stepmother – as possessions but he doesn't care what we feel or think. I've refused to be a good little possession and do as I'm bid and he has finished with me. I don't need to know him well to realise that. Some things, one just knows.'

'Do you mind?'

'A little. Not much. How can I mind that I've been cast off by a stranger?'

The masculine anchors in her life had been Matthew and Benjamin and Matthew at least was still there. But her father had never been much more than an occasional disruption to the domestic routine.

'Your father has failed you badly,' Eleanor said harshly. 'Just as mine did. Damn them! We're young, Hen. There are things we need and can't have unless we're married; things we mustn't even admit we want, not if we're to remain respectable. The court ladies the King amuses himself with; they can admit the truth, but not us. Our respective fathers had a duty to find good husbands for us and they only found bad ones.'

'I want him. Benjamin, I mean.' Henrietta had not known she was tired, but now she found that she was exhausted. Too much had happened too swiftly: Benjamin's defection; being whisked to Taunton; the horrible advent of Mr Gale; her translation to Broom Cottage; the mountains of work they had moved since they got here . . .

She found herself crying, her face pressed against her friend's dove-grey brocade. 'I *want* him. I know it's no use to think of him but I can't stop wanting him. I don't know how.'

'Come.' Eleanor half-lifted her to her feet. 'It's time you were in bed.'

When Henrietta was alone in her room, she drew back the curtains of window and bed alike and let the moon shine in. It was disturbing in a way, because it seemed to make the hungry ache inside her worse, and it was like a face gazing at her. But she welcomed it because that same face had looked on her and Benjamin in the cornfield.

With a soft creak, her door opened. 'Hen? Are you still awake?'

'Yes.'

Eleanor came quietly in and sat down on the edge of the bed. 'I was afraid you might be crying yourself to sleep. I wouldn't want that. I want you to be content here with me. I didn't like to think of you lonely and yearning.'

Then, smoothly, she lifted the coverlet and slipped in beside Henrietta. They put their arms round each other. This too was comforting, Henrietta thought. If only that hungry ache would stop, or could be somehow satisfied.

'We have needs,' whispered Eleanor. 'But we can do without men. Let me show you.'

Chapter Twenty-Three
Ships on the Horizon

Life in Broom Cottage settled down, taking its own shape, adapting itself as the nights drew in and the equinoctial gales began to sweep clouds of autumn rain up the Bristol Channel. They stored the apples and preserved the plums from the fruit trees which they had discovered at the foot of the unkempt garden, chivvied their aged gardener into pruning them, helped him weed and hoe, sniffed the woodsmoke of the end-of-summer bonfires.

They read, practised music, sang, bought material for extra curtains and new gowns, incurred Mrs Johns' disapproval by intermittently taking over the kitchen to experiment with recipes, walked on the hillside or into the village, and rode the sturdy horses which Eleanor and the groom had now found and purchased. 'Well-bred horses aren't the best purchases for this part of the world,' she had told Henrietta. 'What's needed for these hills is surefootedness and stamina.'

Eleanor's skewbald gelding, Splash, and the liver chestnut, Captain, which Henrietta rode, were cobs, broad in chest and back and strong in the leg. But each had Arab blood on one side of his ancestry, which showed in their shapely heads and their clean fetlocks. Hairy fetlocks were a nuisance to grooms in muddy weather.

Ricky Cuscombe, the groom, who treated Eleanor and Henrietta as if they were his daughters, took them riding, accompanying them on another cob, a brown mare called Dusty, heavier in build than the others, and with a mealy nose which suggested that moorland pony featured in her ancestry.

With Ricky, they learned the byways of the Quantocks ('When I was Mrs Jacob, we only rode out visiting, on the main tracks,' Eleanor told Henrietta). Ricky had once been an Exmoor huntsman and he knew all the country from the Quantocks to Ilfracombe, far away to the west. He showed them short cuts through sunken lanes and along tracks which were only narrow ledges on steep hillsides, introduced them to a secret web of sheep-runs and deer paths, led them up and down gradients so fierce that they found themselves gripping their pommels for support. He taught them how to recognise changes in the weather, and the sound of a stag belling.

Once, he led them down from the Quantocks towards Exmoor to visit some cousins of his near a little town called Wiveliscombe. They were entertained in a tiny cottage to cider and potato cakes by an elderly labourer and his wife, who were almost overcome at finding two such

301

well-dressed ladies under their roof, until Eleanor asked to see their kitchen range and Henrietta told Ricky to talk to his family while she unsaddled the horses, after which the cousins relaxed and the party grew merry.

'Jacob would have been *horrified*,' said Eleanor, giggling, on the way home in the late afternoon. 'He used to make me work in the kitchen alongside the servants, because work was godly, but I always had to keep my dignity and make sure they kept their place. And it can be mighty difficult, let me tell you, when you're rolling pastry and the cook's dressing a chicken on the same table!'

'You've had too much cider,' said Henrietta.

'I know. Jacob would have been horrified at that, too. Isn't it fun? What a lovely day this has been. Where shall we go tomorrow? Ricky, let's ride to the sea! We could get there in two hours, couldn't we?'

On their return home Eleanor went to lie down, slept until the next morning and woke up with a bad headache. But when it had worn off, they set out with Ricky, reached the Bristol Channel and walked their horses in the sea. Captain, who despite his solid build had a skittish streak, danced when he felt the water and afterwards took off along the beach at full gallop. 'It's lucky you ride well, Hen,' said Eleanor when Henrietta had stopped him and the others had caught up.

'I learned during my summers in Essex,' said Henrietta and then broke off, abruptly. To speak of Essex was to think of Benjamin and it would be better to forget him.

This became gradually easier, for even though Eleanor's year of mourning was not yet ended, their social commitments were increasing. In quiet fashion, they called upon the Dyers and the Handleys, invited other guests and were invited back, dined at Mary Blake's school, began to convince the neighbourhood and much of Taunton that although extraordinary, they were nevertheless models of propriety. When days were so full, there was less time to brood.

In the evenings, by the fire, in the candlelit parlour, they ignored Mrs Dyer's pessimistic warnings regarding their eyesight and set about embroidering their elaborated version of the Whitmead device on every piece of linen in the house. Two elderly sisters from Chugg's Fiddle ('They're what I mean by biddies,' said Eleanor) twice took the trouble to walk up from the village after dark, carrying lanterns, 'just to pay you a call, dears; these dark evenings are so lonely', but on both occasions found Eleanor and Henrietta seated on opposite sites of the hearth, plying their needles in this most innocent and feminine occupation. Their credit rose accordingly.

Deep in the night, when all nosy and censorious neighbours were virtuously in bed, and Mrs Johns and Dotty were safely up in their attic room, Eleanor and Henrietta were free to be lovers and the deception they thereby practised on the rest of the world was an endless source of mirth.

'I can understand how much my grandfather and grandmother must have enjoyed making music and dancing in secret in the Puritan times,' Henrietta said. 'The secrecy makes it even more thrilling.'

One night in November, she had a disquieting dream in which she stood on a hill looking down at the sea, and at a little harbour just below. It was night, but a full moon was shining, casting a silvered path across the water. She saw a ship, of curious, archaic design, square-rigged and with a crenellated forecastle, glide quietly out of the harbour and along the moon-path and knew to her grief that her grandfather Ninian was on it. He was sailing away for ever and she would never see him again. She woke to find herself in tears, but then Eleanor turned over and reached for her, groaning, and drove the dream away with caresses.

Later, Eleanor gave voice to a new emotional demand.

'I'm always afraid you'll leave me, Hen. Another Benjamin will come along and you'll go to him.'

'Oh, *Eleanor* . . . who knows what will happen in years to come? You might be the one to leave. Perhaps Sir John Handley will produce a wealthy, handsome, unmarried cousin who will fall in love with you on sight and sweep you off to church. Or we might quarrel one day. If ever I left – or you threw me out – I'd stop taking the income you've given me, of course and even pay back what I've had, if I could – I worry about that sometimes because perhaps I couldn't. I know I'd want to. But—'

'Don't say that!' Eleanor sat up indignantly, her hair, which was long and chestnut and strongly waved, swirling round her like a cloak. 'Don't say that, not ever again. That income's yours; I've made it yours always. If you left me tomorrow I'd still be grateful for what we'd had. I've enough for myself and money has nothing to do with us. I'm not buying you. I just wanted you to have dignity and independence. I don't want you to stay because you can't afford to go. But oh, if only you could love me enough to want to stay always.'

'I'm sorry. I didn't mean . . .'

'No, no, my darling, I know. Oh, Henrietta, you're the best thing that ever happened to me and I love you so much. You're all I have. I can't even love my mother now. She let me be given to Jacob; she told me it was my duty to marry him. So did Aunt Becky. And they would have kept me at Peace-Through-Praise if they could; you weren't there when they cried and railed at me the day I said I wanted to have my own home. As for my grandmother; she almost accused me of wanting to set up as a whore. You're the only person who has ever loved *me*, as I am. I'm grateful. And if ever you want to leave, I'll let go gracefully. I promise!'

'Don't promise!' said Henrietta, holding her and stroking the chestnut hair. 'If I ever did leave, you'd be terribly upset, I know it. You don't even like it when I get letters from Matthew and he's only my brother!'

'I know. I'm jealous and I'm a fool. What's a brother, after all? Exchange all the letters you like with him,' said Eleanor.

But Henrietta heard the rough edge in her friend's voice when a letter arrived from Matthew only a week later. As was usual on such occasions, Eleanor walked pointedly out of the room. Henrietta stayed

where she was, beside the parlour fire, to read what Matthew had to say.
When Eleanor at last came back, she found that Henrietta had moved to
the window and was seated there, quite still, staring blankly out at a
rainswept garden.

'Hen? What is it?'

'My grandfather Ninian is dead,' said Henrietta. 'He died a week
ago. My father wrote to Matthew in Oxford and Matthew wrote at once
to me. Grandfather died one night in his sleep and oh, Eleanor, I believe
I dreamed about it, that same night.'

'*Dreamed* about it? Do you make a habit of that sort of thing? You
never mentioned this dream to me.'

'No. I woke up and then, well, you gave me other things to think
about.'

'A good thing, perhaps! I don't really believe in prophetic dreams,'
said Eleanor. 'I'm sorry about your grandfather, though. But wasn't he
very old?'

'Eighty-four. He was born in 1600. Yes, he was very old,' Henrietta
said.

She knew instinctively that she should not grieve too much in
Eleanor's presence. To Eleanor, the fewer links of affection Henrietta
had with other people, the better.

Of the two of them, Eleanor was the elder, the more beautiful, and,
because she had been married, the more experienced. Yet at times
Henrietta felt that she herself was the elder and most knowledgeable.
Eleanor's jealousy did not make her angry because she saw through it to
the loneliness beyond. She had begun by admiring Eleanor and looking
up to her. Now she was learning to pity her as well.

In the tones of normal conversation, she said: 'When I was looking
out into the garden just now I noticed how many berries there still are
on the rowan. I hope it isn't a sign of another bad winter. Last winter
was terrible.'

'Even in London?' said Eleanor. 'My dear, you know nothing about
terrible winters until you've seen one in the country. Last year I was
snowed in with Jacob for weeks on end. We put on all the clothes we
could, layer on layer until our arms stuck out at right angles . . .'

'Oh, Eleanor, what an exaggeration!'

'No, it isn't. That's exactly what we did do, because the supplies of
firewood were going down and anyway, Jacob's house had enormous
rooms and the fires never seemed to heat more than the bits beside the
hearths. We had old tapestries piled on the beds for extra warmth. We
almost ran out of food too except that in the end the men managed to dig
their way out to a patch of our woodland and then on to a lane where
other people had been digging before us. Then we could cut some fuel
and fetch supplies in from Taunton with a pony and sledge. But still,'
said Eleanor blandly, 'I suppose I should be grateful to that winter. It
finished Jacob off for me.'

It was not, after all, as bad a winter as its predecessor. There were many
days fit for walking or riding and few Sundays when the weather kept

Eleanor and Henrietta from attending church in Chugg's Fiddle. The village accepted them now; there were friendly nods, invitations to this house or that cottage after the service, for mulled ale and cakes; sometimes to dinner. Eleanor wore her dove brocade on special occasions but otherwise kept to her widow's black and intended to do so until February, when a full year would have passed since Jacob's death. Chugg's Fiddle approved. 'It's worth it,' Eleanor said, 'even if I do hate black and even if it's pure hypocrisy to pretend I'm grieving.'

At home, they learned several new songs and tried their hand at compositions of their own; planned a complete reconstruction of the garden for next summer ('We must have a sundial,' said Eleanor, 'and rosebeds near it'); and embroidered a bridge and river in the corner of their very last sheet. Mr Dyer lent them a history of the district which he had written himself and had printed at his own expense, and from it they discovered that the name Chugg's Fiddle, which had amused them so heartily, had an entirely dignified provenance, since it was a worn-down version of Choquant's Fealty.

According to Mr Dyer, the village and surrounding land had in the twelfth century been granted to a man called Reginald le Choquant as a reward for valour in battle alongside Henry the Second. 'The Le Choquant family have long since been extinct and the estate broken up and most local records were destroyed by Parliamentarian soldiers, who sacked the church and the vicarage. It is known, however, that Choquant meant shocking and it is interesting but vain,' said Mr Dyer, 'to speculate on the reason why his contemporaries called him thus.'

Henrietta and Eleanor speculated frequently, inventing increasingly absurd or melodramatic stories about the long-departed Reginald. But the name Chugg's Fiddle itself ceased to be ridiculous and became interesting.

'Life itself is interesting, don't you agree?' said Eleanor when Henrietta remarked on this.

'Yes, indeed,' Henrietta agreed.

And strange, she sometimes thought. What would those friendly villagers say if they knew what Mrs Henderson and Miss Whitmead, so charming, so decorous, did after dark, when all the candles were out and the house was silent? 'If you had married your Benjamin,' Eleanor said to her once, as they descended together from a dizzy peak of ecstasy, 'would he have shown you such delight as this?'

'I don't know. No, he wouldn't,' said Henrietta, and tried not to listen to the inner voice which persistently told her that Benjamin would nevertheless have been better, because Benjamin was male and secretly, still, it was a hard male body which she desired, and the vigorous male smell.

The last time Benjamin had embraced her, when her senses had reeled in that astonishing and hitherto unknown way, he had smelt of sweat and saddlery. Eleanor's body was not soft, exactly, but it was too smooth, too prettily perfumed with lavender water and lemon balm, and being shaped like Henrietta's own, offered no voyage of discovery. But Eleanor must never know, because she would be hurt and furious and everything they had here at Broom Cottage would be spoiled. 'And then where would I go?' said Henrietta to the nagging inner voice. 'And what could I do? What would I live on? I couldn't go on taking the income Eleanor has arranged for me then. It was a generous gesture but whatever Eleanor says, it's a wage. She pays me to stay with her, even if she won't admit it. I refuse to be a burden to Matthew or to apply to Father and so I have to remain where I am. That can't be changed, so be quiet!'

'I wonder if you'll still be here in ten years' time, or twenty?' asked the voice insidiously. 'Will you still be lying bravely to Eleanor then?'

'Be quiet, I say! Leave me alone!'

'Some man might come along, of course, and rescue you. If only Andrew Gale *had* been a good-looking twenty-five . . .'

'*Be quiet and go away. Oh, Benjamin, Benjamin!*' Henrietta almost shouted it aloud, was panic-stricken for a moment in case she had actually done so, and then, realising thankfully that she hadn't, drew her friend's head on to her shoulder and held Eleanor close, murmuring endearments, until they both slid into sleep.

They kept Christmas quietly. In January, Eleanor, prowling in the garden in clogs, gleefully reported snowdrops. 'Spring sometimes comes early in this part of England. It didn't last year, but it can. Primroses will be our next excitement.'

But they were not. King Charles the Second died at noon on Friday the 6th of February 1685 and although Taunton was a hundred and fifty miles from London and Chugg's Fiddle a few miles more, the news arrived so swiftly that Mr Dyer gave it out from his pulpit on Sunday the 8th.

'Oh no,' wailed Eleanor, as soon as she and Henrietta were back at home. 'Oh, *no*! I was going to throw away this horrible black at the end of the month and now I can't. Everyone will go into mourning, mark my words. Until May, very likely! You'll have to wear it, too. There isn't a yard of black cloth in the house; we shall have to rush to Taunton tomorrow or the drapers will all be sold out before we can get there. We could make over some of my dresses to fit you, perhaps. I'm taller, so it will only mean taking in and cutting down . . .'

'I suspect,' said Henrietta, 'that we'll all have more to worry about than wearing black for a few weeks.'

Eleanor became serious. 'You mean the succession? James the Duke of York, or . . . ?'

'I don't know. But I've listened to what people like Mr Dyer and Sir John Handley keep on saying and . . .' Henrietta hesitated and then said diffidently '. . . Matthew said in his last letter that there is endless talk in Oxford about what should be done regarding the succession.'

'Oh, yes, Matthew. He keeps up with political affairs, I take it?'

'Yes. And I think there may be trouble,' said Henrietta.

Others, as they soon discovered, shared Henrietta's fears. The two of them made haste to Taunton the next day, starting out early. The town was as Eleanor had expected, full of people on the same errand. Those among the drapers and haberdashers who had noted earlier reports of the King's fading health and put in extra stocks of black accordingly were doing a brisk trade, while those who had been more optimistic or less alert had already sold out.

But there was little zest to it. The activity was only a thin surface over an underlying anxiety. Faces were strained and every street corner seemed to have a worried little knot of people, talking in hushed tones. Others hurried about their business alone and preoccupied, exchanging no greetings, apparently aware of nothing outside their own thoughts.

'It's like a town of ghosts,' said Henrietta when they had purchased a bolt of dark wool cloth and were carrying their booty to where Ricky awaited them with the horses. 'It gives me the shivers. Is it grief or fear, Eleanor, do you think?'

'I don't know. Time will tell. At least in our quiet cottage we ought to be well out of it.'

'I expect when the Civil War started, a lot of people wanted to keep out of it. My grandfather did, I think. But he couldn't.'

'Take heart,' said Eleanor. 'Civil war hasn't broken out yet.'

'I'm going to write to Matthew.' Henrietta stopped short in the street and turned to her friend. 'He's finished with university and he's in London now. He'll know what's going on. I shall ask him.'

'I'm sure he'll inform you without being asked. He writes regularly, after all.'

'He won't if I don't make an effort as well. Eleanor, he's only my brother! He's not . . .' Henrietta swallowed, seeing Eleanor frown, but went on doggedly. 'He's not your rival!'

'No, I know!' Eleanor glanced at her angrily and then, as Henrietta's gaze remained steady, the anger dissolved into a contrite smile. 'I'm sorry, my dear. Forgive me.'

'Of course. The wind's cold,' said Henrietta, walking on. 'Let's hurry.'

'It's like a storm waiting to break,' said Samuel Whitmead, returning home after a visit to Chelmsford, undertaken not for any business purpose but simply to hear whatever news was circulating. 'I don't know what to think. They're saying that King Charles himself accepted Catholicism on his deathbed, and we all know what religion James and his queen follow. It's appalling, and yet Charles was our proper king and so by the law of the land is James.'

'But the only alternative is supporting Monmouth and he's not legitimate.' Charity was genuinely shocked. 'If a son born out of wedlock is allowed to inherit . . . !'

'There'll be lawsuits from end to end of the country, I should think,' said Benjamin humorously and Beatrice, helping his sisters to serve the food, laughed. He smiled at her. After all, it had been all right. The first few nights had been difficult, with Benjamin forcing himself and Beatrice not sure if it would be improper to encourage him, but in the end they had become friends.

307

Part of him still ached sometimes for Henrietta and she occasionally invaded his dreams. But Beatrice was too warm and steady to be resisted for long. Henrietta had had a magical quality, a foreign air, a touch of unpredictability. He sometimes found himself wondering if, after all, these would have been hardwearing enough for mundane everyday life at Whitmead, year after year. Perhaps, after all, things had worked out well.

Charity said with mild reproof: 'One shouldn't joke about immorality, Ben. I can find no cause for laughter anywhere in this unhappy situation. Of course, there is the Princess Mary and her husband William of Orange. They would be a lawful alternative.'

'They've sent Monmouth away from their court,' said Samuel gloomily. 'He was with them when his father died. It seems that William wishes to recognise James and have normal diplomatic relations with England.'

'If James respects the Anglican religion,' said Charity hopefully, 'perhaps all will go well after all.'

'When was there ever a king who didn't want to lead his country to his own beliefs?' said Samuel, more gloomily still. 'Besides, he'll want to defend them and the one will slide into the other. You heard our vicar, only last Sunday, preaching against Popery. I said to him afterwards: maybe it would be best to wait a bit and see what happens before you start breathing quite so much fire, but he said he wasn't breathing fire; he was trying to put one out before it got a hold. And he's not the only one, or so I gather from what my friends in Chelmsford say. It sounds as if every vicar in the land has had the same idea.'

'They could well,' said Benjamin gravely, 'be putting oil on the flames instead of extinguishing them.'

Charity, suspecting levity over yet another serious subject, gave him a sharp look. He met her eyes calmly. His sisters and Beatrice kept their faces serious although their eyes danced.

'Let us hope not,' said Samuel, and then rose to say Grace and changed the atmosphere by including a prayer for the happiness of his elder daughter Cherry, who was to be married in the spring.

In Somerset, the anti-Papist sermons were equally impassioned and the sense of approaching trouble was even stronger. Mr Dyer himself was no fire-breather but the grave warnings he issued from his pulpit against the dangers of Catholicism were in their way as effective as the eternal hellfire with which other, more emotional vicars threatened their congregations.

Not that the congregations appeared to need the threats. Ricky Cuscombe, who frequented the tavern in Chugg's Fiddle, told Eleanor and Henrietta: 'No one round hereabouts has any time for they Papists; you ought to hear what the men in the village call them. Hereabouts, men are all for Monmouth.'

Very soon, the point was reached when no one could invite guests for the simplest social occasion, but King James's religious proclivities dominated the conversation. After word came that the new King was going openly to Mass instead of following his unpopular religion in decent privacy, it was widely reported that at a dinner held by the Handleys, Sir John had proposed a toast to Monmouth coupled with damnation for all Papists, and out of his eleven male guests, not one as much as hesitated to drink it.

Matthew wrote to Henrietta from London and Eleanor, as eager as anyone now for information, greeted the letter with positive enthusiasm but the news itself was worrying. The King had summoned the Archbishop of Canterbury and told him outright that although he intended to undertake nothing against the established Anglican church, he would not protect it if the Anglicans didn't do their duty towards the throne.

'This is thought to refer to all the sermons which are being preached against Popery,' said Matthew. 'The King wishes the Archbishop to order them to stop but judging from some of the sermons I've heard lately, I can't imagine the order being heeded even if it's issued. People are very angry. Coffee-houses fairly hum and the sermons are getting more inflammatory, instead of less.'

There was a breathing space at Easter. 'We will turn our thoughts,' said Mr Dyer from his pulpit, 'from the worldly matters which have filled our minds of late, and fix them instead on the world to come and the Redemption which was won for us on Calvary.'

But it was a very short pause. There was a further letter from Matthew a week later.

'London is seething worse than ever. The King tried to persuade his ministers to accompany him to his Papist chapel at Easter. The Earl of Sunderland went as far as the chapel door and then turned back and Rochester got out of it by going into the country for Easter, but that the King should even urge them has shocked everyone.'

'This is dreadful,' said Eleanor. 'Something must happen, Hen. It can't go on like this.'

'No, I know.'

'What's the matter? Hen, you look quite frightened.'

'I am. I don't know why. Living here in this quiet cottage, we ought to be able to keep out of trouble if anyone can, but I do feel afraid. I keep having bad dreams which I can't remember when I wake in the morning.'

'You will keep eating cheese at supper,' said Eleanor. 'The results are notorious.'

Henrietta laughed. 'Well, we are expected to dine with Mary Blake and Susanna today, and they always feed us so well that we hardly need supper. I can avoid cheese tonight! I wonder if they've heard this latest piece of news?'

'If they haven't, let's not tell them. Let's talk about something quite different.'

But they had heard.

The house where Mary Blake and Susanna Musgrave taught their twenty-seven pupils, mostly the daughters of Taunton merchants and master craftsmen, was a comfortable, slate-roofed building over a hundred years old. Some of the girls boarded and they slept in a long upstairs room with a row of dormer windows looking out from the roof. Mary and Susanna shared private rooms on the ground floor, with a separate front door.

'Do you know,' Eleanor said as with Ricky in attendance they rode towards the school, 'when I was a pupil here, we were never allowed to come near this entrance. We were fond of Mary Blake but we were afraid of her too. She has so much presence. At this moment, I half expect her to come out and ask me what I'm doing here.'

'Really? You never told me that before,' said Henrietta. 'But I know what you mean when you say she has presence. She must be a good teacher.'

'Yes, she is. She made lessons interesting. Here we are. Ricky!'

Ricky dismounted, helped them alight and led the three horses off to the little stable where Susanna and Mary kept their own mounts. Before they reached the door, Mary herself opened it, and followed her words of welcome almost instantly, with: 'Have you heard the news?'

'What news?' asked Eleanor, as they came inside and handed their cloaks to a hovering maid.

'Why, this scandalous business of the King trying to make his earls attend a Papistical Easter service!' Mary ushered them into the parlour, where Susanna was kneeling by the hearth, mending the fire. 'Come in and get warm. What a grey, chilly day it is. It's often the way on a Saturday, when we stop lessons early and the girls want to play out of doors. One would think the weather did it on purpose. We're always up to date with public events. Some of our pupils are from families with wide connections. The world of commerce is like a spider's web. A twitch in one place makes the whole web vibrate. We hear what's afoot in London almost as fast as the Londoners do.'

'And there's not a girl in the school whose family isn't horrified at the King's behaviour,' said Susanna pugnaciously, rising to her feet. 'He'll live to regret it.'

Something in the atmosphere was markedly odd. The presence which Eleanor had admired seemed to have deserted Miss Blake. Her manner was too effusive and her angular face was bright with a girlish excitement which would have sat better on the face of one of her pupils. Susanna, on the other hand, exuded an air of fierce satisfaction. Eleanor and Henrietta, taking chairs by the fire, looked at their hostesses in surprise.

'We had heard about it as it happens,' Eleanor said. 'But how do you mean: live to regret it? Are you smuggling arms to Monmouth? Well, we promise not to denounce you!'

'It isn't a game!' said Susanna.

'You mean you *are*?' Eleanor pulled a grave, judicial face, though her eyes were merry. 'Would your pupils' fathers, even the most nonconformist ones, approve of that? My husband always said that women shouldn't become involved in politics.'

310

'I can't see why not. We have to live by the laws men make,' said Susanna, still pugnaciously. 'So why can't we have a hand in deciding which men make them?'

'Don't let's have a dispute.' Henrietta was uneasy. 'If Monmouth is planning anything, it certainly isn't a game. But I'm sure that none of us are concerned in any way.'

'There are rumours that Monmouth is in Amsterdam, putting a fleet together, with or without the help of William of Orange. Opinion is divided on that and no one knows for sure,' said Mary. 'But there'll be plenty of backing for him in this part of England if he lands. Somerset and Devon have a strong nonconformist element. They hate Papists.'

'So you would approve if Monmouth came? Oh, don't be afraid of us!' cried Eleanor. 'Even if you *are* somehow concerned. Susanna, we know it isn't funny. We are not fools. We know what your opinions are already, anyway. You told us last year, over my dinner table. If Monmouth could move quickly enough, he could seize England just as Henry the Seventh did at Bosworth. That's what you said, or words to that effect.'

'But King Charles was still alive then,' said Henrietta soberly. 'It wasn't real. Now things are different. We would rather keep ourselves right out of it. But we would never betray our friends, no, of course not.'

'Oh, let us show them, Susanna!' exclaimed Mary. 'All our girls know and their families. If it comes to the point, the whole of Taunton will rise for Monmouth. Come and see what the girls have been doing in their embroidery lessons. It's improved their skill. Children always work better if they are shown a purpose for their work.'

'Embroidery lessons?' said Eleanor, while Henrietta blinked.

'We're not smuggling arms,' said Mary in laughing tones as she led them out of the parlour. Susanna, somewhat dubiously, brought up the rear. 'That would not be at all fitting. Eleanor may have been joking when she repeated that dictum that women shouldn't involve themselves in politics but there is much truth in it. Oh yes, there is, Susanna. But a marginal involvement, using womanly skills, may be permissible. There!'

She opened the door of a big, south-facing room which in brighter weather would have been full of sunshine. In the middle was a table covered with a white cloth, with seats set round it. Mary Blake whisked the cloth off the table.

Beneath were several folded pieces of brightly coloured fabric, with threaded needles stuck into them. Susanna, shrugging, lifted the nearest and shook it out.

It was a long, tapering triangle of scarlet cloth and traced on it in faint ink were the words: *Defender of the Protestant Faith*. The first three letters of *Defender* had been embroidered over in gold thread.

'We are doing banners for Monmouth,' said Mary. 'Some girls are working individually, some in groups on the bigger banners. Each one is different. This next one' – she shook out a second piece of fabric – 'says "Hail to our true King James" and will be in silver on blue. Three

311

girls are sharing the work. Oh dear, Joan Fuller is one of them. She'll have to unpick that H. She's not clever with her needle, alas.'

'I think it's madness,' said Henrietta as they rode home. She spoke softly so that Ricky shouldn't hear. 'It's treason, you know. Oh, I shall never whisper a word to anyone. Don't worry about that. But I still think they're mad.'

'You're a funny one,' said Eleanor thoughtfully. 'More practical than I am, and yet more fey. You're afraid, aren't you? But we can keep out of it, living quietly in Broom Cottage. I hope no one tries to requisition our horses! That sort of thing happened during the Civil War, I've been told. Look, those banners won't count as treason if Monmouth wins.'

'He hasn't won yet. He hasn't even landed!'

Chapter Twenty-Four
Monmouth

'One can feel the excitement in the air. It's as though he's pushing a bow wave of it in front of him,' Eleanor said, nudging Splash with her heel to persuade him to hurry. The Quantocks still had the new-minted look of early morning, but already the road into Taunton was becoming busy as people streamed from village and farmstead, quarry and mine, in the hope of glimpsing King Charles the Second's famous son the Duke of Monmouth, who was marching to Taunton through the June sunlight, from his landing place at Lyme.

'What a poetic turn of phrase!' said Henrietta, jogging alongside on Captain as they drew near the outskirts of the town. 'I wonder if the Dyers will be there? Poor Mrs Dyer; she cried her eyes out when Philip went to join the Duke's army.'

'I should think they'll be there,' said Eleanor, 'if only in the hopes of seeing Philip. If they can pick him out of the multitude. The whole of the West is up and the Devon militia have run away; isn't that so, Ricky?'

The nose of Ricky's mare was level with Splash's girth and the groom was within easy earshot. 'So I hear,' he said in prim tones, which mingled oddly with his broad Somerset accent.

'Ricky doesn't approve; I can tell that by his voice. But Ricky, you can't like the idea of the whole country being pushed back to Popery.'

'I don't. But it b'ain't happened yet and it's not right, a byblow going after the throne. Lucy Walter weren't never married to the King. I say that, and my old dad were killed fighting agin Popery back in the Civil War days. Fell here at Taunton, he did, defending it under Robert Blake. And still I tell 'ee, this b'ain't right and I hear the Mayor and the town council of Taunton think the same. They're only greeting the Duke because the townsfolk won't have it any other way. And if you want my opinion, the townsfolk are a lot o' girt fools,' said Ricky bluntly. 'Seems to me, Mrs Dyer's got something to cry about.'

'I think much as you do,' Henrietta said, while Eleanor rolled her eyes heavenwards. 'But we'd better not say so in public, Ricky.'

'You don't want to worry,' said the groom. 'I'll hold my peace when others is around. But I can tell 'ee one thing. It b'ain't just religion. Times are hard for some and there'll be men coming from the fields and mines thinking that this new Duke'll wave a wand and put an end to poverty. But he b'ain't a magician, any more than anyone else. They'll lose what little they've got if they b'ain't careful. It's poor men mostly as

313

is following the Duke. Sir John Handley; he's talked a lot about being anti-Papist, but he's still at home and so are all the gentry that I know of.'

'Oh, you two!' cried Eleanor. 'Well, we're only spectators. We can't sway things either way. Oh, just look at Taunton!'

Taunton was en fête for the Duke of Monmouth. It was open for business, with awnings up over street stalls, shop doors open and the sound of sawing from a carpenter's shed. Behind the wall which hid a monumental mason's yard and the half-finished tombstones in it from the gaze of passers-by, someone was chiselling; a dyeworks was giving off its usual noticeable smell; and a loom clattered briskly in every other cottage.

But it was obvious that everyone was ready to down tools and rush to a vantage point as soon as the word went round that the Duke had marched in. Eager expectancy filled the air. People in the midst of buying and selling kept pausing, heads cocked, to listen for distant fanfares, and every cottage door had been festooned with garlands of flowers; roses and carnations, foxglove and lavender, the white meadowsweet, and chains of daisies and buttercups made by the children. Street entertainers, fiddlers, tumblers, a man with a dancing bear, were on every corner.

Many of the townsfolk were in their best clothes: only on festival days were such bright silks and satins and so much newly laundered linen and lace to be seen in the street. The people not in festive dress were mostly the farm-workers and miners who had come in from outside. These were mainly in their workaday homespuns and some, Henrietta noticed for the first time, looked undernourished and their clothes were patched. But they too had a light in their eyes, and their voices as they called to each other had a harsh vigour.

'Look!' Eleanor cried as they made their way towards the town centre. 'Look, it's Mary Blake and Susanna and the whole school walking in a procession! Mary! Good day!'

'Eleanor, my dear! And Miss Whitmead.' Mary Blake stopped, waving Susanna on with the procession. It was obviously a formal expedition, for all the girls wore white dresses and chaplets of wild flowers, and some of them carried furled banners, presumably the results of their embroidery lessons. Susanna had what looked like a cloth-wrapped book under her arm, and Mary Blake, improbably and somewhat awkwardly, was carrying a sword in an ornamental scabbard.

'What on earth is that for?' said Eleanor, pointing.

'Get yourselves down from those horses and come and see,' said Mary Blake. 'We are part of the Mayor's reception for the Duke, I'll have you know. This was my father's sword, and he was given it as a keepsake after Admiral Robert Blake died. It belonged to the Admiral, and they were cousins.'

'In my view,' said Ricky, 'it 'ud be as well if you did get down, Mrs Henderson, and Miss Whitmead too, and I'll find somewhere to bait the 'osses. They've had a longish road already this morning and it's going to be hot. I'll find 'ee in the town centre all right.'

Eleanor and Henrietta slipped out of their saddles, handed Ricky their reins, and fell in at the back of the school procession. 'It's like old times,' Eleanor said to Henrietta, chuckling. 'I remember when I was one of Mary's boarders, going out for walks like this or else to church, two and two, all looking as virtuous as angels and talking in quiet, ladylike voices. We were usually planning how best to make life a burden to our visiting dancing master.'

By the time the little procession reached the market place in the town centre, it was moving in a tight-packed crowd. Trumpets could now be heard in the distance. They passed the place where, on their right, there would once have been a view of the towers of Taunton Castle, except that Charles the Second, displeased because Taunton had supported those he considered his father's murderers, had had most of it pulled down. The hall and the gatehouse remained, but they were shut and empty. There was no overlord now to order the townsfolk what to think or where to place their loyalties. They had decided that for themselves.

Miss Blake's little procession came into the square just as the Duke, riding on a tall grey horse and accompanied by a trumpeter and a standard-bearer whose banner, whenever the light wind blew it out straight, boldly proclaimed the words *Fear nothing but God*, entered from the other side, followed by a column of mounted troops.

On their own, Eleanor and Henrietta would have been hemmed in at the back of the crowd, but Mary Blake was on official business and her imperious cries of: 'Way! Make way!' opened a path through which she, Susanna, Henrietta, Eleanor and all twenty-seven pupils could pass. They halted at the front of the throng, with a clear view of the Duke and his men.

They were impressive at first sight. The sun flashed on ceremonial breastplates and polished stirrups, on swordhilts and well-shone helmets and on the gem of a ring on the Duke's right hand. Monmouth himself was good-looking in a swarthy fashion, with the large, dark Stuart eyes, in which melancholy was curiously mingled with gaiety, and a princely bearing. All twenty-seven of Mary's girls looked up at him with candid admiration and Susanna, unexpectedly sentimental, sighed and whispered: 'How handsome he is.'

Eleanor was nodding agreement, but Henrietta, studying the Duke's face, found that she could make no response to him. Benjamin had looks more to her taste. Henrietta's idea of perfect male looks included fox-red hair, brown eyes and fine, lightly freckled skin and a certain kindliness of expression.

To Henrietta, the Duke was only moderately handsome, and though he sat well on his horse, he still seemed only life-size. A monarch, above all a monarch who proposed to marshal a country behind him and snatch a throne from under a rival by force, ought to be more than that.

Then she saw the crowd of foot-soldiers jostling into the square behind the horsemen, and inside her, doubt ossified into hopelessness. If she hadn't been at the front of the multitude and quite unable to leave, she would have turned round and walked away. These, presumably, were the cream of the Duke's infantry. They had obviously been drawn from mine and farm, because the weapons they carried so proudly were mainly the implements of their trades. A few had swords and muskets, mostly old and speckled with rust; hand-me-downs, no doubt, from fathers and grandfathers who had fought in the Civil War. But the majority bore axes, scythes, pitchforks, hammers. If the Duke had any artillery worthy of the name, he wasn't parading it this morning.

In London, she had seen processions of real soldiers. These were scarcely even imitations.

But the crowd was cheering. She glimpsed the Dyers, waving to someone in the infantry; Philip, presumably. The Mayor and his Councillors came forward, or rather, were pushed. They all looked unhappy and the Mayor stammered as he welcomed the Duke. The trumpeter blew a fanfare for silence and an officer rode forward and handed Monmouth a scroll. Monmouth undid it, cleared his throat, and announced that this was the manifesto which he had read in public when he landed at Lyme. He now proposed to read again, and launched into it forthwith.

It was long and wordy, but its meaning was simple enough. The self-styled King James the Second was a usurper who had seized the crown after Papist traitors had poisoned King Charles. 'I, James Scott, Duke of Monmouth, am the true heir, the genuine King James the Second, by right of being the eldest and only legitimate son of King Charles, to whom Mrs Lucy Walter, my mother, was lawfully married.'

'But it's nonsense about the Catholics poisoning the King,' Eleanor whispered, disconcerted. 'That rumour was laughed out of existence before King Charles was even buried.'

'I know. And King Charles himself declared that he was never married to Lucy Walter,' Henrietta whispered back.

The Duke was building up to his climax, describing all followers of the present King James as traitors, denouncing Popishness, calling on all honest men to take up arms and follow his banner, as he marched on Bristol in order to claim the whole West Country before conquering the south-east and sweeping the usurper away. *'Fear nothing but God!'* he ended, standing up in his stirrups and drawing his sword in order to point at the wording on his standard.

Cheers broke out anew. The Duke rolled up the scroll and handed it back to his officer, and the crowd heaved and lurched as numerous eager young men thrust their way through to join the Duke's following. The Mayor cleared his throat and declared: 'Sir, there is a presentation from Miss Mary Blake, a well-respected teacher in this town, and from Susanna Musgrave her assistant, and twenty-seven Maids of Taunton. Will you receive it?'

Mary, a flush of excitement on her cheekbones, stepped up to the Duke's stirrup without waiting for him to say yes, curtsied deeply and offered him the Admiral's sword. 'Here is a weapon for your royal hand! It was once borne by Robert Blake who fought so bravely for the Protestant cause, here in Taunton itself!'

Monmouth had instincts of graciousness. He dismounted to receive the sword, tossing his reins to the officer, raised Mary Blake to her feet and kissed her. Susanna pressed forward, unwrapping the book she carried, which turned out to be a Bible.

'Your Majesty, here is a copy of the Word of God, for which so many martyrs died, that we should have the right to read it.'

The Duke kissed Susanna too, and then found himself confronted by Mary's pupils, lined up in order of age, the youngest first, waiting to give him the banners they had embroidered. All had completed their task, even, apparently, the incompetent Joan. 'Will you let my girls present gifts to you?' Mary Blake asked. 'They have been working to make them, these many months, with your cause in mind.'

'Of course, of course.' Monmouth's expression was slightly bewildered but the graciousness held. One after another, the girls curtsied to him and handed over their banners. Monmouth, having signalled somebody forward to take charge of the gifts so that he could keep his hands free, kissed all the girls as well, asked their names and kept count.

'Twenty-seven,' he said. 'Twenty-seven of the fairest maids of the West Country. I congratulate you, Miss Blake, Miss Musgrave.'

The Mayor, in response to urgings from the crowd, once more came forward and, albeit in a depressed voice, invited the Duke to accompany him to where refreshments waited. The Duke remounted his horse and edged forward through the throng, and Mary Blake fell back beside Eleanor and Henrietta.

'That's done. It went off well, didn't it? Come back to the school with us and share our celebration dinner. We have cider, fresh hot bread and a pork pasty which is a great favourite with us all.'

'Thank you. We should like to.' Eleanor decided for them both. Mary and Susanna gathered their charges and they all began to move through what was now a swiftly emptying square. They caught sight of Ricky making his way towards them and as he came up, Henrietta explained where they were going. 'I'll fetch the hosses round there, then,' Ricky said, and disappeared again.

'My dear,' said Mary Blake to Henrietta, 'why is that old man over there staring at you so? The one in the green coat. Do you know him?'

Henrietta looked once at the upright figure with the fashionable clothes, the curly black mane of a wig and the wrinkled face beneath it and then looked away. 'So he's settled in this district anyway! That is Mr Gale, the man my father wanted me to marry. He's the reason why I am living with Eleanor and not with my family.'

'That old man?' Susanna had heard. She gave Mr Gale a swift glance and shuddered visibly. 'That's shameful. He looks about a hundred and fifty. Whatever did your father want you to marry him for?'

'He's rich,' said Henrietta shortly. 'And capable of siring children, apparently,' she added.

'And how would your father know the truth of that?' inquired Susanna. Two of the girls were near enough to hear and giggled. Mary clicked her tongue reprovingly. 'Susanna, we'll discuss the matter elsewhere, if at all.'

317

'He's turned his back. He's going away,' said Henrietta. 'Let's forget him; I'd much rather. I wonder what will happen next? Will there be fighting?'

Information was not long in coming. In the days that followed, Ricky went almost every day to Taunton and brought back the news. The Duke had surveyed the topography of the land from the top of St Mary's church tower in Taunton. He had marched on towards Bridgwater. Men were coming in swarms to his aid. 'It's as if they'm sprouting out of ditches and dropping down out of the trees.'

And then: the change of note. The King's commander, a man called Feversham, was organising his forces. Bristol was ready to resist Monmouth and a bridge had been broken to obstruct his route to it. A volunteer army had been raised in Oxford, with half the university, dons and students alike, turning out to support the reigning King. Reinforcements were marching from London.

And then came the news that the Duke had tried to attack Feversham's troops by night, through mist and darkness, on the Sedgemoor outside Bridgwater.

He had been taken.

'I'm going to Bridgwater. If they could get here, so could our Philip, if he's on his feet at all. I've got to know.'

Mrs Dyer, short, plump, pale with anxiety, lips folded determinedly together, shut the back door of the vicarage. The two frightened and hungry fugitives whom they had illegally succoured were on their way again. They had had food and a sleep in the stable loft and now, Lord be praised, they were off the premises leaving no trace behind, on their way back to the Exmoor farms they should never have left.

The Dyers had only yesterday heard the proclamation read by a trooper in the middle of Chugg's Fiddle, to the effect that anyone who aided or comforted one of Monmouth's defeated rebels was liable to be taken up for treason and suffer the full penalty thereof, but it wasn't possible to regard two white-faced lads, appealing for food in broad country accents, as anything so solemn as rebels or traitors.

Accordingly, the Dyers had put themselves in danger of the law. 'They're someone's sons,' William Dyer had said. 'We'd want people to do as much for our own. But where is our Philip? That's what I'd like to know.'

'I'm going to find him,' Mrs Dyer said now. 'If he's a prisoner, or wounded, or dead on that battlefield, I'm going to find him. I've *got* to know.'

'Very well.' William Dyer knew his wife. If one of her children were in need, nothing would stop Peggy Dyer, usually so devoted to her home and her husband's wishes, from going forth to the rescue. He had no more chance of dissuading her than of deflecting a cannonball with his bare hands. 'But I'm coming with you.'

'It might be better if you didn't. You ought to stay here and tell anyone that asks that you wouldn't dream of harbouring a rebel and

Philip's no son of yours.' A pained line appeared between Peggy's brows. It hurt her to pronounce such words even when they were a lie. 'I can't let you go into danger without me, Peggy. What kind of husband would I be?'

'A wise one. I can be the wife who went off against your advice. If you go after your son, someone might say you're in sympathy with Monmouth, but if I go, there's a chance no one will think I'm more than just a silly woman besotted with her son and knowing nothing about politics,' said Peggy, displaying an uncomfortably accurate knowledge of the way most people felt about her. 'I'll take Wheeler to escort me. He'll be a servant doing as he's bid and shouldn't come to any harm.'

'Mrs Wheeler won't like it,' warned Dyer. Of the couple who looked after the vicarage, cooked the meals and groomed the two horses, Mrs Wheeler was undoubtedly the stronger personality.

'Mrs Wheeler will have to put up with it,' retorted Peggy.

Nevertheless, it was true that Peggy Dyer was a domesticated woman, of limited experience and imagination. After bearing seven children, her body had become cushionly, and so had her mind. As the wife of a vicar, she had comforted many victims of tragedy, but to hold a newly bereaved widow in her arms, to dry the tears of a grief-stricken child, even to help nurse a man dying in pain but in his own bed, belonged to the normal order of things. She had not understood that such things as Sedgemoor battlefield existed.

The battlefield wasn't hard to find. If the soldiers and the horrified local people she met in the lanes as she skirted Bridgwater hadn't been able to tell her where the Sedgemoor was, the circling crows would have done so. The battle had taken place last night and the two fugitives who sought shelter at the vicarage had stumbled to the back door at dawn. This was the afternoon of the same day. Most of the dead and many of the wounded still lay where they had fallen. She and Wheeler reached the edge of the Sedgemoor and then reined in, staring across it in despair.

The major error she had made, in her simplicity, lay in the way she had visualised things. She knew she was coming to a battlefield but she had seen it in her mind as an actual field, a meadow. She knew too that there would be dead men there but the picture in her head was that of corpses neatly laid-out with their hands folded in peace.

The real battlefield was the whole of the Sedgemoor, and it was as its name implied, an expanse of marshy moorland. There were acres and acres of it: tussocky grass with reedy pools in the dips, a few gorse bushes and bilberry patches and an occasional clump of trees amid a network of ditches and stretches of swamp; and the dead who littered it were not peaceful but hideous. Bodies which yesterday had been those of living men lay like heaps of old clothing or broken dolls, some in attitudes and with faces which bore the stigma of death in slow agony.

Peggy Dyer and Wheeler stared down at a young man lying half in and half out of a ditch, his hands clutched over a glistening mass of intestines which protruded from his ripped stomach, and his dead mouth stretched in a nightmare rictus. They looked away, quickly, and found themselves staring towards a clump of trees. Beyond them, a tent had been pitched, and from their lower branches, in full view of whoever occupied the tent, hung half a dozen bodies. Peggy put a hand over her mouth.

'Mistress.' Wheeler's voice was husky. He was thought an active man but he was not young and now an extra twenty years seemed to have stamped themselves on his face. His voice shook. 'Mistress, you can do no good here. Best come away.'

'I can't. Philip may be here. Listen!'

The field was neither silent nor still. There were the crows, for one thing, flapping down, hopping about, rising and cawing. There were also carts, accompanied by soldiers, moving over the ground in a purposeful fashion, gathering up the bodies, and there were a few sad, bent-shouldered people apparently searching for their dead.

And, worse than any of this, was the moaning. Some of those lying there were wounded, still marginally living.

Hoofbeats and shouts made them turn. Two troopers rode up to them, putting their horses across the path. 'And what have we here?' The foremost trooper had a lopsided smile and a face with creases on the side where the smile was most active. In private life, the effect might have been merely idiosyncratic. In these circumstances, it was villainous. 'One manservant with straggling grey hair,' he said rudely, 'and one short, fat woman perched on his pillion. Employer, aunt or mother? Names and business!'

Peggy Dyer and Wheeler stared back at him without answering and the second trooper, a sharp-featured, younger man, snapped: 'We're asking you your names and business! Speak up!'

Both the soldiers were still in battledress: buff coats, helmets, cuirasses, steel elbow-gauntlets. Coat and armour and even the stubbly faces of the men themselves were splashed with the brownish stains of dried blood. The man with the creased face was stained all up his right arm and side. But neither man showed signs of being wounded. The blood was not their own. Wheeler, swallowing, remained speechless. Peggy Dyer said: 'My name is Mrs Dyer and this is my servant Wheeler. We are trying to find my son, Philip Dyer.'

'King's man, is he, ma'am?' said Creased-Face.

'I just want to search the battlefield for him,' said Peggy in a low voice.

'So he's a cursed rebel! Well,' Creased-Face informed her, 'you can't search the field without Colonel Kirke's permission. D'you want to see him?'

'I wouldn't, in your place. He doesn't like rebels, or their families. Likely you're wasting your time, anyway. We've hanged quite a few out of hand and we didn't ask their names first.' The younger man said it with satisfaction.

'Come now. We mustn't discourage the lady too much.' The lopsided smile was in evidence again. 'There's a few cartloads of wounded being taken into Bridgwater. If they live, they'll be tried for treason. Their names are being taken, of course, and the first lists have been brought to the Colonel. He's over there.' He jerked his head towards the dreadful clump of trees and the tent beyond. 'He might see you, if we ask him nicely. Depends how much an interview's worth to you.'

'You mean you want a bribe? I can't bribe you,' said Peggy in a low voice. 'I have no money with me beyond a few small coins.'

Wheeler hesitated, torn between a longing to go home and his loyalty to his mistress. Loyalty won. 'I have,' he said.

When, after a considerable wait, they were ushered into the tent, they found that it had been furnished in rough and ready fashion as an office, with a desk behind which Colonel Kirke was sitting, on the only chair. He was a beefy man, his face dully flushed with over-indulgence in alcohol although at the moment he was sipping coffee from a mug in an effort to defy exhaustion. He had been up most of the night and like his troopers was unshaven and heavy-eyed. He looked at his visitors with disfavour.

'What's all this? You're the mother of one of these damned Monmouth-lovers, are you, ma'am? You're looking for him?'

'Yes. I want to find my son.' Peggy was sick at heart and frightened, but she had come too far to turn back. 'He ran off to join Monmouth and he hasn't come home. If he's a prisoner, I'll try to find money to buy comforts for him. If he's wounded, I'll tend him. If he's dead, I want to bury him. Can you help me, Colonel?'

'Why the devil should I?' His voice was rough and chesty and carried a remarkable charge of sheer, murderous hatred. 'Your son hasn't come home, you say? And if he had done, what then, pray? Would you have harboured him? You know what the penalty is for harbouring an enemy of the King, I trust?'

'Mistress, we shouldn't have come.'

'Be quiet, Wheeler. Colonel, I know what the penalty is on earth for harbouring the King's enemies. I wonder what the penalty is in the hereafter for denying a mother the right to love her children? Of course I would have harboured him, as you put it. What else would a mother do?'

'I should warn you, ma'am, that the law takes no account of maternal feelings. There will be vengeance for this uprising against the King's majesty, such as men will talk of for a thousand years.' He pulled a sheet of paper towards him and ran a thick forefinger down it. 'This is the first list of names from Bridgwater gaol. Dyer . . . No, he's not there—yet.'

'If I must, I'll go to Bridgwater myself to look for him. But first, I must ask permission to search the battlefield for his body. I know he is not . . .' Peggy's voice faltered, '. . . among those . . . hanging outside. Wheeler . . . looked. I saw some of the dead being taken away, too. Is anyone trying to find out who . . . who they are?'

'No, ma'am. One does not bother to put names to rubbish.'

'Rubbish?' Peggy gaped at him and then her plump face suffused with anger. 'How *dare* you?'

'Mistress, please,' said Wheeler tremulously.

'Are you speaking to me, ma'am?' inquired Kirke.

'Yes, Colonel, I am. I don't know if your mother is still alive, but if she could hear you now she'd be ashamed of you. And if she's in heaven then I daresay she can hear you and no doubt she's asking God to forgive you. A decent man doesn't look a mother in the face and call her son rubbish. Nor does a decent man say that the law takes no account of a mother's feelings, as though this were something admirable. It isn't admirable at all. I know nothing of kings and dukes and rebellions; such matters have no interest for me. But I do know that my son went to war thinking he was doing right by God and I won't be told he's rubbish. Nor will I be told that I'd be committing a crime if I *harboured* him. I carried him for nine months in my womb . . . yes, Colonel Kirke, go on, blush. You men! You'll look on an obscene mess like that battlefield out there and laugh, but let someone mention some of the real facts of life in your presence and you blush like a spinster who's found a naked man under her bed . . .'

'Ma'am!' Colonel Kirke had shot to his feet. 'This is the outside of enough. Unless you wish to be placed under instant arrest . . . !'

'I've nearly finished,' said Peggy Dyer. She was herself astounded at her temerity. This sense of righteousness, she supposed, was the grace which had sustained those who in the past had died for their faiths. It was quite possible that this furious bull of a man might have her killed but she no longer cared. Contemptuously, she said: 'I carried my son for nine months and I pushed him into the world at risk of my own life – two days and nights it took me and I was at the brink of death when he was born – and then I fed him at my breast for six months after. I'll harbour him any time I like and don't tell me that the law can't recognise my feelings! Maybe you'd better get women to make some of the laws. Maybe they'd reflect the real world then!'

Mrs Dyer stopped, breathless. She and the Colonel stared at each other in mutual loathing. Wheeler whimpered.

'Turnbull!' Kirke simultaneously scribbled something on a sheet of paper and raised his voice in a shout and Creased-Face appeared in answer. 'Take this termagant away! She has permission to search the battlefield. Here's my authority. But make sure I never set eyes on her again or I may decide to string her up as well. And you, ma'am: if you find your son alive, don't try to remove him. Trooper, make sure she doesn't. His body, his life, are the property of His Majesty King James the Second of England. Be on your way, woman.'

'My thanks,' said Peggy. She curtsied briefly, and then turned on her heel and walked with as much dignity as a short, plump woman could ever muster, out of the Colonel's tent.

Wheeler, trembling so much that even his mouth shook, followed. Creased-Face came with them.

'You were lucky,' he said seriously as he led them away from the tent. 'He's weary to the bone and he's ordered so many hangings today, that he's sated with them. Otherwise I wouldn't have given a farthing for your chances in there.'

'Mistress,' pleaded Wheeler. 'Can't we go home?'

322

'No,' said Peggy. 'I've got to find Philip. We've got permission to search, now, and you spent three months' wages getting us into that tent; I saw what you gave the trooper. Thank you for that, Wheeler. I'll repay you when we go home. When we've . . . finished.' Hopelessly she looked out across the Sedgemoor. 'The battlefield first, and then Bridgwater. Oh God, where do we start?'

In the end there was no long search, no journey to Bridgwater, no doomed attempt to rescue a beloved son in the face of armed troopers invested with the King's mandate. They found him quite soon. He was dead, although he did not look as though he had been dead very long. One arm had been shot away below the elbow and someone, perhaps Philip himself, had put a rough tourniquet on with a piece of cloth hacked from his coat. There was a deep wound too in his right thigh and beneath it on the ground a huge, dark stain.

She was allowed to take him home for burial.

Chapter Twenty-Five
The Fugitive

'Mrs Dyer must be as brave as a lioness,' Henrietta said. 'To go to the battlefield and brave Colonel Kirke in his very tent and give him a piece of her mind like that!'

'The poor Dyers.' Mrs Johns took a pie out of the oven and straightened up, grunting as she did so because she had had to bend double, and Mrs Johns was a woman of ample proportions. 'Losing their eldest boy in such a fashion. Though at that he was luckier than some. You've been down at Chugg's all day, Miss Henrietta, at Philip's funeral, and you was the lucky one. Mrs Eleanor kept her arrangement to see her mother, so she's been across Taunton and she'll tell 'ee what's been going on there. Now, Dotty, get your cloak off and put that sugar and flour 'ee've brought into the larder, and put they warm plates on the table. Terrible times these may be, but empty bellies won't make them any better.'

'Why, what happened in Taunton?' Henrietta turned startled eyes on Eleanor.

'I doubt if Mrs Dyer's remarks had much effect,' said Eleanor grimly. She sat down at the table. 'Oh, my mother is all right, and Aunt Becky and my grandmother, but it was a near thing. Two days ago they gave some water and food to a couple of Monmouth's men who were trying to escape home from the battle, and just after I arrived, six of Kirke's troopers came pounding at the door. Mother told them that Peace-Through-Praise was a household of elderly women and one ageing manservant with no interest in politics but then my grandmother started cursing the soldiers for being the pet dogs of the Pope . . .'

'Oh, no!' Henrietta gasped.

Eleanor's face was very tired and her vivid blue eyes seemed to have sunk into it. 'Becky hustled Grandmother upstairs and Mother told the men the old lady was mentally afflicted, which may well be true! To shout such things into the faces of Kirke's men . . . ! Well, the soldiers searched the house, in case we were hiding anyone. They threw bedding and books all about and broke some glassware when they were dragging a cupboard away from a wall in case there was a door behind it. They didn't find anything.

'They went away in the end, after warning us about what might happen to anyone caught helping fugitives. Treason, it would be: hanging and drawing for men and the stake for women. They herded us all together to tell us – made the servants listen too and fetched my grandmother downstairs again. Poor old Joshua Graves was grey with terror; I thought he was going to faint. After they'd gone, we all went into the parlour and knelt down and Mother read the psalm beginning *Deliver me from mine enemies, O my God: defend me from them that rise up against me*, and which goes on *Deliver me from the workers of iniquity and save me from bloody men.*

'For once,' said Eleanor, 'I was glad to listen to a psalm. A lot of honest people are going to need God's help in the near future, some of them for doing nothing worse than show a bit of Christian kindness to a few frightened lads who remind them of their own sons. But that wasn't all. Coming back, we went to buy that sugar and flour in Taunton and . . .'

'It was horrible!' burst out Dotty, dropping a pile of plates on the table with a clatter. 'Oh, those poor men, those poor men. I *knew* one of them; he come from the zame farm where my dad works . . .'

She sat down next to Eleanor and put her face in her hands. Eleanor put an arm round her. 'Fortunately,' she said wryly, 'we'd bought the stores first. But on the way out through Taunton, we went through the centre and there's a tavern, the White Hart . . . well, Kirke was sitting outside it, drinking wine.' Eleanor was speaking rapidly, as though to empty the words out of herself. 'Opposite the tavern a gallows had been rigged up, and men were being hanged. They were so young,' she added fiercely. 'Two of them were nothing more than boys. And they were so frightened and bewildered. They were crying and they were filthy dirty – I don't think they'd been given anything; not even a mouthful of water or a crust since they were taken. There wasn't even a chaplain . . . bloody Kirke! He isn't human!'

'Best not think about it too much.' Ricky had come quietly in at the back door, which stood open because the day was warm and the kitchen, with its glowing hearth, even warmer. He was wiping his feet. He too looked haunted but his voice was steadying. 'There's nothing to be done except look after ourselves as best we can. Is that a meat pie you've just taken out of that oven, Mrs Johns?'

'It is. It's the remains of the mutton roast we had yesterday. Nothing like a bit of roast for making a tender pie filling.' Mrs Johns heaved the dish on to the table. 'And good beans and cabbage to go with 'un. There now, Dotty, don't go pushing your plate away. You may not feel like eating now but one mouthful of this and you'll change your mind. Mrs Eleanor, if you'll say Grace and ask God's protection on us all, we'll fall to and be the better for it.'

After the meal, they all stayed together, clearing and washing up and then sitting down once more round the table which Dotty, encouraged by Mrs Johns, had just scrubbed. In times like these, the distinctions between kitchen and parlour became blurred. In the three days since the battle of Sedgemoor, Eleanor and Henrietta had abandoned the parlour and taken to eating and sitting in the kitchen, glad of companionship, obeying the instinct to draw together in the face of horror.

'It's nearly evening already,' Eleanor said, trying to speak cheerfully. 'We ate our dinner at a peculiar hour, Mrs Johns. I'm glad it didn't spoil the pie.'

'I timed it for Miss Henrietta, since I didn't think she'd be back for dinner at the regular time. One can't hurry away from a burial; it isn't decent.'

'The burial itself was over very quickly,' Henrietta said. 'As if people were afraid that even laying poor Philip to rest with any sort of ceremony might be counted as treasonable! But then Mrs Dyer wanted to sit and tell me all about going to Sedgemoor. She's been so brave! She amazed me.'

Eleanor gazed out of the back door. 'How peaceful everything seems. It's hard to believe in the things we saw this morning. Look, there's a family of starlings on our hazel bush. The fledgelings are bigger than their parents but the parents are still feeding them – Dotty, can you see them? Just look at the young ones with their beaks wide open . . . oh, they've flown off.'

'Something startled them.' Ricky half rose.

'The cats from Chugg's wander miles,' Mrs Johns said comfortably. 'No call to be jumpy, Mr Cuscombe.'

'There's a shadow, look!' said Eleanor sharply. 'There's someone in the garden!'

'Who's there? Who is it?' Ricky went to the door.

A frightened voice, that of a woman, said: 'Only me. Can I come in?' Ricky stepped quickly outside and came back a moment later, supporting Susanna Musgrave over the threshold.

'Susanna!' Eleanor rose to her feet. Susanna was grubby and untidy, her hair tangled and her dress covered with twigs and burrs as if she had been scrambling through bushes, and she appeared to be exhausted. 'Mrs Johns, bring some brandy,' said Eleanor. 'Susanna, whatever's the matter? No, it's all right, don't cry . . .'

'It's not all right!' Susanna let Ricky help her into a chair and sat there shivering. 'I shouldn't be here. I'm a danger to you but I didn't know where else to go. I've run away and I'm so frightened . . .'

'You have this, now.' Mrs Johns had brought the brandy. Susanna gulped it as if it were water.

'Mary's been arrested,' she said.

'Arrested? Lord have mercy, what's the world coming to? A lady like Miss Blake arrested!'

'But what for?' Henrietta asked blankly.

'Colonel Kirke's in Taunton,' Susanna said. 'Did you know?'

'Yes.' Eleanor did not elaborate.

'You were there,' said Susanna, 'the day Monmouth came. You saw Mary and myself and the girls present things to him. Someone reported it to Kirke. He sent men to the school today. They've taken Mary and twelve of the older girls away. They'd have taken me too only I was out in the grounds watching some of the little ones at play.' Susanna gulped more brandy. 'One of the maids came running to warn me. She said the younger ones were just to be sent home; she'd see after them but go,

Miss Susanna, she said to me, go, go, quick as you can, just as you are. So I did. I didn't dare go to the stable for a horse. I went straight through the bushes at the end of the grounds and up that bit of hill behind the school, keeping low, under the shelter of a wall. I got into some of the alleyways and brushed myself down . . .'

She glanced at her dress and let out a somewhat hysterical laugh. 'I've been through a few more bushes since then. I just . . . just scuttled along until I was out of the town. Then I went cross-country, through field and wood, and I came here because I couldn't think where else to go. I'm sorry. I shouldn't have come.'

'Of course you should,' said Eleanor. But she had gone very pale. So had Dotty. They were both remembering the words of Kirke's troopers at Peace-Through-Praise, explaining in detail what would happen to those who sheltered fugitives; and the sight of Kirke's ugly entertainment in Taunton.

Although the others had learned of these things at second hand, the effect on them was not much less. Henrietta and Mrs Johns exchanged worried glances, and Ricky went quickly outside again and walked all round the house before returning to say: 'No soldiers on the way here as far as I can see. We're safe enough so far.'

Susanna got up. 'I must go. I can't stay here, putting all of you in danger.'

It had the effect of making them all pull themselves together. 'You don't go anywhere till 'ee've some food inside 'ee,' said Mrs Johns, and was piling food on to a plate on the instant. 'When did 'ee last eat, I wonder?'

'Of course you can't go, just like that.' Eleanor too adopted a brisk tone. 'You must make plans first. You certainly ought to get well away from this area. You've an uncle somewhere along the coast, haven't you? A sailor, isn't he? Could he arrange a passage abroad for you?'

'He's a ship's captain.' Susanna ate thankfully. 'But I don't know where he lives or the name of his ship and he might be at sea, anyway. My grandparents might know more about him. They're in Dulverton. I'd better make for there.'

'Dulverton's miles,' said Eleanor seriously, 'and right in the middle of the moor. Do you know the way, Susanna?'

'Not really. I came to Taunton as a child and I haven't been back since.'

'You can't make Dulverton on foot,' said Ricky. 'It's too far.'

'What else am I to do?' Susanna flashed at him. 'I've got to get away. They've taken Mary to prison!'

'Easy now, easy. No call to get in a panic.'

Eleanor caught Henrietta's eye with a lift of an eyebrow, which said: 'Why not?'

'If Mrs Eleanor'll give me leave, and the use of the mare,' said Ricky calmly, 'I'll get 'ee to Dulverton, by ways no one'll expect. The best route'd be cross-country to Wiveliscombe where my cousins live and where we can put up, maybe in an inn in the town, so as to keep my cousins out of it. The inn'd be safe if we look respectable. They're

328

looking for a woman running away, not a decent lady travelling openly with her groom. Next day, we go on over the moor to the Exe valley and across it to Dulverton. It'll be a roughish ride with bogs to get round and hills to manage but we'd take some finding. We can make Wiveliscombe from here before sunset, and Dulverton by midday tomorrow if the weather don't fail us.'

A faint expression of hope had appeared on Susanna's face. 'If only . . . but I can't mix you up in this, any of you. Oh, my God, I feel as if I'm trapped in a nightmare. If you could lend me a horse and Ricky can tell me the way . . .'

'Well, I can't,' said Ricky frankly. 'I know the tracks because I've known them all my life. On your own you'd never do it.'

Shakily, but valiantly, Eleanor said: 'We're your friends, Susanna. We must see you safe away. I'll come as well. We'll all go. The more of a respectable party we look, the fewer suspicions we'll arouse. I daresay there won't be that many ordinary travellers about these days, but there'll be some – people are still visiting relatives and going to the markets. Mrs Johns, you'd better go to your sister in Chugg's and take Dotty with you, and Henrietta and I will set out with these two . . .'

'No.' Henrietta was trying to think clearly, and to suppress an inward cringing. 'We want to look innocent, so that we can go on living here in peace afterwards. I think . . . I'd better stay here. If Kirke's men come, I'll account for your absence, Eleanor, and mislead them. I'll tell them that you've gone on a visit to . . . to . . . I know, the Handleys. I'll say you were frightened by what you saw in Taunton today and wanted to get away.'

'That wouldn't be a lie,' said Eleanor with feeling. 'But . . . no, it's too dangerous for you, Hen.'

Henrietta shook her head. 'I'll be in no more danger, respectably at home, than out on the roads with Susanna. I can say I haven't seen her but you can't, not if you're caught in her company. Whoever stays here will be safer, I think.' She paused and then forced herself to add: 'If you like, I'll go and you can stay.'

'No, I'd rather go with Susanna. I've a preference for action,' said Eleanor.

'It's a sensible enough arrangement, either way,' Ricky observed.

'Ricky, about the horses.' Henrietta was still thinking. 'Splash and Dusty have been to Taunton and back today, a couple of hours each way. You can leave Splash at least, and take Captain. He's only had a short outing today.'

'Aye, that might be best.' Ricky nodded. 'Dusty'll have to tackle some extra work but she's sturdy enough; got a good strain of Exmoor pony in her, Dusty has. She'll go all day, even under a pillion.'

'I could be Eleanor's maid,' said Susanna. 'It would look right; a lady travelling with a groom and a maid. But . . . oh, I shouldn't let you do it, I know I shouldn't. If I bring any of you to harm, I'll never forgive myself.'

'My mother's helped fugitives, and look at Mrs Dyer!' said Eleanor. 'I'll tell you about Mrs Dyer as we go, Susanna. What they can do, we can do. We'll adopt Henrietta's plan. The thing is, we just mustn't get caught.'

There was a silence. Once again the terror of the soldiers' warning at her mother's home that morning echoed in all their minds. Dotty was biting her lips.

Then Mrs Johns said: 'You'd best take some food with you. I'll put up a flask of wine and some bread and cheese and what's left of the pie,' and Henrietta, determinedly bright, said: 'I'm sure Eleanor would never allow her maid to have a dirty face and a dress with burrs all over it. Come upstairs with me, Susanna, and we'll make you tidy.'

'I'll get the horses saddled,' Ricky said.

When the little party had gone, Henrietta closed the back door and said: 'That's that. We can only pray they get through safely. There's nothing more that we can do. Since I'm staying, of course, there's no need for you two to go to Chugg's. We'll have a quiet, normal evening.'

'You go and set in the parlour, Miss Henrietta,' Mrs Johns recommended. 'I'll bring 'ee a nice honey and milk posset to help 'ee sleep easy tonight.'

'It won't be dark for hours,' said Henrietta, 'and I'm not going to bed yet. We can all have possets, but I'll drink mine in the kitchen with you. I'll sit here and do a bit of stitching. I'm putting our little bridge and river device on that new linen we bought last month.'

'Well, that'll be companionable,' said Mrs Johns. 'And Dotty can get on with some mending. There's those napkins to finish, Dotty.'

'I left my sewing in the parlour. I'll get it,' Henrietta said.

She was trying to be natural. But her nerves were on the stretch and every sense was unusually alert. She was crossing the little hallway to the parlour when she heard the hoofbeats.

With her heart jolting in alarm, she darted into the dining room, which faced the front. Stepping to one side of the window, for all the world as though she had been engaged in nefarious adventures all her life, she peered stealthily out, seeing without being seen.

Yes. Half a dozen troopers, making straight for Broom Cottage. They had got Susanna away barely in time.

She rushed to the parlour, grabbed her work-basket, and ran to the kitchen. 'Soldiers are coming here. Mrs Johns, start making the possets. Dotty, just keep darning. We've got to look ordinary.'

'S . . . soldiers!' Dotty dropped a napkin on the floor. Henrietta picked it up, shoved Dotty back on to her stool and rammed the napkin into her hands, retrieving the needle before it could come unthreaded. 'Get on with it, Dotty!'

'But, Miss Henrietta, my hand's shaking so . . .'

'Then stop it shaking! Pull yourself together and go on darning as if it were the most important thing in the world or I'll personally break your neck!'

'Do as Miss Henrietta says,' said Mrs Johns kindly, as she poured milk into a pan and stirred the fire. At Peace-Through-Praise, Judith had been inclined to bully Dotty, but Mrs Johns had the virtue of preferring to bully her employers instead. With Dotty, she was gentle. 'No harm'll come to 'ee,' she said reassuringly. 'Don't 'ee be frightened.' As if mesmerised, Dotty began to stitch. 'There's something we've not thought of, Miss Henrietta,' Mrs Johns observed. 'If Mrs Eleanor's run off to stay with the Handleys, why didn't 'ee go with 'un?'

'I wasn't with Eleanor this morning at her mother's home or in Taunton. I couldn't see the need.'

'But it 'ud still be natural for you to go with her,' said Mrs Johns persistently. 'Tell 'ee what. You had a stomach ache come on this afternoon, that's what it is. That's what I'm making this posset for; to soothe it down. You didn't feel up to riding anywhere.'

'All right.' Henrietta sank into a chair and began on her embroidery. 'I wasn't well enough to travel. Oh, my God, they're here!'

Someone had begun pounding on the door. A man's voice shouted: 'Open in the name of the King!' Henrietta half rose but Mrs Johns shook her head. 'No, you'm not up to running to the door. I'll go. *Do* stop that sniffing, Dotty, there's a good girl.' She whisked her milk pan off the fire, and stumped flatfootedly out of the room. 'I'm coming! No need to bellow like a bull and knock the door down!'

She had left the kitchen door ajar and through the gap Henrietta and Dotty saw her partly open the front door, but plant herself massively in the aperture while she demanded to know the meaning of all this racket.

'Out of the way, woman.' The answering voice was clipped and correct. 'We demand entrance in the name of King James!'

'And who might you be and what business has King James with us?'

'I am Captain Luke Pargeter. This is my second-in-command Sergeant Wavetree, and these are my troopers. We are here on His Majesty's lawful business, seeking an escaped miscreant. Stand aside.'

'Well, 'ee'll find no escaped whatsits here, though I suppose I can't stop 'ee searching . . . well, if that don't beat all . . . !'

She had been shoved aside. Booted feet were in the hall. The clipped voice was ordering the Sergeant to take some of the men and search the garden and stables. The front door slammed. Then Mrs Johns, very red and indignant, was pushed into the kitchen ahead of the Captain and two troopers.

'They just forced their way in! I'm that sorry, madam!' Mrs Johns kept up a scolding tone, but a thin stream of sweat ran down each temple. Dotty dropped her work again and sat open-mouthed. Henrietta rested her hands on her embroidery, and said: 'Good evening, Captain. Forgive me if I don't get up but I have been unwell today. How can we help you?'

The Captain jerked his head at his troopers. 'Search the other rooms, downstairs and up. Now, ladies, attend to me if you please. First, your names.'

'I am Henrietta Whitmead. This is Mrs Johns, who cooks for us, and Dotty Larrimore who is maidservant here.'

'There's a Mrs Henderson who lives here too. You see that I am well-informed. Where is she?'

'She left this afternoon intending to go to our friends Sir John and Lady Handley near Washford. A spur-of-the-moment decision,' said Henrietta quietly. She reached out to Dotty, and patted her hand. 'She had visited Taunton this morning and she came home in great distress.'

'I were with her. Horrible, it was!' said Dotty, and then stopped with a gasp, afraid of having said the wrong thing.

Henrietta smiled at her and said: 'Quite. That is what Mrs Henderson said. They witnessed the hangings in the town, and also, Mrs Henderson was visiting her mother when soldiers burst in and searched the house, with no more reason than you have shown in coming here. She wanted to get away from Taunton. I would have gone too but I decided to wait until I felt better. I shall follow tomorrow or the day after.'

'I see.' Captain Pargeter was quite young, but his sharply chiselled features had the expression of one who is used to authority and he did not look as though he were capable of smiling. His incisive voice was that of a Londoner. He glanced towards the window, caught sight of his sergeant crossing the lawn, and pushed the casement open. 'Sergeant! Come here! So, Mrs Henderson was distressed at the sight of traitors to the King receiving their deserts, was she?'

'No,' said Henrietta frigidly. Her heart was still thudding but she must not show that she was afraid. Better show dislike instead, as though she had nothing to hide and cared nothing for him. Had she really said that whoever stayed at Broom Cottage would be safer? She felt anything but safe. 'She was distressed to see terrified young boys being choked to death. We are not interested in political matters, sir.'

'Indeed? So she set off for – Washford?' The Sergeant appeared at the window and Pargeter turned to him. 'Wavetree, you're local. Where is Washford and who is Sir John Handley?'

'Washford's near the coast, sir, not on it, zactly, but nigh to it, north-west of here, like, maybe eight or nine miles as the crow flies though the road b'ain't that straight . . .'

The Sergeant's slow West Country burr was a curious contrast to Pargeter's incisive voice, but Pargeter listened attentively, clearly respecting Wavetree's knowledge. 'And Handley?' he asked.

'Gentry, zur. Local gentry, living round those parts.'

'And are those parts anywhere near Dulverton?'

'No, zur, nowhere near. Dulverton's right inland, in the heart of the moor.'

'Thank you, Sergeant. Continue with the search.' Pargeter turned back to Henrietta. 'You're sure Mrs Henderson set off for Washford, are you, ma'am? Not Dulverton? And you're sure she didn't have a companion by the name of Susanna Musgrave, who has family in the town of *Dulverton*?'

He said the word as though he were hitting her with it. To her horror, Henrietta felt herself go hot all over. Black dots whirled in front of her eyes. She mustn't faint. *She must not faint.* 'Susanna?' she repeated.

'You know Susanna Musgrave, I believe. The assistant teacher at

Mary Blake's school in Taunton. Miss Blake, for your information, is under arrest.'

'*Under arrest?*' She had steadied herself now. She had no difficulty in bringing the words out with a properly flabbergasted intonation. It still seemed incredible. 'Whatever for?'

'For welcoming the traitor Monmouth with kindness and making gifts to him, signifying disloyalty to King James and support for his enemies. She involved her pupils and twelve girls have been taken in as well. It is known that both she and Susanna Musgrave are associates of yours. It has been reported that you were seen with her that day.'

'Who reported it?' The troopers had made short work of the downstairs rooms and could now be heard tramping about overhead. Well, they'd find nothing up there.

'That's not your business, ma'am. Susanna Musgrave has escaped and we are searching for her. Have you seen or heard anything of her? I warn you that to conceal information of her whereabouts would constitute a most serious offence.'

Memory had come to Henrietta's aid. 'Gale. Andrew Gale. Was he your informant?'

'I repeat, ma'am, that it isn't your business.'

'Because if it was, he probably said it out of spite. We are acquainted with Susanna and Mary, of course, but it's quite a slight acquaintance. I believe we spoke to them that day, yes, and I remember that Mr Gale saw us. Well, I once refused to marry Mr Gale and no doubt he resented it. If he was your informant, then this is just a piece of mischief-making.'

To her immense relief, the Captain looked a little disconcerted. Heartened, she pressed on. 'I assure you, there's no reason why Susanna should have come to us and in fact she has not. We have seen nothing of her, Captain Pargeter. I'm sorry we can be of so little help. Will you not take a little ale with us? And Mrs Johns, you and I and Dotty could all do with that warm posset.'

'In five minutes, my lamb,' said Mrs Johns, who had been listening by the stove, arms folded. She now unfolded them and put her milk pan back on the fire. Dotty rose and went sidling to help her, eyeing the Captain nervously and not venturing to speak.

The troopers came down the stairs and looked in at the kitchen. 'Nothing suspicious in the house, sir.'

'I see. I wonder how the others are faring. No, I've no time for ale, ma'am. Ah.' Someone was knocking at the back door and he opened it, admitting the Sergeant.

'We've not found much, zur, but the groom's not in his quarters and there are two horses gone from the stable, we reckon. At least there's two empty stalls with straw bedding down, pretty fresh.'

'The groom went with Mrs Henderson,' said Henrietta. 'They took a horse each.'

'I see.' Pargeter considered her coldly. 'If Susanna Musgrave contacts you, it's your duty to hold her and report her presence to the authorities in Taunton and I'd advise you to remember it. I have noticed that in this part of the world, people stick together even in the face of the law and I find it disgraceful. You need civilising.'

There seemed no point in answering this. Mrs Johns, her mouth shut tight, added honey to the posset. Sergeant Wavetree said: 'Zur!'

'Yes?'

'If she's got family in Dulverton, likely she's made straight for it, whether she came this way or no. Be a long walk but she might do it. She's a wiry enough lass; I know her by zight.'

'Ah, so do I,' agreed one of the troopers. 'She's not one of these big buxom wenches but . . .'

'That will do. It's grandparents that she has in Dulverton.' Pargeter frowned. 'Or so the girls said when we questioned them at the school. They said it was a long way. I'd have expected her to seek help somewhere but . . .' He stared round the kitchen as if expecting to see Susanna hiding behind a chair. 'But you may be right. Who knows what people, even young women, will undertake in this wild place? Yes. Dulverton.'

'They've gone,' said Mrs Johns, coming back from the dining room.

'To Dulverton.' Henrietta was standing up in front of the kitchen hearth but her legs felt so wobbly that she could almost believe in her own lie about being unwell.

'They won't catch them,' said Mrs Johns comfortingly. 'I was listening as they were getting on their horses. That there roan brute the Captain's made a nice mess of the front garden, too. Trampled all over them foxgloves Mrs Eleanor likes so much. But I heard enough. They're making for Dulverton right enough, but they're going by Tolland and Brompton Ralph, and that'll take them well north of Wiveliscombe. They won't come nigh our people.'

'No, they'll outpace them,' said Henrietta. She leant on the mantelpiece for support. 'They'll get to Dulverton first and be waiting. They can requisition fresh horses from farms along the way and they will. Oh, my God.'

Mrs Johns, grasping the point, sat down with a thud in her chair. 'If Miss Susanna gets there first, her folk'll hide her or get her away, that's for sure. But if that Pargeter and his men are there already and watching the paths in . . . some of them know her by sight. They'll get her, Miss Henrietta!'

'How long since the others left?' Henrietta looked up at the kitchen clock. 'They've been gone an hour. Only that long! It seems like a hundred years. I've got to go after them. They mustn't go to Dulverton, wherever else they go. I'll have to take Splash. Poor Splash; what a hard day's work for him.'

'But there's no one to escort 'ee, Miss Henrietta!'

'I'll have to do without. Fill a wineflask and put up a lot more bread and cheese and some ham – plenty, please, because Lord knows where we'll end up – and some corn for the horses and Dotty, fetch my cloak and hat. Bring it all out to the stable. Don't *argue*!' said Henrietta. 'It's life and death, maybe for all of us. *Hurry!*'

334

★ ★ ★

Ricky didn't like his 'young ladies' to saddle or unsaddle their horses for themselves but Henrietta sometimes did so all the same. She had learned to do it at Whitmead. Benjamin had taught her.

Splash was somewhat annoyed at being dragged from his hay-rack and his stable and obviously considered that Taunton and back was enough for one day but Henrietta, ignoring his laid-back ears, put on his tack, hauled him out into the yard despite his attempts to hang back at the end of a taut rein, and was tightening his girth by the time Mrs Johns and Dotty came out with the cloak and the provisions.

'Miss Henrietta!' Mrs Johns protested. 'You're never going to ride astride like a gipsy woman!'

'Yes, I am.' At Whitmead, as a girl, Henrietta had often kilted her skirts and ridden astride, sometimes even bareback. She had regretted the convention that once grown up, she must ride side-saddle. The cross-saddle was easier when one had to mount or dismount alone and a knee on each side of the horse gave one a stronger control. Fortunately, there were a couple of cross-saddles in the tackroom, provided so that Ricky could exercise any of the horses and find a saddle to fit. 'I'll be alone and I need speed,' she snapped.

She stuffed the provisions into the saddlebags, donned cloak and hat and was in the saddle without benefit of mounting block. 'Take care of yourselves, you two. If those troopers come back and ask questions, you know nothing. Be frightened and bewildered. Say I got panicky and rushed off after Mrs Eleanor and just left you by yourselves. Or you can both go to Chugg's after all.'

'Oh, Miss Henrietta, if only there were someone here to advise you!'

'Well there's only me and I'll have to advise myself. Goodbye!' cried Henrietta, and raising a hand to them, clattered out of the gate.

It was a soft evening, but with a little coolness in the wind and a haze of cloud to the north. There might be mist that night. For the moment, however, visibility was good. Henrietta took the downward zig-zag track which would lead her off the Quantocks and south-west towards Wiveliscombe. Pargeter and his men might not be taking the same route as herself, but they could be inconveniently close to it. She hadn't been to Brompton Ralph but their rides with Ricky had once or twice included Tolland and she knew where it was. As she rode, she was alert for any sign of the enemy.

But she saw nothing of them. She made the best speed she could, cantering where possible, cursing the fact that Splash was in a sulk and kept on trying to turn his head for home. Eleanor had chosen him because his skewbald coat was showy 'but Captain's a much better horse than you are,' Henrietta growled, attempting with whip and heel to impart a sense of urgency to her mount.

At a steady pace, it was roughly two hours to Wiveliscombe. If she pushed Splash hard enough she might just overtake the others before they got there. She hoped so because otherwise she would have to search Wiveliscombe for them. It wasn't a big place and she could only remember seeing one inn but still, it could be awkward. She would have to go to the inn, a young woman on her own, and inquire. 'Oh, Splash, will you get on with it!' she said angrily.

Splash, after a time, seemed to grasp that his rider was on serious business and that the stable and hay-rack for which he yearned were more likely to lie ahead of him than behind. He gave up sulking and began to go forward with a degree of energy. Henrietta found that she could remember the way quite easily. The paths nearer home were very familiar to her, and further on there were landmarks that she recognised: a huge hollowed oak, a ruined cottage with ivy creeping over its broken walls, a little hamlet beneath a hillside where a church stood.

She avoided the hamlet, for the fewer people who saw her, the better. Later, at a crossroad, she passed a gibbet where a hanged sheep-stealer had been left to dangle in chains, as a warning. It was a common enough sight which normally she would have passed without much interest but now she was on the wrong side of the law herself and she rode by shuddering and looking the other way.

One did things – like presenting a Bible to a handsome young duke – and thought of them just as unimportant outbursts of sentiment which didn't matter because they could have no real effect on anything. Susanna's Bible, Mary Blake's sword, even the embroidered banners, weren't likely to sway the outcome of a battle. And then, suddenly, they acquired a hideous significance. To the likes of Captain Pargeter they were Treason, writ large, with a capital T, laying one's quiet domestic world open to violation by terrible threats of captivity and death.

Urging Splash on at the best pace he could sustain over a long distance, Henrietta was so very frightened that the sensation was actually physical, like a genuine ache in the stomach. She would have sold her soul to be home in bed, with her head under the covers, and never to have heard of either Monmouth or Susanna Musgrave.

She passed along sunken lanes between banks thickly grown with meadowsweet and cow parsley and overhung with tangled scrub where dog-roses twined; thin paths, edged with foxgloves, leading over hillsides covered with heather and long, golden moor grass and dotted with clumps of gorse; paths almost invisible, winding through thick bracken where gnats bit and she had to pull bracken fronds to use as a fly switch, even though the evening was now cooling. She traversed steep tracks strewn with pinkish stones, where Splash must put his head down to climb, and descend with forelegs braced to keep his footing; beaten earth paths through woodlands of birch and beech and stunted oak; little stone bridges and brown purling fords. Now the shadows were lengthening and the expected mist was rolling in from the north-west, from the sea. And here was another hamlet where she must take care.

Henrietta drew rein and Splash, who had been kept at a steady lope for a very long time, stopped with relief.

She was at the top of a sloping track, looking down into the village. It was quiet, but not empty. Even from here she could see several women standing at their doors to chat to their neighbours and if she rode straight through they would certainly greet her and would be surprised to see her riding alone and astride. They would remember her and if the troopers came this way after all, and questioned them . . .

There was no obvious path round this village but she had better find one, just the same. The trouble was, it wasted time. She looked for a possible track and failed to find one. There was a stream to her right, running between steep and overgrown banks and she could see no way of crossing it, but there were cornfields to the left; she could try skirting the edge of those. She found a gate and then discovered that it was impossible to open it while riding Splash, who did not understand either how to back or to turn on his forehand.

Henrietta muttered several words she had heard her father use when annoyed, dismounted, led her aggravating horse through, shut the gate, got back into the saddle and put Splash into a canter along the edge of the corn. A few minutes later she discovered a path on the far side of the field, and saw from its direction that it would probably rejoin the track she had left, after bypassing the village. She urged Splash into a gallop. As they came round the last curve of the path a squat stone building came into sight with a man standing in the doorway.

Splash reared up, and she clutched at the saddle pommel and a handful of his brown and white mane. She stayed on somehow and pulled up, and the man himself came forward quickly to catch her bridle and make soothing noises. 'Steady, there, steady. Zilly old beast, thee be, then. Fancy a'shying at zight of a forge, then. Who puts thy shoes on for 'ee? The fairies?'

He looked rather like a pixie himself, being small and wiry and nothing like the conventional pattern of a blacksmith, until you looked again and saw the stoutness of his short legs and the massive pads of muscle on his shoulders and the size of the biceps in his arms.

'Thank you. I'm afraid we must have startled you. I'm so sorry,' said Henrietta. He went on holding her bridle and she wished he'd let go. This was the main track again and the forge was actually the last building in the village, but separated from the rest of it by about two hundred yards. The track she wanted ran on, invitingly lonely. 'I'm quite all right now,' she said pointedly.

'I've zeen 'ee afore,' said the smith maddeningly, smoothing Splash's nose. 'Zeen 'ee ride through with Mr Cuscombe, han't I?'

'Ricky Cuscombe? Are you a friend of his?'

'Known Ricky all my life, lass. Zilas Thorne, blacksmith, I be and I used to shoe his 'osses when he wur a huntsman. Lived in these parts, he did. You'll be one of his young ladies from up Quantox way. You trying to catch 'un up?'

The curiosity in his blue eyes was entirely benign. In Henrietta, panic began to change to hope. 'Has he been through here? How long ago?'

'Not ten minutes. His mare had a loose shoe and I fixed it for 'un. In a right taking, Mr Cuscombe were, and the lasses with him all in a fuss at the delay. My wife gave 'un scones and cream to pass the time, and we wouldn't do that for just anyone.'

'Ten minutes! I'll catch them yet! Forgive me, Mr Thorne, but I must go on, quickly. Please let go of my rein.'

'Gently, lass. Let the horse get 'un's breath. They were taking it steady; 'ee'll catch up quick enough, don't fret.'

'You say you're a friend of Mr Cuscombe's?'

'Zince the both of us were young.'

'Then, you haven't seen him, or the girls with him, or me. If anyone asks. You haven't seen any of us. Will you say that?'

'Ah. I reckoned zummat were up; you ridin' so hard after 'un, all alone and dodging round the village like, and thy face as white as lambswool. Troublous times.' Mr Thorne shook his head gravely. 'I'll axe 'ee no questions.' He stepped back, releasing the bridle. 'No, I han't zeen 'ee, nor Mr Cuscombe nor any young ladies.'

'Thank you. God's blessing on you,' said Henrietta, gathering her reins.

'And God go with 'ee.'

'Thank you. Goodbye,' said Henrietta, and once more put Splash into a gallop, although this time with more caution. If he shied again and she came off and lost hold of him, her whole errand might be lost as well.

But she caught up with her quarry only a quarter of an hour later. She saw them in the distance, on the brow of an open hill, looking back at the sound of hoofbeats. She stood up in the stirrups, waving and shouting, afraid that they would mistake her for an enemy and bolt for it, but they waited. She thundered up to them and pulled the grunting Splash to a halt.

'Miss Henrietta!' Ricky was both alarmed and concerned. 'What's happened?'

'You changed your mind and decided to come?' asked Eleanor. On Ricky's pillion, Susanna remained silent, her face pinched with worry.

'Troopers came to Broom Cottage.' Rapidly, she told them what had happened. 'Whatever you do, don't go to Dulverton. I'm so thankful I caught you up before you reached Wiveliscombe. I don't think it's safe even to stay in an inn here. Mrs Johns heard them say they were going another way but there could be troopers anywhere, these days; and if Susanna's description has been given out, nowhere that's public is safe.'

'But where *can* I go?' cried Susanna. 'There's only my uncle and I don't know where to find him or even if he's ashore!'

'What's his name?' Ricky asked. He touched a heel to Dusty and began to lead them down the hill. 'We'd best not sit here on the skyline. Not that it'll matter for long; that fog'll be here in a minute.' He nodded towards the north, where the hills were fading out of sight. 'We've got to get into shelter of some sort soon.'

'My uncle's name is Captain Richard Musgrave,' said Susanna. 'And that's about all I know, except that he sails from one of the Exmoor ports but I don't know which.'

Ricky was counting off names on his fingers. 'Watchet, Dunster,

338

Minehead, Porlock or Lynmouth, it'll be. But if he's got his own ship, likely his name's known all along the coast. We can ask. But meanwhile, what do we do tonight? It looks as if I'll have to pull my cousins into it, which I'll be sorry to do. But I've got to get you ladies under cover before that fog comes up.'

They could smell it already, tingling in their nostrils, and the first tendrils of mist were drifting round the trees of the next hillside.

'Have your cousins got a barn?' Henrietta asked.

'Aye, that they have. But what about food? Supper we've had and we've some food with us, but there's all tomorrow. We'll have to buy something to eat, or ask for it somewhere.'

'The barn'll do to sleep in,' said Henrietta. 'If only there's hay or straw or something to keep us warm and as for food, I've brought enough to last us all at least until tomorrow night.'

Mist deadened sound. The horses' hooves seemed muffled and in the little wood through which they were riding, there was only the faint drip, now and then, of water from the motionless leaves. Even the birds were hushed.

Henrietta, riding at the rear of the tired little cavalcade, felt as though she were a ghost, in a party of phantoms. Her eyes were sore with sleeplessness and she was cold. The morning was chill and she had had nothing hot to eat or drink since yesterday, and the hay in the barn where they had slept, unknown to Ricky's cousins, hadn't been as snug as they had hoped. She rested a cold hand on Splash's warm skewbald neck. His mane was dewed with grey droplets just like Henrietta's own dark curls, but unlike Henrietta, he didn't seem to mind.

Ricky, leading the way with Susanna perched behind him, quietly drew rein. 'Are we lost?' inquired Eleanor.

'Best keep your voice down, Mrs Eleanor. No, I know where we are and we're about to come on to the track between Tolland village and Brompton Ralph. Pray God the soldiers went this way last night and b'ain't hanging about yur.'

'Why should they be?' asked Eleanor.

'They shouldn't, but it won't do to be careless.' Ricky glanced from side to side, at the trees. 'Can't be sure they *all* went to Dulverton, can we? When there's a manhunt, a good officer spreads his men wide, 'specially if he b'ain't sure which covert his quarry's in. Bit of wind stirring now. This is a sea-fog that's rolled inland. Be gone in half an hour, this will.'

'Can we get off the track?' asked Henrietta quietly, urging Splash up close to them.

'Not so easy, just hereabout,' Ricky said. 'It's either crops or rough heath with bogs. There's just this one little wood. Come on. I can't hear anything like other horses near. Let's get this stretch over.'

As Ricky had so astutely surmised, the enemy had not all gone to Dulverton.

'Coming here?' Sir John Handley had said, when Pargeter arrived at

Handley Court the previous evening. 'Eleanor Henderson? Well, she'd be welcome any time, but she hasn't arrived yet. Nor have we seen anything of Susanna Musgrave. You'll stay the night, of course, Captain Pargeter? If you want to look round the house, and make sure I'm telling the truth, I've no objection.'

Pargeter availed himself of both invitations, conducting the search politely but as thoroughly as possible, in view of the fact that it was already dark. He also collected all the servants, from Robbins the butler and Sapphira her ladyship's maid down to the spitboy and the grooms, in the firelit kitchen, and warned them what to expect if they had knowledge of this affair and didn't instantly reveal it but their faces just gaped blankly at him. However, he took some comfort from the fact that Eleanor did not arrive. It looked as though her friend Miss Whitmead had been lying.

'Dulverton,' he said to the two men he had brought with him. 'It'll be Dulverton, as we guessed the first time. That's where she's gone, and the Musgrave woman with her or I'm a Dutchman. They may be in Sergeant Wavetree's hands by now.'

He left early the next morning, with thanks for the hospitality and a final warning against the heinous crime of shielding fugitives.

'I'm a law-abiding gentleman, Captain. If we come across Miss Musgrave, rest assured we shall do the right thing,' said Sir John, and Lady Handley, standing by in her unsmiling fashion, inclined her head in agreement.

Riding away, with a scarf over his nose against the dank mist, Captain Pargeter wondered if they meant it. He didn't trust anyone, not anyone at all in this county of Somerset which had given the impression, from the first moment he set foot in it, of having a life, a culture, of its own and a hidden lattice of friendships and loyalties capable of rendering laws as impotent as fish in a net.

'We'll make straight for Dulverton now, to join up with Wavetree,' he said. 'Flaxton here says he knows the way.'

'Zo I do, zur,' said the trooper who had described Susanna as not being a big buxom lass.

'Even in that?' Pargeter pointed ahead to where a low drift of cloud obscured the hills.

Flaxton, who was young and cheerful, laughed. 'It'd be mortal easy to miss our path in that but there's a breath of wind already. It'll lift soon. If we take it at an easy jog, it'll be gone avore we have to ride into it.'

'An easy jog. Hm. How long will it take to reach Dulverton from here?'

'Be a matter of six hour, zur.'

'Damn,' said Pargeter.

Had he made an error of judgement? From the start, it had been more likely that Susanna would be found there. Perhaps he should have gone straight there himself. But Sergeant Wavetree, armed with the warrant, was more than capable of arresting her or spurring the parish constable of Dulverton into mounting a search and there had been something definitely odd about Eleanor Henderson's sudden departure from home. He'd wanted to check the story and calling on Sir John Handley wasn't a task to be delegated to a sergeant.

'Have 'ee thought, zur,' said Flaxton, as they rode on, with a breeze now rustling the leaves on the trees and the mist beginning to flow past, 'maybe Mrs Henderson's just slipped off to meet a lover, with a sympathetic groom to escort her?'

'I hope not,' said Pargeter sincerely.

They were safely past the dangerous stretch between Tolland and Brompton Ralph and moving briskly along a good valley track between steep, rounded hills where corn was ripening on the slopes. A few patches of woodland clung to the hillsides, the tree-trunks rising, resolutely perpendicular, out of dramatic inclines. A little mist still hung about on the higher ground but the weather was clearing fast. Thin sunlight broke through the cloud to warm them.

There was little conversation, however, for they were all anxious, except for Eleanor, who seemed suddenly to be enjoying herself.

'It's an adventure,' she said to Henrietta. Bits of hay clung to her clothes; her hair needed combing and her face was white with tiredness, but her blue eyes were blazingly alive. 'Well, isn't it? This is a change from sitting round the fire embroidering rivers and bridges on napkins, if you like!'

'I wish I *were* sitting over my embroidery,' said Henrietta in heartfelt tones, and Susanna, with a sigh, said: 'You should be. I shouldn't have let any of you come.'

'Sensible folk avoid adventures, Mrs Eleanor.' Ricky had heard and reined back to say so. 'If we ride into the arms of they troopers, we'll all end up in Dorchester gaol. That's where they're taking the prisoners, so I hear. That'll be an adventure and a half, that will.'

But Eleanor only laughed and made Captain prance. Henrietta had that morning suggested that they ride their usual mounts but Eleanor had pleaded for one more day on Captain. 'I like his spirit so much. Please, Hen?'

Splash was sulking again and as she kicked him along, Henrietta was irritated at being denied her own horse, but could well understand why Eleanor found Captain such a pleasant change. She looked sidelong at her friend and was surprised at her own depth of feeling for her. Hitherto, she had been by turns dazzled by Eleanor's spirit and beauty, swept away by her lovemaking, annoyed and even alarmed by her possessiveness, and then filled with a sense of responsibility for her, for there were times when all these attributes – the spirit, the beauty, the passion, the jealousy – seemed like perilous flaws which made Eleanor vulnerable to hurt, and from which a friend must strive to protect her.

But at this moment, watching Eleanor sitting so straight and easily on Captain's back, hearing her laugh in the face of danger, Henrietta knew that she loved her.

Presently, the mist melted even from the hilltops, and the sun began to beat strongly down. Away to the west they could see the hills rising to the purple uplands of Exmoor, and beginning to twinkle in the heat. Ricky was leading them by an indirect route, taking the least-used paths, in order, he said, to bring them to Washford from the inland side.

As time went on, they noticed that whenever they passed a side track leading downwards, their mounts exhibited a marked desire to follow it. 'The horses are thirsty,' Ricky said. 'There's a place near here where we can get down to a ford and let them drink.'

A few yards further on, a path appeared, sloping down to the left and he led them on to it. They descended through a little wood of stunted oak, to where a translucent brown stream ran over a pebbly bed. The horses splashed eagerly into it and their riders let them drop their heads to drink.

'We can get off in a minute, when they're out of the stream, and get a drink ourselves,' Ricky said.

They were back on the bank, taking turns to hold each other's horses so that they could all scoop up palmfuls of the clear, cold water, when they heard the sound of other horses, and jingling bits on the road above.

The mare Dusty stiffened, ears pricked. Ricky rose quickly from where he was kneeling by the brink, and gripped her nostrils. 'Do the same, all of 'ee. Don't let them whinny!' he whispered.

They waited, silently, peering upwards. Above, was a line of bright light where the trees ended at the track, and they could see the legs of the horses passing along it, and the booted feet of the riders.

'Soldiers,' said Ricky in a low voice.

Henrietta said shakily: 'One of the horses was roan. Pargeter had a roan.'

'Plenty of horses like that about,' said Ricky.

'But it might be him. He could have tried Handley Court instead of going straight to Dulverton,' said Henrietta.

'They've gone back along the way we came,' whispered Eleanor. 'We'd have met them if we'd gone on. As it is, they're past and out of the way. We can go straight on. It's no more than a mile and a half from here.'

'What if they've left someone there?'

'We've got to go on now,' said Ricky. 'Not to Handley Court if it b'ain't safe, but to the coast. We'll find somewhere safe to stay while I make some inquiries about this uncle of yours, Miss Susanna. Can't hear any sound of they troopers now but I do know a way hereabouts of getting off the main track and maybe we should, if there's going to be troopers all over the bloody place. We can go on over the ford here and up through the wood the other side. It brings us out on to a hill. We can go over it to Handley Court, or branch off for Washford village and the coast.'

They were out of the trees and jogging up on to the shoulder of a grassy hillside when they heard the shouts.

For once, Ricky's knowledge of short-cuts and alternative paths had failed him. The path he had chosen was little-used, certainly, so much so that it was almost invisible. But it crossed land which was too open for safety. Anyone on it was visible for a considerable distance. They had been seen. Three helmeted men, shouting and hallooing, were galloping after them, headlong, straight across the cornfield that spread over the lower part of the hillside.

'Oh, God. It *is* Pargeter!' Henrietta gasped.

'And they've seen us,' Ricky muttered. 'My fault! My damned fault! Should have stopped under cover by the river for an hour or so.'

'What do we do now?' demanded Eleanor.

'I knew it. I'm sorry. I'm sorry,' Susanna moaned.

'Handley Court's our only chance,' said Eleanor recklessly. 'We'll have to risk it. It's not a mile off now. I'll give us an excuse to get there at full gallop!' As she spoke, she was kicking Captain and simultaneously jagging his mouth. He half-reared, prancing indignantly in protest at these contradictory signals. Eleanor clutched at her hat as if to keep it on, removed a hatpin from it and brought her hand down swiftly, driving the pin into Captain's rump. He bucked once and bolted.

'Oh, dear God!' said Ricky and with that they were all tearing in pursuit. Ricky, in genuine alarm, was shouting advice at the top of his voice. 'Bring 'un round in a circle, Mrs Eleanor! Haul 'un round! Or jump off, jump off for the love of Heaven!'

As they tore over the crest of the hill, Henrietta managed a brief glance back and saw that the troopers were no longer gaining. And Handley Court was indeed close. There were its chimneys below. Captain was still going full tilt. Eleanor's hat had blown off and she was leaning back in the saddle apparently trying to rein in, but Henrietta saw her let go with her right hand for a moment and make another jabbing movement behind the saddle. Her infuriated mount accelerated, displaying a turn of speed which would have done credit to his Arabian sire as he hurtled downhill and veered on to a track which led straight to the gates of Handley Court.

There was a porter's lodge, but by day, the gates commonly stood open. Within them, the track curved elegantly through a small park with grass and scattered trees. The porter emerged from his lodge but jumped aside as Eleanor and Captain tore past. Captain ignored the curve and thundered straight on across the grass. Splash, leaving his laziness behind in the excitement of the chase, overtook Dusty with her double load, and was next through the gates. Henrietta, urging him on, saw the front door of the house ahead and people already running from it. Someone had recognised that whoever was arriving was out of control. They were trying to head Captain off into the corner where the house met the stableyard wall, so that he would be forced to a stop.

He saw them and plunged sideways to avoid them, plunged again to avoid a tree, skittered off balance, feet going one way and body another, and fell, rolling, with Eleanor beneath.

Henrietta was drawing rein at the place almost at once, but Sir John Handley was before her, already kneeling at Eleanor's side, along with an exclaiming woman servant and the butler, Robbins, who was incongruously clutching a silver-polishing cloth. Captain was on his feet again, snorting, red-rimmed nostrils spattered with foam, eyes rolling at the two grooms who were attempting to catch him. Eleanor seemed to be unconscious.

The troopers must be almost at the gates. Henrietta said shortly: 'We have Susanna Musgrave with us. She's wanted by the King's men and they're on our heels.'

Sir John glanced up, first at Henrietta and then past her to where Ricky was pulling up with Susanna still behind him. His eyes narrowed. 'Get her into the house. Ask my wife to help. Quick. Robbins, tell those grooms to leave the horse and fetch a door or a hurdle or something to use as a stretcher.'

Henrietta dragged Susanna down from the pillion and ran her to the house. Lady Handley was standing at the open door. Swiftly, Henrietta repeated what she had just said to Sir John. Lady Handley pulled them in and shut the door after them instantly. Her face was as hard as ever, but her voice was reassuring.

'We know about it. Pargeter was here. Don't be afraid, Susanna. We don't betray our friends. Give me your hat and cloak, quick. That's it. Dear Lord, where have you been in them? They're filthy. Never mind. Go through to the back parlour, out of the window and into the shrubbery. It joins on at the far end to a stretch of our woodland. Get into the wood and hide. Up a tree if necessary – like our good King Charles did, when he was a prince and the Roundheads were hunting him. You're young and spry enough. Make haste!'

Susanna was trembling but obeyed without a word. Lady Handley, the dirty hat and cloak in her hands, shouted up the stairs for her maid Sapphira. Henrietta, peering through a window beside the front door, saw that Pargeter and the two troopers with him had arrived but had been halted by Sir John, close to the knot of people round Eleanor who still lay where she had fallen. Somebody had after all caught Captain and was leading him away. She glanced questioningly round at Lady Handley and at the plump maidservant who was now descending the stairs.

'Here's Sapphira,' Lady Handley said. 'Sapphira, you were here when Captain Pargeter said he was looking for Miss Musgrave.'

'Yes, madam,' said Sapphira, looking curiously at the battered clothes her mistress held.

'She's just arrived, pursued by troopers, and we're hiding her. She was on a groom's pillion. Now then, Sapphira, you used to be an actress.'

'Yes, madam.'

'You're about to have the opportunity of a lifetime.' Lady Handley shot out a well-manicured hand, seized hold of the startled Sapphira's hair and proceeded to make an untidy mess of it. 'Now put these things on. You are going to be the girl who arrived on Ricky's pillion. You're

Mrs Eleanor's maid and your name is . . . is . . . Nellie. Yes, Nellie Merridew.'

'But, madam, them troopers saw me yesterday and questioned me, along of all the other servants!'

'Pargeter's coming towards the house with his men,' said Henrietta. 'They saw you in the kitchen, by firelight, in a crowd. They'd hardly take note of your face unless you had a squint or you were a raving beauty. They won't remember you. You're Nellie Merridew and you're in a state because your mistress has had an accident. Run out, go to Mrs Eleanor, and act as if you *were* her maid! Pretend you only came into the house to call help. Use a Somerset accent. Do as you're bid or I'll turn you off. Henrietta, go and make sure that the parlour window's shut. Sapphira! *Now. Go!*'

He'd made a fool of himself, Pargeter concluded grimly. He stood surrounded by people exclaiming and calling Mrs Henderson's name, and the girl who'd been on the groom's pillion was only Mrs Henderson's maid, and was a silly hysterical wench who'd first, apparently, rushed screaming indoors and then rushed screaming out again to crouch beside her mistress, crying on God to bring her round and cursing that there vicious horse. Lady Handley was telling one of the grooms to ride to Washford for the physician and Sir John was barking orders about carrying Mrs Henderson indoors. She was still unconscious, with blood trickling from a cut on her head. And Henrietta Whitmead was coldly explaining that no one had been running away from the troopers.

'We meant to wait for you, though we couldn't imagine what you were hallooing at us for. But a rabbit shot across the path and frightened Eleanor's horse. The horse was off as if he'd been fired from a cannon.'

'But how is it that you're here, ma'am?' Pargeter still had lingering suspicions. 'We left you yesterday sitting at home saying you were ill.'

'I'd *been* ill, Captain Pargeter. Ladies occasionally are, for a day or two. But I was beginning to recover when you came and I must say your visit disturbed me very much. Searching the house and bullying us like that. I took horse and decided to go after Mrs Henderson.'

'Astride, ma'am?'

'I frequently ride astride,' said Henrietta untruthfully. 'This is very rough country, as you may have noticed. We leave London ways behind, in Somerset.'

'That I have noticed!'

'Miss Henrietta caught us up at a forge, somewhere back there.' Ricky joined in, waving a casual arm in the general direction from which they had come. 'My mare were losing a shoe or we'd have reached yur last night. Mist come up and we all put up for the night in some godforsaken cottage or other. Look at the mare's shoes, if 'ee don't believe me,' he added unpleasantly. 'Her off fore, it be; see for thyself. I don't know what the world's coming to; decent ladies frightened half out of their senses by soldiers of the King – King's men ought to know

345

better in my opinion – and folk making a plain honest visit, being chased round the countryside like deer by a bloody hound pack!'

'That'll do. Watch your manners, my friend.' More to preserve his dignity than anything else, Pargeter signed impatiently to Trooper Flaxton to examine Dusty's feet. Flaxton did so and straightened up, shaking his head. 'New shoe on off fore; the rest are all pretty worn.'

'Satisfied?' said Sir John sarcastically. 'I must say I'd be glad if you'd all leave. We have a very sick young woman here to look after and frankly, you are not helping.'

Susanna Musgrave was not here. 'We've made a false cast,' said Pargeter to his men. 'We'll waste no more time. Flaxton, once more, be good enough to show us the road to Dulverton.'

'Thank God. They've gone.' Sir John strode into the parlour where Eleanor had been laid on a sofa. Strained faces turned towards him.

'Truly? We're safe?' said Lady Handley. Her face was much less hard than usual. Robbins was dabbing a wet brow and two of the maidservants were holding hands, like children. They were all, every one of them, more frightened than ever before in their lives.

But no one had faltered; no one had let the others down. As Sir John said: 'Yes, they've truly gone and good riddance,' there were sighs of relief. 'How is Mrs Henderson?' he asked.

'She's coming to,' said Henrietta.

Eleanor's eyelids were flickering. As Henrietta turned back to her and spoke her name, they opened.

'Hen? Wh . . . where am I? What happened?'

'You fell off your horse and knocked yourself out but you're all right. You're safe in Handley Court. Can you remember? We were coming here.'

Eleanor raised a hand to her head. 'I can't . . . remember much. Oh, how my head aches.'

'Have you any other pain?' asked Henrietta anxiously, kneeling down beside the sofa. 'Are you hurt otherwise?'

'No. I've no other pain. I . . .'

Terror suddenly filled the brilliant blue eyes. A hand came up and clutched at Henrietta.

'I can't move my legs! I can't feel them, even! Hen!'

'It's all right, I'm here. The Handleys are here and the physician has been sent for.'

'But what if . . . Hen, don't leave me, promise you won't leave me!'

'Hush, hush.' Henrietta was painfully aware of their audience. 'I shall always be your good friend and I will look after you as long as you need it,' she said, in a carefully prim voice.

As she spoke, prescience broke over her like a wave. Because of the nature of their bond, the promise she had just made was as binding as though she had said *I will* to a man, in church. She had bound herself to stay by Eleanor's side until she was no longer needed. They all

346

understood, Eleanor as well as any of them, what loss of feeling and movement in the legs could mean. It could mean a broken back and in that case, the sufferer would never stand on his or her two feet again. Eleanor feared it, but Henrietta knew. She would have to stay with Eleanor now, until death did them part.

Chapter Twenty-Six
The Last Wave

Benjamin Whitmead had once spent a month in the house in Wych Street, but that was getting on for thirty years ago. He would have said, if anyone had asked him, that he didn't remember the house at all, yet to his surprise he found it instantly familiar. The same rug lay on the polished floorboards of the hall; the stairs ahead of him were lit by the same shaft of light from the landing window. The place even smelt the same, of beeswax and books. It was as though time had run backwards.

He had lagged behind the rest of his family. In her late seventies, of course, his mother Charity was much too frail to make the journey from Essex, and his four children had not come either. He had left the elder ones to deal with the work of the harvest, while his youngest son was still at school. But his sister Cherry had come with her husband John, and although his other sister Frances and her husband were both dead, their son Miles, a real foxy-haired Whitmead even though his surname was actually Cutler, had accompanied him, too.

Crossing the hall in their wake, he joined them as they mingled with the other mourners into the biggest of the downstairs rooms where the butler was drawing back the curtains to let in the bright October day. Once more, as he had tried to do at the graveside, he attempted to murmur condolences to the lean, blue-jawed man whom he had recognised at once, despite the lapse of time, as Matthew and once more, Matthew, as if by accident, turned away just as he approached. He found himself offering his sympathy instead to Matthew's half-sister Caroline, and her husband and distant cousin, Hugh Browne.

Hugh was his usual amiable self, but Caroline, always somewhat reserved towards Ben, had of late become formidable. He had seen her fairly often in the days when she and Hugh visited Essex frequently to see Hugh's parents. But time went on; people didn't keep their parents for ever and once Hugh's had gone, Hugh had simply sold the Essex property, in which he was not interested. Ben hadn't set eyes on Caroline for the last four years and was startled to find that she had altered from a sturdy but diffident woman into this stately matron with a bust like a ship's figurehead and the presence of a good-natured but very majestic queen.

She bent a gracious head. 'It was kind of you to come, Benjamin. We appreciate it.'

'It's a sad day for you. I'm so sorry.' She bent her head again, dismissing him and Hugh gave him a smile, and he moved on to make way for somebody else. He found himself alone, standing at the side of the room, searching the faces. Searching, stupidly, for the one person who was missing. He knew quite well that he wouldn't find her. He had sought her without success already, when they were all standing round the grave.

Charles Whitmead, retired ship's captain, formerly of the East India Company, had been laid in his last resting place, in a churchyard close to the River Thames down which he had so often set sail for the east. But his daughter Henrietta, Matthew's twin, had not come to her father's funeral.

It was incredible. How could such a thing be? It was nearly three decades since he last saw Henrietta, and he was missing her, aching with it, as though she were a tooth just drawn and the socket was still raw.

Which was ridiculous, for a lifetime lay between them now; the long, calm years of his married life – astonishingly happy after all – at Whitmead; the birth of his children, of whom four were thriving yet; his father's death and then, most grievously, the death of his dear Beatrice at thirty-seven, along with a stillborn child. That was nine years ago now and he had given up grieving; but his hair had begun to turn grey soon after he was widowed, and he still, quite often, caught himself thinking: I must tell that to Beatrice, or turning round to speak to her. It ought to be Beatrice he was missing now.

But it was not. Bewildered, in need of something or someone normal and familiar to steady him, he looked round for a member of his own family to talk to. He could only see Miles, who was talking to Matthew and apparently being introduced to Matthew's family. Hugh had kindly pointed them out when the family were gathering at the church for the service. 'That's Matthew's wife Deb, and their son and daughter-in-law are with them. The daughter-in-law is called Araminta and the son's called James.'

He couldn't say he was impressed with them. Deb and Araminta looked like a pair of meek mice and James struck him as a supercilious whelp; at this moment, he was sipping wine as though the vintage didn't meet with his approval.

He didn't know whether Matthew had cold-shouldered him deliberately or not, but it had made him uncomfortable and he didn't want to incur another rebuff. He turned away and discovered Hugh now in conference with a couple of City gentlemen. A word or two drifted his way; they were discussing East India Company business. Ben moved towards them.

Life played curious tricks. Once, he had been so much in love with Henrietta, but it was Hugh, and not himself, who had married one of Charles' daughters. After his parting from Henrietta, Ben had wanted nothing to do with the London family, and his father had never liked Charles anyway. But the Brownes had chosen to cultivate Charles, who had eventually helped young Hugh Browne to a post in the London office of the East India Company. Here Hugh displayed such promise

350

that at the age of only twenty-two he had been accepted as Caroline's husband. The wedding took place in London, and Ben did not attend it, although Cherry and Frances did.

He loved Beatrice. She was a dear girl and he didn't care a straw for Henrietta any more. And yet, the old sense of hurt still lingered, detached from its cause, like a chicken which persisted in running about after it had been beheaded. It was strong enough to make him go on avoiding contact with the London family. He did not go even to Cousin Ninian's funeral. When Christabella died, he didn't find out for months afterwards, because nobody troubled to tell him.

But when Caroline sent word that Charles was dying, Benjamin paused to take stock of himself. Charles Whitmead, said to be a devil with the women, but wealthy, successful, a famous ship's captain and a shipowner, whose name was widely known, was a landmark in the family and his going was not something to be ignored. Now that he thought about it, Ben's boyhood romance with Henrietta seemed very long ago, very trivial. Yes, he had said to himself. This time, he would attend. Caroline would appreciate it if he paid his last respects to her father.

Standing casually at Hugh's elbow, waiting to join in the conversation, he heard the talk turn to the disposition of Charles' wealth. Caroline and Matthew would be very rich, now, one of the City gentlemen remarked jocularly. No one mentioned Henrietta. It was assumed, apparently, that her father's will would not include her.

She was still alive; he knew that much. She lived a long way from London and had remained unmarried; he knew that, too. The projected marriage with a man called Gale hadn't taken place and Henrietta had become estranged from her family. Caroline wrote to Cherry quite often, but that was all she had ever said about her sister.

. And now . . . He had come here sincerely believing that he had left his youthful sweethearting behind, but one foot across the threshold of the house which once had been Henrietta's home, and she was long ago and trivial no longer. He kept on seeing her in his mind: Henrietta with the blue-black curls and dark eyes; that lovely skin with its touch of duskiness; and her sweet, brave smile. How could he have forgotten that smile? She had been both as feminine as a rose and as gallant as a soldier, his little cousin Henrietta, his first love. And, he would have said, as loyal as a good soldier should be. He had never understood . . . never understood . . .

And with that, he discovered that he had got to understand. Today or never. While Beatrice was alive, he couldn't have asked; nor in the first years of mourning for her. But now, here, in this room, like a dragonfly emerging from a chrysalis, the time had come. He had only to decide to whom he should put his question.

The answer to that was unexpectedly easy. Caroline might know, but although he had now caught sight of her, she was in the midst of a group of ladies. Besides, a man talked more easily with another man, and while he was about it, he would also challenge Matthew's inexplicable hostility. If it were not his imagination, then he would find out the reason. He murmured an excuse to Hugh, and made straight for Matthew – who presented his back and walked away.

It was blatant, a snub there was no mistaking. He certainly wasn't imagining things. Striding after him, Ben laid a hand on Matthew's arm. 'May I have a word with you, in private, please?'

Matthew quivered, glancing down at Benjamin's hand as if it were an insect he would like to flick off his sleeve. 'I have no wish to speak to you, in private or out of it.'

'I'm sorry to hear it and I can't pretend to understand your attitude. But the matter is important. I must insist.'

'A gentleman cannot start a quarrel at a funeral,' said Matthew in an undertone. 'Very well. There is a small room across the hall which we can use.'

The small room had been Charles' study. It had been made ready in case anyone wished for a private conversation. A small fire burned on the hearth, easy chairs waited on either side, and straight chairs were arranged in businesslike fashion round what had been Charles' desk. Matthew and Ben, by tacit consent, took seats on opposite sides of the desk. 'Well?' said Matthew.

Benjamin's brow furrowed. 'Look, I don't understand at all why you are being so discourteous, and presently I shall ask you to explain it, but there is something else which to me is more important and I wish to ask you about that, first.'

'Indeed? And what is this something?'

'It will seem a strange inquiry, I expect. It even seems strange to me. It was all so long ago. But . . .'

He was losing himself in words. What use was it, after all, to dredge up the past like this? Matthew's inimical stare was difficult to endure. Matthew Whitmead, lawyer, for whatever reason, quite obviously regarded Benjamin Whitmead, gentleman farmer, with the utmost dislike, not to say contempt.

'It's about Henrietta,' he said, beginning again. 'Is she not coming? I had hoped to see her here.'

'Henrietta? You *hoped* to see Henrietta?' said Matthew brusquely. 'She is not expected. She lives with a crippled woman friend and never leaves her side. Why did you want to see her?'

'Why? Can you ask that?'

'And what does that mean?'

'My wife Beatrice was very dear to me,' said Benjamin, slowly. 'But once, I hoped to marry Henrietta and she called it off and said she was going to marry somebody else. Or so my father told me. She never told me herself, or even wrote; only passed the message and some kind of apology through him. I heard later, roundabout – through Hugh – that the man's name was Gale but that that marriage never came off either. But Henrietta and I were in love. I married Beatrice instead and I can't regret that, but I never understood what happened, why Henrietta changed her mind. Can you tell me? I've wondered all my life.'

'What in the devil's name are you talking about?' said Matthew.

'I beg your pardon?'

'You may well beg my pardon but it would have been more to the point if you'd begged Henrietta's pardon, and a long time ago, at that. Are you out of your mind?'

'No, I am not out of my mind but you seem to be out of yours. Why are you angry? What's the matter with you, Matthew?'

'What's the *matter* with me? Why am I angry? You don't understand why I'm so discourteous, as you put it? My sister never called off her engagement to you. She never passed you a message through your father or anybody else. She wept her heart out because you sent word through Father that you had thought better of it and intended to marry somebody else. The Beatrice who was so dear to you, presumably!'

'*What?*' shouted Benjamin.

'We have all wanted, all through the years, to ask you how you could have done it, so cruelly, without even a line in your own writing,' said Caroline candidly. 'But there was Beatrice. I realised, the first time I met her, how sweet she was, and she was married to you by then. What was the use of discussing Henrietta? I thought it best to hold my tongue.'

Matthew had fetched her, and the three of them had closed the door between themselves and the rest of the gathering. The atmosphere between them was still awkward. Long years of silent resentment couldn't be wiped out in a moment.

'But what *happened?*' Ben insisted.

Matthew shook his head. 'I can't tell you. Father wanted Henrietta to marry a man called Andrew Gale, but he didn't mention Mr Gale, to her or anyone else, until after you were safely married yourself. She refused Gale and no wonder. Oh, he was as rich as Midas but he was old enough to be her grandfather. She was staying with relatives near Taunton at the time and Father sent me ahead to warn her that he was about to arrive with a prospective bridegroom. I hadn't seen the said bridegroom myself, until he actually arrived and when I did see him, I nearly burst with fury. I was a callow sort of lad and too well brought up to ask him to his face how he dared try offer himself for a young girl like my sister, but I thought it . . . oh, my God, I thought it.'

'And then,' Caroline said, 'because she wouldn't have this Mr Gale, Father cast her off. I was told never to mention her name again. Matthew managed to defy Father over that, but I never could. The only news I ever had of Rietta came through Matt. After the quarrel she went to live with a Mrs Henderson, a cousin on our mother's side of the family.'

'I didn't like her, either,' said Matthew. 'She was a handsome young woman and I think she rather dazzled my sister. I remember that Henrietta kept glancing from one of us to the other, pleading with her eyes for us to like one another. But I didn't take to Eleanor Henderson at all and she didn't take to me.'

'I remember you telling me that,' said Caroline thoughtfully. 'How strange. I had forgotten it until now.'

'Things come in between,' said Ben. 'Marriage and children and daily life tend to fill one's mind pretty thoroughly.'

353

'That's true,' Caroline said. 'I have always preferred to do whatever is to hand rather than wonder about people far away. For years now, Henrietta has been just a sister living a long way off, with whom I've lost touch. Yet we were very fond of each other as children.'

'Anyway,' Matthew said, gradually thawing towards Ben, 'whatever my views, Henrietta made her home with Eleanor Henderson. Mrs Henderson had a riding accident later and was crippled, and Henrietta has looked after her ever since. She and I correspond a little and once in maybe four or five years I visit them but . . . well, Henrietta has drifted away from us, that's all. Even from me, her twin. I can see that my visits aren't really welcome. It's as though there were a wall of glass between us. It's not my imagination. I took my wife with me once – the only time she and Henrietta have ever met. For all Deb is so gentle and quiet, she has a very keen wit. She said afterwards that she felt as if we had intruded into a private world, or a strange country whose customs we didn't understand. She didn't want to go there again.'

'It seems,' said Benjamin, 'that all this arose because lies were told by somebody. All these years, I've thought ill of Henrietta and the Lord knows what she has thought of me.'

Caroline's expression was concerned. 'The lies were told by Father. And today is his funeral. How . . . how ironic. We are sorry, Benjamin, for having thought so hardly of you all these years.'

'I wanted to come and thrash you,' said Matthew. 'But first of all I couldn't get away from university and after that, well, we heard you were married . . . and it all seemed so pointless.'

'I wouldn't go to your wedding,' Caroline put in wryly, 'and I noticed that you didn't come to mine.'

'And so it was left to fester all these years. Well, I suppose Beatrice was the better for it,' Ben said. 'But now, things are different. I should like to see her. Henrietta, I mean. Will you give me her direction, Matthew?'

'It will do no good to you or her.'

'She is a grown woman and I am a grown man. That should be for us to say. For God's sake!' Benjamin burst into anger. 'That was what your father did, yes, and maybe mine too. They decided what was best for us and left us no say!'

Matthew thought it over and then yielded. 'Very well. You shall see her if you like. The rest will be your business, and hers.'

Caroline was wrinkling her brows. 'Ben, there seems no doubt that a deception was practised on you and Henrietta but – do you believe that your father was involved too? I could believe it of mine; yes, I say that even though the grave's not yet filled in. But do you think your father lied as well?'

'My father disliked yours,' said Ben grimly. 'I recall that I had hard work to persuade him to come to London to meet your father and make my proposal on my behalf. I am wondering now if he ever did make it. I'd like to know what was really said when they met. Clearly, I have some more questions to ask and there is just one person who may know the answers.'

He approached the task of inquiring with some unease, however. His mother, after all, was now seventy-eight and although still able to do small household tasks, she had to rest in bed each afternoon. To look at, she was as fragile as a dried leaf, with a skin so thin that they had to keep a fleece under her bedsheet to prevent bedsores from developing.

He could not bully her. He could only ask questions and accept her answers. She and his father had been close (just as he and Beatrice had). Surely, Samuel would have confided in her, if there were anything to confide. But would she share it with her son?

He chose the morning, the time when she was most alert, and found her sitting in her favourite parlour chair, away from draughts, busily knitting, with her eyeglasses on her nose. She put her knitting down to listen to his question and said: 'You were happy with Beatrice and if you'd married Henrietta, where would Sam and your other children be now?'

'Where are the children I would have had with Henrietta? One could put it both ways. I still want an answer to my question. I will repeat it. It seems that Henrietta did not after all change her mind over marrying me. Father only told me she had. Did he believe it? Did Charles Whitmead lie to him? Or were they in collusion? I wish to know. I am not a boy now, Mother. I am a man in my fifties and for more than half my life, Henrietta, for whom I had and have the greatest regard, has thought of me as a fickle, shallow fellow lacking even the courage to tell her face to face that my feelings had changed. Which they had *not*. I was told that Henrietta's consent was sought and that she refused it and that was a lie. Just what *was* said when our two fathers met? I have a right to the truth, if you know it.'

'Of course I know it. Yes, your father lied to you, but in your own best interests.' Charity had picked up her knitting again She had not fallen victim to the joint-evil which was so prevalent among the aged and her fingers worked smoothly. She spoke with dignity. There may have been a trace of guilty conscience but if so, she wasn't going to admit it.

'But why? *Why?* What do you mean: my best interests?'

'They met in a coffee-house,' said Charity. 'Your father was quite frank. He said that you and Henrietta had entered into an illicit engagement and that it didn't please him. He asked if it pleased Charles. It did not. Charles wished Henrietta to marry elsewhere.'

'But why all the lies? I don't understand. My father and Charles could just have forbidden the match. At least it wouldn't have left me and Henrietta believing the worst of each other.'

'We wanted you to think the worst of each other,' said Charity. She looked like a frail, sweet, simple old lady, thought Benjamin, gazing at her in appalled fascination. But her words were cold and rigid. 'If we had simply forbidden the marriage, what would you have done?'

'Gone straight to Henrietta and run off with her, I expect!' said Benjamin promptly. 'We'd have declared ourselves married before the first witnesses we could find. That was legal by then. Even if she'd been sent away, I'd have found her somehow. Grandfather Ninian knew about us. He would have helped me.'

'I daresay. And even if you hadn't succeeded in running away with her, we and Charles might have found it hard to get the two of you to marry other people. You and Henrietta were both headstrong. You would never have agreed to marry Beatrice and that would have been your loss. I heard that Henrietta actually did refuse the match her father wanted.'

'According to Matthew, the man was as old as her grandfather.'

'Really? That was very foolish of Charles, but no more than one would expect of such an unpleasant man. He said very little to Samuel about his plans for Henrietta. Instead . . .' Charity's voice grew sharp – '. . . he chose to play with your father. He made Samuel pay him before he would agree to tell Henrietta that you had withdrawn your suit . . .'

'*What?*'

'Yes. Disgraceful. There could hardly be a clearer sign that we were right to prevent such a marriage. Henrietta has bad blood. Hugh's union with Caroline has turned out quite well, of course, but in our opinion, he was taking a grave risk. Neither your father nor I approved of that marriage, though it was not our business, and we never said anything to Hugh's parents.'

'Never said what? What do you mean: bad blood? What was wrong with Henrietta? I know you disliked her father and that there was some kind of dispute between you the first time he came here, although you never told any of us what it was about. But that can't have been Henrietta's fault, or Caroline's either. Why, you used to have them here every summer!'

'Yes, to give them a chance to acquire the ways of a decent Christian household. But to show people kindness is one thing and to marry them is quite another.'

'And you felt so strongly that you dared to tell lies to me? To blacken my character with Henrietta? To . . . to *buy* the slander that smeared me! I don't know how to look at you, my own mother, sitting there and saying such things. I ask you yet again: what was wrong with my poor Henrietta?'

Charity dropped a stitch. Clicking her tongue, she repaired the damage. She did not look at him as she said: 'The world's changed since I was young. It's become godless and scornful. It's all science and reason nowadays: the discoveries of that man Isaac Newton, for instance, who said he knew why apples fall down instead of flying straight upwards. As if God himself didn't arrange it that way to keep our feet on the ground and the world sane. Some things haven't changed, however much people scoff. The Bible is still the Bible and if you believe in God you must believe in His Word.'

'Mother, what are you talking about?'

'I always did think,' said Charity, 'that the name of the street where the Whitmeads lived in London was very suitable.'

Her thin, old voice was as chill as an east wind but she was visibly tiring and he thought she had begun to ramble, until she explained.

'That's done.' Henrietta put the damp towel and the basin of soapy water out of the way and began to help Eleanor into her clothes. The all-over sponge bath was a weekly affair, summer and winter, because Eleanor's skin became sore and developed little polyps if it were not cared for.

She also, before Eleanor could mention it, mended the fire.

In all but the warmest weather, bath-days required a good fire in the bedchamber. Before her accident, Eleanor had never felt the cold but now she complained incessantly.

'How can I keep warm when I can't move and keep the blood running in my veins? Fetch me another blanket, Hen, and perhaps I'd better have a warming pan. What does it matter that it's July? The sky's grey and I can hear the wind and I'm cold, I tell you! Where's my shawl? Hen, why do you continually put things out of my reach? Do you just do it to annoy me? Oh no, Hen, don't look like that, I'm sorry, I'm sorry, I grumble too much. Oh, Hen, please forgive me. I know I'm a nuisance. I don't like anyone but you doing things for me and I know that's not fair but if you knew what it was like to be helpless, just stuck in this bed, or in the chair, unable to walk; it isn't just dull, it's frightening. I'm always afraid you'll leave me. Oh, Hen, promise you'll never leave me, please, please, promise you won't desert me!'

And always, Henrietta returned the same soothing answer. 'I'll never desert you. You're upsetting yourself for nothing, Eleanor. You can be sure of me.'

She had developed a special, bright voice and a special, bright smile, for Eleanor's benefit. She employed them now, as she put more wood on the hearth, and went back to adjust Eleanor's skirts over the white, useless legs which she had to lift, one at a time, in order to pull the gown down under them. 'That's it – there we go. You should wear this dress oftener, my love. Blue suits you. Dotty says she saw a woollen material of almost the same shade in Taunton the other day. I think I'll send her to buy a roll of it.'

'You'd better go yourself and have a day out. You ought to go out more; I know that.'

If she did anything of the sort, Eleanor would fret all day. Diplomatically, Henrietta said: 'But I've always a thousand things to do here. I no sooner finish preserving the plums than it's time to start the autumn pruning in the garden. Then we'll begin the Christmas baking and once the winter sets in, the tracks get so muddy that I don't want to ride to Taunton anyway. I'd just as soon send Dotty or Mrs Johns. They always enjoy an outing. We're lucky to have kept them for so long.'

'We almost didn't keep Dotty,' said Eleanor, referring to the crisis twenty years before when Henrietta and Mrs Johns had discovered Dotty, in floods of tears and very drunk on sloe gin, jumping violently on and off the kitchen table.

'Now, Dotty, don't do that, please,' said Mrs Johns, putting restraining arms round her kitchen-maid, and then added shrewdly: 'Come now, tell us, who's the man? He'd better marry you.'

'He can't, he's wed already but I didn't know it when I went to Harvest Supper with 'un over at Smokeham Farm! His wife weren't there because she were lying-in!' wept Dotty.

'And now you're in a fair way to be lying-in as well, in a few months time,' said Mrs Johns and was provoked into adding: 'Oh, Dotty, you really do be as silly a wench as ever I did see. We'll just have to look round for someone for you.'

'Or you can just stay here and have it,' said Henrietta. 'This is an odd household anyway. A baby more or less won't make it much odder.'

This was true, for although only Henrietta and Eleanor themselves had ever known the precise nature of the oddness, Broom Cottage had long been known as the sort of place where: 'There's a sort of atmosphere. One can't put one's finger on it, but there's something. Miss Whitmead is very respectable and Mr Dyer says the way she cares for that cousin of hers is an example to any Christian, but still . . .'

If their maidservant took to producing unofficial babies, there would be some shaking of heads, but not much surprise.

'So don't worry too much, Dotty,' said Henrietta, 'we will manage,' and if her voice sounded a little depressed it was less on account of the reputation of Broom Cottage than the prospect of having to cope with Dotty's confinement and then a small child, as well as with Eleanor's needs and vapours.

None of it happened, because that night, Dotty's efforts with the sloe gin and the kitchen table actually worked. But it was a messy, painful and alarming business and Dotty nearly died. 'Just don't ever do anything that stupid again,' said Mrs Johns, when at last there were signs that the pale, exhausted patient would after all survive. 'I've lost pounds, worrying.' Broom Cottage still had both of them, and though Ricky had fallen sick and died, ten years back, a nephew of his, another Cuscombe, had taken his place in their stableyard.

'I think Dotty has settled down with us now,' Henrietta said, smiling. 'She's forty now, for goodness' sake. There. Let me just run a comb through your hair and put a ribbon in it and then I'll help you into your chair.'

The chair was a sophisticated affair with wheels, so that Eleanor could be pushed from room to room or out into the garden. Henrietta had had it made by a wheelwright in Chugg's, drawing on dim memories of her grandfather Ninian and his wheeled chair, and she was rather proud of it. She pulled it to the bedside but Eleanor resisted, her face pained. 'I need a bedpan first.'

'Here we are.' Henrietta provided what was needed and then, as usual, went tactfully away.

She took the towel and basin to the kitchen, which was empty, since Mrs Johns and Dotty were sweeping the upstairs floors. Putting down her burdens, she closed her eyes and leant against the wall. From time to time nowadays she was overcome by waves of sheer exhaustion and was glad to be alone for a few minutes in order to conquer them.

It was partly her age. She was forty-five now and her body was beginning a process of change, draining energy out of her. But the loss of strength was due to more than that. It was a weariness of the mind, too, as she faced the final slamming of a door. She could not recall ever having wanted children, except that once, long ago, she had hoped to have Benjamin's. She certainly didn't want them now. Yet the end of fertility mattered.

It was difficult, sometimes, not to think: if it hadn't been for Eleanor, I might have married. If she hadn't fallen off that horse; if there had been someone else to help me look after her.

Her captivity was mainly her own fault; she knew that. She had felt herself bound by the love she had at one time felt for Eleanor, and bound by that promise, made in the Handleys' house. Ruth and Becky would have been willing to take Eleanor back to Peace-Through-Praise, but the suggestion drove Eleanor almost frantic.

'I can't go back there, I can't! They made me marry Jacob and then when he died they tried to keep me there against my will. I want to be with you, Hen; it's you I love. You promised to stay; oh, Hen, please!'

And stayed she had, and within two years the option of Peace-Through-Praise had gone. Grandmother Faith had failed to get through a long and bitter winter; Ruth succumbed to a violent bout of influenza the following spring, and then the bereaved Becky, obviously ailing herself although no one could name the disease, came to Broom Cottage but did not last out the year.

After that, there wasn't even the phantom of choice for Henrietta. She was as much Eleanor's prisoner now as if she had been put in chains and sold to her in an Ancient Roman slave market. There were times when she envied Susanna Musgrave. Ricky had found Susanna's seafaring uncle and Captain Musgrave had got her on a ship for the West Indies. No news had ever come back of her fortunes there, but Henrietta often thought that she would have changed places with her regardless, because whatever Susanna's fate might be, it would at least be a new experience.

No one, least of all Eleanor, had ever guessed how many times over twenty-five long years since the accident Henrietta had lain awake, watching the stars march across the sky outside her window and prayed, yes, prayed, that Eleanor would die and set her free. Nor had anyone ever seen Henrietta, in the privacy of her room, weep silently and shake her fist in the air with rage because those prayers were never answered.

She had maintained her bright voice and her smile. She had cared for Eleanor with patience and apparent love and she would go on doing it, for the rest of her life if she must. But every now and then, the split between her outward life and her innermost thoughts became so great that it took all her strength to hold herself together, and now, sometimes, the strength wasn't quite enough.

And so she would lean against a wall like this, and close her eyes and think that since Eleanor was obviously never going to die, it would be best if she died herself, or fell ill or went insane; anything to be free of this burden.

The whinny of a horse roused her. Callers were apparently arriving. Henrietta opened her eyes and straightened her shoulders. Calling to Mrs Johns to come down and open the front door, she made haste back to Eleanor, to remove and hide the bedpan and make her cousin presentable. She had just tidied the bed and settled Eleanor in her wheelchair when Mrs Johns came into what had once been the parlour and was now simply 'Mrs Henderson's room'. 'Mr Matthew Whitmead and Mr Benjamin Whitmead have called.'

'Who?' Henrietta stared at her.

'Mr Matthew and Mr Benjamin Whitmead,' said Mrs Johns patiently. 'I've put them in the dining room but . . .'

'Oh. Well . . . Bring them in and fetch some refreshments. Wine . . . cakes . . . anything.'

'Matthew and Benjamin?' Eleanor whispered as Mrs Johns went out. 'Your Benjamin?'

'Not mine, not now. Hardly!' Henrietta kept her voice brisk, to conceal a curious weakness in her knees and an unruly thumping in her pulse. 'And here they are. How nice to see you, Matthew. It's so long since you were last here. And Benjamin! Well, what a surprise!'

It was indeed a great surprise, because she wouldn't have recognised him. When she last saw him he had been less than thirty years old and it was that Benjamin, wiry and vigorous, with hair the colour of a fox's coat, that she remembered. The man who now held out his hand to her was thick-bodied, his face weathered by years of farming amid the east winds of Essex, and what little hair he still possessed had faded to pepper and salt. He was a stranger.

But the surprise in her own eyes was mirrored in his. She was not what he remembered, either, she thought. She had never gained much weight, but her pinned-up coil of iron-grey air must be a shock to someone who had last seen it blue-black and flowing, and she knew that her smooth, ivory-tinted complexion had long since been marred by lines. 'Henrietta?' he said, and the faint question in his tone wrung her heart.

'Yes, indeed. Let me introduce you to my cousin and dear friend. Eleanor, Benjamin is also a cousin of mine. Benjamin, this is Mrs Henderson.'

'I am delighted to meet you, Mrs Henderson. Matthew has told me about you, of course.'

There could be no settling down to reminiscences until the proper dues had been paid to Eleanor. It was taken for granted that all visitors to Broom Cottage had come to see Mrs Henderson and for the first hour at least, they must sit and talk to her, ask after her health and her interests, let her hold court and be the hostess. The private talk with Benjamin must come. He had undoubtedly come here with a purpose. But they would have to wait.

It soon became clear to Henrietta that unless she took some kind of decisive action, it would be a lengthy wait. Eleanor too understood that Benjamin must have a reason for his visit and she intended to frustrate it. Even when Henrietta proposed showing her guests round the garden, she insisted on being wrapped up and wheeled along too, despite Henrietta's objections that the weather was too cold.

It was absurd, of course. What on earth did it matter that she and Benjamin had once been sweethearts? It was all a thousand years ago. Did Eleanor imagine that if they were left alone together they would fall into each other's arms like Romeo and Juliet, and run off together?

The trouble was that Eleanor probably did. She was afraid of anything that might pull Henrietta back to the outside world. It was to soothe Eleanor that Henrietta had gently discouraged even Matthew's visits. As they came back indoors, with Matthew now wheeling the chair, she decided that she would just have to be firm, whatever tears and sulks might follow. She was drawing breath to announce that she and Benjamin must have a few words apart, when Matthew got in first.

'Henrietta, this isn't just a social call. We are here on business connected with Father's death. It was such a pity that you couldn't attend the funeral. We need to have a private talk with you, if Mrs Henderson will kindly excuse us for a little while.'

'Of course. Shall I bring your embroidery frame, Eleanor?'

'No, the light's not good enough. I've a book here; I'll read,' said Eleanor politely. Only Henrietta, her ears sharpened by years of experience, could hear the discontented undertone.

She took the two men into the dining room, motioning them to chairs and looking at them expectantly.

'You're not in mourning,' Matthew observed.

Henrietta stiffened. 'For Father? I haven't set eyes on him for over a quarter of a century. He abandoned me and didn't care what became of me. No, I'm not in mourning. Why should I be?'

Then she saw the amusement in her twin's eyes, and subsided. 'I take it,' she said, 'that you didn't come all this way, and bring Benjamin with you, just to see if I were observing the proprieties.'

'No, I didn't,' said Matthew. 'That was an observation, not a criticism. Although I did think you might be wondering about Father's will. I have to tell you that he didn't leave you anything. But I have with me a document explaining how Caroline and I propose to make over some of our inheritance to you.' Henrietta opened her mouth but he raised a hand. 'You're not to argue about it, Henny. We're determined. Lord knows, there's enough. Father was rich.'

'What can I say? I didn't expect that. It's generous of you both.' Henrietta hesitated and then asked: 'Did he ever mention me? When he was ill, for instance?'

Matthew shook his head. 'No. I'm afraid he didn't.'

'I knew it would be like that,' Henrietta said. 'He swore he would forget I ever existed and he kept his word.'

'Obstinate brute,' said Matthew casually, and rose to his feet, pulling a paper from his coat. He laid it down on a table beside her. 'Here's the document for you to read at leisure. That's the family business concluded. And now, I rather think you would like to talk to Benjamin alone. I shall go to the kitchen and renew my acquaintance with Mrs Johns and Dotty.'

He left the room. Benjamin instantly came over to Henrietta and took her hands in his. 'Henrietta! It's been so long.'

'It has indeed.' Quietly, she withdrew her hands, and sat down again. 'What brings you here, Ben?'

'Oh God. I knew it would be difficult. You haven't forgotten or forgiven and why should you? But that's why I've come: to clear up the misunderstanding.'

'Misunderstanding?'

'Yes! Henrietta, I have found out lately that for years and years you have believed that I broke our engagement, and did not even have the grace to do it in person. It isn't true. All through the years, in fact, I have believed the same thing about you.'

'You what?' It was all so sudden that she was bewildered. 'Whatever can you be talking about?'

'Your father,' said Benjamin, 'wished you to marry somebody else – Gale, I think his name was. My parents co-operated with your father in lying to us both. Each of us was told that the other wished to break the engagement. I just wanted you to know, that's all.'

Half an hour later, oblivious of Eleanor abandoned in the next room, they were still talking. Henrietta, who had heard, through Matthew, only the briefest details about Ben's marriage and Beatrice's death, now learned that he had been happy, and was regaled with details of his children, and found that when she said: 'I'm glad it all turned out so well,' she could speak with sincerity. In return, she told him of her own life in the intervening years, including some facts which she had never mentioned before, even to Matthew.

'It's extraordinary,' she said. 'No one would care now. But – well, you remember what it was like after the Monmouth rebellion, when Judge Jeffreys came to the West Country?'

'No one is ever likely to forget,' said Benjamin. 'Even in Essex we shuddered to hear of it. You were in the midst of it and it must have been terrible.'

'It was,' said Henrietta. 'It was a waking nightmare, to ride about the countryside here at that time. Wherever one went, there were gibbets.' Ben nodded. The horror of Jeffreys' vengeance on Monmouth's supporters had started the surge of opinion which eventually rose so high against King James that he had at last abandoned country and throne to his daughter Mary and her husband William of Orange.

'And even William and Mary are gone now,' said Henrietta, marvelling, 'and we have Queen Anne to rule us and no one would come after me or Eleanor because once we helped a poor fugitive from the King's forces after Sedgemoor. But what I saw after Judge Jeffreys came here and held his assizes in what was left of Taunton Castle has kept me silent all these years. All I ever said to Matthew was that Eleanor was thrown from her horse when we were visiting the Handleys. But now, I want to tell you what really happened.'

He sat, listening and marvelling as she told him of Susanna Musgrave's escape, and how Mary Blake had died in Dorchester gaol, and how twelve of their pupils had been taken into custody and had to be ransomed by their families.

'And you and Mrs Henderson were in the thick of it?' he said at the end. 'I always thought you were brave, Henrietta. Even when you were sixteen, and pledged yourself to me in that cornfield.'

They fell suddenly silent. Next door, they could hear Matthew's voice; he had evidently gone in to talk to Eleanor.

'Henrietta,' Ben said at last. 'Oh, my dear.'

'I won't ask you what you mean by that. I know. All the years, all the things that can't be changed and many that we wouldn't even wish changed. The way we've grown older.' She pointed to a cushion on an empty chair. It was embroidered, boldly and expertly, with a picture of a blue river flowing under a bridge of brick in a soft, sandy yellow shade. 'Look at that embroidery. Eleanor and I did it; we worked it up from an old Whitmead device. That's like our lives. It's all water under a bridge now, Ben.'

'Is it? Henrietta, you were kind enough to say you are glad that I have been happy. But you didn't say you were happy too. Have you been so?'

'Sometimes. Not always.'

Impossible to give details. Impossible to explain to anyone how difficult, demanding and jealous Eleanor was, and how, at the same time, she could be touching. And impossible to explain the big, quiet joys of Broom Cottage. She had been able to endure only because of them. It was always a delight when the first spring flowers showed in the garden or when the fruit ripened in the orchard and the house was filled with a happy bustle of making preserves and jam. She found pleasure in the woodsmoke of the autumn bonfires and the excitement of making Christmas dinner ready. Impossible to explain that one could lie awake at night cursing one's servitude, and then, the very next day, be thrilled because a rose had bloomed or she had a new book to read, or because when she went out into the garden she saw an unusual bird, or a stag on the hillside. One couldn't convey the whole texture of a life in words.

Ben was leaning forward, hands on widely spaced and solid knees. 'Because if you're not happy, Henrietta, you need not stay. You know what I'm asking?'

'Ben, my dear. I couldn't leave Eleanor.'

'Eleanor could come too. There's plenty of room in Whitmead.'

'Give up her home and go to live in someone else's? She would never agree. And besides . . .'

'Yes, my love?'

'Do you really wish to turn your life upside down and introduce me and Eleanor into Whitmead? Do you, Ben? Will you be truly heartbroken if I say no?'

'I want peace and happiness for you. I have thought hard things of you, so often.'

'Under the circumstances, I'm not surprised!'

'I wish,' said Benjamin with passion, 'that the man Gale, that your father wanted you to wed, had been suitable for you. Matthew told me he was old. I wish he'd been young and handsome and won your heart so that you could have had a good marriage, too.'

Henrietta laughed. 'You're very dear, and I'm more glad than I can say that we now know the truth about each other. But – water under the bridge, as I said. I will keep my life as it is, and I think you would prefer to keep yours.'

'You've been a very faithful friend to Mrs Henderson. She's fortunate to have you.'

Henrietta did not reply to this. She had become serious again. 'There's one thing, Ben.'

'Yes, my dear?'

'Your father and mine conspired to separate us. It's odd, you know. I remember, when my father called me to tell me that my betrothal – my illicit betrothal was how he described it – was ended; I somehow felt as though he were responsible and not you. I was right, it seems! Well, he wanted me to make a wealthy match. But why were *your* parents against our marriage? Do you know?'

'I hoped you wouldn't ask that.'

'So you do know. Tell me, Ben.'

'It wasn't your fault. It was nothing that you did or said or were. It was all so silly! I got it out of my mother in the end – when she told me, I just stood up and walked out of the room. I packed my things and set out for London that same day and Matthew passed his clients to his partner and we came straight here. He was coming anyway, to bring you that document about the inheritance, but he set out three days early because of me. He was so shaken by what I told him. Dear God!'

'But what *was* it?'

'You had a foreign grandmother, born a heathen . . .'

'Is that all? But she became a Christian! That's what Grandfather always said, anyway.'

'Did he also say under what circumstances she died?'

'It was in the Civil War. Oh, Grandfather told me the whole story. They'd been involved in a Royalist rising and they were escaping from the Roundheads.'

'That was partly true but not the whole story. Your father, long ago, let the rest of the story out to my parents. The Roundheads weren't just after them because they were Royalists. There had been a charge of witchcraft laid against your grandmother.'

'*Witchcraft!* But that's nonsense. I mean, it can't have been true. Everyone knows now that there are no such things as witches!'

'My parents came of Puritan stock and they were always old-fashioned in some ways. They clung to the old ideas. My mother still believes in witches. She quoted the Bible at me. "Thou shalt not suffer a witch to live," she said to me, and then that quotation about visiting the sins of the fathers – or the grandmothers in this case – unto the third and fourth generation.'

'Meaning me?'

'I'm afraid so. Henrietta, you look amused!'

'Well, I am. Oh, dear. I know I shouldn't laugh. I don't suppose my grandmother laughed, or Grandfather Ninian. But there's a ridiculous side as well. And you have just suggested that I should, well, come to Whitmead after all? To share it with your mother, who thinks of me as . . . my dear Ben! Can you imagine it?'

'She said,' said Ben wryly, 'that she had always thought the London Whitmeads had a most appropriate address. I couldn't understand her and then she said: *Wych* Street.'

They gazed at each other, saddened now because they both knew that their lives had divided too long ago and that their futures could not now merge.

'Our whole lives,' said Henrietta. 'So much that might have been. Neatly wrapped up in a worn-out old piece of cloth called superstition, and put away in a cupboard called eternity.'

'That's a poetic turn of phrase,' said Benjamin.

'Oh no. I've no interest in poetry. I'm very down to earth. Eleanor is the imaginative one.'

'But your grandfather Ninian would have appreciated that phrase, all the same, and he was very fond of poetry. You have Indian looks,' said Benjamin 'I suppose you take after your grandmother. But you remind me of Ninian all the same.'

'Do I? But describing things in pretty words doesn't change them, does it? Wych Street! It's even more absurd than I thought. And yet . . .' Henrietta became very sober. 'Thinking about it – no, after all, I don't feel much like laughing. Do you?'

'No,' said Benjamin.

'Well, they're gone. Just a brief visit. Shall I get you ready for the night now, Eleanor? Let me brush your hair.'

'Have they gone for good? Or did they say they'd come back? Are you going to visit either of them?'

'No, Eleanor, I am not. Oh, *Eleanor*! You didn't think that just because I had a girlhood romance with Benjamin, I'd run off and marry him now that I'm middle-aged, did you? Matthew came to tell me that he and Caroline intend to share their inheritance with me and Benjamin just came for . . . for a visit of condolence. I didn't need it, but it was nice to see him. That's all there was to it, though. The past is past. They've gone away and that's the end of it.'

'You'll stay with me, then?' said Eleanor. 'I know I am often a trouble. I know I am. I can't help it. But . . .'

Her eyes, as vividly blue as ever, were frightened and pleading. Her hand reached out to Henrietta.

'I'll always stay,' said Henrietta, patting the hand. Then she took up the brush and began carefully to tidy Eleanor's long hair. 'Your hair is still chestnut,' she said. 'It's always been beautiful. My darling Eleanor, I would no more go off with Benjamin than I'd go off to the Americas. He doesn't even look like the man I remember.'

No point in saying: *but I might have found someone else if you hadn't stolen away the years of my youth.*

No point either in lying awake tonight and cursing fate, or Eleanor, or her father, or even her poor dead grandmother, who was responsible for most of this and yet completely innocent.

Extraordinary, how Ben had changed. He'd grown so heavy she'd hardly have known him. At least she'd never grown fat.

She'd settle Eleanor down and then she'd go to bed herself, and sleep well, and in the morning once more take up the burden which in sheer humanity she could not lay down.

EPILOGUE
The Strange Valediction
1742

Death, be not proud, though some have called thee
Mighty and dreadful, for thou art not so . . .

John Donne

The wedding of George Whitmead, son of James and Araminta and grandson of Matthew and Deb Whitmead, to Lucy-Anne Browne, daughter of Hugo and Lucilla and granddaughter of Hugh and Caroline Browne, was a huge and costly occasion, involving so many horses and carriages and such a crowd of interested bystanders that the traffic round St Clement Danes virtually ceased until the ceremony was over.

The bride's gown was of the most expensive ivory-coloured Indian silk, embroidered with seed-pearls, its immense skirts adorned with innumerable lace flounces. Six little girls, cousins from her mother's side of the family, carried her train, and the bride's lacy cloud of a veil was held in place by a circlet of pearls. Most of the admiring exclamations concerned her finery. Lucy-Anne herself, being small and pale and petrified and only seventeen, was virtually extinguished by it.

The bridegroom on the other hand, being twenty-nine and a much-travelled gentleman who had spent six years in India, wore his wedding clothes with aplomb: green coat and gold-braid edging, white silk stockings and buckled shoes, and a peruke wig, smoothly rolled and the same pale red as his own hair. Not a single wrinkle was to be seen in the coat or the stockings, which fitted his thick shoulders and his stout calves as if painted on them.

There was a triumphant smile on his face as he came out of the church with his bride on his arm. Her father Hugo had made money as a London merchant and could give his daughter a mouth-watering dowry. Though admittedly, Hugo's town house was not quite big enough to accommodate such a crowd of wedding guests. George's home, however, where the reception was held, absorbed them with ease.

One of the guests was the couple's mutual great-aunt Henrietta, aged seventy-seven, up from Somerset for the occasion. She had come by easy stages for she grew tired rather easily now, but she had not, as so many elderly people did, become either lame or clouded in mind. Her mind was active still, which was why she became very annoyed when in the course of the wedding reception, she found that the bridegroom was patronising her.

'You would hardly believe, Great-Aunt Henrietta, what the palace of the Nawab of Arcot is like. I have been fortunate enough to be bidden there more than once to the Nawab's banquets. You can scarcely imagine the grace of the stone lattices and the fretted arches; and the paintings, depicting tiger-hunts with the aid of elephants, contrasted with the most delicate delineations of exotic flowers, which are painted on the walls. And there are designs of semi-precious stones set in the walls too, and always the constant tinkle of water from some little flowing channel nearby, for you must know, the Indian climate is extremely hot. One can hear the water flowing because there are so many open archways, to permit the cool circulation of air.'

'My dear boy,' said Henrietta, 'you sound exactly like a textbook. My father knew India well and described all these things to me when I was a girl. But I expect Lucy-Anne will enjoy listening to you. Do you intend to educate her?'

Sarcasm was lost on George. 'I shall no doubt have to do so. She is, after all, very young. Of course, I shall have only a limited amount of time with her, since I must soon return to my duties with the East India Company in Madras, but I shall place her in the care of my dear mother, whom God has so graciously spared to see this day.'

Henrietta, glancing across the spacious, high-ceilinged room at Araminta, wouldn't have placed a heavy bet on her care lasting very long. She had seen Araminta last at Deb's funeral, two years before. Araminta then had been much as she had been all her life, both as wife and widow: anxious of expression and too inclined to agree with everything said to her, but she had looked healthy. Now she had grown thin and her hair was dull. But George, Henrietta suspected, only saw what he wanted to see.

He was now excusing himself, with many unnecessary bows, explaining that he wished to greet other acquaintances, obviously feeling that he had done his duty by this elderly spinster aunt in her plain grey satin. As soon as he had turned his back, she rose and made her way to the next room, in search of her twin brother.

Matthew was sitting on a gilt and velvet chair, looking on at the dancing. He greeted her with a smile and she sat down beside him, at first in silence. They had grown close again in the fifteen years since Eleanor's death. Matthew came often to Broom Cottage, and sometimes he and Henrietta would sit together for long periods of time, not talking, but communicating all the same, in a way which neither could explain but which pleased them both deeply.

Presently, however, Henrietta spoke her thoughts aloud.

'I see that the bride is dancing with an uncle. Did George lead her out to start the set?'

'Naturally. It's correct. George would always do the correct thing.'

'I believe you. I've been talking to him,' said Henrietta. 'He's the most pompous young man I've ever met. I'm sorry for Lucy-Anne.'

'She's captured a rich husband,' Matthew pointed out.

'I daresay he thinks that he's the one who did the capturing. Your branch of the family,' said Henrietta, 'seems to make a habit of marrying mice.'

Matthew laughed. 'Everyone thinks Deb was a mouse; even you, and you got to know her quite well eventually. But it was only because she never said very much. She was sharp enough, my dear sister. I become impatient with people who say women can't reason. Deb could.' With his eyes on the dancers, he added: 'I never had any illusions about my son, you know. James was an arrogant devil. He got that arrogance from Father, I suspect – I don't think I have it but I must have been carrying it, like one of those diseases that jump a generation. But all the same, he did have some cause for pride. He was one of the most intelligent men I've ever known and I don't say that just because he was my son. He had amazing business acumen. George had a good start in life. Well, James got his intelligence from Deb, in my opinion.'

'All right,' said Henrietta. 'So Deb wasn't a mouse. But what about Araminta?'

'Oh, God, yes. Poor Araminta. Yes, James; No, James; James, you are very right; James always said so and so; I'm sure that this is – or isn't – what dear James would have wished . . . ! But no other kind of woman would have been any use to him. He couldn't have borne one who had any opinions of her own.'

'And can George?'

'No, probably not. For Lucy-Anne's sake, we must hope you're right and she's a mouse. Come to think of it, he once told me that in India, women are so retiring and obedient that English girls seemed strident and demanding by comparison. He came home on purpose to find a wife, you know, and he turned down a lot of possibles, in spite of their good dowries. But when Hugo and Lucilla offered him Lucy-Anne, he fairly pounced on her. Her portion is excellent, of course, but maybe she matches his biddable ideal as well.'

'Highly likely, I should think. Ah well. I shan't be here to see the end of it,' said Henrietta.

Matthew turned sharply towards her. 'There was something in the way you said that. Are you in good health, Henny?'

'In general, yes, but I tire more and more quickly and I find events like these depressing. So many people have gone. Thank heavens I still have you. But I miss Caroline and Hugh. I've had my supper. I think I shall go to bed soon.'

'Before the last ceremony?'

'Come, come. They can bed the happy couple without my help. But I want to speak to Lucy-Anne first. I haven't exchanged a single word with my great-niece yet. Ah, the dance is over and by the look of it, she's going to supper. I'll speak to her now. Goodnight, Matt.'

The bride was leaving the room on the arm of her elderly maternal uncle. Following her into the supper room, Henrietta caught up just as the uncle was settling his niece at a table and asking what food and wine she would like. He withdrew to fetch it and Lucy-Anne, with a timid smile, said: 'You are my Great-Aunt Henrietta, are you not? Father pointed you out earlier. But we have not spoken before.'

'You've had other matters to attend to,' said Henrietta with amusement. 'I'm getting on in years, my dear, and I can't keep the late hours you younger people can, so I'm about to retire. But I had to wish you happy before I went.'

'That is kind of you, Great-Aunt. Oh, I must thank you for your gift.

Such beautiful linen and with such a charming device embroidered on it. So pretty; with the blue water flowing under the bridge.'

'It's some sort of Whitmead badge,' said Henrietta. 'So my grandfather told me. It was used back in the days of Good Queen Bess. He was born while she was still on the throne, you know and he could even remember seeing women in ruffs. I had the device embroidered on to new sheets and napkins for you. I couldn't stitch it myself; my eyesight isn't up to it these days. But I've made sure the workmanship is all it should be.'

'I'm sorry about your eyesight,' said Lucy-Anne shyly.

'It's the way of the world, my child. But never mind. Your life is ahead of you. I feel sure,' said Henrietta, saying the right thing, 'that George will take care of you.'

'Oh, oh yes, I'm certain he will.'

Lucy-Anne bit her lip and Henrietta, as though she had momentarily entered her great-niece's mind, sensed her fear of the night to come and the years ahead with George, who was probably little more than a stranger to her; simply a man her parents had told her to marry.

'It will be all right,' said Henrietta bracingly. 'Courage, child.'

She moved out of the way of a footman who was on his way round the room with a taper, lighting the candles in the wall sconces. She looked worriedly at this little relative, whose life, like Henrietta's own, was being officiously arranged for her by other people. Henrietta's own life had been changed without her knowledge by earlier generations; and later, she had been trapped by the demands of a love which she had only partly reciprocated. She had known little more freedom of choice than Lucy-Anne herself.

They were about to be interrupted. Lucy-Anne's uncle was still pottering at the supper-table, selecting dishes, but her mother was now surging towards them through the open double-doors from the hallway. Lucilla Browne, née Compton, was magnificently hooped and coiffeured. Her much-curled hair had grey streaks amid the brown, but it was the pearl and diamond hair ornament, flashing in the candle-light, which caught the eye. A huge diamond ring blazed on the hand which held up her wide blue satin skirts. There was nothing of the mouse about Lucilla Browne. It was quite possible, indeed, that Lucilla's powerful personality accounted for Lucy-Anne's lack of one.

Henrietta found that she was far too tired to hold a conversation with Lucilla. Quickly, she stooped to give her great-niece a kiss, and whispered a few words into her ear. Then she withdrew and lost herself in the crowd, leaving Lucy-Anne to gaze after her in astonishment.

'Was that Henrietta Whitmead?' inquired Lucilla, sitting down beside her daughter. 'Extraordinary woman. Led an extraordinary life, by all accounts. Spent most of it buried in some unbelievable place called Chugg's Fiddle, nursing a crippled friend, or cousin, or something. Too peculiar ever to get married, I imagine. She's wealthy enough – her father was a regular Croesus – but you'd never guess it to look at her. You look quite bewildered, child. What in the world did she whisper to you, just now?'

'I didn't understand it,' said Lucy-Anne.

'Well, what *was* it?'

'She said she wished me well,' said Lucy-Anne slowly, 'and then she said she wished me something else too. She wished me power and freedom. It didn't make sense. Women can't have that. Except for Good Queen Bess, I suppose.'

'I told you she was peculiar,' said Lucilla.

Henrietta, falling asleep in a fourposter bed in one of George's spare bedchambers, knew she was going to dream of a ship. She had had the same dream for many nights now in succession. She was standing on a quay, watching the vessel glide in along a path of moonlight. It had a square sail and a crenellated forecastle, as ships had had in olden days.

Soon, now very soon, Henrietta would dream that she was going on board that ship. It would set sail with her and neither she nor it would ever return to the world. She knew this and if anything, it was a relief. But there was one thing, she thought drowsily as she settled herself, that she must attend to before she went up that ghostly gangplank. She must change her will to give Lucy-Anne a really worthwhile legacy. The girl looked so vulnerable. She should have some money of her own, tied up so that George couldn't get at it.

Poor little thing. Henrietta hoped very much that in the years she would not see, life might be kind to Lucy-Anne.